D0804249

AND SO IT WAS
WRITTEN

A Novel by

Ellen Brazer

And So It Was Written

Cover Art Designed by Mario Chiaradia and Henri Almanzar
Graphic Design by Hope Lane

For information go to:
www.ellenbrazer.com
or write to the author at
ellenb9815@bellsouth.net

ISBN: 978-0-615-67183-3

Printed in the United States of America

Other books written by Ellen Brazer

Hearts of Fire
Clouds Across the Sun.

For Mel: my husband, best friend and the love of my life.

I see him, but not now;
I behold him, but not nigh.
There shall step forth a star out of Jacob;
and a scepter shall rise out of Israel,
and shall smite through the corners of Moab,
and break down all the sons of Seth.
The Star Prophecy of Numbers 24:17

Chapter 1

The Jewish Enclave of En Gedi
In the Year 128 CE

A two-day walk from the holy city of Jerusalem, on the western shore of the Dead Sea, stood the lush oasis of En Gedi. Fed by a jeweled waterfall, the grass was green as emeralds; the palm and date trees flourished and the vineyards were lush. Amid miles and miles of naked, treeless mountains of rock, herds of ibex grazed. This was the Judean Desert–unchanged since the time of Joshua.

As the clouds shifted and the sun blazed, Livel and his brother Masabala patrolled the perimeter of the olive groves searching for any sign of approaching Roman soldiers.

At sixteen, Livel was narrow in the hips and shoulders. A newly sprouting beard sat upon an angular face, his chin a little too sharp, his brow a bit too wide. He had large, expressive coal-colored eyes and an imposing nose that curved at the end. His appearance teetered on the edge of homeliness–until he smiled, an act that transformed his face.

In contrast, fifteen-year-old Masabala was handsome, with thick ebony hair, sable eyes, long legs and a sleek hard body. Even though he was younger by a year, he was already two inches taller than Livel.

Masabala weaved towards Livel with a sharpened stick in his hand, graceful as a panther, slashing the air like a sword. "Take that, you Roman swine!" he hissed, arm extended feigning an at-tack. He lunged, driving hard and stopping just short as he gently poked Livel's chest with the tip of his weapon. Faking a sneer, he hissed, "Had you been the enemy, you would be dead!"

Livel shook his head and laughed. "With a stick?"

"A stick today, tomorrow a mighty sword. Let's go. There's a cave I want to explore." Masabala yanked Livel by the arm.

Livel dug in his heels. "We shouldn't leave the grove."

"You afraid?" Masabala jeered.

"Not afraid, just cautious. As you should be." Livel knew his remarks would go unheeded. Once Masabala had set his mind to something, he was relentless, and it was fruitless to try to dissuade him. Memories flashed of the times Masabala had put them in harm's way–climbing dangerous cliffs where one misstep would have meant death, hanging precariously from tree limbs as they built a forbidden tree house, their bodies scarred from scratches and falls.

Livel would never admit that he loved the danger, or that he silently rejoiced in his brother's bravado. He did not have Masabala's great physical strength, but he did have the courage and aptitude of a warrior, and he often fantasized what it would be like to act as impulsively as Masabala. But impulsivity went against Livel's nature. He protested for the sake of protesting, telling himself that he was going along to keep Masabala out of trouble. In truth, he wanted to go. "We have to be back before dark."

Masabala shot his brother a smile. "We will be." He knew that Livel was more adventurous than he would ever admit, but there were great expectations surrounding his brother, and for that reason alone Masabala was willing to take the blame for all their bloodied knees and bruises.

They ran side by side towards a ridge of low cliffs. Masabala was swift as a gazelle, his stride long and elegant. Livel kept up by sheer determination.

Without warning, Masabala slid in the sand. Livel came to a stop beside him.

"No matter what our parents say, my destiny is to become a great warrior!" Masabala proclaimed, raising a clenched fist in the air. As a Kohen, his family was directly descended from Aaron, the older brother of Moses. Being a part of that lineage came with certain obligations and becoming a soldier was not one of them.

"I'm sure the entire Roman garrison will one day know your name, and they will tremble in your presence." Livel faked a bow and then playfully punched Masabala's arm.

"And one day all of Judea will know *your* name as well," Masabala said, respect tingeing his words. "Father says even now the rabbis in Jerusalem speak of you in whispers."

As the first-born son of a respected rabbi, Livel's fate was sealed at birth–he would follow in his father's footsteps. What set him apart from others was his unique gift. Information stayed in his head, stored in compartments, available verbatim as needed. With perfect recall, he could recite all six hundred and thirteen commandments–the ethics, laws and spiritual practices of the Jewish people. He spoke Hebrew, Aramaic and he had learned to speak Latin and Greek from the traders who frequented En Gedi. By this time next year, he would be studying under the tutelage of the great rabbis in Jerusalem.

Masabala ran backwards. "Come on great scholar, I'll race you!"

The boys sprinted toward the ridge that led to the cave they were going to explore. When they were halfway between En Gedi and the cave, they heard the thundering of horses' hooves and the unmistakable clanging of armor. Horrified, the boys froze. Sound carried far in the desert, bouncing off the sheer walls, making it impossible to gauge how far away the soldiers were.

The Romans controlled Judea and were unmerciful adversaries. They would overrun villages at will, and there were stories of young boys being beaten and forced to become sex slaves for the men.

Terrified, the brothers ran toward En Gedi. Livel turned for a quick look, trying to spot their enemy. That decision was catastrophic as he collided with a boulder and tripped. Masabala reached down and yanked him up. Livel screamed when he put pressure on his foot.

"I'm hurt. I can't keep up!" Livel cried, grabbing his brother by the shoulders. "Go!"

"And leave you behind?" Masabala shook his head wildly. "We can hide."

"There's no place to hide and you know it!" He looked into the desert, to the dust kicked up by the distant riders, their spears and shields reflecting the sun. He would not be the reason his brother got captured. "I'll be right behind you." He gave Masabala a shove. "Just once, listen to me! Run!"

"I'll get help and be back before they get here," Masabala said, as he ran toward home.

Livel took a tentative step on his swelling ankle. Walking would be a painful option, and running was out of the question. He hobbled a few steps trying to decide what to do. If he turned toward En Gedi, they would spot Masabala, so instead, he headed in the opposite direction. For ten minutes he crawled, hopped and limped, determined to put as much distance between himself and Masabala as possible. All the while he was hoping his brother would return before the soldiers found him.

He squinted into the distance. The horses and soldiers were so close now he could count their numbers. There were twelve. He looked toward En Gedi. His eyes searched for a wisp of dust, anything that might give proof of a rescue. There was only stillness.

The shouts and clattering of armor closed in on him, and soon he was surrounded. A soldier wearing a bronze breastplate and helmet dismounted. He reached for his *pilum*, a wooden spear with an iron tip. Livel stood paralyzed, gutted by the greatest fear he had ever known.

"What do you think he's doing out here alone? Or is he alone?" the soldier asked his comrades in Greek. He poked Livel with the tip of his sword as he looked toward En Gedi.

"I'm injured, and my friend went for help," Livel replied in Greek. All eyes were now riveted on him.

The soldier smiled, menace turning his eyes to fire. "My, my, a well-educated young Jew."

An older soldier dismounted and approached. The men made way in obvious deference to their leader. "My name is Marcus Gracchus," the man said. "And yours is?"

"Livel son of Eleazar."

"Tell me Livel, how many languages do you speak?

"Four," Livel replied.

Marcus Gracchus smiled. He was in need of another tutor for his sons, and it seemed that good fortune had come his way. "Put him on the extra mount. We will take Livel with us."

Everything was happening too quickly. Hands were coming at him and faces blurred as he was tossed onto the horse, his ankle throbbing. Livel understood as clearly as he had ever understood anything in his life that there was no point in resisting. He twisted in the saddle to get what he knew would be a last look at En Gedi.

Tears burned the back of his eyes, but he forced them away. He would not let them see him cry. Not now. Not ever. Livel could hear his father's voice: *when you are lost or frightened, confused or disheartened–turn to the Holy One, Blessed by He. He will always be with you.*

Livel began to pray.

They traveled throughout the night, moving rapidly whenever the rugged terrain allowed them to do so. Livel prayed until exhaustion overcame him, and he fell asleep slumped over the soft mane of the horse. The ensuing nightmares were intense, whips and fire, his parent's anguish, Masabala's rage.

At dawn, the Roman troop halted, and Livel awakened with a start. Torrents of anguish washed over him, and the sleep world dissolved. They were outside a Roman encampment waiting for a bridge to be lowered. It would allow them to pass over a ditch that encircled the entire perimeter. His horse tethered to the saddle of a soldier, they entered the camp filled with hundreds of tents. As they moved over the paved roads, they passed stalls where the pounding of anvils could be heard. There were blacksmiths and butchers, bakers and wine sellers. They turned left, and passed a street of bathhouses and barbers. Another left and they were on a street with hospitals, workshops and endless mule-drawn carts heaped with food, armament and every sort of supply.

Livel was torn from his mount, thrown into a tent and chained to a post. The only visitor came once a day to deliver food and empty the pot where he defecated. The rest of the time he lay alone on a mat of straw, withdrawing into a shadow world. He teetered on the edge of starvation, eating only enough to remain alive. The Judaism he so deeply believed in forbade suicide.

On the tenth day of his incarceration, the commanding officer, Marcus Gracchus ordered that Livel be bathed, dressed in a clean tunic and brought into his tent.

Gracchus lay on a chaise, impressive in a white robe trimmed with gold thread. He had a square face, angry sea-green eyes, a chiseled nose and soft, almost feminine lips. It was as if his face were divided: stone-like from the nose up, gentle from the nose down. His black hair was slicked with oil.

As a senator of Rome and an accomplished Legion Commander, he was in Judea by direct edict of Emperor Hadrian. The objective was to ascertain the situation in Judea and report back to the emperor. Domitius, his youngest son, had accompanied him. Scipio, his oldest, was sent to the northern border to take part in the building of a defensive wall for Rome.

The tent was lavish with carpets on the floor, pillows scattered about, draperies and tapestries hanging from the walls. Incense burned, the scent of myrrh and frankincense wafting through the enclosure.

"It's been reported to me that you are barely eating. Have a seat," he said in Greek, pointing to a stack of feather-filled pillows.

Livel didn't move. He just stared at the man, defiance in his eyes.

"You *will* learn to follow orders," he said, his demeanor turning ominous. "Sit!"

Livel sat.

"I am returning to Rome and taking three hundred of my men with me. When we get to Rome, if you're healthy, I will allow you to become a tutor to my sons."

Livel knew he was on precarious ground. This was not a man to defy; yet his anger seethed and he couldn't help himself. "I may be enslaved, but you can't make me eat!"

Marcus slowly lifted a whip that sat beside the chaise. As if he were swatting a fly, he cocked his wrist. The whip slashed across Livel's bare arm.

Livel cried out, as much from shock as from the pain.

"You will do as I say, or I'll sell you as fodder. Is that what you want, boy, to be fed to a hungry lion in the center arena of the great Coliseum in Rome?"

Livel shook his head.

I will eat. I will live. And one day, I will go home!

Chapter 2

Masabala

Masabala ran until his chest ached and his legs threatened to collapse. He bolted through the olive groves and raced down crowded streets until he reached the center square of the village.

"Abba, Abba!" he screamed, spotting his father, Rabbi Eleazar. He stood beneath the shade of a tree, a group of students at his feet. In his fortieth year, the rabbi was a tall man with protruding ears, a prominent nose and a receding hairline.

"What's wrong? Where's your brother?" the rabbi cried as Masabala charged to his side.

Masabala yanked on his father's arm. "We spotted Romans! Livel is hurt. He couldn't run so I left him in the desert while I came for help." For a split second Masabala thought he saw condemnation flash in his father's eyes. Shame seeped over him as he bit back tears.

"Horses! Get the horses!" Eleazar yelled, sprinting toward the barn.

* * *

Masabala, Rabbi Eleazar and the rabbi's closest friend, Yehuda, galloped into the desert. Masabala rode beside his father, his knees locked hard against the saddle as they flew over the rock-strewn terrain.

Ten minutes into their rescue, Masabala pulled back on the reins, and his horse slowed to a walk. He scanned the distance between En Gedi and the caves. "There, Abba. I left him there! I remember that clump of rocks where he fell!"

They were moving forward slowly when the rabbi reined in his horse and slid off the saddle. He knelt on the ground, tracing tracks in the sand with trembling hands.

Yehuda crouched beside him. "It appears to have been a small group, no more than eight or ten. They're heading north," he said.

"We will follow." The rabbi looked straight at Masabala. "And when we find them, we will help your brother escape."

* * *

They moved through the valley between Masada and En Gedi as the sun was setting, the waning light making it more and more difficult to see the tracks left by Livel's captors. Blanketed in despair, no one spoke, the only sounds the panting of horses and the calls of an occasional flock of birds passing overhead.

Then without warning, there was a subtle shift in the wind. The sand began to vibrate and lift, drifting across the barren ground, the winds increased, hurling grains of needle-like sand and small pieces of rock into the air. For men who inhabited the desert, they knew there was no choice but to seek shelter. The rabbi pointed toward the caves, his shouts barely heard over the now shrieking storm. Pulling the tunics over their faces for protection, they coaxed their mounts toward the cliff walls.

At the mouth of a cave, protected by vast boulders, they dismounted and led their horses inside.

"Father," Masabala screamed, "we can't just give up!"

The rabbi pulled Masabala into the cave. "We are not giving up! But I will not risk your life or Yehuda's life."

"We can't just stand here and let them take Livel!" Masabala cried, frustration burning his face crimson.

"We have no choice but to wait and place our trust in the Holy One, Blessed be He." The rabbi turned toward Jerusalem. A truly pious man, Eleazar lived with one foot in the secular world and the other in the spiritual realm. Prayer was his form of communication with God, and he believed without question that his lamentations would be heard.

I raise my eyes upon the mountains; whence will come my help? My help is from Adonai, Maker of heaven and earth. He covered his eyes with his right hand, preparing to recite the invocation that was the cornerstone of Judaism, a prayer that proclaimed the ideology of one God.

"*Sh'ma Yis-ra-eil, A-do-nai E-lo-hei-nu, A-do-nai E-chad.* Hear O Israel, the Lord is our God, the Lord is One. *Ba-ruch sheim k'vod mal-chu-to l'o-lam va-ed.* Blessed be the name of the glory of His kingdom forever and ever."

The rabbi reached out a hand to his son. Masabala stared at his father and then slowly turned away.

His father would rather pray than fight.

Masabala had no use for a God that would forsake his brother.

* * *

Hours later the howling winds finally subsided. The silence that followed their journey was eerie; it hung over the riders as they traveled through the shadowed night.

"I'm so sorry, my friend," Yehuda said, moving next to the rabbi. "Perhaps we can try again at daybreak."

"It's over," the rabbi said, silent tears falling. "There are no tracks to follow. My son is in the hands of the Holy One, Blessed be He."

"No!" Masabala shouted. "We must keep looking."

"Which direction shall we go?" the rabbi asked gently.

Masabala looked north and then east and west. There were hundreds of Roman encampments between here and Jerusalem, and he had no idea where they might have taken Livel. He wanted to shout at his father, to scream every obscenity he knew. Instead, he kicked his horse and rode ahead, embracing his anger, allowing it to plant itself in his gut. The closer they came to En Gedi, the angrier he became, as if he were being consumed from the inside out.

Anger was easier to accept than guilt.

Two months later

Alone in the kitchen of the two-storied stone house, Miriam stooped over a pot that hung in the hearth. Barely four and a half feet tall, she had black curly hair that she kept covered with a scarf for modesty, gentle grey eyes, thick brows and Livel's ingratiating smile–a smile that had died the day her son disappeared.

With a heavy sigh, she brushed the hair from her eyes, reached for a spoon, dropped it in the stew and stirred. It was an act that took enormous willpower, because in truth, Miriam didn't care if it boiled over or not. In fact, she didn't really care much about anything anymore. She missed her son. She missed him so much that at times she would see a shadow and turn her head quickly, certain that it was Livel. Other times, she was certain she heard him call, and she would run upstairs to his room. Each time, the disappointment assailed her anew, and she would collapse in a heap on the floor.

Miriam kept all of this to herself, including her belief that God was punishing her because she had forgotten the greatest of all virtues, humility. Even Saul, Israel's first King, had preached that his heart not be lifted above his brethren. Yet she had been self-important, as if Livel's great talents were her doing and not the Holy One, Blessed be He.

Miriam was so entrenched in her own grief, that the simple act of a smile made her feel disrespectful to the memory of Livel. Even her husband, Eleazar, was becoming impatient with her. Yet, she could not be intimate, could not bring down the walls that surrounded her. If she did, she would shatter.

* * *

It was the day after Sabbath, and Masabala stood at the entrance to Market Street. The place was teeming with buyers, some from as far away as Beersheba. They came to the fertile oasis to haggle prices with the merchants for dates, oranges, mangos, goat's milk and cheese. Masabala was here to escape his loneliness, even for just a little while.

He watched Joseph, the cheese purveyor, slice a hunk and wrap it in cloth, muttering about the buyer taking food from the mouth of his children. Masabala smiled, knowing that Joseph lived well off the profits from his cheese. He moved into the fray, sidestepping jugglers and barbers chairs. As he entered a bakery, he felt a tap on the shoulder.

He turned to see Sarah staring at him. "I miss Livel," she whispered, her eyes filling with tears. Sarah was a slender fifteen-year-old with big brown eyes, a round face, high cheekbones and a crooked smile

Masabala took her arm. In silence, they dodged mules being loaded with supplies and squeezed between shoppers. Without words, they traversed several backyards, climbed over a stone wall and kept walking until they were standing beneath their tree house.

Sarah found a toehold and climbed to the first low hanging branch. Years earlier, Livel had secured a plank of wood where the branch met the trunk, so that Sarah could ascend easily. When she reached the platform, she sat cross-legged under the canopy of branches. She watched as Masabala climbed into the fortress and then sat beside her.

For so many years it had been just the three of them, their private fort where they were allowed to talk about anything, no matter how inconsequential or irreverent.

"It's not the same without Livel," Sarah said, "but if I close my eyes and pretend—"

"We're not children anymore," Masabala snapped. "Livel's gone, and he's never coming back!"

Sarah knew that Masabala's anger was not aimed at her. He still blamed himself for Livel's capture. "If things had been different and you had been the one hurt, would you have let Livel stay with you?"

Masabala shook his head. "But we wouldn't have been there in the first place, if not for me."

"And Livel could have said no, but he didn't."

Masabala didn't want to hear her. Anger was his refuge, and the need for revenge all consuming. He stood and kicked at a tree branch until it broke.

"Stop it," Sarah admonished. "You're going to ruin everything."

"Everything is already ruined," Masabala shouted, yanking a board from the corner of the tree house and heaving it to the ground. "This is a stupid, useless place, and I want it gone!"

Sarah grabbed his arm. "You don't mean that!"

He jerked away, his mouth in a snarl. "Get out! Now! Before you get hurt."

Sarah saw a knife on the table and reached for it, wondering at first why Miriam would have left the chopping knife out. Then the realization struck her. Tens of thousands of zealots had cut off a finger, a way of proving their loyalty and showing they were worthy of joining Bar Kokhba's army.

She glared at Masabala. "You better not be about to do what I think you're about to do!"

"This is my business." He said, taking the knife from her hand. "You could never understand."

"You're the son of a rabbi. You're not allowed to mutilate yourself!" Sarah bit down hard on her lip. She wanted to wish away the stubborn set to his jaw; an expression that she knew meant he had made up his mind. "You're not even sixteen yet, and besides, it would be a terrible thing to do to your parents!"

"My mother can't even look at me. All I do is remind her of the son she lost, the son she loved best."

"That's not true. Your mother loves you too. She's just grieving." Sarah touched his knee. "If you go away, what will happen to me? I can't lose you too!"

Masabala momentarily lost himself in the familiar face. Sarah could be impetuous and often talk too much, but there were times when he was so infatuated with her, he could barely think. He reached for her hands. "You have to go, Sarah."

"Why are you always sending me away?" she cried, slamming her fist on the table. She stared at the knife. "Go ahead! But I'm not going anywhere. I'll be outside."

* * *

Sweat dripped into Masabala's eyes. He stood and rested his left hand beside the table's edge, made a fist and placed his smallest finger on the table. He held the knife over the second knuckle. It was the most terrifying thing Masabala had ever contemplated.

He held the knife in his trembling hand. *I deserted my brother.* Anger seethed. He lifted the knife, the blade catching a flash of sunlight. *I will never be a coward again!* He struck the blow and heard the crunch of bone. The tip of his finger flew across the table. In shock, he stared at it thinking it looked like something to be thrown into a stew pot. It took seconds for what he had done to register in his brain, and then the agony hit. Time shrank, and his vision blurred. The pain shot up his arm. His heart raced, the pounding in his ears deafening, as a crimson puddle grew at his feet. He howled.

Groping for the strip of white cloth that he had cut beforehand, he used his mouth to tighten the knot at the base of his finger to stop the flow of blood. He was trying to wrap another strip of cloth around the bloodied stump, when Sarah charged into the room. She saw the tip of his finger lying on the table, ran back outside and retched in the grass.

Taking huge gulps of air, Sarah forced herself back into the room. Pushing back her shoulders in defiance to her cowardice, she took the bandage from Masabala and secured it around the nub of his finger. With tears streaming down her face, she kissed his cheek.

He would become a soldier, and she would lose him. She only hoped not forever.

* * *

Simon Bar Kokhba sat tall in the saddle as he entered En Gedi. His commanders surrounded him, a dozen soldiers selected for their loyalty, exceptional physical strength and mental prowess. As disciples of Bar Kokhba, the men were valiant, self-righteous and pious. They observed the Sabbath and all the Jewish holidays. To pay for schools and synagogues, they had the responsibility for collecting *Tzedakah*, charity, from every soldier.

Bar Kokhba had his detractors, gossipmongers who thought him an impervious dictator with an aggrandized opinion of himself. His followers, fifty thousand strong and growing every day, fervently disagreed. They believed Bar Kokhba to be the Messiah, a humble servant to his people, a brilliant military tactician and a charismatic leader anointed by God.

The entourage moved single file, turning left at the first street and right at the next one. Bar Kokhba paid careful attention to the storefronts they passed, memorizing where medicines, bitumen and salt from the Dead Sea were sold, so he could requisition them for his troops as needed.

They continued on past the flourmill and the balsam building, where all of Judea's perfume and medicines were produced. A group of pubescent boys were congregated in the street, blocking the way. They were leading camels and donkeys laden with sacks of grain and jugs of date palm honey. Bar Kokhba lifted his arms and shouted for them to stand aside. At over six feet three inches tall, his height in the saddle alone would have been enough to terrify the boys. Then they recognized the auburn-bearded man with the shock of red hair, tied back with a leather strip.

"It's him!" one of the boys shouted.

Crowding around Bar Kokhba, the boys reached out to touch the great man.

"Work hard and study," Bar Kokhba said, patting heads. "I'm going to need all of you to join my army when you've grown."

Their faces flushed with pride. The awestruck boys stepped aside, waving as the entourage passed, headed toward the synagogue.

The men dismounted when they arrived at the rock terrace where the synagogue compound was located. The compound was a series of single-roomed stone buildings that opened into a large courtyard. Surrounded by a wall, the only entranceway into the compound was a doorway that led into a square chamber.

Rabbi Eleazar stood at that doorway. He had received a message from Rabbi Akiva and was prepared for the meeting. He lovingly touched the pouch he wore around his waist. "Shalom," he said, greeting Bar Kokhba with a handshake and an embrace. "It's good that you have come."

"I am so sorry for your great loss." Bar Kokhba said, saddened by the misery he saw in the rabbi's eyes. "If words could change anything..."

Eleazar sighed, remembering the hundreds of funerals he had officiated; offering solace to the grieving and telling them that time heals. Only in his own misery did he come to realize that grief was a language unto itself.

Chapter 4

In silence, the two men walked through the chamber and down a set of stairs that led to a tree-shaded garden. A table had been set with pitchers of wine and sweets. The men sat. Bar Kokhba accepted a glass a wine from Eleazar, and together they said the blessing before drinking. The stillness hung over them like a shroud, as a bird chirped and the trees rustled.

"Hundreds have assembled in the synagogue to greet you," Eleazar said, realizing that at least for now he must push aside his grief, regardless of how impossible that seemed.

"And there is much I have to say to my followers. But first, you and I must talk."

Eleazar forced himself to relax, knowing that Bar Kokhba would not get straight to the point. It was not his way.

"The Torah tells us that God instructed Moses to build a tabernacle as a dwelling place to hold the Ten Commandments," Bar Kokhba said with great passion, using his hands to dramatically punctuate his words.

As a learned rabbi, Eleazar was not hearing anything he did not know. Bar Kokhba was himself magical, and Eleazar was under his spell.

"For two hundred years, we worshiped at that alter offering sacrifices as a way to approach God. Then David, the prophet, pointed out to our people that we had built our own houses. Now it was the time to build a house for God in Jerusalem. David drew the plans, gathered the materials and was ready to begin."

Bar Kokhba placed both hands on the table and continued. "A soothsayer warned David that as a man of war, he could not build the Temple. So he turned the project over to his son, Solomon. I am a man of war like David." Bar Kokhba paused, and a huge smile turned the corners of his mouth. "Unlike David, after we have defeated the Romans and Judea is ours," he took a breath, and Eleazar leaned closer. "I have the blessings of the Holy One, Blessed be He, to build the Third Temple!"

Eleazar gasped. Speaking to God was blasphemy. It was self-serving. But this was the *nasi,* the prince, the Messiah of the Jews. Eleazar believed him.

The First Temple had stood in Jerusalem for over four hundred years. The Ark of the Covenant was enthroned in the Holy of Holies–the one place in the world where God's presence dwelled. Miracles abounded, and the priests communicated directly with the Holy One, Blessed be He, through the sacred rights of sacrifice. It was a time like no other–until the Temple was destroyed and the Ark was lost.

When the Second Temple was built there was no Ark, few prophecies or miracles. Still the Jews continued to maintain some of their old ways. After the destruction of the Second Temple, they established synagogues and prayer–not sacrifice. That became the new way of communicating with the Holy One, Blessed be He.

"Envision what is going to happen once the Ark is back in the Holy of Holies!" Bar Kokhba's eyes were afire. "God's presence will return, and we will conquer our enemies. Justice and harmony will prevail, and Israel will be restored. The dead shall rise, and justice will reign!" Bar Kokhba put out his mighty hand. "This is the moment."

Rabbi Eleazar trembled and was overcome by trepidation. He had spent his adult life keeping his secret, but it was time for him to break the oath of silence.

Rabbi Eleazar began, his voice shaking. "When the First Temple was destroyed over five hundred years ago and the Ark of the Covenant disappeared, everyone assumed the Babylonians had taken it. That is what our sages told us, and that is what we believed. But that is not what happened." He looked hard at Bar Kokhba wondering just how much Rabbi Akiva had told him. It was impossible to tell from his intense and curious expression. "The High Priest was shown a vision by God: he foresaw the impending attack on the First Temple and knew that he had to hide the Ark. To protect the secret, the High Priest told no one but his closest advisors residing inside the Temple compound. To insure that no one would become suspicious that the Tablets no longer dwelled inside the Holy of Holies, they continued to hold the services and sacrifices.

"What I am going to tell you now came from my father, as told to him by his father." He paused, noting that Bar Kokhba seemed as tense as a tiger. "There were two brothers, Kohens like me, directly descended from Moses' brother, Aaron. They were working inside the compound. It was their revered job to prepare and sort the wood that would be used for the sacred Altar.

"One day the older priest noticed that there was a loose marble tile on the floor near where they were working. Peering through the crack, they saw a passageway below. Rumors among the priests were rampant that the Ark had been hidden beneath the Temple. They knew it was not their right to know the location of the Holy Tablets, but they could not resist the temptation. They tried to move the huge stone. When their attempt failed, the brothers tried to smash the tile. The metal of the ax hit the stone, and it caused a great spark to flash and kill the older brother.

"How much of this is true and how much is conjecture, we will never know. But the story goes that the younger brother saw his brother's death as a sign from God. He believed that it was divinely decreed that the Ark must remain hidden until the coming of the Messiah.

"To insure that the location would never be lost to the Jewish people, he wrote down the exact location of the Ark on tiny pieces of parchment. He made three copies. For generations, that information had been passed down through the Kohen lineage, three men always entrusted with the knowledge." Rabbi Eleazar wiped his sweating brow as he watched the expressions coloring Bar

Kokhba's face. He saw excitement, expectation and triumph on the Messiah's face.

"Over time, it was decreed that one man must always have residence in Judea, and the other two must live in the Diaspora. To insure that the information was never lost, each man had an obligation to tell only one other person–the sage considered the greatest rabbi of that time. I was given the parchment by my father on my twenty-fifth birthday, and in turn, I went to Rabbi Akiva." Eleazar moved his hand protectively to the pouch on his waist.

"You must trust me," Bar Kokhba said, sensing Eleazar's hesitation. "It will be a time of great jubilation when we build the Third Temple and return the Ark to its rightful place in the Holy of Holies!"

The rabbi had always expected to pass down the great secret to his son Livel. He fumbled with the pouch, fingers resisting his bidding. Using every ounce of his concentration, he managed to remove the velvet purse that held the sacrosanct parchment. It was the first time he had the sacred document in his hand in over twenty years, keeping the pouch hidden inside a box in the ground beneath his bed. The only one knowing its location was Rabbi Akiva.

And so it was written, and so it was prophesized. The Messiah had come; the Temple would be restored. He handed the parchment to Shimon Bar Kokhba, Messiah of the Jewish people.

Both men had tears in their eyes.

* * *

The synagogue was a rectangular shaped room with stone benches that sat in rows across the center of the room and along the walls. Every seat was taken.

Guards stood watch. As Bar Kokhba and Rabbi Eleazar entered, a hush fell over the crowd.

"Please," the rabbi said, sweeping his hand forward for Bar Kokhba to precede him, "they are all so anxious to hear the news."

Bar Kokhba walked down the aisle and turned. Three hundred faces stared back at him.

"Shalom, my brothers," he said in Hebrew, his eyes scanning the room. "I stand before you today with a heavy heart." He looked at Eleazar. "The loss of Livel is a tragedy. The loss of any Jew into the bowels of slavery is a tragedy! For each one is someone's son or daughter, brother or sister, mother or father, grandmother or grandfather. Will we sit back and do nothing?" he shouted.

"No!" the assembled shouted, standing with their fists in the air.

Bar Kokhba walked slowly down the aisle. "We must stop the Romans from enslaving our people!"

Heads bobbed in agreement, and there was more shouting.

"Just yesterday, one of my spies returned from Rome." Bar Kokhba put his hands behind his back and waited for silence. "Emperor Hadrian," he spat the name, "has sent a proclamation that no new rabbis are to be ordained. Disobeying this decree is punishable by death!"

A hum filled the sanctuary, rising to a crescendo of outrage. Bar Kokhba, masterful orator that he was, allowed the fury to build before holding up his hand for silence.

"Our people," he said softly, "have never asked for much. We have our beliefs, our one God, and we have never forced those beliefs on others." His face hardened. "Hadrian promised to protect Jerusalem and to allow us to rebuild our Temple–the Temple that Titus destroyed over sixty years ago."

With every face on him, he lifted his eyes toward the heavens. "He has gone back on that promise. Hadrian intends to rename our Jerusalem, *Aelie Capitolina,* and the sacred ground where our Temple stood is to be desecrated by a temple dedicated to Jupiter." Fury burned from Bar Kokhba's eyes. The room was silent. "This vow I make to you today. This is our land, and the time has come for us to claim it!"

"How can we fight the Romans when we have no weapons?" someone yelled.

"We will be slaughtered!" another voice added.

"We have weapons–thousands of them, and thousands more will be ours before we mount a campaign." Bar Kokhba could see the disbelief in the eyes of his followers.

"Where did these weapons come from?" came another shouted query from the crowd.

"From the Romans," Bar Kokhba proclaimed.

A buzz of disbelief filled the room.

Eleazar put his hand on Bar Kokhba's arm. "Please explain."

"The Romans commissioned us to make arms for their army. We did just that, but we made every third weapon defective." He smiled for the first time. "As I anticipated," he said with the emphasis on I, "the arms were rejected by their generals and given back to us for repair." He rubbed his hand through his thick red beard and waited a few heartbeats. "The weapons are repaired. Just this morning, we stored hundreds of them in a cave not far from here."

"How much longer before we fight?" a man called from the front row.

"Soon, but we still have preparations to make. For that I need more volunteers!"

Two hundred men cheered.

A bloody-handed boy joined with them. It was a decision that would change his life forever.

Chapter 5

Egypt

Livel stood on the docks of the deepwater seaport in Alexandria, Egypt with a hundred other slaves: men, women and children, all spoils of war swept up in Rome's conquest of expansion. The water flowed in dapples of light, reflecting the sun. Around him were the sounds of departure, from the crisp cascade of flapping sails to the rusting wails of anchors dislodging from the stubborn sea floor. The excited voices of sailors yelped tawdry lyrics as they loaded exotic spices: cloves, ginger, nutmeg, turmeric and pepper. All were destined for the spice markets of Rome.

The vessel they were about to board was a three-mast square-sailed ship with a symmetrical hull and identical bow. The stern-post ended in a swan's head that faced mid-ships. The steering oars were located in the belly of the ship where cables, tillers and rudders regulated the steering.

With the sound of whips cracking over their heads, the Rome-bound slaves were herded aboard and then immediately taken below deck. They were shoved into a vast wooden-planked room with only one porthole, the limited light casting every shape into the semblance of grotesque statues. Within seconds, the lack of fresh air and the closeness of so many perspiring bodies turned the space into a pulsating inferno. Mothers wailed, grasping their children's hands tightly as they slipped on the slimy sewage that lay like silt along the floor. Adding to the hellish surroundings were the frenzied screams of monkeys and the earsplitting roars of lions coming from cages set along the walls. All were being transported to Rome for games in the Coliseum.

Livel had been the only one given bedding and a blanket. He found a spot for himself and squatted on his haunches, burying his face in his hands. With deep concentration, he managed to suspend his thoughts and numb his emotions.

Once the ship had set sail, the rocking motion twisted Livel's insides. His unrelenting seasickness combined with the accumulating filth and the overpowering stink from the animals compounded his wretchedness. Throughout the entire first day, he vomited his stomach empty, not able to keep even a sip of water down. By nightfall, encircled by pitiful moans and perplexing dialects of his fellow captives, Livel managed to fall into a fitful sleep.

For the next two days, Livel lay in his misery. Too sick to move, his body dehydrated, he teetered on the edge of consciousness. In the midst of hallucinating, he heard his mother's voice and saw flashes of his father's face. He felt a tiny flutter of a hand on his forehead and opened his eyes. Staring back at him was a child no older than nine. She had a cherubic face with saucer-like eyes and a dusky coal-tinted complexion. Her mouth edged upward revealing white teeth that glowed against the blackness of her skin.

The child began an unintelligible dialogue, the inflection insistent as she held a cup of water to his mouth. Livel shook his head certain that if he vomited one more time, his insides would spill out. The tiny girl refused to be dissuaded, sticking her fingers in the water and then putting some water in Livel's mouth. The simplicity of her actions and the determination etched on her troubled little face both inspired and embarrassed him. Unable to withstand her scrutiny, he closed his eyes as she repeatedly dipped her tiny fingers in the water and put them in his mouth. When the glass was empty, she snuggled against the curve of his body.

When morning came, the child was in his arms. With great determination, she helped him to sit up and brought him a bowl of watery gruel. He took intermittent spoonfuls and managed to keep the food down.

He felt better and smiled. "Livel," he said, pointing to himself, trying to imagine what he must look like to the child. His beard was straggly. He hadn't bathed in weeks and grime covered his body turning his own complexion muddy. He pointed a finger at her.

The child made a series of clicking sounds followed by a word that sounded like Tillie.

Livel patted his chest, said his name again and then pronounced hers. "Tillie."

"Tillie," she repeated with a grin.

While communication was impossible between them, it became obvious to Livel that she was alone, even though she occasionally went to speak with others of her skin color. Those conversations always ended with the child in tears. With loneliness and fear as their ally, Tillie and Livel were never more than a few paces from each other's side.

Food was served twice a day, at daybreak and sundown. The sailors carried in the huge pots and doled out gruel into dirty food-encrusted bowls. A week into their voyage to Rome, as they were waiting for their rations, a herd of boisterous soldiers barreled into the hold. Tillie grabbed Livel's hand in terror.

There were soldiers everywhere. One minute Livel had Tillie's hand, and the next instant she was gone. Livel screamed her name and smashed into the nearest soldier. She screamed back. Livel lunged forward kicking and punching his way to the door. He was struck from behind and fell to the ground in a heap.

When Livel regained his footing, it was too late. Ten children, boys and girls, had been taken. Livel expected cries of protest from the other slaves, but instead, there was only silence. Even the animals were still. Livel went to his tiny section of floor and sat.

She's an innocent and harmless little girl. When they get her into the daylight, they will see that and bring her back. Livel had to believe that, or he would go mad.

For the next day and night he kept vigil, never closing his eyes. At times he prayed, and at other times he cursed and paced. On the morning of the second day, Tillie and the others were thrown into the hold.

Livel carried Tillie and placed her limp body on a small square of hay that he had stolen from the lion's cage. She opened her eyes and tried to smile at him through a mouth torn wide. Her front teeth were missing. Blood oozed beneath her. When Livel tried to place a wet rag between her legs, Tillie thrashed and screamed. A black woman approached and shooed Livel away.

He stood off to the side watching as the woman turned Tillie over to her belly and lifted the tunic. Tillie's rectum was shredded and raw, blood spilling from the rupture. The woman turned Tillie on her back and moved toward Livel. She shook her head, her eyes filling with tears.

"No!" Livel shrieked. "She is not going to die!"

Livel gently padded every bleeding orifice with rags and dripped water into Tillie's mouth, just as she had done for him. There were moments when he thought she was rallying. Then she would begin to slip away, with her chest barely rising. When death finally came, it was subtle, yet sudden. Her breathing stopped, and her body turned cold.

Livel ran to the door, screaming for a guard, pounding with unrelenting fury.

Five soldiers rushed into the hold, shoving him aside as they swept among the captives. Four of the ten children were dead.

A young soldier, with blond hair and treacherous green eyes, stood over the dead child.

Livel ran back to Tillie and lifted her in his arms. "Look what you've done!" he howled. "You're all animals!"

The green-eyed soldier shrugged, moved to turn away and then turned back. "You think I'm an animal?" He kicked Livel in the groin and smashed a fist into his face. Tillie dropped from his arms. Livel ducked his head and tried to charge the soldier, but strong arms pinned him from behind. The soldier stared hard at Livel, his expression murderous.

"Hold him! Don't let him move!" the soldier ordered as he bent over and lifted Tillie.

"Don't touch her!" Livel wailed. He tried to kick free but to no avail.

The soldier kept his eyes on Livel as he moved toward the lion's cage with Tillie in his arms. He opened the feeding door and shoved the little girl's lifeless body inside.

"No!" Livel howled, twisting and fighting to free himself.

Then his world went black.

Rome

Livel disembarked in Ostia, twenty-two miles from Rome. The port was at the mouth of the Tiber River on the coast of the Tyrrhenian Sea. Once Livel was on the dock, his captor Marcus Gracchus loaded him into a wagon along with supplies and bounty pillaged by the commander's troops.

Rome was an expansive, multifaceted and diverse metropolis. Set among seven hills, with a population just under a million people, the city was filled with structures of monumental proportions. There was the Forum of Trajan with its basilica, libraries and a six-storied complex of shops, depots and offices. On the Campus Martius sat the Pantheon, a temple rebuilt by Emperor Hadrian to all the gods of Rome. It boasted the largest unsupported dome in the world, built as a likeness to the heavens. In the center of the city was the Flavian Amphitheater, the tallest structure in Rome and the Coliseum, constructed of limestone, brick and marble. It could hold over sixty thousand spectators for the gladiatorial games.

Eleven aqueducts served the city, their water carried from the surrounding hillsides. The water was used for washing, drinking and flushing the sewer system.

Throughout Rome, tucked into every available piece of land, were brothels, baths, theaters, gymnasiums and taverns. The inhabitants lived in modest homes, enormous villas, imperial residences and blocks and blocks of apartment dwellings.

Just walking down some of the congested sidewalks was dangerous, as random tiles fell from rooftops and occupants heaved sewage from open windows above the streets. The din of horses' hooves and the pandemonium of clanging chariot wheels kept the city in a state of infernal noise.

* * *

The Gracchus estate consisted of four colonnades that supported the two-story main house where the family and a select number of house slaves lived.

Nine bedrooms with adjacent sitting rooms occupied the first floor, all fitted with pipes to receive hot steam in the winter. There was a gymnasium, two gilded dining rooms and the kitchen where the house servants ate their meals. Beside the kitchen were storerooms for grain and wine. Three reception areas and the huge bath completed the ground level. The slave quarters were on the west side of the second story. On the east side of the second floor were two more expansive dining rooms, a study and a library.

When Livel arrived, he was taken directly to the stables. He gagged and coughed, loathing the stink of the animals and the memories the smells evoked.

An old man approached. He had stooped shoulders, a round silver-bearded face and a waddled jaw line. "My, my, my, you are certainly in great need of a bath and some clean clothing," he said in Latin, noting the purple and yellow bruises surrounding both of Livel's eyes. "I am the tutor, Zosima."

"Livel." It was the first word he had uttered since Tillie's death.

"Please come with me," Zosima said, moving beside Livel. They walked down a graveled pathway, both sides lined with lush green bushes and blooming trees.

Five minutes later, they arrived at an entranceway with two large wooden doors. Inside they moved through a series of rooms with marble walls, frescoed ceilings and tiled floors. Each room had a bath.

"The family prefers the public baths so these are seldom used except by a select few servants who are allowed access," Zosima said when they entered the third room. "Remove your clothes. I will have them burned."

Astonished by the opulent surroundings and aching to be rid of the gory reminder of his time on the ship, Livel stripped naked. He looked toward the tutor.

"Get in," the man said, pointing to the bath.

Livel slid into the warm water and ducked his head. The filth crusted from his body forming a gritty film in the water.

The tutor slipped off his sandals and dangled his legs in the pool.

"How long have you been a slave?" Livel asked, shocked by the gruffness of his own voice as he rubbed grime from his hair.

"I was brought from Greece and have been here for twenty years. And while it was a lifetime ago, I can still remember the angst and trepidation I felt on the day of my arrival."

"Twenty years!" Livel blurted. The words of Exodus echoed in his head. *If thou buy a Hebrew servant, six years he shall serve: and in the seventh, he shall go out free for nothing. If he came in by himself, he shall go out by himself."* But this was not Judea. Too much had transpired over the last few days for him to think clearly, let alone speak without sounding like a lunatic. He remained silent. Tillie's death had debilitated him in ways he was still trying to comprehend. Broken-hearted, missing his family, disoriented and soaking in a bath in a foreign land–it was all too much for him to assimilate.

After scrubbing and soaking for quarter of an hour Zosima offered Livel a towel. Escorted to a table, he was instructed to lie down. With practiced hands, the tutor massaged and perfumed oil into Livel's back and shoulders. Then he had him turn over and continued working on his legs, chest and arms. The warmth of a human touch made Livel long for his family. He fought the lump forming in his throat.

"This is a strigil," Zosima said, holding up a small curved metal tool. "I will use this to scrape off the grime."

Livel looked at the apparatus with apprehension. It seemed more appropriate as an instrument of torture. He moved to sit up.

Zosima put a strong hand to his chest. "I won't hurt you."

The old man's eyes captured his. He saw kindness there and lay back down.

When Zosima was finished, he showed him into another room. The floor was hot and the bath warmer than the first one.

"I'll be back in a little while," Zosima said.

Livel slipped beneath the surface. Rage and hate, sorrow and despondency assailed him like talons gripping his throat. No amount of scrubbing could ever free him from the filth he had witnessed. Judaism had taught Livel that when a person sinned against another, he was not to remain silent or to let hate linger in his heart. He should face his enemy and rebuke him. Finally, if an enemy asked for forgiveness, one was required to absolve him.

It seemed like such a simple concept when his father cited the teachings of Leviticus. In that other world, long ago, Livel imagined himself a rabbi one day, repeating those same ethics to his students.

That was then, before the savage murder of innocent little Tillie. Livel tried to envision what his father would say to him if he were here, but no words came. So he did the only thing he knew to do. Livel prayed. He begged God to help him remain a faithful Jew and to help him find a way back home to his family.

* * *

Livel and Zosima shared a room on the second floor above the kitchen on the west side of the sprawling manor. There were two couches that served as beds; the only other pieces of furniture were a long wooden table used for study and two chairs.

Lying in bed but unaccustomed to the stillness after so many days at sea, Livel could not fall asleep. With great resolve, he tried to focus on the present, on what would happen in the morning rather than a year from now. But with every passing hour, the anxiety deepened, and Livel found himself entrenched in the world of *what-if* and *if-only*.

By first light, Livel stood with his back to the open window watching the old man sleep, taking comfort in the cadence of his snores. The birthing sun filtered into the room, and the tutor opened his eyes. He flashed a smile and stretched his skinny purple-veined arms flabby and vulnerable in the dawning light.

"Ready to begin the day I see," Zosima said, planting his feet on the ground. "Give me a few minutes, and we'll go to the kitchen for breakfast."

After a meal of salted bread, dried fruit and cheese, Zosima took Livel to the Gracchus family barber where his beard was trimmed and his hair cut short.

"You will spend the morning reading the books and scrolls that I assign to you. If you are to become teacher to the Gracchus sons, there is much you must master first," Zosima said as they walked back to their room. "After lunch, we will discuss what you've learned. In the late afternoon, I will take you to the baths. After supper, you will be free to rest."

There was something about the idea of a routine that gave Livel solace–at least he would know what to expect.

* * *

Livel, dressed in a white wool tunic, sat cross-legged on the couch in his room.

"We must talk," Zosima said, sitting on a chair across from him. "You have been here a week and still, you barely sleep. I have tried to allow you time to adjust. I have not pried for fear of interfering, but I can no longer remain silent. You will become ill if you don't learn to accept your fate."

"Accept my fate as a slave?" Livel shook his head. "Never! I am the son of a rabbi. The only master I will ever have is the Holy One, Blessed be He."

"It's your God that brought you here," Zosima said softly.

"And my God will lead me home." Livel's voice hardened. "I will walk in my own shadow, not in the shadow of another."

"And I hope that someday you do. But in the meantime, there is more than one way to live a meaningful life," Zosima said. "You may see me as a failure, an old man with deteriorating eyesight, who relinquished his life willingly. But that is not who I am."

Zosima stood, lifted his tunic and turned his back to Livel, revealing dozens of jagged scars, obviously the result of whippings. "I tried to run away–more than once. This was the result."

"I meant no disrespect to you," Livel said, imagining the agony of those beatings. After spending his life schooled in the oral traditions of Judaism, the sage Hillel's words echoed, *do not judge your fellow human being until you have reached that person's place.* It was a profound lesson worth remembering.

"I have had only one thought in my mind for years: freedom," Zosima continued, pulling down his tunic. "I finally accepted that escape was not possible. This was to be my life. The Gracchus family has come to respect me, and I too have learned to respect myself. A slave who respects himself is an honored man!"

Zosima's eyes clouded. "I have spent years trying to educate Scipio Gracchus, oldest son of Marcus, and Domitius, the younger son. The task has been difficult. They are both reluctant learners. With my patience now gone, I celebrate when they are away. Even as we speak, they are off again to the family's summer estate. The boys will be gone for three months. That is how long I have to educate you in the ways of Rome and prepare you to assume my duties. Only then can I leave this place–allowed to live out the rest of my life as a free man."

"You were beaten for trying to escape, and now you are being granted your freedom?" Livel asked, unable to make sense of the tutor's remarks.

"In our studies you will learn Greek philosophy, about the Epicureans and the Stoics and how they have influenced Roman thought. Stoicism proclaims slaves are equal to other men. Slaves who save enough money are allowed to purchase their freedom or be freed by their captors. Marcus Gracchus is a follower of the philosophy and has agreed to set me free."

"I will do nothing to stand in the way of that freedom," Livel said, staring at Zosima.

Chapter 6

Three months later
129 CE

Livel sat among a dozen opened scrolls scattered about the couch. His eyes were blurred from reading and his voice was hoarse from arguing with Zosima. "The Stoics profess to believe in God, but I will never accept the concept of pantheism, that nature and God are identical, and the entire universe is animated by a world soul!" Livel said. He studied as he always did, with one eye on philosophy and his mind's-eye on the Torah, the five books of Moses.

"If you would simply open your mind," Zosima replied, "the philosophy has great merit."

"One doesn't need an open mind to accept what seems like an absurd notion!" Livel retorted.

"Why must you continue to equate everything with Judaism?" Zosima shook his head in frustration. "Just try to imagine the tranquility you would feel if you acknowledged the Stoic belief that *fate* is the key to human happiness. Then you could stop trying to control events and learn to maintain your equanimity and accept your destiny."

"The Torah teaches us that though we have the ability to do evil, we should do no evil. Making decisions about living our lives demonstrates free will," Livel stated. "I believe in the transcendence of God, and I believe He acts in the world on behalf of His people." After many months, he and Zosima were still worlds apart in their beliefs.

"It takes courage to be so certain that your way is the right way," Zosima said. A slight smile crossed his face and then disappeared as quickly as it came. "And despite your stubbornness, I want to commend you. You've learned more in just a few months than the Gracchus boys have managed to learn in a lifetime of my teaching.

"And even though others will now teach the boys the concepts of judicial forms and procedure, I am proud that you have grasped an understanding of judgments and legal decisions of the court.

"In my opinion, you are ready to become their tutor for philosophy and literature. Your ability to quote the works of Homer and Hesiod are quite remarkable. In addition, the fact that you have memorized all the works of the Roman poet Ennius is even more commendable, as it's something I could never hope to do."

Zosima rarely gave compliments, so Livel basked in the praise.

"I've been informed that the boys have returned," Zosima continued. "I will tell our master, Marcus Gracchus, that you are ready to begin your duties as teacher to Scipio and Domitius."

"And you will finally have your independence," Livel said, reaching across the scrolls to pat the old man's arm. He was frightened and thrilled at the prospect of taking over for his mentor.

"There is something more," Zosima said. "It has been decided by Marcus Gracchus that you will become Scipio's protector."

"Protector?"

"You will teach both boys, but your primary responsibility will be to accompany Scipio throughout his life. Much like a beloved brother would do."

"Brother! Don't you mean indentured slave?" Livel retorted. The very thought sent shivers down Livel's spine. "Take my word, Zosima, I will not be spending my life with Scipio!"

"It is a great honor," the tutor replied, regarding Livel angrily, "regardless of your high-handed strategy to escape, and believe me young man: I hope one day you will. You must put that aside for now. All that separates you from living this life," he swept his arm around the room, "or facing the gallows, will be how you perform as a teacher."

"And when Scipio goes off to fight for Rome?"

"You teach him to use his head. He will teach you to ride a chariot, shoot an arrow and survive in combat," Zosima said.

Livel thought about how his brother had only one dream; to become a great soldier. *Imagine that, Masabala. Your studious destined-to-be-a-rabbi brother is going to be trained as a fighter. And when I am schooled in the ways of war, I will escape the bondage of slavery, just as my forefathers did in Egypt.*

Silence hung in the air for a moment until Zosima added, "Have you come to trust me?"

"You are the only friend I have."

"Then you must listen carefully," Zosima said. "Your task will be formidable. Scipio only cares about becoming a soldier, and he views all else as a waste of his time. I've tried everything to convince him that intellectual pursuits are as important as physical pursuits, but my words have fallen on deaf ears. Scipio is stubborn and at times childish, but he is harmless."

The old tutor looked around, leaned toward Livel and whispered, "Domitius, on the other hand, is anything but harmless. He is an angry, ambitious young man who will not be satisfied until he is rid of his rival, Scipio."

"You have never spoken of this before," Livel said.

"And I wish I did not have to speak of it now, but the wife is back." Zosima hesitated, searching for a place to begin. "Scipio's mother died in childbirth," he said finally. "Marcus Gracchus then married Athena, a strong-willed woman with an acid tongue, who took every opportunity to be cruel to Scipio. She has a notorious temper and takes delight in personally beating her slaves.

"When Scipio was two, Athena gave birth to Domitius. From the moment her son was born, she has been conniving to make him the favored son of Marcus Gracchus. The father seems to enjoy the brutal competition between the half-brothers.

"Domitius is far more cunning and ruthless than Scipio. It is imperative that you never show favoritism." The tutor's face turned grave. "There is a double-edged sword in all of this. If you can't motivate Scipio to learn, then your position here will be short-lived. And believe me; Domitius will not miss an opportunity to undermine your attempts. If you do manage to inspire Scipio, it will elevate him in his father's eyes. You then become a threat to Domitius. I have seen what he is capable of doing when he is threatened!"

* * *

Perspiration beaded Livel's forehead as he and Zosima walked under the shady vines of the pergola that overhung the garden of the atrium. They followed a path edged by groomed hedges of box and rosemary that separated the east and west wings of the estate. Carefully, they stepped across the ground covering, dodging the mulberry and fig bushes. Together they sat on an ornately carved stone bench beside a marble statue of Jupiter, and waited. The sounds of boots crunching on the path brought them to their feet.

Scipio Gracchus walked with the confidence of a warrior, each step planted with aplomb. He had a classic Roman face: wide forehead, sensuous mouth, straight nose and square chin. His eyes were steel gray, large and owl-like with thick highly arched brows. His curly raven hair was short, and his beard and mustache were closely trimmed. At twenty-one, he was Livel's height with a broad chest and muscular arms.

He smiled at Zosima, examining Livel unabashedly. "As my new tutor and protector, I was told that you are brilliant. I didn't expect you to be so young," Scipio said, his eyes laughing. "With me as a student, you will age quickly." He poked Livel's chest and stared at his scrawny arms. "You have about as much chance of making me a scholar as I have of making you a soldier!"

Livel grinned, instantly liking him. "I'm certain it will be challenging for both of us, but I'm willing to try if you are."

"Did you hear that Zosima? He's negotiating with me already." Scipio turned to Livel. "I like your optimism, since I'm sure you've been forewarned of my ineptitude in matters of intellect."

"Forewarned but not discouraged," Livel replied.

"We'll see if you still feel that way a month from now." Scipio's expression turned serious. "We need to go. My father wishes to speak with us, and he doesn't like to be kept waiting."

* * *

A slave bowed to Scipio, Zosima, and Livel as they entered the library. Built in the round, the room had a domed ceiling and a wall of windows that drenched the room in sunlight. Behind an ornately carved desk sat Marcus Gracchus.

Across from Marcus sat his son Domitius on a wooden platform piled high with pillows, his back to the doorway. Domitius was light skinned with curly blond hair, a sharp nose, full lips and a wide forehead. Although he favored his mother, he had his father's intense green eyes and stocky build. He was as tall as Scipio.

"Scipio is it too much to expect you to be as punctual as your brother?" asked Marcus, displeasure evident in his lifted brows and creased forehead.

"Father, Domitius," Scipio said, crossing his right arm over his chest in greeting, as he moved beside Domitius. As a slave placed a pillow under his feet and adjusted the pillows behind his back, Scipio shot his half-brother a murderous look, knowing that he had intentionally arrived early to gain favor with their father.

Marcus directed his eyes at Livel and Zosima, who stood near a wall of scrolls, a respectful distance away. "This is my son, Domitius. Domitius, this is Livel, your new teacher."

Domitius turned toward Livel with a deprecatory nod.

Livel's heart pounded wildly. *Those eyes! I know those eyes!* His stomach knotted, strangling him. He glared at the man who had vindictively fed Tillie to the lion. He waited for recognition to dawn on Domitius' face. Instead, he barely glanced at Livel and simply looked away.

Of course you don't remember me. I was covered in filth and the color of mud. But I will never forget what you did!

The words from Deuteronomy echoed in Livel's head: *vengeance belongs to Me.* Livel wanted to believe that God would avenge Tillie's death. Yet standing here in the presence of this man who was to become his student, all Livel could think about was *ayin tachat ayin*, an eye for an eye.

Zosima blanched at the hateful expression on Livel's face. He leaned in, his lips barely moving. "Whatever's going on with you, stop it now!" he whispered.

Trembling, his teeth clenched and breathing heavy, Livel was conflicted by the opposing doctrines. Was it his right for revenge or God's right for revenge? He spotted the spear in the hands of the slave near the door and without thinking took a step forward.

"Think before you act," Zosima whispered, his eyes blazing.

In that instant, rationality set in. If he proceeded, it would mean certain death—not for Domitius but for himself. Livel had no idea how he would ever command the strength to be in the same room with Domitius. For now, he had only one thing to focus on: keeping himself under control.

"As a Senator and a soldier, I've spent my life serving our people," Marcus said, bringing Livel back to the present. "I'm loved and respected, and I have earned that adoration." His green eyes shifted from Domitius to Scipio.

Expectation hung in the air as Marcus moved from his chair and approached his sons.

"There is only one position in government I deem worthy for a son of mine and that is the highest office in the state—consul. One of you will earn that right. Which one of you it will be remains to be seen. Do not disappoint me again. Livel is your last chance," Marcus said, shaking a fist at them.

Domitius stood. "I embrace the challenge. You need look no further. I intend to be consul."

Scipio's face turned crimson, as he moved to stand beside his half-brother. "I am the first born son. It is my honor and my duty to become consul."

"Enough! Neither one of you is close to earning the right. You must first learn to speak with eloquence and comprehend the intricacies of reason. To become consul, you must prove yourself not only on the battlefield but in the courts as well. For that, you will need to study with true dedication."

Livel had learned that in the Roman world, a son did not make his own decisions. The father even had to approve whom they married. If that wife displeased Marcus, the marriage could be nullified. A father's control did not stop there. It reached into the next generation, to any children that Scipio and Domitius would father. Still worse, Marcus Gracchus, with ample justification, could even order his sons killed.

Marcus Gracchus moved beside the desk with his arms crossed, green eyes burning. "I know that you both dream of becoming soldiers. When you are ready, you will be sent to serve with Julius Severus, governor of Britannia, the finest commander in the Roman Empire." He pointed a stubby finger at Livel. "This is their last chance and your *only* chance. Teach my sons well." His nostrils flared. "Convince them that knowledge is power!"

Chapter 7

"What happened to you in there?" Zosima asked, his weathered face filled with concern as they entered the room they shared. After today, the room would be unoccupied as Zosima began his life as a free man, and Livel moved into Scipio's room.

Livel bit down hard on his lip as the memories screamed. With stilted words and numerous pauses, he recounted what happened to Tillie on the ship and what transpired between Tillie and Domitius. When Livel finished his commentary, the wise tutor's expression crumpled. "This just reaffirms everything I told you," Zosima said through hate-streaked tears. "Domitius is demented and dangerous."

"What am I to do?" Livel asked. He was not able to create even one scenario in his mind where he could survive teaching such a man.

Zosima intertwined his fingers in contemplation. "I have only one answer for you. Perhaps your God wants you to learn humility. Do you know how many times we argued, and you professed the very words, *greater is the one who is slower to anger than a mighty warrior, and greater is one who rules his spirit than a conqueror of a city?*"

Livel gave his mentor an incredulous look. "You are citing Judaism for your own purpose now. I know you don't believe those words."

Zosima smiled sadly. "No. I don't. But you do! And it would serve you to remember that. There is one thing I do know. If you don't find a way to get past this, you will never live to go home. I can promise you that!"

Livel began to pace, trying to make sense of the irony that Domitius was now to be his student. Was God testing his resolve? Could he maintain the façade needed to rise above his contempt? Livel knew he stood at a crossroads. He could embrace the teachings of his religion or he could turn away. But could he ever really turn away? He was the son of a great rabbi, and he did believe in the word of God.

"It is time for both of us to move on," Zosima said, his kindly eyes moist. "I will miss our discussions. But most of all, I will miss you."

Livel grasped his tutor's hand. "I will never forget you, my friend."

"And I will never forget you."

* * *

"Get up, young scholar. We have an appointment with two horses and a chariot. Today I ride, and today you learn to ride," Scipio said, standing over Livel with a mischievous grin on his face.

Livel jumped up, mortified that he had over-slept. He looked around at the unfamiliar surroundings. His bed lay tucked in a corner under a window, twenty feet from where Scipio slept. His bed was inlaid with ivory and gold and was covered in red brocade damask. There were three couches piled high with tassel-trimmed pillows. The floor was white, gold and red mosaic, and the walls were painted in scenes depicting a peaceful Roman countryside. There were under-the-floor hypocausts that generated heat when the weather turned cold, a room with running water, private bath and a toilet complete with sewage disposal.

Livel rubbed the sleep from his eyes. "My instructions are to begin our studies immediately," Livel said, his head spinning. He had seen the ridiculous contraptions pulled by horses, and he had no intention of riding in one.

Scipio laughed. "If you want my cooperation, then you will have to accommodate me. We can study in the waning glow of afternoon. To ride and to train, this must be done at first light, when the body is at its strongest. I've been granted special dispensation from my father to teach you. Come. Get up. We'll be late!"

* * *

Livel stood in the kitchen with the staff. He gobbled down a breakfast of bread smothered in honey and a bowl of figs. He was determined to follow the Jewish dietary laws that forbade him to eat any animal that did not have a divided hoof and chewed its cud. He instructed the kitchen servants not to serve him rabbit or pig. From the waters, he would only eat fish that had fins and scales. For fowl, he could eat capon, chicken, dove, duck, geese and pigeon, but he would not eat them because they had not been killed in a ritual manner. Whenever the menu did not fulfill his requirements, he ate vegetables and fruit. He washed down his breakfast with a glass of goat's milk.

Livel made his way to the circular track located near the stables. Once there, he stood near the railing where Scipio was preparing to race.

Scipio wore only a light helmet for protection, as he balanced in the chariot behind a pair of perfectly matched stallions. He wrapped the reins tightly around his waist and leaned forward, the excess reins held loosely in his hands. He shouted and the horses began to trot.

Livel gasped. *Scipio has tied himself in! If the chariot flips, he'll be dragged or trampled! If I'm forced to ride, then I shall surely die today!*

Livel watched in terror. On the tenth pass, Scipio pulled to a stop in front of him, the wheels kicking up mud and the horses baying in exhaustion. Scipio disentangled himself from the reins.

"Your turn!" he said, a smug expression on his handsome face, sweat dripping into his eyes.

"This is not going to turn out well!" Livel shook from head to toe.

"Come. I'm simply going to teach you how to hold the reins and balance on the boards."

Livel moved forward, his eyes never leaving Scipio's face. "If you're lying...."

Scipio slapped Livel on the back. "Trust! After all, would I do anything to endanger my new friend?"

Livel looked at the chariot leaning at a precarious angle as it balanced on the ground, the horses snorting and neighing. Using mathematical calculations, he knew that his weight would balance the cart if he stood in the exact center and did not lean too far forward or back. He placed one foot in the center of the chariot and then the other, holding on to the lip of the frame with all his might.

Scipio offered him the reins. All Livel could do was shake his head.

Scipio laughed, prying Livel's fingers loose. For Livel, this was now like standing on a precipice, waiting for disaster. He grabbed the reins to steady himself. The horses misread his movement and began to walk.

"Stop them!" Livel shrieked. The shout spooked the horses, and they began to run. Scipio jumped on the back of the chariot, just as the horses were gaining speed.

Livel could feel Scipio's body leaning into him as he reached to take the reins from his hands. The rhythm of the horses steadied, and within moments, they were racing around the track. At first, he was too terrified to open his eyes, but the sensation of the wheels tearing over the dirt and the wind howling in his face was the most exhilarating feeling Livel had ever experienced. He laughed in delight.

"I'll make a soldier out of you yet!" Scipio yelled in his ear, as the horses raced for yet another turn.

As they drew to a stop, Livel spotted Domitius standing near a tree watching. The intensity in his eyes and the evil grin on his face sent a shudder down his spine.

* * *

Livel entered the library, still invigorated by the morning's adventure. He moved past Marcus Gracchus' desk, toward a table off to the left, in the circular room. With great care, he placed the scrolls he had brought for their first lesson on the table and arranged three chairs. It seemed the perfect place to instruct. There was ample light and little distraction. But something felt wrong. Livel kept looking over his shoulder, expecting Marcus Gracchus to enter at any moment. He would have to find another place to teach. He needed a place that did not have the imprint of his captor or Zosima–a place that would belong to him. He thought about the room he had shared with the tutor. It was now vacant and would serve as the perfect alternative. He would ask Scipio to seek permission from his father.

Livel glanced out the windows. The sun had begun its decent toward the horizon, and his students would arrive at any moment. Livel forced himself to concentrate on his role as teacher. He must learn to play just one small part of the role. Domitius could only hold influence over him if he allowed it, and Livel did not intend to let that happen. He would train himself to see his enemy with pity, not hate, and with sympathy, not retribution.

A door opened and the brothers entered.

"One hour. That's as long as I intend to stay," Domitius said, throwing a disparaging glance Livel's way. "I have better things to do than spend my time with some over-educated Hebrew that my father has taken a liking to!"

"Forgive Domitius," Scipio said, "rudeness is one of his *better* attributes."

Domitius scowled and muttered something unintelligible under his breath.

"Take a seat please," Livel said, making a concerted effort to push the anger from his voice. "I am to teach you philosophy and literature. We will begin with Homer's epic, the *Iliad.* You will read about the Greek hero, Achilles, and learn about the Greek and Trojan War."

"And you think this will be of interest?" Scipio asked, rolling his eyes like an insolent child.

"According to your father, neither of you can be consul until you are considered an intellect. To become an intellect, you will be expected to quote Homer's poetry and expound upon his writings. There is just one more thing before we begin." Livel hesitated until he had their full attention. "Upon Zosima's instructions, I will be giving your father monthly reports on your individual progress."

"Why would you do that? Zosima never did!" Domitius said, uncertainty wiping the smug look from his face.

"It seems your father intends to keep both of you accountable for your progress."

* * *

Marcus Gracchus's ploy to be given a monthly report worked. The half-brothers took to their studies with vigor. Domitius continued to be belligerent towards Livel, and their relationship, on the best day, remained superficial and strained. Yet regardless of Livel's opinion of Domitius, he could not deny his quick mind and his aptitude for memorization, even if he didn't always seem to comprehend that which he spewed forth with such little effort.

On the other hand, Scipio had to spend more time studying. While he was not as astute as his half-brother, he could grasp the philosophies in ways Domitius could not even fathom, and he had a predilection for languages. The reports Livel gave to Marcus on his sons were glowing. But there was a dilemma–Livel did not intend to allow Domitius to succeed at becoming consul.

Under the shade of a mulberry tree, Livel sat across from Scipio. He began to recite verses of Homer in Aramaic.

"Desist!" Scipio ordered. "I have enough trouble understanding the Latin. Now you add another language."

Livel switched to Hebrew and kept reciting. He could see the confusion on Scipio's face. After a particularly long verse, Livel folded his hands in his lap and waited.

"What was all that about?"

"In Syria they speak Aramaic, and in Judea they speak Hebrew," Livel said.

Confusion creased Scipio's brow. "And please tell me why I am supposed to care?"

"Because you espouse to me that you will be the Gracchus son that becomes consul. You say that the citizens of Rome will know your name and the names of the battles that you've won."

"It is so."

"What if you are posted in Mesopotamia or even Judea? Would it not serve you well to speak these languages? Would it not put you above all others?"

Scipio's eyes sparkled. Livel was teaching him something that would give him the upper hand over Domitius. "Finally, you suggest something worth learning!"

"*Kol hakavod*, congratulations," Livel said in Hebrew.

"*Kol hakavod* to you," Scipio repeated with a grin.

* * *

Livel and Scipio parried in the open expanse at the center of the chariot track. Each held a wooden sword in one hand and a wicker shield in the other. Both weapons were filled with lead and weighed twice the normal weight of the actual weapons. They practiced thrusting at a wooden post until Livel collapsed in exhaustion. He touched his aching arm, surprised by the muscle bulging under his fingers.

"That is how you expect to make a soldier out of the Jew?" Domitius shouted, surprising them as he strode across the expanse carrying two swords. He dropped a sword at Livel's feet. "Get up and let me show you how a Roman soldier fights!"

Livel rose, sword in hand, his eyes never leaving Domitius' face. Livel could hear Scipio's voice in his head: regulate your breathing and keep your feet shoulder width apart for balance. Always extend the blade toward your enemy's throat or eye, elbows in and close to the body. Watch your opponent's movements looking for a way to launch a preemptive strike. Most importantly, establish a flow from one move to the next and be aggressive and intimidating.

"He intends to make a fool out of you. You don't have to do this," Scipio said, putting a restraining hand on Livel's shoulder.

Domitius thrust his sword at Livel, taking away any opportunity for him to walk away from the challenge. The look in Domitius' eyes was that of a madman trying to kill or maim his opponent. Weaving and ducking, Livel's mind turned to Tillie's lifeless body being thrown into the lion's cage. Blinded by that vision, his opportunity for revenge too tempting to ignore, he slashed and lunged. Either by luck or circumstance, Livel found an opening in Domitius' stance. He pounced, nicking Domitius' upper arm. Realizing that he was wounded, Domitius shrieked. Slicing the air with his blade, he leapt toward Livel.

"Enough!" Scipio howled, hoisting his own sword, as he shoved Livel out of harm's way. The half-brothers stared at each other with hate dripping from their eyes. "Can you defeat both of us? Would you care to try?" Scipio hissed.

"This is not over," Domitius said, his voice raw with hatred. "You will pay one day!" The threat was clearly aimed at both Livel and Scipio.

* * *

Livel lay in bed, his hands and feet blistered, his body aching from the encounter with Domitius. He kept reliving the fight and the emotions surrounding the near catastrophic event. The realization that he had not been afraid astounded him. That he had lost his temper and therefore, all rational thought was also astounding. Livel would need time to reconcile this new never-before-revealed side of his personality. *I faced death with the courage of a soldier. Masabala would be proud of me!* It was his last thought before falling asleep.

Noises pulled him from his sleep. He opened his eyes. The room was drenched in the soft mellow tones of moonlight. Lying still, he listened to the rutting sounds coming from Scipio's bed. He had heard these sounds before; muffled through the walls on the nights his parents copulated. These were different. There were loud sighs, muffled screams and the rustling of bodies. It went on and on and on until Livel thought he would go mad. He wasn't certain if he was angry at the total disregard of his presence, or if he was jealous. His body ached as he turned toward the wall. Resisting the need for release, he began to count and reached one thousand before falling into a fitful sleep.

Livel was in the midst of a dream when he felt a soft body snuggle against his back, soft and contoured in places he had only imagined. The fragrance was intoxicating: flowers, wine and intimacy. A kiss touched his neck. A tongue teased his ear. He dared not move for fear that this was a fantasy, and he would awaken. Hands slid around his buttocks to his stiffened penis.

"Ah. A large intellect is not the only gift the gods have blessed you with," the velvet voice whispered in an accent he did not recognize.

Livel would never be sure how long it took him to reach a climax, but his best guess would be seconds.

"Your first time?" she whispered, no accusation in her tone.

He nodded into the darkness, beginning to turn, desperate to see the glorious creature that had given him such pleasure.

"You may not look at me," she cooed, pushing him back to his side. "Take good care of your master, and perhaps one day we shall see each other again."

She slipped into the night. Livel turned and looked at Scipio across the room.

"You're welcome," Scipio said, an impish grin on his handsome face.

* * *

When he awoke that morning, Scipio's bed was empty. Livel dressed quickly and went into the kitchen.

The cook Arthenia hollered orders and dozens of servants scurried about. "Have you seen my master?" Livel shouted above the din.

"Can you not see that I am busy?" She pointed her nose towards the door. "When royalty is in residence, even your *master* must attend."

"Royalty?" That Livel did not know about the visit was a stinging reminder of his lowly position as a slave.

The cook shot a killing look at Livel. "The entourage arrived early last night. They're from Hispania–relatives of Emperor Hadrian. They'll depart after breakfast. Now, go! I have no time to talk this morning."

Livel walked into the cool morning air. Songbirds chirped from the treetops, and the sounds of harps could be heard coming from the reception hall. He leaned against a tree and waited.

Scipio sent her to me. Is she royalty or a slave girl? Would I know her if I saw her?

Carriages began to arrive. The drivers climbed down and stood beside their horses. The front doors to the villa opened. Livel watched as two-dozen men and three women descended the steps, accompanied by the Gracchus family.

Livel could see a resemblance between the older woman and the two younger women by her side. The girls were dressed in identical purple tunics, belted and adorned with gold embroidery and pinned to reveal the ripeness of their shapes. All three were bejeweled, wearing necklaces, earrings and bracelets, the gold sparkling in the sunlight. Sadly for Livel, all three wore the customary shawls to cover their heads in public. Thus, their faces were shaded from his sight, to remain a mystery.

Scipio stood to one side, his eyes masked, as if disinterested. Livel watched to see if he would pay special attention to either girl. There was no special look and no sideways glance, as the women climbed into the carriage.

Disappointment seared his thoughts. *Perhaps it was just a dream.*

Chapter 8

Masabala 130 CE

Emperor Hadrian, on tour of his eastern Provinces, made a stop in Judea. Upon arrival, he began making proclamations. He changed the name of the province from Judea to Palestine and turned the Jewish holy city of Jerusalem into a Roman colony. He officially renamed it *Aeliea Capitolina* after himself, Publius Aelius Hadrianus. He then ordered a *pomerium*, a furrow, placed around the city to mark its new boundaries.

He also prohibited circumcision, a covenant between God and the Jewish people that required a son to be circumcised on the eighth day after birth. Already outraged by the oppressive Roman taxes and rules, the new edict further inflamed the Jews.

* * *

Masabala worked in the village of Gamla, eighty-three miles northeast of Jerusalem and six miles northeast of the Sea of Galilee. He worked in secret, as did so many young zealots in villages and enclaves throughout the Holy Land. They were digging underground cities that would be stocked with food, water and weapons in preparation for war.

Masabala had always dreamt of greatness–slaying Romans and being heralded by his peers as an illustrious warrior. Now it seemed an absurd notion. He was just another anonymous soldier.

The soldiers toiled without complaint, the backbreaking work strengthening their resolve and their bodies. Seventeen-year-old Masabala's chest expanded and his physique swelled. He wore his long ebony hair tied back with a leather band; a thick beard covered his handsome face. With every rock he dug and every pail he filled, Masabala's determination intensified. Fueled by his guilt over the kidnapping of Livel, self-recrimination was his constant companion.

Herodian

After months of laborious work, Masabala and his group of rag-tag soldiers were transferred south of Jerusalem to the abandoned mountain fortress known as Herodian. The Romans had built the palace for King Herod the Great a hundred years earlier. The palace was located in the Judean hills, a natural dividing point between the coastal plains and the Jordan valley. The hills proved a varied and demanding place where the paths were steep and narrow. The hillsides boasted pine forests, oak and carob trees and rockroses that bloomed in early morning, dropping their flowers only hours after opening.

King Herod's builders had constructed steps leading to an intricate underground cistern. The mission of the Jewish zealots was to dig a shallow, wider second cistern that could only be accessed from underground tunnels–ensuring a water supply that could not be cut off in time of war.

It was rumored that Herodian was to be Bar Kokhba's headquarters when the revolt began. A camp was set up in the central courtyard–fifty tents that housed four hundred young men. The recruits worked from sunrise until sunset.

Masabala was asleep on a straw mat when he heard the call to rise. After a breakfast of dates, stale bread and goat's milk, he made his way to the tunnel.

Masabala climbed down the steps into the belly of the excavation. Once inside, he trailed two empty buckets and a pick, the space so tight he was forced to crawl on hands and knees. He inched along in the darkness, using every ounce of his resolve to keep moving forward.

Dusty grit filled his mouth, and the stench of the soldiers permeated his nostrils. The pounding and smashing of rock reverberated in his skull, and the shifting earth beneath his knees compromised his sense of balance. One hundred feet from the entranceway, he finally saw the light from the torches. Masabala steadied his breathing, waiting for his heart to stop pounding from exertion and fear.

Rising to a standing slouch, he ducked to keep from gashing his head on the ragged stones that protruded from the ceilings and walls. He lifted his pick. His motions were short and choppy, limited by space and the nearness of his comrades. Still the stones broke free from the walls, and soon he had filled his buckets. Dragging his pails, he handed them off to his fellow-diggers who transferred the stones and dirt back to the surface. Empty pails were then passed back to the diggers.

Masabala worked for two hours without stopping. His hands had grown numb, and his arms were too weak to strike another blow. He nodded to a replacement and crawled out to the surface.

Gulping fresh air, Masabala maneuvered around the mountain of stones from the excavation to a water trough. He dipped his entire head into the water before filling the attached cup and drinking. He collapsed on a patch of grass and was asleep in seconds, a nap that lasted less than a quarter of an hour.

On his next rotation, Masabala was half way down the stairs when there was a deafening roar. The ground shook, and an explosion of dust shot forth from the tunnel like a raging windstorm. Blinded and coughing, Masabala clawed his way up the stairs and out of the tunnel.

In shock and bloodied from flying rock, Masabala laid spread-eagled on the ground. For a few heartbeats, he lay there listening to the crashing sounds and watching the dust twirl in smoky circles above and around him. Moving to sit up, he shook his head trying to clear his thoughts. That was when he saw a leg sticking out from the rubble.

Too traumatized to stand, he crawled toward the body. "There's been a cave in! I need help!" Masabala howled in a voice sounding distant to his deafened ears.

There were a hundred men within earshot, and using bare hands they tore away the shattered stones. Within minutes, they managed to save a pale and barely breathing soldier.

"Where is the commander?" Masabala shouted.

"In the tunnel," came the reply from a wild-eyed soldier.

Masabala jumped up. "You and you and you!" he ordered, yanking panicked soldiers by the arm. "Dig! There may be men still alive down there."

Masabala ran to the perimeter line where at the end of each day of digging, they paced off how far they had progressed and marked it with a pile of crossed stones. He fought to steady his mind, to concentrate, to think like his brother Livel, with forethought and careful calculation. Masabala knew the first hurdle would be getting fresh air into the tunnel without causing another cave-in.

He stared at the marker. *The men would be right below here.* "I need the longest, sturdiest bough you can find," he shouted, as a stunned group gathered. "We have to open an airway into the tunnel, and we have to do it now!"

He dug at a patch of dirt with his pick, and then used his fingers to scratch away at the rubble. Like a mad man, he kept at it, digging until his hands were bloodied and raw.

A soldier dropped a heavy branch at Masabala's feet. "Tear off the leaves and sharpen the end into a point," Masabala ordered. "And get me a rock this big." He made a circle with his fingers.

He kept digging. When he felt that he was getting close to opening a breach, Masabala began to pound the stick into the soil with the rock. With a particularly powerful strike, the branch disappeared into the earth. He had broken through. The men began to shout and applaud. Masabala held up his hand for silence, putting his ear near the opening. He could hear calls for help. He placed his mouth to the hole and shouted, "We are going to get you out!"

Masabala took the pick and lightly tapped the ground. A soldier knelt beside him pushing the graveled dirt aside. "We need an opening large enough to pull out one man at a time," he said, finding strength of purpose that had eluded him ever since his brother Livel had been taken. "We have to proceed in haste but with caution, so we don't cause another cave-in."

A young soldier squatted, mimicking Masabala's gentle strokes. Soon others joined, each taking a tiny square of earth as their own. Masabala glanced at his fellow soldiers and realized for the first time that they were all young boys, the innocence that should still be in their eyes now gone.

By the time they had an opening large enough to begin their rescue, the moon had crested in a star-streaked sky. Masabala lay on his belly and reached into the void. "Take my hands," he cried. For a few moments nothing happened. Then he felt a hand grasp his. "Hold tight. I'm going to get you out of there!"

Hands reached around and over Masabala, and within moments they had rescued their first survivor. For another hour, they pulled men up. They were injured and stunned, but they would all live.

"Now what?" a soldier asked when no one else came to the surface.

"I'm going down there. When I get in, drop me a torch."

Masabala slid through the opening. Once he had the torch in hand, he looked around. There were crushed and mangled bodies everywhere, the commander among them–an unimaginable horror. Standing in the death pit in shock, he began to wander around in a stupor, seeking any sign of life. He heard soft whimpering and weakened cries. There were men still alive, trapped under the rocks. "I need help down here," he howled.

Masabala stuck the torch in the ground. To his right was a boy-soldier pinned down by a boulder that rested on his belly and chest.

"Get it off!" he begged.

Masabala pushed with all his might, and the rock rolled off, snapping ribs and crunching bones. There was a horrific scream and then silence. Masabala took the lifeless boy's hand in his. He wanted to weep for the lives that would never be lived, but there would be time for that later. Right now, he had to organize his comrades to save as many men as they could. The work was grisly and spirits broke.

In the dawning light, Masabala organized the recovery of bodies. The weary soldiers-turned tunnel-diggers became gravediggers.

Masabala oversaw the burial of their commander and the other dead soldiers. In doing so, he broke with the covenant from God. The covenant stipulated that as a Kohen, he was not allowed to touch a dead body or attend a burial.

Masabala ordered fires built and food cooked. Then the entire camp, the survivors and those that had worked so valiantly to save them, ate together in a mournful silence and then slept.

The next morning, a soldier shook Masabala awake. "Hurry! Get up. He's here!"

"Who's here?" Masabala asked in dread, his mind still wrapped around the nightmare of the past day.

"Bar Kokhba!"

By the time Masabala rose to his feet, the *nasi* was standing beside him.

"I hear you took charge. I am told it was your leadership that saved the lives of a dozen of our soldiers."

"I did my duty, but fifty still died," Masabala said, too weary and grief-stricken to say more.

Bar Kokhba turned and leaned into the man standing beside him. He whispered something, and the man walked away. Then he turned toward Masabala.

"Masabala, son of Rabbi Eleazar, what you did here, under these dire circumstances, has sealed your destiny. From this moment forth, you shall remain by my side until I deem you ready for your own command."

Masabala stared straight ahead, death clinging to him like a cloak of tar. He could not comprehend the full meaning of Bar Kokhba's words, only the realization that the *nasi,* the prince, finally knew his name.

Chapter 9

Maresha, Judea

Masabala accompanied Bar Kokhba and his commanders to the caves of Maresha located near the city of Beersheba. It was a place of bell-shaped underground caverns, some with ceilings that soared as high as sixty feet. Although it was in ruins now, Maresha was a thriving city with over five thousand separate rooms. It stood during the First Temple period, a thousand years earlier. Because most of the rooms were inaccessible, remote, dilapidated and deserted, it was the ideal hideout for Bar Kokhba and his officers. Maresha was the perfect place to strategize plans for an eventual attack on the Roman army ruling Judea.

Masabala issued orders for the caves to be stocked with weapons and food. He brought in men who would put the ancient olive presses back into operation and repair the water cisterns.

Each day the commanders, Masabala the youngest by years, would meet in an underground cavern that was dank and smelled of rot. They sat around stone tables planning as light from the torches danced off the walls and flickered across the ceiling. With a half million soldiers scattered throughout Judea, all waiting for Bar Kokhba's orders, the pressure on the *nasi* was mounting.

"We must consider the resources of Judea," Bar Kokhba said, hands flat against the table as if he were about to rise.

"We have storehouses filled with wheat, barley, olives and dates," one of his men replied.

"The grapes will be harvested in the next few weeks," another commander added.

"What about our livestock?" Bar Kokhba queried.

"Our herds are healthy. We should have more than enough milk, butter, cheese and wool," replied the commander sitting next to Bar Kokhba.

Bar Kokhba nodded. ""We must decide how to set up a distribution network."

"Why not distribute provisions to each village and make them responsible for their own welfare?" said one of the commanders, with a grey beard and puffy eyes.

"You have been by my side for years!" reprimanded Bar Kokhba. "Have you not learned that in time of war, people are terrified, and chaos and anarchy reign?"

The man paled under the rebuke.

"We can assign troops to distribute rations," another commander offered, his voice hesitant as he waited for the *nasi's* retort.

"And if those troops are attacked, our people will starve," Bar Kokhba said. He pushed himself up and glanced around the table. "Send out the fishermen. When they return with their catch, I want the fish salted and stored. Have the farmers harvest their crops. Gather blankets and warm clothing for the winter. Once that is done, we will discuss distribution."

Masabala was tired of all the incessant discussions. He was tired of hearing how wars were won through careful planning.

He wanted a weapon in his hands.

* * *

It was the Sabbath and Masabala walked with great purpose through the corridors that led from the officers' cave to the cavern serving as a makeshift synagogue. Chairs were fashioned from boulders, rank determining the row in which you sat. Many of the men were already seated, all wearing clean clothing and speaking in hushed tones. Masabala moved to the second row.

Sitting in a chair, on an elevated platform at the front of the room was Bar Kokhba. Rabbi Akiva, with his snow-white side curls and unkempt beard, stood by his side. Even though Masabala was often in the rabbi's presence, he was still in awe of the man who was the first to systemize Jewish law.

"In this moment of imminent conflict, we must turn to the teachings of the Holy One, Blessed be He for our truths," Rabbi Akiva began, his web-encircled eyes glistening as he continued. "*Adonai* is my light and my salvation; whom shall I fear? *Adonai* is the stronghold of my life; of whom shall I be afraid? When evildoers came upon me to eat up my flesh, even my adversaries and my foes, they stumbled and fell. Though a host should encamp against me, my heart shall not fear; though war should rise up against me, even then will I be confident."

Masabala felt a lump in his throat. His father never held a teaching that did not include those same words. He missed home, the mundane things: watching his mother prepare a meal and hearing his father's musings about Masabala's bad temper. Most of all, he missed Sarah. Time and distance had served as a catalyst, making him realize that he was in love with her; perhaps had always been. He imagined their reunion, imagined holding her and telling her how he felt. It kept him warm on cold nights and sane when boredom and frustration threatened to overwhelm him. He caught only the end of Akiva's sentence and admonished himself, turning his attention back to the rabbi.

"The law is clear, in all cases it is our obligation to . . ."

The teachings went on for hours.

That evening Masabala wandered alone, striding along the rugged ridge with his hands behind his back, the autumn wind blowing in his face. He thought about his parents and friends at their table for the Sabbath meal, speaking about Torah. After everyone would leave, his father would sit in the dark and pray late into the night.

These were the traditions of his family, and those rituals had brought meaning to the days and weeks and years of Masabala's life. Livel had always been a part of those traditions, a smiling face resplendent in his unwavering faith in God. But Livel was now gone, and the pain Masabala felt was ever present. He raised his eyes to the star-carpeted sky. *If only I knew you were unharmed and safe.*

With profound sadness, Masabala turned back toward the caves of Maresha. It was then the nasi appeared, red hair whipping in the wind, his white tunic bright against the evening sky.

"I was told I would find you out here. You and I need to talk," Bar Kokhba said, pushing hair from his eyes.

Masabala had grown several inches over the previous year, and he was now almost as tall as his mentor. He had not spent time alone with Bar Kokhba since arriving in Maresha, and this opportunity to be singled out both thrilled and unnerved him.

"I feel discontentment in you, Masabala son of Eleazar," Bar Kokhba said.

Masabala felt the heat of shame rise in his cheeks. "I am honored to be serving you *Nasi*, my prince," Masabala said, addressing him by the name only his closest advisors used.

"I am not questioning your loyalty, only your impatience," Bar Kokhba said, leaning against a tree. "I have a story I want to share with you."

Masabala stood rigid, his eyes never leaving Bar Kokhba's face.

"Sixteen years ago, when I was not much older than you," Bar Kokhba said, his voice soft as he peered into the distance, "Trajan was emperor of Rome. The Jews raised up an army intending to defeat not only Rome, but also the Greeks in Africa, Cyprus, Libya, Egypt and Mesopotamia. And what a mighty army we had! We destroyed their temples and set fire to their cities." Bar Kokhba paused and closed his eyes. When he continued, his voice was soft. "The lust for revenge is like a fiend without a heart. In my dreams, I can still hear the screams of people burning alive and begging for help. I can smell the stink of sizzling skin. I took part in that massacre. And in the midst of bloodlust, I never stopped to think, to question or to save the life of even one child." Regret spilled over his words. "We were heady with victory and thought we were invincible! We let our guard down, and we became complacent."

He sighed, and his eyes turned dark and angry. "While we celebrated, the Roman general, Turbo, sailed into Alexandria with fresh legions, thousands and thousands of men. He mounted an attack against us and annihilated an entire generation of our people! Do you think I have forgotten that lesson?" Bar Kokhba stared at Masabala, as if daring him to disagree. "Do you think I ever will?"

"Even if you were more vigilant, you were still outnumbered," Masabala said, compelled to reply by the defeated expression on the *nasi's* face.

"And we will be outnumbered again!" Bar Kokhba retorted. "That is exactly why I spend my days examining how we can outmaneuver a stronger force. So while you may find this waiting agony, I want you to remember that I chose you for your character and bravery. I know you are hungry for revenge but–"

"Yes. I want revenge," Masabala shot back in a voice louder than he intended, his temper getting the best of him. "I joined this army to fight. It has been an entire year, and I have yet to pick up a weapon!"

"Weapons!" Bar Kokhba scoffed. "You want to learn to handle a sword and shield? That can be arranged. But the success of your command will not lie in how well *you* fight–victory will lie in the decisions you make before leading your men into battle.

"These soldiers will be under your command," he continued. "Some will become your friends, and others will have names you may never know. As a commander, it is your responsibility to try and keep them alive." Bar Kokhba's breath caught, and he sighed. "But no matter how hard you try, many will die."

He shook his head as one might at a defiant child. "There is so much you do not understand. War is like the roaring waves of a storm, so powerful that once it has begun, there is no stopping it. People die. Not just your enemies, but innocents. The old and the young will starve, children will die in their mother's arms, and disease will strike down those not already maimed. You think you know of these things, that you can imagine war. But you cannot! You will curse the day when you do understand. Your heart will break a thousand times; it will harden, and you will never be the same. Remember this discussion. It will change nothing, but it may give you pause and a moment to reflect."

For a brief moment, Masabala envisioned the hell of Bar Kokhba's words. Almost immediately, he disregarded them, blinded by the retribution that had planted itself in his heart and became the driving force in his life. "May I speak freely?"

Bar Kokhba gave a quick nod.

"You said yourself that Hadrian is taking his legions back to Rome. Would that not be the perfect time to strike? By the time he realizes what has happened, it will be too late, and we will be in control of Judea. Israel will be ours!"

Bar Kokhba's expression turned cold. "When I deem the time is right, I will unleash this storm. When I am ready." Bar Kokhba stood. "Not one minute before." The conversation was clearly over.

Chapter 10

Nineteen year-old Livel sat in the room he had shared with Zosima, the room now converted to a classroom for the Gracchus brothers. The room contained a table and chairs and a wall full of books and scrolls. Livel let his mind wander over the past year. Five days a week, at seven o'clock in the morning, he and Scipio met at the track near the stables. They practiced for four hours before Livel went to the baths. After the mid-day meal in the kitchen with the other house servants, he retired to the classroom and spent the next two hours in preparation for his lessons with Scipio and Domitius. The three of them studied until the evening meal. At night, Livel worked alone with Scipio on Hebrew and Aramaic.

Livel opened a book on Homer, staring at his hands rather than the words written on the page. He examined the calluses that sat like a mountain ridge above his palm. These were no longer the hands of a scholar but rather, the hands of a soldier.

Learning to become a soldier was grueling, episodes that resulted in bruises and sore muscles that never seemed to go away. Livel smiled and made a fist, flexing his arm and watching the muscles bulge.

At least he had managed to continue the daily rituals of Judaism, praying upon awakening and before sleeping, before washing his hands and before meals. But living in an idol-worshipping society of debauchery, gluttony and self-indulgence had been difficult. In his estimation, everyone drank to extreme and fornicated without shame. It was not unusual to find Scipio or Domitius groping some maiden's breast in broad daylight or to come upon them in a compromising position in the garden.

Domitius continued to be a problem. His vindictiveness towards Livel was like a volcano threatening to erupt. The only thing keeping him under control was his need for Livel's favorable reports to his father, so Domitius remained marginally civil.

As for missing his family, it was the most difficult transition of all. Livel kept his sanity by promising himself that one day he would escape. With vast effort, he learned to tuck away his grief until the moments just before sleep. For that brief period each day, Livel allowed himself to wallow in his loneliness and misery.

* * *

Livel knocked on the door and entered the study. The room was drenched in the gloom of an impending rainstorm. Marcus Gracchus looked up from his desk, beckoning Livel to approach with a wave of his hand.

"I'm very busy," he barked. "What of my sons' progress?"

Livel hesitated. Just that morning, he had heard gossip from the servants that Marcus Gracchus was nearing a decision on which son was to be groomed as consul.

"Both sons continue to progress admirably."

"As you say each month. Yet, is it not true that Domitius is the most accomplished?"

"In some ways that is true. But Scipio has a great gift for languages. Upon his request, I have been teaching him both Aramaic and Hebrew," Livel said, making his move to prevent Domitius from realizing his dream.

Marcus Gracchus leaned forward on his elbows. "Knowledge that would certainly serve any commander well," he said. "You may go."

The Following Day

Livel and Scipio sat at the desk reciting a verse from the Odyssey by Homer when Domitius stormed into the classroom. His face was livid, his green eyes blazing.

"What did you say to my father?" he screamed, pointing a raging finger at Livel.

"Are you referring to my monthly report?" Livel asked, reveling in Domitius' distress.

"Do not be coy with me," he threatened, taking a step forward.

Scipio rose. "What is this all about?"

"Ask the Jew!"

Livel sighed, pretending boredom. "I gave both of you favorable reports."

"Liar!" Domitius howled. "You told my father some stupid story about Livel being able to speak Hebrew and Aramaic!"

"That's not a lie," Scipio said.

"That was your plan all along, to outmaneuver me for consul. Well, you won't get away with this!" Domitius shook a fist at Scipio and then turned on Livel. "You don't have to worry about having me for a student any longer. I will never be in the same room with you again, Jew," he hissed, charging from the room.

"He's really mad," Scipio said, squinting at Livel. "Telling my father might have been a big mistake."

"Not if you want to become consul," Livel said, placing a hand on Scipio's shoulder, basking in the glow of retribution and self-satisfaction.

* * *

Livel stood in the middle of the Flavian Amphitheater, located in the center of Rome, just east of the Forum. He looked into the stands. On the days when gladiatorial contests were held, there were fifty thousand spectators. Today the seats were empty. He shivered.

Livel was dressed in full fighting regalia–iron chain mail armor that was fastened at the front and back by brass hooks and leather laces, a scarf to protect his neck from the armor, a metal helmet and woolen trousers. A sword belt hung at his waist. In his left hand was a shield and in his right a sword. He stood among two hundred soldiers who were faced-off against a line of two hundred-soon-to-be approaching soldiers.

They were called war games. No one was supposed to be killed, but Livel knew that men did die. He had practiced over a year for this day. While he was not a great soldier, he was certainly competent. He could ride a horse and shoot an arrow at the same time without falling off, and occasionally, he even hit a target. He could parry with sword in one hand and shield in the other. While he was no Goliath, he had mastered the skill. This time it was an actual confrontation where the swords were real, even if the enemy was not.

Scipio moved beside him. "I just heard that Domitius requested to be on the opposing team. I'll try and stay next to you, but if we get separated—!"

Livel stared across the expanse. Fear tugged at his gut. "Zosima warned me not to show favoritism. I should have listened."

Scipio grinned. "How could you help it? I'm just too charming."

"Right now, I don't need your charm. Right now, I need your protection!" Livel swung his sword, its gleaming metal whistling.

A horn sounded, and the clanging of cymbals filled the air. The columns moved forward, screaming men charging across the field, their armor shimmering in the sunlight.

Livel was swept into the fray, his world instantly insular, only as large as the length of his arm and the sweep of his sword. His encounters were swift and controlled, and before long, exhaustion obliterated his fear. It was then that a soldier broke through the ranks and bore down on him. Domitius swung at Livel, metal smashing against metal. Livel hefted his shield just as Domitius lunged to spear him.

"Are you crazy?" Livel shrieked, leaping to his left.

Livel tripped on his own feet, his leg twisted precariously, and he tumbled to the ground.

"Not so brave now, are you?" Domitius said, hovering over Livel, menace seeping from his eyes. "I won't kill you, but I am going to hurt you!" he said viciously. He stomped on Livel's twisted leg, tearing tendons and ligaments in his knee.

* * *

Livel opened his eyes slowly. He was in his bed, and Scipio was sitting on a chair staring at him.

"Thank the gods! For a while, it looked like you weren't going to make it."

"Water," Livel croaked.

Scipio put a hand under Livel's head and held the glass to his lips. "You're going to recover. I swear you will! Did Domitius do this to you?"

Even in his state of pain and confusion, Livel understood that to accuse Domitius would be a mistake. Marcus Gracchus might reprimand his son, but it would be Livel who would be cast out. "I don't know who it was," Livel croaked.

* * *

When next Livel opened his eyes, the room was cast in the shadows of evening. Beside him stood a man with an oblong-shaped face, highly arched brows and intelligent, kind blue eyes. His beard and hair were white, and deep lines creased his forehead.

"This is Doctor Claudius Galen, the most famous physician in the kingdom," Scipio said, pride lacing his words. "He is here to take care of you."

Claudius Galen was born in Pergamum and studied medicine while traveling throughout Greece, Asia Minor and Palestine. He possessed great knowledge in physiology, pharmacy and anatomy and was respected as a compiler of medical information. He professed that all illness was caused by the four bodily fluids; yellow bile, black bile, phlegm and blood.

"You've been gravely injured," the doctor said, scowling. "Your chin will heal as will the wound on your chest. I've stitched them both closed, and so far, there is no green puss or angry red edges. Unfortunately, your knee is badly damaged."

Livel visualized that moment, the agony when Domitius put the full weight of his body on his twisted leg. He tore away the blanket to get a look at the damage to his knee.

The doctor grabbed his hands. "You must remain still so the body can adjust to the blood loss and the injury. I've fashioned a splint to keep the leg straight. This will help you heal."

"Will I walk again?"

The doctor smiled. "Of course you will walk again! There may be pain and a limp, but you're young and strong, and you will adjust." He took a powder and mixed it into water. "This will help you sleep. I'll be back tomorrow to check on you." He looked at Scipio as he gathered his instruments. "Assign a slave to him, and perhaps you should consider moving him to the slave quarters, so his recuperation won't interfere with you."

Scipio flashed a smile. "I wouldn't think of it. If he is here, I can watch out for him."

* * *

Doctor Galen visited every day. With great pomp and formality, he unfurled his leather cloth filled with torturous-looking tools. He used a retractor to pluck at Livel's stitches.

"I am not happy with the swelling and redness of the knee, but the other wounds are healing," he said, removing two of the stitches. "I will begin to regulate your medicines."

"How?" Livel asked, fascinated by the idea that someone would know enough about herbs to regulate their dosage.

"There are different degrees of potency, and I am able to manipulate the ingredients depending on the needs of my patient."

"Why do you apply cold to my knee?" Livel asked as the doctor accepted chilled stones brought in by a slave.

"Because it is hot, and the muscles are swollen. Feel for your-self." The doctor took Livel's hand and placed it on his knee.

"It's warm and feels spongy," Livel said, palpating the tissues around his knee.

"I have a supposition I refer to as the opposite theory of medi-cine," Doctor Galen said. "When fever, swelling or possible infec-tion is present, I believe cold should be introduced. When a patient is cold, I introduce heat."

"And when a patient has trouble breathing?" Livel asked.

"I have them sing!"

Livel laughed.

"Can you tell me about your tools?" Livel asked.

"Not tools, dear boy, instruments! I am a musician, and these are what I use to make music." The doctor lifted a long thin metal probe. "This is a bone hook. It has a blunt end, and it's used for dissection and for raising blood vessels." He slid it into a leather pouch and held up another instrument. "This one has a sharpened end. It's used to hold and lift small pieces of skin, so that I can extract and retract the edges of wounds."

"And the rest?" Livel asked, pulling out an odd shaped probe.

"I've never had a patient so interested! We have drills and forceps, scalpels, rectal speculums, probes and curettes. Perhaps when you've recuperated, you will come to my offices. Then I'll show you everything."

Livel was enthralled by the doctor's knowledge and intrigued by the opportunity to be a seeker rather than teacher.

The doctor motioned to the slave. "Come. I will require some assistance." He looked hard at Livel. "You have become weak, and I believe it is time to introduce exercise that will help you grow stronger."

"Livel shot his arm forward as the two men approached. "Are you sure I am ready?" The doctor put his arm behind Livel's back. "It's been a month. I am going to help you sit up. Now," he said to the slave, "we're going to move him to the edge of the bed. Ready?"

The doctor lifted Livel's injured leg, and the slave lifted the other as they shifted him to the side of the bed. For the first time in almost a month, Livel was sitting, even if one leg was splinted and unable to bend.

"How do you feel?" Doctor Galen asked.

Livel shrugged and swallowed hard. "I'm dizzy."

"That is enough for today," Doctor Galen said.

"No. I want to try."

Livel placed one hand on the slave's shoulder and the other on the doctor's shoulder. He pulled himself up and was able to stand on the good leg for a few seconds before he inadvertently transferred weight to the injured one. The pain was excruciating. He screamed.

They helped him lie down.

"Well done," Doctor Galen said. "Tomorrow, I'll bring you a crutch for assistance."

* * *

Livel stood beside his bed, a crutch under one arm, as Scipio held the other arm for support. He had lost weight, and his muscles had shriveled. It took every bit of his diminished strength to remain upright. Scipio stood next to him like a falcon protecting its young.

"You look more miserable than I feel!" Livel said looking at Scipio. "Go find something worthwhile to do."

"I'm so sorry for all of this," Scipio said. "It's my fault. You were never meant to be a soldier, and now I have lost you!"

"What are you talking about?"

"I'm leaving within the year for Britannia to serve under the Governor, Sextus Julius Severus. You are going to have to remain behind."

"Why?"

"With your injury, you cannot fight."

"So now I am worthless. Perhaps my brain is also useless, along with my leg?" Livel shouted.

"I did not say that," Scipio shouted back.

"Then stop talking like a fool!"

"It is no use. I tried to persuade my father to let you accompany me. He would not even allow me to finish my request."

"Are there no doctors on the battlefield?" Livel said, voicing an idea that had been churning in his head for weeks.

"There are, but what does that have to do with anything?" Scipio's expression froze. "You want to become a physician? You are certainly smart enough."

"And who would be better to teach me than Doctor Galen?" Livel asked.

"Interesting idea." Scipio put a finger beside his nose. "After all, Claudius Galen did become famous as a surgeon treating the gladiators in Asia Minor."

"Convince your father. Make him see how important it would be for you to have a well-trained doctor at your side," Livel said, imagining a tolerable future, for the first time since being forced into slavery.

Chapter 11

Scipio walked alongside his father at the port of Ostia. A ship sat low in the water at the dockside mooring, its hold pregnant with cargo. Marcus Gracchus wore a tailored ivory tunic decorated with silver thread. His neck was adorned with a thick gold chain, and on his middle finger was a ring with an emerald the size of a walnut. Scipio was dressed in a white tunic with a leather belt cinched at his hip holding a knife with a pearl and sapphire encrusted handle.

Father and son watched as slaves unloaded crates and baskets marked with the Gracchus family name. Domitius had remained in Rome, ill with a fever. Marcus stopped one of the slaves and with great anticipation untied the laces on a bulging leather pouch. Leaning over, he inhaled deeply, his green eyes dancing as he reached inside and took out a handful of saffron. "Look at the color of this," he said to Scipio.

Scipio pinched the precious golden yellow spice between thumb and forefinger.

"This will be used in perfumes, ointments and medicines. It is more valuable than gold!" Marcus said, dusting the saffron from his fingers into the pouch.

They labored over their inventory into the late afternoon: pearls from the Persian Gulf, emeralds and vivid green peridot from Egypt and amber from the fringes of the empire. Their job complete, Marcus led Scipio through the crowded streets overrun with fishmongers, prostitutes and sailors. Down a long and winding street, they came to the Caelius Inn where Marcus always stayed. It was not until they were sitting in the dining room and his father was on his second glass of wine, that Scipio decided to broach the subject of Livel.

"Sir," Scipio said, "I've had an idea that I think may be of interest to you."

"Some new spice you've come across? Perhaps a new breed of horse?"

"No. But I have found a way to parley a bad situation into a good one."

"Then I'm certainly interested," Marcus said.

"I think I've found another use for Livel." Scipio knew that his father viewed Livel as an investment, and that he was angry his investment was now damaged. "I think he is well suited to become a physician." Scipio paused, giving his father time to absorb the suggestion. "With your great influence, I'm certain you can convince Doctor Galen to take him on as a student. Once trained, Livel will become invaluable to our family. Instead of being a burden, he will become an asset," Scipio said, tugging at his beard, a habit he had when nervous.

"An interesting suggestion," Marcus replied. "I could certainly arrange for him to be assigned to your regiment. That way, he could keep an eye on you and Domitius." He took a deep drink of wine, wiping the drops that dribbled down his chin with the back of his hand. "There would be just one codicil attached to this agreement. If I am going to expend such great expense on the Jew's training, I want your word that my investment will come back alive and well, accompanied by both my sons!"

"No one wants that to happen more than I do," Scipio retorted.

Marcus lifted his glass. "Distinguish yourself on the battlefield, my son, and the honor of consul will be yours."

Scipio wanted to shout for joy and pump his fists into the air at his father's words of endorsement, imagining the look that would be on Domitius' face when he heard that Scipio was the favorite son. He lifted his glass. "I will make you proud."

* * *

Livel was getting ready to retire for the evening when Scipio charged into the room. "It's done!" he said, his expression triumphant.

"That's nice," Livel said, unlacing his sandals. He was accustomed to Scipio's proclamations at all hours of the night. And since Scipio had not been home the night before, Livel was fairly certain he was referring to some new female conquest.

"I used my immeasurable charm and personality to convince my father that you should become the Gracchus family physician, and all you have to say is *that's nice?*"

Livel stopped unlacing his shoes and gazed at Scipio. "You did what?"

"Does the word *physician* resonate in any way with you?"

Livel started to laugh as he hobbled over to Scipio and shook his hand. "*Baruch Hashem*, blessed be to God."

"Don't thank your god, thank me. I was the one who convinced my father. But don't worry, you don't owe me anything."

Livel scrunched his eyes. "What exactly does that mean?"

"You forced me to learn Hebrew and Aramaic, and because of your constant nagging," Scipio said, tapping his chest, "I am now my father's choice for consul."

Livel was ecstatic that his plan to elevate Scipio had worked. Knowing that Domitius would suffer the rejection served to heighten his satisfaction. "You are the right choice."

"There is only one way now that Domitius would ever become consul—I would have to die."

* * *

The Galen dining room shimmered in the lamplight as servants hovered about ladling soup and pouring wine for the evening meal. Doctor Galen watched as his daughter Arria lifted her goblet. Holding it delicately, her eyes shifted towards him. Her expression was so similar to the mother she had never known that he felt as if one foot were in the present and the other in the past. He swallowed hard, fending off the rush of emotions that always overtook him at times like this.

Julia Galen had died giving birth to Arria, and although it had been sixteen years, Claudius Galen still grieved for her. Over the years, his wife's memory had become the personification of perfection, and because no woman could compete with such an illusion, he had never remarried.

Doctor Galen smiled at his beautiful daughter, wondering for the hundredth time if his doting ways and indulgent demeanor had spoiled her to such a degree that no man would be able to handle her. That she could be charming and even witty when it served her was helpful. But she was too much like him: outspoken and headstrong, and she cared more about intellectual pursuits than about what people thought of her.

"How was your day, Father?" Arria asked, taking a delicate sip of wine.

"Remarkable!" he boomed, compelling himself back to the present. "I have a patient with a badly damaged knee and chest and facial lacerations. I've been treating him for the past six weeks at the Gracchus villa. I'm fascinated by the boy."

"Is he one of the sons?" Arria asked, having seen the brothers at gatherings and been intrigued by their good looks.

Galen shook his head. "He's a slave, a Jew serving as tutor to Marcus Gracchus' two sons."

"You've been treating their slave?" Arria asked with disdain, putting down the goblet. "Father, that is beneath you!"

"First of all, Marcus Gracchus is my patient and my friend. When a friend asks for a favor, you do not refuse." He forced the anger from his voice before continuing. "His name is Livel, and he is quite remarkable. He speaks Hebrew, Aramaic, Latin and Greek and is more interested in my instruments and my methods of healing than he is about healing himself!

"The other day, when I removed one of the stitches from his chest, he actually asked for a mirror so he could watch. Then he asked me to show him, with a piece of parchment, how I made the stitch. His curiosity astounds me, and his questions are thought provoking and challenging. He may have the finest young mind I have ever encountered."

Finer than mine? Arria cringed, infuriated by her father's remark. She had never been relegated to second position before, and she viewed the competition with this Livel person as a personal assault.

She began to calculate in her head. *He's been injured for six weeks; father will soon have no need to attend to him. Then I will never have to hear his name again!* She smiled in relief. "I'm certain you'll miss him once he's discharged from your care," Arria said, biting back the sarcasm from her tone.

"I certainly would have."

"Would have?" Arria asked, astounded by her father's remarks.

"Marcus asked me if I would take the boy into my school."

"Well that isn't possible," Arria said icily, "since your session is well underway. I hope you recommended one of the other schools."

The doctor frowned. "I most certainly did not! I can't imagine giving someone else the opportunity of training such an exceptional mind."

Exceptional mind! Arria was seized by jealousy–a scorpion snapping its pincers. Hearing about this Livel was one thing. Having him in their lives was something else entirely.

* * *

It was an early autumn morning, and the sun was ascending in a water-blue, cloud-dusted sky as Livel rode in a wagon through the city of Rome. It was to be the first day of his apprenticeship and his first outing since arriving in Rome a year earlier. On that day, he had been so overwrought and filled with foreboding that his mind barely registered his surroundings. Now his heart pounded in anxious anticipation, his mind racing at what lay ahead.

He did not know where to glance first, enchanted by the chaotic frenzy of the burgeoning capital. Everywhere he looked, there was something to see. Men rode chariots jockeying for dominance over horses and their riders. Peddlers dodged this way and that, their carts overflowing with everything from rags to food.

As they neared the center of the city, Livel thought his eyes might bulge right out of his head. He was awestruck by the massive marble buildings, the height-defying gabled roofs and the elaborate stonework and statues that seemed to adorn every archway and entrance.

A vast array of shops lined both sides of the street. There were bakeries, barbershops, butchers, cobblers, fishmongers and food shops, furniture sellers, olive oil stands, perfume purveyors, taverns and storefronts for moneylenders. A block past the senate office building, the wagon pulled to a stop.

"Up there," the driver said, pointing.

Livel grabbed his crutch. He no longer wore the splint but his knee was still stiff and swollen, and it hurt him to walk. Limping up the small hill to a two-storied building, he knocked, waited a few moments and then pounded again.

The door opened. "You the new student?" Bolo asked. He was a huge black man with kindly eyes and a knowing smile.

"Yes. I'm Livel."

"Come in, the doctor's expecting you." He eyed the crutch.

Livel repositioned himself so that he stood taller, suddenly self-conscious and annoyed by the look of pity on the servant's face.

Intent on keeping up, Livel disregarded the pain as he hobbled down the hallway. They moved past closed doors and through the sunlit atrium. Unlike the Gracchus villa, this atrium had no box hedges and blooming flowers, just a small pool to collect rainwater and a few stone benches.

"That staircase leads to the family quarters, and in there is the doctor's private office," Bolo said.

He pointed to his left just as the door opened and a young girl stepped into the hallway. She had a heart-shaped face, charcoal-colored hair, almond-shaped eyes the color of jade and pouty lips that seemed to frown and smile in unison. She wore a pleated azure tunic that brushed the floor, her tiny waist was wrapped in golden ribbons and a palla was draped over her shoulders, held in place by a pearl brooch. He guessed her to be about sixteen.

Livel smiled and nodded, so overcome by her beauty, he was unable to find his voice.

She in turn shot him a discordant look and walked back into the office, slamming the door.

"Who was that?" Livel whispered to the slave. "Is she always so rude?"

"The doctor's daughter," Bolo said, his tone suddenly protective as they moved toward the classroom. "This is where the doctor teaches."

Livel pushed open the door and stepped over the threshold into a room large enough to amply accommodate the twenty students gathered inside.

"Ah! Look who's here," Doctor Galen boomed proudly from behind his waist-high table at the front of the room. "You're just in time. I'm about to cut into the brain of this dog."

Livel limped toward the line of students.

"Bring our newest student something to sit on," the doctor shouted to a servant.

As Livel joined the group, a few students nodded, and some said, "Hello." He scanned the room. The floor was an intricate mosaic pattern and wooden shelves lined both walls. The shelves to his left were filled with rolls of papyrus, some with projecting knobs of ivory and others with knobs of ebony, all wrapped in purple covers with scarlet strings. He had never seen so many books–not even in his father's library at the synagogue. To his right were shelves lined with flasks and jars of every size and shape.

Livel placed his crutch on the floor and perched on a stool just as the doctor began to excise the brain from the dog.

"It has been six-hundred years since Hippocrates gave us a glimpse into the power we mere mortals might have over injury and illness," Doctor Galen espoused. "That brilliant man opened the door for us into the fundamentals of healing. But if we're truly going to progress and understand, we must study firsthand the structure and workings of the human body.

"There is a great difference in the size and weight of a dog's brain when compared to the human brain," the doctor proclaimed, holding up the excised organ that looked to Livel like a turtle with its head peeking from its shell. "Now let's take a look at the heart."

Livel had lived his entire life for this very moment. He felt suspended in time as he memorized every word and every movement. All too quickly, the session was over and the other students gathered their belongings and left. Livel wanted to prolong the day for as long as possible, so he remained seated–a satiated lover too drained to move.

"Clear this away," the doctor ordered a hovering servant, "and bring my writing instruments." He glanced towards Livel. "You're still here?"

"If I may, Doctor."

"Well then, come closer. I'm writing a book called the *Faculties of Nature,* and I'm about to record today's findings. Would you like to assist?"

Livel could not believe his good fortune as he limped to the doctor's side. "It would be my honor, sir."

After the students filed out, Arria returned to the classroom. She stood in the shadows listening to her father and Livel in an animated conversation. Jealousy raged, a serpent devouring her from the inside. This was her time with her father, the time when he would teach Arria lessons from the day, and she did not intend to have an interloper change that. Arria's anger took hold as she stepped from the doorway and strode to her father's side.

"Father, why is he still here?" Her voice startled the two men who looked up at her. She shot Livel a furious look. "And more importantly, what is he doing in my place?"

"Calm down, sweet girl. Would it be so terrible if you were both to assist me?"

Arria pointed her eyes at Livel. She wanted to scream out, "Yes!" But there was something in her father's expression that stopped her. "And if he tells someone about me?"

Doctor Galen put down his quill and walked over to his daughter. He took Arria's hand in his and turned toward Livel. "This is my daughter, Arria. I think she is concerned that you might expose our little secret–that we have disregarded that which society deems customary. You see, while I have taught Arria to read and write, which is acceptable to some, she has also been taught to do so in several languages: Latin, Aramaic, Greek and of special interest to you, even Hebrew." He looked at his daughter and smiled. "She is also the most gifted surgeon I've ever trained. Of course, she has only practiced on animals thus far, but that doesn't preclude me from espousing her talent. Now young man, do you think you can keep that information to yourself?"

"I'll take her secret to my grave." Livel had no idea why this beautiful young woman had learned the language of his people, but he was ecstatic that she had.

"Be certain of those words," Arria sneered, "because if you ever tell a soul, I'll be the one to send you to that grave!"

Chapter 12

It was twilight by the time Livel arrived back at the villa. In the kitchen, he devoured a meal before rushing to his lesson with Scipio.

In the classroom, he moved to the table and found a piece of parchment. With trembling hands, he dipped the quill into ink and began to draw, amazed when an image slowly emerged. Using his gift of perfect recall, Livel created a replica of the dog's brain. Satisfied and feeling a bit smug, he stretched out his stiffened leg. Noticing Scipio was almost an hour late, he was about to go and search out his errant student when Scipio entered the room.

"How was your first lesson?" Scipio asked.

Livel handed him his drawing. "Take a look. It's a dog's brain."

Scipio picked up the parchment and whistled. "You did this?"

Livel nodded. Until today, he did not even know he had the skill to draw. He had always thought his destiny was to become a rabbi, but now he felt certain that God had other plans for him.

"Perhaps this injury of yours will turn out to be a good thing."

"Perhaps it will," Livel said. "Now it's late, and I still have the responsibility to be your teacher. Have you memorized the first two stanzas of *Shir ha-Shirim*, the Song of Songs in Hebrew?"

"I have."

"Write it for me, please."

"Oh! It's not good enough that I speak and read this most difficult language, but now you insist I must write it!"

"It will help you to become consul. Is that not a good enough reason?"

Scipio took up the quill, dipped it in ink and scratched out a few letters. Then he hesitated. Livel took his hand. "Like this. The aleph is a line here and an open circle next to it."

Ten minutes later Scipio put down the quill, a look of satisfaction on his face.

"Recite it aloud in Hebrew," Livel said.

"Let him kiss me with the kisses of his mouth–for thy love is better than wine," Scipio said, his eyes lusty. "Thine ointments have a goodly fragrance; thy name is as ointment poured forth: therefore do the maidens love thee."

"Very good," Livel beamed. "Your accent is excellent."

"Speaking of maidens, did you meet Doctor Galen's daughter yet?" Scipio asked, making a circle with the fingers of his left hand and jabbing the pointer finger of his right into the hole.

The obscene gesture embarrassed Livel. "I didn't have the honor," he lied, hoping that would end the conversation.

"Wait until you do. Half the men in Rome have lined up to be her suitor. She shuns them all. Perhaps it's time for me to meet her." He laughed. "She'll never be able to resist my charms."

"I'm certain that's true," Livel said, still puzzled by Arria's open hostility towards him.

Scipio stood. "All this talk about a beautiful woman stirs my manhood. I'll see you later."

Livel heard his laugh all the way down the hallway.

* * *

After six months, Livel no longer used a crutch, and the pain on most days was tolerable. But the limp remained. He didn't mind. The injury was a doorway to great opportunity–allowing him to use the gift of his genius that the Master of the Universe had bestowed upon him.

When Doctor Galen arrived, he was sitting on a stool at the front of the room while the other students mingled with one another. Wearing blood-splattered clothing, exhaustion pouring from his red-rimmed eyes, the doctor moved to the front of the class. With great flourish, he placed the bundle he held in his arms on the table and unfurled it.

"This, my good students," the doctor said, holding up a human arm, "is our lesson for today. My hope now is that the gods allow the noble man associated with this appendage to survive." He looked at Livel. "Perhaps you will assist me," he said. "I am quite tired."

Livel moved to the doctor's side.

The other students, all slaves sent by their masters to improve the techniques they had learned from actual field battle experience, had grown to accept Livel's elevated status as their most gifted student.

Doctor Galen pointed. "Make the first incision here. We'll remove the skin from the arm and forearm. Then we'll examine the superficial veins, the cutaneous nerves, and lastly the triceps and the biceps brachii muscles. Shall we begin?"

* * *

After class, Livel paced as he waited for Arria to arrive. It was the highlight of his day–every day–just being in the same room with her, even though she never missed an opportunity to belittle him.

Arria pushed open the door. She wore an old stained tunic, and her hair was covered in a bright red scarf. She pulled the scarf off as she came to his side, her eyes boring into his. There was no hello. "Where's my father?"

"He's gone to check on a patient," Livel said.

"Teach me what you learned today," she demanded.

Livel explained every detail of their dissection, showing her the excised veins and the exposed muscles of the arm.

Arria picked up the retractor and spent the next half hour engrossed in the anatomy. Livel stood by silently watching in admiration as she prodded and explored the veins and muscles of the arm, her face an explosion of joyous emotion.

Just as Arria was about to slice open a quadrant of the bicep muscle, her father entered and moved to her side. "Very good. Now cut here. Look at the way the muscle is entwined with the fibrous tissues."

They worked together for another fifteen minutes before the doctor said, "Later, my dear. It's growing dark, and we need to begin our writing."

Livel reached under the table and picked up his leather pouch. He handed it to the doctor.

"What's this?" asked the doctor.

"I've been working on these in the evenings. I thought it was time to show them to you."

Doctor Galen moved to an adjacent table and pulled out the parchments one at a time. "Arria come and look–it's a perfect depiction of a heart–and this lung! Look at the brain! You are a veritable genius!" he said, gazing with appreciation, his eyes never leaving the drawings. "Arria, can you believe the magnificence of his details? You did all of this from memory?"

"I did," Livel said, praying that Arria was as impressed as her father.

"Arria look at the stomach, and this one of the intestines, and the liver, and this glorious depiction of the muscle fibers of the leg and torso!" Doctor Galen looked at Livel with pride. "I never imagined that taking you to the morgue to view the bodies of the poor souls butchered by outlaws would have such an astounding outcome. Now I no longer care if Rome passes laws that disallow us access to cadavers, because thanks to you, we have these perfect illustrations! Do you have any idea what this means?" Doctor Galen asked, beaming at Livel as he caressed each drawing with the tips of his fingers. "I can only dictate my work to others during my lifetime, but thanks to your gifted artistry, generations of future physicians will learn." Warmly, he put his arm around Livel's shoulder.

"You must stay for supper. I want to tell you all about my newest work with pulses and how I'm using that knowledge to diagnose illness." He turned his attention to Arria and kissed her forehead. "I have a few more notes to make. Please show Livel to the dining room."

Once alone, Arria turned her face toward Livel. It was a mask of blackened fury. Livel went cold.

"Those pictures!" she spat. "I know what you're trying to do, but you'll never take my place!"

"That is not my intention! I swear it."

"Don't lie to me! I know exactly what you are–a conniving, hawk-nosed cripple who's trying to take my father from me!" Arria sneered, the vitriolic words pouring out with no regard for the effect they were having on Livel.

Livel wanted to shout back–wanted to slap her face–wanted to find a way to hurt her. Instead, he held his expression neutral and his voice steady. "Please extend my apologies to your father. I won't be staying for supper."

He didn't remember leaving the house and almost stumbled down the stairs as he made his way to the waiting carriage–Arria's accusation and disparaging words cut deeper than any sword ever could.

Chapter 13

En Gedi
Summer Year 131 CE

Just as the desert sky turned dusty pink, and the sun began its plunge into the distant horizon, Sarah moved along the trail that led to the tree house Masabala had destroyed. She came here every night seeking the silence and innocent memories of childhood, trying to make sense of being in love with Masabala for as long as she could remember.

It was also a time when Sarah tried honestly to evaluate her attributes and her failings. Although Sarah realized that she talked too much and should listen more, once she began speaking, there was no stopping her. She was impetuous and curious by nature, and that seemed to exacerbate her constant bantering.

Sarah always prided herself on being even-tempered and patient. Having a temper was not usually an issue, but when Masabala decided to cut off his finger, she was infuriated. Sarah found her moods changing over the past year. It now took little to incite her into a rage, an anger that was always followed by sulking and dark moods.

She recognized that some of the anger stemmed from jealousy. She was eighteen years old, and all of her friends were married and talking about becoming mothers.

"You must stop this foolishness!" her mother had said just that morning. "We can't keep turning down offers of marriage. You need a man to take care of you and give you children. It's madness to wait for Masabala when you don't even know if he intends to marry you!"

"If Masabala doesn't want me, then I shall never marry, and you will never have grandchildren!" Sarah had shouted, storming out the door.

She wiped away a tear that fell across her cheek; at the memory of the hateful way she had treated her mother. After all, it had been over a year since she had last seen Masabala, and her mother could be right; he might not want her. To make matters worse, the rabbi and his wife had no information about when their son might return. All the worry was taking a toll on Masabala's mother, Miriam. She had grown painfully thin, pale and sickly and often said that no mother should face the possibility of losing two sons. Sarah understood Miriam's agony, having lost both her best friend Livel and the only man she would ever love, Masabala.

News had begun to filter back from the cities that the Jews were preparing to wage war against Rome. Sarah was frantic that Masabala would not return before the fighting began. She wanted to tell him that she loved him; just once, she wanted to say those words.

Sarah was turning back toward En Gedi when she spied a figure walking amongst the trees. In the dusk, she couldn't distinguish the features, and her heart began to race. How often her mother had warned her not to wander through the orchards alone, fearful that some wayward Roman soldier might come lurking and do unspeakable things to her.

Sarah hovered behind the biggest tree trunk she could find, so panicked she could almost taste her fear. As the man neared, Sarah was aghast by his huge stature, imagining how he could break her neck with one hand. She didn't breathe–terrified that he might hear her. The man turned in circles as if he were looking for someone. In the waning light, she could see that he had long black hair tied back with a band.

Then she heard her name called by a voice as familiar as her own.

Sarah moved into the clearing. "Masabala?" she cried, running to him and hugging him with all her might. Immediately embarrassed by her impetuousness, she let him go and took a step backward.

Sarah could not believe how much Masabala had changed. His beard was thick and his facial features as prominent as the muscles in his arms. They looked like they had been carved by a sculptor's tool.

Masabala stared at Sarah, and his breath caught. His little cherub had become a beautiful woman, her face more angular, the high cheekbones and sable eyes alluring, her breasts full against the fabric of her tunic.

"I went to the house first. They said I would find you out here," Masabala said, his voice anxious and strained.

"I was so afraid you weren't coming back," Sarah said, her entire body trembling as if her very blood was boiling. "I have thought about you every single day, and I have prayed morning noon and night that you would be safe. You just can't imagine what it's been like here without you. I have been so unhappy. I just want you to know—"

"Shh," Masabala laughed, touching her lips with his fingers.

She pushed his hand away. "I have so many things I need to say to you," she insisted. "Things I should have told you before you went away."

"Sarah, a lot has happened to me over the past year. I've changed."

"If you are going to tell me that you have found someone else, I don't want to hear it!" She put her hands over her ears and scowled.

Masabala shook his head and gently took her hands. "That's not what I was going to say. I was going to tell you that I never realized how much you meant to me until you weren't there. I've missed you, Sarah. I know now that I love you, and I always have. Marry me, Sarah, become my wife."

Sarah's mouth dropped open. "You mean that? Do you really, really mean that?" she asked. Bursting into tears, she took him by the hands and jumped up and down, just like she used to do when they were young.

Masabala laughed, realizing that while she might look like a woman, the little girl would always be lurking inside.

* * *

Two days later, in the garden of the rabbi's home, Sarah and Masabala stood beneath the wedding *Chuppah*, a canopy of woven linen attached at the corners to four cedar poles. Sarah was dressed in a white tunic covered by an over-mantle edged in white fringe. Around her waist, she wore a braided belt interspersed with blue and silver threads. Golden rosettes hung from her ears, and a golden necklace draped her neck. Her head and face were covered with a silk veil.

Rabbi Eleazar stood before the bride and groom under the *Chuppah*. He wore the white robe traditionally worn on the sacred holiday of Yom Kippur. Sarah's mother, Alma, stood to her daughter's left, and Masabala's mother, Miriam, stood to her son's right. Two Kohanim were also in attendance to serve as witnesses.

"My heart sings with joy today as I welcome Sarah into our family," the rabbi said, as he smiled at her. "As is our custom, you will circle Masabala seven times to represent the seven days of creation and to declare Masabala is now the center of your world. May your lives be blessed by Hashem."

Sarah walked around Masabala seven times, her eyes never leaving his face. It was the culmination of a lifetime of loving him. Had Livel been present in this moment, everything would have been perfect.

The rabbi chanted blessings and then offered a cup of wine to the bride and groom. They each took a sip.

Masabala then placed a coin in Sarah's hand. "Behold, you are betrothed unto me according to the laws of Moses and Israel."

The rabbi read the Ketubah aloud and then presented it to Masabala for his signature. The sacred document listed the responsibilities and rights of the groom toward his bride. The two witnesses came forward and signed.

The rabbi set the cup down on a table beside him and began reciting the seven blessings. On the sixth blessing he hesitated, reaching out his hand to Sarah and Masabala. "Blessed art Thou Lord our God, King of the universe who created joy and gladness, groom and bride, rejoicing, glad song, pleasure, delight, love, brotherhood, peace and companionship. Soon, Lord our God, let there be heard in the cities of Judah and in the streets of Jerusalem the sound of joy and the sound of gladness, the voice of the groom and the voice of the bride. Blessed art Thou, Lord, who gladdens the groom with the bride."

Again Rabbi Eleazar held the cup of wine for Masabala and Sarah to drink.

The goblet was placed on the ground. Masabala stepped on it, smashing it with his right foot as an act of remembrance. Even at the most joyous moment in life, a Jew must always remember the sorrow surrounding the destruction of the sacred Temple. Masabala kissed Sarah, consecrating her forevermore as the wife of a Kohen, descendent of Aaron, brother to Moses, from the tribe of Levi.

* * *

Their wedding night was spent in Masabala and Livel's child-hood bedroom. The two beds were pushed together, and a vase of flowers sat on a table beside the bed. The oil lamp burned, flickering in the smothering breeze of the open window.

"This is the happiest day of my life," Sarah said, lying in Masabala's arms. "I love you so much."

Masabala ran his fingers through Sarah's hair, burying his face into her neck. "You smell like flowers," he cooed, trying to block out remembrance of the odors from soldiering that had attached to him like a second skin.

"Do you remember the day I punched Livel in the stomach, in this very room when I was nine?" Sarah said, the memories from the room unfolding like the opening of a book. "I can still see the look on his face."

"And he pulled your hair, if I recall correctly?" Masabala's voice caught. "I think he'd be very happy for us."

"He always knew," she whispered.

"Knew what?"

"That I loved you," Sarah said, momentarily losing herself to the cherished friendship. Exhausted, her eyes unwillingly began to close. She twitched herself awake. Masabala would be leaving in a few hours, and she was not going to miss even one second of the limited time they had left. "How am I going to say goodbye when you go back to your command?"

"This is our beginning, Sarah. I will come back to you!"

They wrapped themselves around each other, husband and wife, merging their bodies into one.

Chapter 14

Masabala sat in a makeshift tent on a mountainside ledge. It overlooked the central highlands of the Jordan Rift Valley that connects the Jordan River to the Sea of Galilee and the Dead Sea. The sun blazed, transforming the surrounding parched earth into a thousand shades of beige.

Even though he had been back at his command for a month, Masabala still found it hard to believe he was actually a married man. For so long, he fantasized what it would be like to explore Sarah's body, to find the places that brought her pleasure. Even now, if he closed his eyes he could still sense Sarah's silken skin against his body and the intimacy of their caresses. But something else had happened that first night they were together; a depth of emotion had overflowed from Masabala like a river breaching its banks. He had fallen in love, not just in word, but also in deed.

He shook his head, coming back to the present. He had a job to do if he ever expected to get home again. Masabala's command was a ragtag group of soldier-boys, less than three hundred in number, all inexperienced in combat and fearless in their ignorance.

They had come to this place in the mountains by order of Bar Kokhba. Like a rabbi leading his minions in worship, the *nasi* had laid forth his plans. He would take his soldiers and strike in the north, near the port city of Akko, one of the main ports of the eastern Mediterranean coast. Thousands of Roman soldiers were stationed in and around that city, and Bar Kokhba intended to attack with an army that would outnumber his enemy three to one.

At the same time the assault was underway, another set of tactical plans was to be set in motion. Bands of Jewish zealots, who were lying in wait all over Judea, had been given an edict: attack small groups of unsuspecting Romans, and then retreat into the underground passageways and caves stockpiled for just that purpose.

The intention lying behind Bar Kokhba's plans for these *attack and hide* raids was simple: inflict ruinous strikes that would obliterate their opponent's morale.

Masabala's first attack would occur somewhere outside of Tiberius, a city known for its hot springs and healing waters, a city inhabited by wealthy Romans and a stronghold of Roman soldiers.

After spending so much time at Bar Kokhba's side studying the strategy of warfare, and then spending another six months learning the art of actual combat, Masabala was anxious to deal a punishing blow.

Master of the sword and the lance, Masabala was also an expert archer. He was able to predict an arrow's trajectory depending on the wind and his choice of arrowhead. He rarely missed the target when using the leaf-shaped arrowhead, standard for fighting lightly clad soldiers, but he was less proficient at releasing the heavier tri-pointed arrowheads that were intended to pierce through body armor. Still, Masabala was better than most, and just as Bar Kokhba predicted, learning to fight had not been that difficult.

Masabala was in the middle of writing a letter to Bar Kokhba announcing his location and intentions when he spotted his scout, Ari, approaching at a run.

"About a hundred Romans have broken from their regiment. They wear no armor and are riding in loose formation!" Ari said, eyes fevered, and his face dripping with perspiration.

"Call in the men from their posts and have them gather on the low ground!" Masabala shouted. He was overcome by a myriad of emotions as he made his way down the mountain path to the clearing below. Yet he was confident that he knew what needed to be done and how to do it.

Under the burning desert sun, surrounded by boulders and tumbling brush, the nasi's words came to Masabala's mind as he waited for his men to assemble: *victory lies in the planning.*

"Pay close attention. Your lives and our victory will depend on your understanding every aspect of our mission," he said, seeking out the eyes of his boy soldiers, seeing fear and expectation, courage and bravado in their expressions and stance.

Masabala picked up a stick and began drawing in the sand. "We will wait until they are here," he said, pointing to an X in the drawing. "When they ride into the valley, we will surround them and cut them off here," he tapped the ground, "at the mouth and the exit. Archers will position themselves in the hills," he made more X's. "Are there any questions?"

No man spoke.

"May the Holy One, Blessed be He guide us to victory," Masabala said. "Mount up! We go!"

* * *

A slovenly group of Roman soldiers moved along the floor of the Jordan valley. Traveling at a leisurely pace with their helmets and chain mail iron shirts dangling from their saddles, they paid little attention to their surroundings. Each man carried a bow and arrows, and darts clipped to the back of his shield, along with a sword and a dagger. Had anyone amongst them been vigilant, they might have spotted in the distance wisps of sand kicked up by the horses of Masabala's scouts who were shadowing their every move.

After the last enemy soldier was within the canyon walls, Masabala dropped his arm as a signal to begin their assault. What followed seemed to happen in altered time. Masabala heard, rather than saw, the sound of arrows shooting through the air, whooshing like the wings of a thousand birds. He heard men shout victoriously as their arrows found their marks.

"For my brother!" Masabala screamed, shooting for the first time at a human target. In detached astonishment, he watched as his arrow shot through the air striking the thigh of a soldier, impaling the rider to his horse. For a millisecond, the soldier seemed stunned. Reacting to what was obvious agony; he tugged at the arrow skewering him. The horse reared back on his hind legs and fell to the ground, crushing its rider.

The entire drama played out in less than a minute. That was how long it took Masabala to regain his perspective and shoot another arrow. From his vantage point, it was like watching a choreographed dance of death. With their escape routes cut off, the Romans circled and tried to protect themselves from the on-slaught. It was to no avail.

Masabala was not prepared for the chaotic bloodlust that en-sued–the noise and confusion, the blood and screams as his men converged on the dead and dying vying for the spoils, cutting off fingers for rings, hording swords and daggers. Masabala was pres-ent during the ensuing carnage, watching but not seeing, basking in the glory of victory yet writhing in the revulsion of death.

It was day one of a war that would be carried out by hundreds of thousands of Jewish zealots, many of whom had come from distant lands, speaking different languages and having different backgrounds. They were unified in their absolute faith in Judaism and their belief in One God. United they all marched the width and breadth of Judea with a singular goal–freedom.

Three months later

The desert sun of late summer sizzled and scorched, burning the sand and blistering the skin. Dehydrated and miserable, even the mildest-mannered under Masabala's command turned belligerent and beastly as they waited impatiently for the order to attack.

Passing in the valley below, beneath their hideout on the high ridges, was an assemblage of twenty-two men and eight women. They were trailing mules whose packs overflowed with goods, a common sight now that the wealthy Roman merchants had de-cided to flee the war-torn country. Two-dozen fully armored and armed soldiers, riding on skittish horses, escorted them.

With the knowledge that his men were fueled by adrenaline and satiated only in battle, Masabala gave the signal to strike. Arrows flew. The ensuing attack was murderous in scope, though only a quarter of an hour in duration. No Roman survived, and no Jew lost his life.

Descending like locusts from their lofty lair in the cliffs, the soldiers began their greed-driven quest to appropriate the bounty: jewels, coins and gold. Masabala turned aside as he always did, unable and unwilling to partake in what was considered the right of every soldier victorious in battle.

Hands behind his back, his tunic stained rusty by the blood of his enemy, Masabala walked into the desert night. Only the sound of sand careening across the desert floor and the rustling of bush could be heard. He stood staring at the stars, thinking how insignificant all of this was in relationship to the universe. Suddenly he heard a grunt. Pulling out his sword, he moved forward, his footsteps light and silent.

At first, Masabala saw only a silhouette, an image that morphed into the darkened night and then reappeared as he moved closer. One of his soldiers, a boy he knew as David, and a particular favorite of Masabala's for his gregarious personality and seemingly innocent demeanor, was having intercourse with a Roman woman. A dead child with dark curly hair, its mouth open in a wordless scream, lay not two feet away.

David was unaware of Masabala's presence, grunting in ecstasy, groping the woman's bloodied breasts as he rode her non-responsive body. Masabala could see that the woman's skin had the marble-white paler of a corpse, her eyes vacant and her lips bluish-purple in death.

He had witnessed horrific things over the past six months of battle and thought he was immune, his heart as calloused as his hands. But even in war, there had to be rules of conduct. Wounded women and children were supposed to be treated and then transported to prisoner of war camps. Sexual contact with the prisoners was forbidden and resulted in immediate discharge.

The heinous act, now taking place before him, tore into the very core of his humanity and morality. David was a Jew, and Jewish boys did not act like this, especially when they were under his command. Masabala was blinded by his own self-righteousness and overcome with the desire to obliterate the obscenity before him.

The beginning words of *Kaddish*, the Jewish prayer for the dead, came into his head, *Yit'gadal v'yitkadash sh'mei raba b'al'ma di v'ra khir'utei,* May His great Name grow exalted and sanctified in the world that He created as He willed.

Masabala prayed that by professing his love for God, he could regain control of himself. It was useless. Blackness descended, a cold anger so enveloping, he could barely breathe. He no longer saw David as human–his face now distorted, eyes shooting fire, hands clawed. Masabala felt his arm raise in the air, heavy with the sword, the avenger intent on revenge. The blow that followed was lethal in its power, obliterating the young soldier's transgression along with his life. In death, David fell foreword, draping the dead woman like a shroud.

Masabala dropped his sword and stared, howling in disbelief, finding it incomprehensible that he had actually killed one of his own men.

His knees buckled, and he slumped to the hard ground, hands grasped in supplication. Then he saw blood seeping from the eyes and mouth and even the fingernails. He knew the blood was not real. Still, Masabala shivered and blinked several times before he was able to shove the images aside. He reached for his dagger and held it, with a trembling hand, to his own throat. He longed for death.

Sarah's face flashed before him. He could feel the salt of her tears upon his face and hear her beseech him not to take his own life. Then Masabala thought of his mother. His suicide would kill her as surely as if he had plunged the blade into her heart himself. He wanted no other deaths on his hemorrhaging conscience. He let the dagger fall to the sand.

He stood and pulled David off the dead woman and hefted him over his shoulder. He would tell his troops that he found David dead in the desert–just one more lie bounded up within the treacherous web that would surely follow. But he would go on to live another day, to lead his men and do his job.

Chapter 15

En Gedi

It had taken only six months for the Jews to rid Judea of her Roman captors. It was an exhilarating time for the new Israel, but the victory had taken an enormous toll on the tiny land. Thousands of young Jewish men had perished, and the laments of anguish and loss seeped from every town, village and city, the sorrow like daggers plunging into the very heart of the nation.

In the midst of the transition, Masabala was reassigned, with his men, to the desert wilderness. They built corrals for their horses and mules, set up tents and established a perimeter line of defense against any remnants of Roman troops that might still be in the area.

With his new headquarters only a short ride from En Gedi, Masabala drove his men relentlessly, counting the moments until he could take his leave. Once the last sentry was in place and the encampment was secure, Masabala mounted his horse and searched for Asher. He found his second in command overseeing the placement of posts used to create more fencing.

Asher, Masabala's closest friend waved a welcome. Raised in Jerusalem, he was the fifth son of a blacksmith. He had a symmetrical face offset by a crooked nose, broken in a fight. His deep-set eyes nested beneath bushy, black eyebrows that met in the middle of his forehead. Asher had fought valiantly alongside Masabala in Ashdod, Beersheba, Tiberius and Hebron.

"I'm going home for a day," Masabala said.

Asher placed a hand over his heart. "Ride in safety, my friend."

* * *

Wearing only his tunic and a wool jacket to stave off the cold of a desert night, Masabala dismounted, tied his horse to a tree and entered En Gedi. He moved down the familiar streets. It was midnight, and the guards smiled and nodded as they welcomed him back home. Masabala was anxious to see his family and would have gladly passed by the guards without regard, but upbringing and proper manners prevailed. He shook some hands, patted backs in recognition and partook in mundane conversations before finally extricating himself.

Masabala stood in the tranquility of the courtyard of his home and stared into the darkened windows. With the silent footsteps of a seasoned warrior, he entered the house and climbed the stairs. He moved past several closed doors until he stood in front of the one that led to his childhood room. Slowly and with great care, he opened the door.

Sarah was lying on her back with a hand carelessly thrown across her face. Hair tumbled over the pillow and lay damp across her neck. The nightdress had fallen off one shoulder, and the rest had bunched up about her, revealing her upper thigh.

Desire overwhelmed him, yet Masabala remained rooted in place. The responsibilities of his command and the chaotic relocation of men and supplies had kept him busy, too busy to think. But now, standing here in the stillness, reality came crashing back, the claws of recrimination strangling him. He felt tainted and dirty, seeing himself as a murderer with no right to pleasure or love. There was no other choice. He could not stay.

Masabala took one last glance at his beloved Sarah before forcing himself to turn away. He had taken only three steps before arms encircled his waist. He felt Sarah's body pressing hot against his back. Masabala allowed himself a few moments to bask in the warmth of skin that felt like velvet, to be embraced by the love he no longer deserved. Then he turned and held Sarah gently by her heaving shoulders.

"You're home," she cried, shrugging off his hands as she stood on tiptoe kissing his eyes, nose, cheeks and mouth.

"Sarah," he said, begging her name. "I just can't be here. Not now. I don't expect you to understand, but unspeakable things have happened. I thought I could put them aside, but I can't! I need time to sort things out." He took a step toward the door.

"This is your home, and I am your wife," Sarah said, blocking his path like a sentry. "You made a vow before the Holy One, Blessed be He, remember? For all eternity, I am yours, and you are mine."

"I've done things–" Masabala uttered, his eyes downcast in shame.

"Tell me what happened. I will help you. Just don't leave me!" Sarah begged, clutching his hands.

Images flew at him, the dead woman being raped, the innocent child lying lifeless beside its mother, the tiny mouth opened in a voiceless cry. The memories that followed were so raw and so real that Masabala hugged himself to keep his arm from lifting to strike. He gasped, his stomach knotted as if he'd been punched. He saw the fear and anguish on Sarah's face and knew then he could never tell her what had happened. It was his burden alone to carry. Masabala felt a flicker of relief now that he had made a definitive decision. No one would ever have to share in the complicity of his murderous actions.

His eyes caressed Sarah, understanding that her love would be a shield against his pain. Masabala lifted Sarah and cradled her in his arms. Carrying her, he placed Sarah tenderly on the bed. She opened her arms to him, and Masabala lay down beside his wife. In love, he found respite. Although it would only be a momentary reprieve, for now, it would have to be enough.

* * *

The room was bathed in the golden light of morning as Sarah nuzzled deeper into Masabala's arms. He opened his eyes, content as he stroked her sable hair and kissed the top of her head. Sarah cooed and turned her face to accept his kisses. Their passion be-

gan as a low vibration, the first sounds of a melody, foretelling the
rapture that lay ahead. With bodies tingling, they reached towards
the crescendo. The ultimate release was rapture, bringing a tiny
cry from Sarah's lips and tears to her eyes.

Masabala kissed her and then stood, his muscular body out-
lined in the dewy light.

"I don't have much time. I have to see my parents and then get
back to my command."

Sarah sensed the barrier rising around Masabala and heard
the sudden coldness in his voice. She pulled a cover around her
and got out of bed. Taking Masabala's calloused hands in hers, she
brought them to her lips. "I love you, and I want to be a part of
whatever happened to you."

The daylight stripped away his respite, the stain of blood again
upon his hands. He jerked them away.

"I won't let you shut me out!" she said, throwing her arms
around his waist, her face warm against his chest. She felt him
cringe. Sarah knew that something was terribly wrong. Even as
they came together as husband and wife, she had felt a barricade
of resistance, as if a layer of ice insulated the warmth of his body
from her. A part of Sarah wanted to stamp her foot and insist that
he tell her what had happened. But there was another part of her
that wanted to remain in denial, fearful that the knowing would
somehow taint their relationship. She vowed to herself to be patient and not pry. She reached for her tunic, gathered her hair with
a ribbon and then placed a scarf over her head. "Everything is going to work itself out," she said, patting his back. "You're stationed
close enough now to come home often. Promise me that you will."

"That's an easy promise to make," Masabala said, putting his
arm around her. "I know this is all very confusing for you, and I'm
sorry."

"You're home, and that's all I care about," Sarah said. They
walked side-by-side through the hallways and then down the
stairs and into the dining room. His mother and father sat at the
table eating.

"My son!" his mother, Miriam cried, jumping up from her chair and rushing into his arms. She held him tightly and then let her hands linger on his face. "Are you alright? You look so—"

"He's fine," Rabbi Eleazar boomed, hugging his son and then kissing his cheek. "Let the boy sit and have something to eat."

"Something is wrong. I can see it in his eyes," Miriam lamented.

Masabala hugged his mother again. "Mother, please don't worry about me. I'm fine."

The rabbi held the chair for his wife to sit down again. "We heard you were setting up a camp nearby, and we have been waiting expectantly for your return. *Baruch Hashem* that you're safe. How long can you stay?" his father asked, distraught by the look in his son's eyes.

"Only for a few hours," Masabala said. He wished he could turn back time and become her innocent son again. How he longed for that altruistic young soldier who had gone off to war believing he would change the world. He smiled at his mother, intent on dispelling her worries. "I'm fine, mother. Really I am. I just need to be surrounded by the people that I love and a good home-cooked meal."

Although Livel's name was not mentioned aloud, each silently grieved his absence.

"Of course that's all you need. Now that you're nearby, everything is going to be better," Miriam said, patting Sarah's hand. "For all of us."

* * *

Miriam and Sarah stood under the wispy palms of a date tree. It was early fall, a time when the evenings were cool. The thirsty desert sand, that had known little rain for almost seven months, stung their eyes and tickled their skin.

Miriam pulled her scarf down to shield her face as she turned to her daughter-in law. "He should be here any moment," she said, knowing that her son would arrive an hour before sundown on the Sabbath, just as he had done each week for the previous two months. She put a protective arm around Sarah. "He's changed," she said softly, her face etched in worry. "He's distant–here, but not here–pretending to be happy but so obviously sad."

Sarah sighed and shrugged, wishing she could pretend that her mother-in-law's observations about Masabala were inaccurate. But he *was* different. There was a sadness that seeped from his smile and a vacant look in his eyes, even when he engaged in conversations. Sarah thought about their years of growing up together. Masabala loved to argue, always insisting on being right and quarreling about a point until Sarah or Livel would yield out of sheer exhaustion. Now he was reticent, giving in too easily, brooding over his remarks as if he had no right to an opinion. "We have to be patient," Sarah said, sounding more like the parent. "It's just going to take time."

Masabala walked into view, leading his horse by its reins. He smiled, convinced that with each passing week he was getting better at putting on a mask of contentment, distancing himself from the memories, pretending to be the same Masabala that had gone to war two years earlier.

He had no idea how miserably he was failing.

* * *

Prayers said, the Sabbath lamp flickering out, the food consumed and the darkness cloaking them in gentleness, the rabbi took a sip of wine and said, "There is much talk among the elders as to when Bar Kokhba will formally announce his plans to form a government. Have you heard anything?"

Masabala shook his head. "We are waiting as well."

A servant entered the room and approached Masabala. "There are men at the door asking for you."

Masabala glanced at his father as he rose and hurried from the room, Sarah close on his heels. A perspiring, mud-streaked soldier, with Asher at his side, stood on the threshold of the front door. Masabala beckoned them in as his parents entered the foyer. Introductions were made.

Masabala leaned into Asher. "What's going on?"

"Please allow me to answer that question," Menachem, the messenger said with great deference, sending a smile Masabala's way. "I am here as an emissary of Bar Kokhba. You are to accompany me to Jerusalem when the Sabbath ends."

"I can see you are both in need of a decent meal," Miriam pronounced, crooking her finger for the men to follow. "No one leaves my home hungry. No one!"

Sarah touched Masabala's chest as tears pooled at the corner of her eyes. "I need to talk to you."

Masabala looked at Sarah and then at his comrades.

"Come," Sarah whispered, pulling him by the hand out the door and into the courtyard. The night songs of hooting owls greeted them, the sky overhead was a mantle of stars and a cool breeze dusted their brows.

"Haven't you done enough, given enough of yourself?" Sarah cried, her breathing ragged. "You went away a boy and came back a brokenhearted man! You've done your part. I don't want you to go!"

"Sarah, I'm a soldier. It's who I am. You knew that before we married. And besides, the war is over and the danger has passed."

"But that's exactly it," she said, her eyes defiant. "They don't need you anymore."

Masabala took her hand, his expression gentled. "You may be right, but I need them."

Sarah stamped her foot. "No, you don't! You could come back here and become a rabbi. We could be together, like a family is supposed to be!"

Masabala's mouth turned downward, and he let go of Sarah's hand. "I'm not a holy man," he said softly, his eyes burning into hers.

"You can learn to be!" She made a prayer tent with her fingers.

"It's too late for that."

"I can't do this alone," Sarah insisted, hugging herself, the color rising in her cheeks.

"What are you talking about? Do what alone?"

"Have a baby," she blurted, her expression vulnerable, yet determined.

Masabala was speechless. His first thought was that it was an ill-conceived ruse, but the look on Sarah's face belied that idea. For a singular moment, he saw himself as a father, a man capable of providing for and protecting a child. The fantasy dissolved in an instant, replaced by a picture of a dead baby lying beside its mother. He blinked away the vision and forced himself to focus his attention on Sarah.

"You're not pleased," Sarah cried, misreading his silence.

"Not pleased? I'm so overjoyed, I couldn't find my voice," he said, taking Sarah into his arms.

"What if Bar Kokhba insists you stay in Jerusalem? What then? What happens to us?" Anger and fear sliced her words.

Masabala cupped Sarah's face in his hands and he gently kissed her lips. "I vow to you on this day, I will never forsake you."

"You will come when the baby is born, no matter what?"

"As God is my witness."

Chapter 16

It was early evening, and Livel had just finished his supper. He looked around the classroom, a self-satisfied grin on his face. In the corner was the new addition–a bed. It had not taken much to convince Scipio that as Doctor Galen's official illustrator, he needed more space and privacy. For Livel, the newfound freedom was exhilarating–however false the illusion of independence was.

The window creaked as he pushed it open. It was a glorious night, the sky over Rome dappled lilac, white and pink as the autumnal sun disappeared behind the grassy, green hills on the horizon. Contemplating what he had learned that day with Doctor Galen, Livel watched with little interest as dozens of *carpentum*, large, four-wheeled, horse-drawn covered coaches lined the graveled driveway of the Gracchus villa.

Just another raucous party where sprawling drunkards will be lying under bushes in the morning.

He was about to turn away when he recognized Doctor Galen stepping from one of the carriages, white robes gleaming, his usually disheveled hair slicked carefully into place. A moment later, Arria emerged. Her tresses were pleated and braided with garlands, and she wore layers of deep orange linen gathered at one shoulder and held in place by a sparkling brooch. A twisted rope of pearls was belted beneath her breasts, accentuating the promise held beneath.

Livel's breathing quickened. The voices in his head screamed for him to look away, but he could not give up the opportunity to watch her. Smitten by her beauty, Livel found he was unable to swallow, as his knees grew weak. He castigated himself for caring about the mean-spirited, acerbic-tongued shrew that belittled him and never missed an opportunity to remind him of his lowly station in life.

Scipio! The thought struck him like an arrow. His tutelage had turned the shallow man into an intellectual. *If anyone can turn Arria's head, it will be Scipio.* Jealousy tore at Livel's gut, and his stomach clenched. His fingernails ground into his palms. He wanted to be at that party, to have her see him as something other than a tongue-tied slave wearing bloodstained clothing.

Distraught, trembling in covetous fury, he strode to the desk and opened a portfolio filled with ink-drawn illustrations of his family–portraitures he had drawn for comfort in times like these.

The first drawing was of his mother lighting the Sabbath lamp, covering her kindly grey eyes with delicate hands. The next drawing was of her standing at the hearth, steam from boiling pots flushing her cheeks and turning her hair damp. He turned to the next page. His father's image stared back, tall and commanding, gentle yet stern, standing before the congregation. Livel smiled, thinking of the one feature that father and son shared-their protruding ears.

The following drawings were of Masabala as a gangly young boy with feet and head too big for his body. On the ensuing parchments were depictions of his brother, some smiling, some angry, but all with a determined glint in his eyes.

Livel ached for home, the longing intense like a knife lodged in his gut, always present, never letting him forget his loss.

He picked up the quill and dipped it into a vial of *atramentum librarium*, black ink. His hand caressed every stroke as he drew Arria stepping from the carriage. Two hours later, he began another drawing of her with scalpel in hand, an exposed body opened upon a table, her tunic dripping in blood, her eyes wild. When he realized the drawing revealed her secret, his first instinct was to tear it up. Holding the parchment between his fingers, he stared at the page, ready to rip it in half. He ran his hands over the drawing. Then he closed the book.

If she's found out, I don't care!

Distant words came to his mind. *Kol man d'rachem v'la kasher ima kina, lav r'cheemutai r'cheemutah.* Whoever loves without any jealousy, his love is no love.

* * *

Scipio stood in the ballroom wearing a crisp white tunic, his beard groomed and his curly brown hair a semblance of neatness. The musicians began playing. While most wealthy Romans had a harpist and flutist; Marcus Gracchus loved music and owned slaves who could play lute, kithara, lyre, trumpets, drums and tambourines as well.

The exotic tones resonated off the marble walls as Scipio made his way past tables laden with food: soft-boiled eggs in pine-nut sauce, lentils with coriander, ostrich, tuna, fried veal with raisins, roasted wild boar, lamb and pheasant. The lavish display was a testament to the fact that Marcus Gracchus loved his food as much as he loved his music.

Scipio barely glanced at the cuisine, heading instead toward the tables where servants were preparing the wine. He took a decanter and poured himself a drink. Wine in hand, he nodded to acquaintances as he moved through the crowd. He admired the lovely ladies with their painted eyes, cheeks and lips and gave an intimate smile and a wink to the ones he had seduced. He took careful count of the ones he had yet to conquer, trying to decide which one would share his bed before the sun rose on a new day.

Scipio was on his second goblet of wine when he spotted Arria standing with her father. His mouth went dry. She was the beauty the eligible men of Rome fantasized about. That Livel described her as moody, quick tempered and unapproachable did not matter. All Scipio could see was a magnificent young girl with flashing eyes and an aura of self-assurance that intrigued him. He sauntered into the throng of people paying homage to the renowned Doctor Galen and his daughter.

Arria glanced toward Scipio. Their gazes locked. She thought him handsome and smiled as he moved to her side.

"I'm Scipio Gracchus," he said formally.

"I know who you are," Arria replied, tipping her head slightly. "Do I need to introduce myself?"

Scipio laughed. "I think not."

"Good. Now that we have that behind us," she said, stepping closer, "perhaps you can tell me how deserving you are of your bad reputation."

"Reputation?" Scipio smirked. "Just gossip. I enjoy a good party, like pretty girls but in truth, I am waiting for that one right woman to come along."

"And when you find her?" Arria asked, her smile flirtatious.

"I shall put the world at her feet."

"And I should believe you because. . . ?"

"Just ask Livel. He will tell you of my character."

Arria shivered at the mention of her archenemy's name. Her eyes turned cold, and the smile evaporated. "Nice to have met you," she said, turning her back on him in hostile disregard for his fatal, courtship-ending reference to the man she hated most in the world.

Scipio stood stone-like, embarrassed by her sudden contempt and confused at what might have caused it. He turned on his heels and stomped away.

Across the room, Domitius stood amidst a bevy of lovely young women, deciding on his conquest for the evening. He noticed his brother's exchange with Arria Galen. He had been watching her discretely all evening and thought her much too attractive. Beautiful women were much too self-absorbed: he had no inclination to fight for the right to bed a woman. Domitius put his arm around the waist of a plump, blue-eyed delicacy who was breast-snuggling him. Slowly, his hand slid to her buttocks, and the girl sighed and licked her lips seductively.

His hand squeezing the ample rear, Domitius watched in awed delight at the short exchange between Scipio and Arria. The ensuing snub and look of confusion and hurt on his stepbrother's face intrigued Domitius. Suddenly, the idea of winning over Arria Galen was titillating. Doing anything to best Scipio was titillating.

Domitius thought about his silver-tongued charismatic mother, Athena, and how hard she worked to manipulate Marcus Gracchus into believing the son they had together was the child most worthy of his affection. With all her cajoling, there was one factor Athena could not control–Marcus had loved Scipio's dead mother more than he would ever love her.

Consumed by jealousy that she was not Marcus' great love, Athena had taken every available opportunity to barrage Scipio with poisonous remarks and disparaging criticism, encouraging Domitius to join in the ridicule. Domitius enjoyed partaking in the cruelty, embracing the sinister inclinations born from being spoon-fed vindictiveness from an early age. But maliciousness was only one aspect of his personality–amicability was the other. When it suited him his charm was impossible to resist. With a wink and a kiss, he excused himself from the girl at his side. Her frown exhibited her apparent disappointment as he walked away.

Arria saw Domitius approach from the corner of her eye. He moved with panther-like grace. Unlike most Roman men who were dark, this young man was fair, with blond hair and blazing emerald eyes.

"I'm Domitius Gracchus. The brother you're *going* to like," he said, offering his arm. "Perhaps I can lure you away for a short while?"

Arria whispered something to her father and took Domitius' arm.

They walked together past the musicians and stood for a brief moment to watch naked slave-dancers twirl and kick, and bounce and weave to the music. Standing so near to him, the raw sexuality unnerved Arria, and she turned away.

"Some wine?" Domitius asked, retrieving two glasses from a passing servant and handing one to Arria. "To the loveliest woman in the empire," he said as he raised the goblet.

"An outrageous pronouncement," Arria scoffed, taking a sip.

"How is it possible that you and I have never met before?"

"I serve as my father's hostess, and I go where he goes," Arria replied. "He is a very busy man, and we don't socialize often."

"Then I shall surely have to rectify that. But we have little time, as my brother and I are commissioned officers and will leave for Britannia within a year." Domitius looked deeply into Arria's eyes. "When I go, will you miss me?" he asked, half teasing–half serious.

"That seems highly unlikely, since I don't even know you," she replied, one hand adjusting a lock of hair that had fallen from its braid, her eyes seeking his.

"Ah, but now that you've found your intellectual equal, a man who is both a soldier and scholar, surely you *must* miss me."

Arria smiled, captivated by Domitius' sarcastic wit. "If what you say is true, and you're not simply some full-of-himself sot of a man-boy, then perhaps you might be worth getting to know. Then and only then might I care that you are gone."

"You are as high-spirited as an unbroken filly and as confident as a gladiator." Domitius laughed. "I like that!"

Domitius was perceptive at reading a woman's subtle signals. Like a skilled hunter, he was an expert at moving in for the kill. That Arria was so sure of herself only made the hunt much more interesting. "Perhaps you will give me the honor of calling on you?" he said, placing a hand over his heart. "You must know that love once found should never be squandered."

"Love? Is that what you always say to women you've just met?" Arria asked, sparring with Domitius.

"Most certainly not! You judge me too harshly."

"Then I pray that my judgment is erroneous because I intend to accept your invitation."

An hour earlier, Domitius had not cared if Arria Galen lived or died. Now, he cared about only one thing–possessing her.

Chapter 17

The evening came to an unceremonious end as guests staggered from the Gracchus villa with cheeks blotched and eyes reddened from the overindulgence of food and drink.

"I was surprised to see you spending so much time with Domitius Gracchus. He has a treacherous reputation," Doctor Galen said as Arria settled beside him in the carriage.

"I had a good time," Arria replied, as they bumped along the road. It was two in the morning, and for her, the night had passed all too quickly. She found Domitius interesting and his self-confidence and easy manner intriguing. In the past, her problem with men was they were too eager to do her bidding. She sensed that Domitius would not yield to her every whim, and that excited her. Arria had always loved a challenge. What thrilled her most about Domitius was that she felt there was a dangerous streak beneath his charm.

"Arria Galen, I have never involved myself in your intrigues, but I must warn you to be careful with Domitius. He comes from a powerful family, and since we both know how quick you lose interest—"

Arria leaned over and kissed her father's cheek. "This just might be different."

Doctor Galen could not remember a time when Arria showed interest in any particular man. He twisted the ring on his finger wondering how he could understand the complicated anatomy of the human body but could not even begin to understand his own daughter.

Arria had begun manipulating him from the moment she learned to talk. As she matured, she mastered the art of getting her way. Now as he sat beside Arria in the dark, the horses' cadence lulled him into the past; he remembered how difficult it had been to raise a motherless daughter. He reflected on the day she began her menses. Most young girls would have been embarrassed, but not Arria. Her face proud, she strutted through the house proclaiming herself to be a woman to anyone who would listen. Her confidence and unaffected personality earned her the love of the servants and all of Doctor Galen's friends. For months after she reached woman-hood, Galen tried pretending that while physically a woman, Arria was still his little girl. It was a foolish notion.

Arria was maturing, and he needed to find her a suitable husband. Once, he had made lists of eligible young men from aristo-cratic families of Rome and announced his intentions to Arria.

"How can you even think of doing that to me?" she had cried, pointing a trembling finger at him. "My entire life, you spoke to me of the great love you had for my mother! Now you want me to marry a stranger!"

She had locked herself in her room and refused to come out until he promised that she would never have a husband forced upon her. They never spoke of it again.

With each passing year, Arria became more alluring and beautiful. Young men came calling, but none could hold Arria's interest for long. She disposed of them as quickly as one disposes of sour milk. Claudius Galen spent many sleepless nights fretting that she would never marry. He knew that one of her major obstacles was that Arria could never claim the title of surgeon, even though she considered herself as skilled a surgeon as any physician in Rome. Marriage would put an end to her secret practice of medicine.

Galen patted Arria's hand. Perhaps Domitius would be the man to turn her head and make marriage and motherhood more compelling than the study of medicine. Feeling that he should offer more advice he said, "Tread carefully, my dear. Courtship is a serious matter."

Arria rested her head against her father's shoulder. "I like him," she said softly.

* * *

Stars twinkled overhead as the tip of the slivered crescent moon peeked out from behind a billowed cloud. Arria wore a white tunic that scooped at the neck, revealing the ample white mounds of her breasts. Her hair was loose, kept off her face by a single pearl clip. Her lips were tinted pomegranate red, and kohl encircled her enormous eyes. Domitius was dressed in uniform, a sword at his waist. They had come to the arena in the dead of night, the reason a mystery that delighted Arria.

Over the past month, Domitius called on her almost every night. They went to parties and picnics and spent quiet evenings in the garden of his estate. Arria never imagined a man could have such an effect on her. Now, instead of spending afternoons covered in blood, she took leisurely baths, allowing her servants to massage her in scented oils and brush and style her hair. Arria had always taken her beauty for granted, but seeing herself reflected in Domitius' eyes had somehow changed her. She wanted to please him, and she wanted him to want her.

She tugged on his arm. "What are we doing here? Do you intend to do battle with me?" she teased, glancing around at the empty stadium that could hold thousands.

Domitius clapped his hands twice, and the silent night was filled with the sound of wheels and the clattering of hooves. "Have you ever ridden in a chariot?" he asked, as he accepted the reins from a servant who bowed his head and quickly disappeared into the darkness.

Arria did not waste a moment telling him, "No." At once, she was swept into the open carriage and needed to grab the bar to balance herself. Her heart was beating wildly, not just for the impending experience, but because Domitius seemed to instinctively know that she thrived on danger.

He chuckled as he moved behind Arria, strong arms grasping the reigns, his body hard against her back, his legs bracing hers.

"Are you ready?" he whispered, his breathe hot upon her neck.

Arria laughed, nodding her head.

Domitius slapped the reins, and the horse began to move. Arria bent her knees, absorbing every rut and ridge in the track. She screamed in delight when he whipped the horse into a gallop. Around and around they went, Arria's exhilaration heightened by an unrelenting faith that Domitius was in control. That he seemed determined to take them to the verge of an accident only intensified the experience. Eventually, the horse began to wheeze, and Domitius slowed him to a walk.

"You're fearless," he said, his voice thick with desire.

"I loved it!" she laughed. "Get a fresh horse, and let's go again!"

"Perhaps later," he said as he handed the reins to the servant who had suddenly reappeared. "I have another surprise for you," Domitius said, helping her down. They walked hand in hand to the center of the arena.

Arria smiled into the night. A blanket and pillows were laid out on the ground, and the lamps flickered. There was a buffet table with cheese, wine, cold duck and a dozen other dishes presented as if the emperor were going to be dining with them.

"My lady," Domitius said, sweeping his hand forward. "Please help yourself to dinner."

Arria was too excited to do something as normal as eating. She felt fearless and alive, and she wanted the adventure to continue.

"Not yet," she said, tracing Domitius' face with her fingers.

He took Arria into his arms. They kissed. The sensation of his tongue in her mouth and his hands moving gently over the curve of her body made Arria feel weak. She sighed, overcome by desire and recklessness. She stepped away from him, bravado seeping from her eyes as she unclasped the brooch that held her tunic in place. It slid off one shoulder and exposed her breast. She noted the delight that showed from Domitius' face. With brazen daring, she allowed the tunic to fall from her other shoulder. Like water cascading over a waterfall, her tunic fell in a heap at her feet. Naked now, she felt wild and free.

He caressed her as she had never been caressed before, his mouth exploring her body. Arria had always found the act of coupling disappointing. The men she had known were always in a rush, and she never reached fulfillment. Domitius was different. He knew what pleased a woman, and he took his time. Lying on the blanket, his face buried in the folds of her womanhood, he brought Arria towards a climax. She cried out, feeling as if waves were crashing against the shore and fire and lightning were exploding in her body.

Only then did he enter her. It was the moment that Arria Galen fell in love.

* * *

Livel perched on the stool at the front of the room as the students studying under Doctor Galen filed from the room. He cast his eyes towards the doorway every few seconds, hoping that Arria would walk through it. At least she is not sick, he thought, remembering how frantic he had been when she first began missing their sessions together.

Scipio was the one who had told Livel that Arria Galen was being courted by his half-brother Domitius. At first, Livel could not believe it. Sure, he understood why Arria might be drawn to Domitius. He had charm and certainly cut a handsome figure. But that she had not realized Domitius was evil was more than Livel could comprehend. Every time he thought about that beast touching Arria, he wanted to punch a wall. To make matters even worse, it seemed that Arria had given up helping her father with his work. Now Livel never got to see her. His face downcast, he picked at a cuticle on his thumb until it bled.

Doctor Galen put a hand on Livel's shoulder. "What's wrong with you lately? You've been so distracted."

"I'm sorry," Livel replied miserably, forcing a smile to his face.

Doctor Galen knew that Livel had fallen under Arria's spell, and that he missed her. It had been obvious from the very first day he became a student at the school. But the doctor had the perfect solution to bring Livel out of his wretchedness.

"I have a very good friend who is not feeling well. I promised to call on him this afternoon. I would like you to go with me."

"I would be honored," Livel replied, feeling the doldrums lift. This would be his first time visiting a patient. Suddenly, Arria's absence was no longer on his mind. Livel paced as the doctor placed all of his writings securely into the locked drawer. He then changed his work tunic for a clean one.

"Let's go," Galen said, striding towards the door.

* * *

They rode for half an hour, up and down dusty lanes. As they moved further from city center, they neared the Tiber River, a tributary of the Tyrrhenian Sea. The streets became narrower, and even riding single file became difficult. The duo had to get off their horses and urge pedestrians aside so they could pass. This was an area of Rome that Livel had not known even existed. There were no glorious buildings, magnificent thoroughfares or elegant women out for afternoon strolls in the parks that dotted the cityscape. Instead, emaciated children crouched beside sewage spilling from gutters, their distended bellies and pale faces sunken and desperate. They stared as Livel and Doctor Galen passed, their parched voices begging for money and food. Livel could not imagine the doctor could have a friend who lived in such squalor.

They finally stopped in front of a tilted house attached on both sides to other houses. After tying up the horses, Livel and Doctor Galen climbed the rickety steps. They were greeted at the door by a very old man with cloudy eyes and stooped shoulders. That he was ill was obvious; his arms were covered with bloodied black splotches, and his face was grey. Doctor Galen took the old man into his arms and held him as one might hold a beloved child. Livel saw tears in his mentor's eyes. Whoever this man was, he was obviously very dear to the doctor.

Galen held the old man's arm as they walked over the dusty rugs that sat atop an uneven cracked stone floor. They moved from the hallway into what appeared to be both kitchen and dining room. There was an enormous table built from planks of rough-hewn wood that sat upon a pedestal fashioned from the remainder of a tree trunk. Ten chairs were placed around the table, and at each setting there were scrolls and parchments, quills and ink. Livel took in the room in a glance, the clutter an obvious place of study. There was something about the space that filled him with a familiarity that made his skin prickle.

"Livel, let me introduce you to the man who was my very first teacher. He has been both friend and adviser to me since my time as a young man in Alexandria. This is Doctor Joshua Matthia."

"It is an honor to meet you," Livel said, trying to imagine that anyone could be smart enough to have taught Doctor Galen. "I'm sorry you are ill."

The old man swatted at the air with a bony hand as Doctor Galen pulled out a chair for him to sit on. "The righteous perish, and no one ponders it in his heart; devout men are taken away and no one understands that the righteous are taken away to be spared from evil. Those who walk uprightly enter into peace; they find rest as they lie in death."

Livel gasped, his head spinning. The words were from Isaiah the prophet. He looked first to Doctor Galen and then towards the old man.

"I thought you might like to help me repay a debt," Doctor Galen said, his eyes twinkling. "For years, Joshua has been treating the sick in the Jewish quarter by himself. He is too ill to continue, and I thought you would be interested in visiting once or twice a week. I am sure we could find the time. What do you think?"

The old man grinned at Livel, showing a mouth with few teeth left. "It would be a mitzvah, my son."

Livel knelt on the floor beside Doctor Matthia so that they would be looking at each other eye to eye. "I have been taught by my blessed father, Rabbi Eleazar, that every Jew is responsible for every other Jew. Being a bystander is not permitted." He kissed the old man's hand. "It will be my honor to come."

Chapter 18

Emperor Hadrian's Villa

Doctor Claudius Galen, responding to a note ordering him to appear before the emperor of Rome, traveled by boat down the river Aniene. It was a cool autumn day with the sky threatening rain.

The Emperor's residence stood on a hillside outside of Tibur, seventeen miles east of Rome. It was certainly most inconvenient for the ruler of the Empire to live far from its capital, but Hadrian detested Rome, its senate and the local aristocracy.

A royal carriage, bearing the gold insignia of the emperor, took Galen directly to the imperial residence. The compound consisted of over thirty buildings spread over two hundred and fifty acres. As they traveled along paved roads, the escort, a snarly servant with protruding ears and a nasal voice, pointed out the buildings along the route: guard barracks, a library, theaters, extravagant bathhouses, pavilions and banquet halls. There was a temple to Venus and a huge rectangular colonnade that had a pool reflecting from in its center. Interspersed between every building and beside every road flowers bloomed, fountains splashed and pools shimmered. Hadrian's love of Greek architecture and statuary was evident everywhere Galen looked.

Emperor Trajan had adopted Hadrian on his deathbed. In the ensuing days after Trajan's death, four Roman aristocrats, who were seen as contenders for the throne, were murdered. Hadrian was thought to be the mastermind behind the assassinations. He arrived in Rome eleven months after Trajan's death. As the appointed emperor, he found himself surrounded by enemies. They saw him as an unsophisticated Spaniard who had stolen the imperial throne. The monarch's reaction was two-fold: he decided to establish his residence far from the city and he traveled to the empire more than any other ruler before him. This was the reason Hadrian had beckoned Claudius Galen to appear before him.

Galen was led through the massive corridor of the residence. The walls were adorned in frescos of birds, nymphs, gardens and flowing streams. The floors were mosaic tile inlaid with slivers of gold. Two spear-carrying soldiers pushed open the carved, ebony wood double-doors. Inside, Emperor Hadrian sat on a sofa amongst a variety of multi-colored pillows. He had an elongated face and a firm, jutting chin adorned by a close-cropped beard and a mustache. His nose was straight, his eyes deep set and his dark hair curled tightly around his head. Sitting beside him on the sofa was a beautiful young man known as Antinous, the cherished slave for Hadrian's unlawful pleasure. Galen had heard that the god-like boy was intelligent, sharp witted and an outstanding hunter and athlete. That Antinous was extraordinary seemed obvious. He had maintained the Emperor's attention for several years.

"Ah, the infamous Doctor Galen," Hadrian called, beckoning him forward with the crook of a finger.

Galen did not cower before any man, yet being in the royal presence made him nervous. He moved slowly forward, keeping his eyes averted.

"I have a question for you," Hadrian said, as Galen neared. "As the emperor of Rome, am I not entitled to have the very best doctor as my personal physician?"

Galen knew there was only one answer he could give. To do otherwise would be blasphemous. If he were appointed Hadrian's personal physician, whenever the ruler traveled, he would be by his side. Hadrian was known to stay away from Rome for years on end. Galen's eyebrows pinched in anguish. He had never been away from his daughter for more than a few weeks at a time. The thought of leaving her devastated him, but at least she now had Domitius.

Claudius Galen's school was another matter. His class was about to graduate, and a new group of students was already registered. Who would teach his class? What would happen to Livel? He couldn't let everything he had worked so hard for just slip away. A plan began to formulate in his mind as he said, "Certainly, there is nothing more essential than the supervision of your health, Majesty."

"I knew you would say that," Hadrian said, stroking his lover's hand. "How quickly can you put your affairs in order?"

"Please do not think me insolent, Majesty. Rome needs well-trained doctors to serve in your army. I am teaching those doctors in a school that I run. As I have no heir, please allow me to find a suitable replacement before I take leave."

"Is there someone capable of overseeing your school?"

That was exactly the question Galen had hoped he would ask. "Yes, there is. He is a young slave with a brilliant mind who would be quite capable."

"Then I see no problem," Hadrian responded, popping a grape into his mouth and dabbing at his lips with a napkin given to him by Antinous. "I insist you adopt the boy! That way you will have a successor, and I will have you!"

"As you wish, Majesty. But the slave does not belong to me."

Hadrian scowled, and his face darkened. "Every man in the kingdom is *my* subject, so they ultimately belong to me!" he bellowed. "I am giving this slave to you!" He clapped his hands three times, and a page appeared from behind a curtain. "Bring my scribe and the royal seal. I will free this slave and bequeath him to you as your lawful son." Hadrian pulled a fistful of gold coins from his pocket and held them out to Doctor Galen. "This should be more than enough to settle the debt for the slave."

Galen accepted the money, slipping the coins into his pocket. He held back a smile, satisfied he could not have choreographed the scenario for a more perfect outcome.

"I will expect you in three weeks time," Hadrian ordered, turning away dismissively.

The interview was over.

The following day

Doctor Galen shifted his weight from one foot to the other waiting for his students to assemble. This was the third group of doctors to graduate from his school, and it would be the last under his mentorship. He would miss teaching, but he missed many things in his life: his wife paramount among them. Doctor Galen had always embraced change, professing that it kept him young. But this change was different. He was moving into a new stage of his life, likely the final phase. He looked around at the twenty men expectantly watching him.

The doctor cleared his raspy throat, just another reminder of his approaching old age. "Let me begin today by congratulating all of you." He let his gaze linger on Livel for a moment. "Each of you has taken the Hippocratic oath to do no harm. You will now be graduating from my school as accomplished surgeons. For now, you will be physicians to our soldiers on the battlefields. Eventually, you will return to serve in your masters' homes and in your villages. What I hope you will take with you, when you leave me today, is the ability to diagnose and cure.

"You've been taught to take a pulse, to feel the strong and steady rhythm of a heart, to know that arteries carry blood and that illness is spread by a dog's bite. You know when it's appropriate to use bloodletting as a cure, and you know when you must cut. As we end our time together, I want to wish you the protection of the gods, and I want to give you one last lesson, one last reminder."

The doctor turned to Livel sitting on the stool beside him, as always. "Livel, please review the proper position to take when performing surgery."

Livel stared at the doctor. During the entire time he had been his assistant, he had never taught in place of Doctor Galen when the doctor was present.

"We're waiting," Doctor Galen said.

Livel stood and faced the class. "During long procedures, there are times when we must sit during surgery." He moved his stool to the center of the room so that everyone had a clear view. "When sitting, knees are slightly separated, forearms are kept at a right angle and elbows never pass in front of the knees." With confidence in his voice, Livel demonstrated the correct position. "Always use two hands. When standing, the same procedures are followed. Always remember to keep both feet on the ground so that balance can be maintained." Livel dragged the stool back to the front of the room.

"That is just one small bit of information I expect all of you to follow. It has been my privilege to instruct you," Doctor Galen said. He sat down heavily and watched under hooded eyes as his students dispersed.

Livel kept watching the door certain that Arria would, at the very least, appear for the final session. Disappointed, he turned his thoughts toward the future. Doctor Galen had convinced Marcus Gracchus to allow Livel to continue his studies until it was time for Livel to depart to Britannia with Scipio and Domitius.

Once the room had emptied, Livel began gathering his papers. Doctor Galen walked to the window and pushed open the shutter. Tugging on his ample beard, he turned toward Livel, shoulders leaning forward, his green eyes intense. "I want you to know that you are the most brilliant student I have ever had the privilege of teaching," Doctor Galen said. "And I have taught many."

Embarrassed, Livel muttered a thank you.

"You have the makings of a great physician, but there is so much more you will need to learn." He spoke softly, as if to himself. "We are just beginning to understand the intricacies of the human body. If only I had more time to spend with you," he said, his voice trailing off to a whisper.

Livel remained silent.

"I took a boat ride yesterday to the Villa Hadriana at the behest of the emperor. I am to become Hadrian's personal physician. Because this emperor likes to travel, I will be away for long periods of time."

Livel bit his lip, certain his future was crumbling. This would be the end of his studies with the great doctor and the end of any hope he had for spending time with Arria.

Doctor Galen looked hard at Livel. "You can remove that crestfallen expression from your face. Do you think I would let my school fail? Do you think that all my years of hard work would be put aside on the whim of a monarch?"

"You have refused the emperor?"

"Of course not as I have no choice in the matter!" He pointed at Livel. "But I do have a solution for my school: You!"

"There is nothing I would not do to help you. But I just don't see how I can be the resolution to your problem."

Doctor Galen handed Livel an official looking document that he had been holding in his hand. "Read it."

Livel's eyes grew wide, and his hands began to shake. "This says that I am free! It says that I am your adopted son, and I have all the privileges of a Roman citizen!" Livel reread the document. "It is signed by the emperor."

The doctor smiled, stroking his beard. "As of today, your name is officially changed to Livel Galen. And just as the document states, you will enjoy the rights and freedoms of an adopted son. When I die, you will inherit, along with your new sister Arria, all my works, words, school and estate."

Livel stood with his mouth open, his entire body vibrating. In an instant, he had gone from slave to free man, from poverty to land owner, from student to teacher. Certainly, that alone would be enough to overwhelm anyone. But added to that information was something he could not comprehend: Arria was now his sister. He did not want her as his sister! The notion was ludicrous, destroying every fantasy he ever had about winning her heart.

Livel thought about his parents; suddenly, he was overcome by shame, slithering inside him like a thousand squirming worms. "I want you to know that I am grateful." He looked at Doctor Galen. "But—"

"Don't be afraid. You can always talk to me."

"I respect you, sir. You are a great man, and I will always be loyal to you. But I already have a father, and no one could or ever would take his place."

Doctor Galen smiled. "That's exactly what I anticipated you would say. I certainly have no intention of trying to replace your father. This is simply a matter of quid pro quo–you help me and I help you."

"And what about the promise I made to help Doctor Matthia with his patients? How can I run the school and still find the time?"

"Here is what I have learned in my life. When you try to force time, time will push you back. When you yield to time, you will find that time is on your side."

The door opened at that moment and Arria entered.

"Sorry, I was certain that everyone would be gone," she said, all but snarling at Livel.

The doctor clucked his tongue and scowled. "Livel, please wait outside. I need a few moments alone with my daughter."

* * *

Livel paced the hallway, trying to comprehend what had just happened. He reread the document for the third time, just beginning to understand its implications. *If I can travel without interference, then I can go home!* His euphoria was interrupted by a scream and Arria shouting the word no, over and over again. Then there was silence.

A short while later, a pale and shaken Doctor Galen came into the hallway. Struggling to maintain eye contact, he escorted Livel inside. Livel had witnessed the relationship between father and daughter, and he could only imagine the unhappiness Arria must be feeling at the thought of her father going away.

He entered the classroom expecting to see a grieving woman. Instead, he was met by a raving shrew, shrieking, "This is what you always intended!" Arria stood inches from his face. "I knew you were trying to steal my father from me. You're nothing more than a driveling Jew!"

"Arria Galen, that is enough! You will not speak to Livel in this manner!" Doctor Galen pushed between Arria and Livel, his temper barely in check. "You will treat him with respect!"

Arria glared at her father, refusing to believe she was being chastised because of Livel. "He's ruining everything." Tears filled her eyes.

"Please. I had no intentions. I came here solely to learn," Livel pleaded. *And now all I want is to go home.*

"Liar!" Arria hissed.

"Not another word out of you," Galen shouted, raising his hand as if he were going to slap Arria. Silence froze the room. The doctor had never lifted a hand to Arria. She gasped in horror.

Galen stepped away and turned his back, visibly shaken. No one moved or said a word. After what seemed like many minutes, he turned to Arria. "There are some things you will have to learn to accept," he said, his voice now gentled. "I have no choice but to serve His Majesty. To save all that I have worked for my entire life I need an heir. No matter how smart or clever you are, you cannot run my school." Doctor Galen took Arria softly by the shoulders. "Livel can. Now, I want you to apologize to him."

Livel wanted to shout out that he could not, would not stay in Rome. Instead he remained silent, understanding that every word he said and action he implemented would impact the rest of his life.

Arria felt as if she were standing in two different worlds. As a woman about to accept a proposal from the man she loved, she wanted her inheritance intact. It was the only way she could hope to maintain a modicum of independence. But she was also a dutiful daughter who loved her father. For now, she had no choice.

"I'm sorry," she said through clenched teeth. *And someday you will be sorry too!* She thought as she glared at Livel.

Chapter 19

Summoned by Bar Kokhba to appear in Jerusalem, Masabala, Asher and the messenger, Menachem, rode throughout the day and into the night. They passed under the shadows of towering sand dunes and snaked around the dry riverbeds that ran across the desert floor. The glistening Dead Sea was to their right and the massive cliffs of the Judean Desert to their left.

Masabala conjured up the various scenarios he thought might await him now that the Jews had defeated Rome. He had proven himself and felt entitled to become a moving force within the newly forming government. He thought of the line from Deuteronomy, "Judges and officers you shall appoint in all your cities." Masabala smiled into the waning light.

The smile faded as quickly as it appeared. The inclination towards evil was called *yetzer hara*, and he had surrendered to that evil when he lifted his hand to strike down a fellow Jew. Deceit then blinded his eyes. He had nowhere to hide from the shame and no right to accept any position that might be offered to him. *Perhaps Sarah was right. I should just resign and return to En Gedi.*

These were the thoughts that engulfed Masabala as they began their ascent over the winding road that led to the golden city of Jerusalem, again the capital of Israel. They stopped just long enough for their horses to drink at a spring nestled in the foothills of the Kidron Valley. With the moonlight as their guide, they crossed a steep narrow ridge and followed the main street that led them to the Dung Gate. It lay in the southeast corner near the Temple Mount.

Passing through the gate, a city of tents stood before them. Masabala handed the reins of his horse to Menachem. "It looks like every soldier in Judea is in Jerusalem tonight," he said, moving into the rowdy crowd. The people were celebrating their victory with laughter, songs and dance, all heroes who had rewritten Jewish history.

A sleepy-eyed soldier approached. "There are a few vacant tents in that quadrant," he said, pointing to his left. "Take whichever one you like."

* * *

Masabala was shaken awake by Menachem just as the sun was beginning its ascent.

"Please come with me," he said.

"Should Asher come, too?"

"Only you," Menachem said.

Near the Temple Mount, they met a few dozen other soldiers, commanders who Masabala recognized. The men greeted each other with pats on the back as they trudged along the twisting narrow streets.

Ten minutes later, they all arrived at a row of warehouses. The men entered a doorway and were led down a short passage into a room that had arms piled on one side and crates of olives on the other side. Chairs were set up in rows with a raised platform at the front of the room. Bar Kokhba stood on the dais along with the venerated scholar and beloved Rabbi Akiva. The soldiers took their seats in silence.

"Welcome victorious warriors!" Bar Kokhba said, his arms outstretched to bless them. The great man's beard was shot with white, the mane of his once blazing red hair now faded and thinning.

"We are so grateful. I know that many of you traveled far, leaving your homes and families in Africa, Syria and Egypt to join us in our fight to defeat Rome and free our people. It is your courage and sacrifice that has led us to the reestablishment of a Jewish homeland. A Jewish homeland," he repeated, as if chanting a prayer.

Masabala felt a lump form in his throat and a shiver went down his spine.

Rabbi Akiva took a step forward, the ravages of time and the anxiety of war engraved on his ancient face. His back was hunched, and his shoulders were stooped. "I too, want to bid you congratulations and welcome," he said. "The Holy One, Blessed be He has shown us, yet again, the Jewish nation lives beyond the influence of those who would defeat us. With the power of the Torah as our intimate companion, *Am Yisrael,* the people of Israel, will determine their destiny as promised in the sacred writings."

He put a trembling hand on Bar Kokhba's shoulder. "As prophesied in our scriptures, there shall come a star out of Jacob, and a scepter shall rise out of Israel. They shall smite the corners of Moab and destroy all the children of Sheth. Shimon ben Kosiba, renamed and anointed Shimon Bar Kokhba, *the son of a star,* our leader, our Messiah and our deliverer."

Shouts and clapping echoed off the walls like thunder as Bar Kokhba, towering over the tiny rabbi, beamed. When the din began to fade, Bar Kokhba moved closer to the edge of the platform.

"I am saddened to report there are still skirmishes taking place in the northern hills."

Faces in the crowd went from smiles to frowns and grunts.

"Did you think that Rome would remain docile and simply allow us to retake our land?" Bar Kokhba raised a fist in the air and jutted his jaw forward. "It does not matter! We are the army of the Holy One, Blessed be He, and we will remain an army, protecting our borders and our people from foreign invaders!"

The men stamped their feet and hissed threats.

Masabala cringed. He had fought his war, and he wanted no part of another. He wanted to talk about the future and about peace. He was suddenly claustrophobic and had an overpowering need to flee. Bile rose in his throat. He felt smothered and needed air to breathe that was not putrid from the smell of unwashed bodies.

"There is much work to do!" Bar Kokhba shouted. "We must organize into administrative districts and begin to collect taxes so that we can commence our governmental operations."

Masabala's head pounded and perspiration beaded on his forehead. He had to get out!

"I have one more pronouncement to make." Bar Kokhba hesitated, his face illuminated as if the sun had entered the room. "Of all that we have accomplished, our most significant task still lies before us."

Masabala was confused. He could not even begin to imagine what could be more important or more difficult than defeating the Romans.

"As a people," Bar Kokhba continued, "our Temple has been the foundation stone of our faith. When the Babylonians destroyed the First Temple six hundred years ago, our people never stopped mourning that loss. As the generations passed, we never lost our faith or our will to rebuild a Second Temple. And rebuild we did, only to have it destroyed by the Romans! Now sixty-two years later, I stand before you vowing that a Third Temple will be built. And this Temple shall stand forevermore!"

Masabala gasped, frozen in place as if his body had tuned to stone. *Was it possible? King Solomon's Temple to be rebuilt?* Every Sabbath, his father had spoken about the glory days of the First and Second Temples. While he was not the Jewish scholar that Livel was, he too, had been enchanted by the stories. He could only imagine the joy he might feel if he were allowed to participate in such a holy undertaking–*the footstool of God's presence to stand again in our physical world.* It could be his penance, an opportunity to purge the demons and again feel worthy of God's love.

Bar Kokhba moved into the crowd of applauding soldiers. Masabala stood just as the *nasi's* eyes found him. The two men embraced. "It has been too long. I am told that you have taken a wife. Mazel tov!"

Masabala was surprised the *nasi* knew anything about his personal life. He felt flattered.

"May you have many sons and daughters," Bar Kokhba said.

Masabala smiled, choosing not to tell him that Sarah was already with child.

"Later we will talk. As for now, I want you in the discussions that will take place this afternoon."

* * *

Masabala spent the rest of the day listening as Bar Kokhba and the elders spoke of ways to organize self-rule, establish a new government and implement guidelines for taxation. He tried to pay close attention, but his mind kept wandering. He imagined the presence of a Third Temple and speculated about what Bar Kokhba would say to him.

There was much talk about money–a sign of sovereignty. It was decided that all the bronze and silver coins from Rome, Syria, Phoenicia and other countries, which were circulating in the new Israel, would be confiscated. The etchings would be filed off and re-stamped with Jewish symbols and Hebrew inscriptions.

The discussions went on for hours about what the symbols would be. It was decided that there would be trumpets heralding their freedom, palm trees, a symbol of water and fertility, grape clusters to show the sanctified spiral of time and the representation of wine used to commemorate the sacred holidays. The *lulav*, the frond of a date palm tree used in the holiday of *Shavuot,* was also selected. It celebrated the bounty of the harvest, the descent of Moses from Mt. Sinai and the giving of the Torah to the Jewish people. Inscriptions would all say, *to the freedom of Jerusalem.*

Late in the afternoon, when it became obvious that everyone was too exhausted to continue, Bar Kokhba stood, bid farewell to his followers and with Rabbi Akiva at his side, headed toward the door. On the way out, he touched Masabala on the back and signaled him to follow with a tilt of his head.

Once outside, the *nasi* turned to Masabala and said, "Everything you have heard, thus far today, will pale when compared to what I have yet to say to you, my son."

* * *

Masabala followed closely behind Rabbi Akiva and Bar Kokhba as they moved down the twisting alleyways. His thoughts in turmoil, he was unable to make sense of the *nasi's* comment, *everything you have heard, thus far today will pale when compared to what I have yet to say to you.* How could anything be more important than the announcement that a Third Temple would be built? Rounding the corner, they were met by a line of soldiers posted on both sides of a doorway.

"Welcome to my home," Bar Kokhba said, leading the two men into a well-tended garden atrium. They washed their hands as a servant appeared placing bowls filled with berries and grapes on the stone table along with wine and goblets.

Rabbi Akiva settled himself on a bench under an olive tree. "Sit with me, Masabala," he said, patting the seat beside him.

Bar Kokhba lifted the carafe and filled three glasses with wine. He intoned the blessings and handed a glass first to Rabbi Akiva and then to Masabala.

The men sipped their drinks in silence; the only sounds the rustling of trees and the bark of a dog in the distance. After what seemed an eternity to Masabala, Bar Kokhba moved to face him, feet apart, hands intertwined, his eyes shining. "I have a glorious tale to tell you. Shrouded in secrecy, it is a story that only a few men have ever heard." He settled into his thoughts and then said, "It was told to me by your father, the blessed Rabbi Eleazar."

"My father?" Masabala asked in wonder, so enraptured and excited, he felt dizzy.

Bar Kokhba began, his voice soft and otherworldly. He shared how the High Priest of the First Temple had a vision the Babylonians would destroy the Temple. He spoke of the Ark of the Covenant being taken from the holy of holies and hidden away and how the woodcutter priests had discovered a loose stone that seemed to lead to a passageway beneath the Temple where it was believed they would find the Ark holding the Ten Commandments lay. He related every detail of the account to Masabala. How the spark from an ax killed one of the brothers and how the other brother saw that as a sign, making the decision that the location of the Ark would never be revealed until the coming of the Messiah.

"The surviving brother wrote the location of the Ark on three pieces of parchment. In each generation, only three men were entrusted with the knowledge," Bar Kokhba said. "One always resided in Judea, and the others lived outside our borders. Each man told only one other person, and that person had to be a holy man." Bar Kokhba grew silent, his gaze on Rabbi Akiva.

The old rabbi placed his hand over his heart. "Your father was the keeper in our generation, and I was his confidant."

Bar Kokhba opened his hand to reveal the ancient parchment. "The words written here will lead us to the Ark of the Covenant." He held Masabala with his eyes. "And *you* have been the one chosen for that task–to find the tablets that hold God's sacred writings."

Masabala stumbled to his feet. He wanted to scream, *you've made the wrong choice,* but all he could do was shake his head. "I can't," he muttered, taking a step toward the gate.

"You can't? You can't?" Bar Kokhba raged, his face contorted as he moved to block Masabala's escape. "I stand before you, the Messiah of our people. I am God's presence on earth. The right to deny my request is not yours to make!"

Masabala cowered, his legs threatening to fold. He tried to find his voice, but it was useless. He was aghast by his own reticence and knew that his silence would damn him forever. His heart felt heavy as if it had turned to stone. To refuse Bar Kokhba was the same as standing before the throne of God and refusing. Yet, he was helpless to do otherwise. He had vowed never to tell anyone what he had done, and he intended to take that secret to his grave.

Rabbi Akiva waved a bony hand at Bar Kokhba as he stood with difficulty and took a few steps. "Please speak with gentle words. He is injured, and anger is not the salve that he needs." The rabbi reached for Masabala's hands. When their fingers touched, Masabala felt inexplicable love. The burden of shame and guilt that weighed so heavily on his shoulders seemed to lighten, just slightly. Hot tears burned Masabala's eyes.

"You can trust me, my son, just as your father trusted me."

"I know," was all Masabala managed to say.

"I have lived a very long, long time, and I have come to understand that wisdom is derived from experience," the rabbi said, his hands now pressed together as if in prayer. "We live, we suffer and then with the blessing of the Holy One, we grow wiser and learn to accept that suffering is as much a part of life as breathing. Then and only then, can we move beyond our pain and learn to appreciate and fully rejoice in our moments of ecstasy, however fleeting they may or may not be.

"You are having difficulty accepting all of this right now, and that is understandable. You have just spent years fighting a brutal war. For some soldiers, the lucky ones, they fight and then they are able to forget. For others, the war within continues turning the victorious soldier into a victim.

"As for the secrets you keep, we all have them." The rabbi continued, glancing at Bar Kokhba. "All of us. And I can tell you from years of knowledge as a rabbi, our secrets make us sick. And while I can only begin to imagine how difficult this is going to be for you, I am begging you to unburden yourself. You must do so to face the holy task that lies before you."

Masabala's throat was so dry he could barely swallow. When he finally managed to say a few words, they were jumbled as if he had forgotten how to speak. Eventually, he was able to put a sentence together and then another. At times, he knew he was not making any sense, but he forged ahead. He whispered the rape and cried when describing the dead baby lying on the ground beside its mother, so close their hands were almost touching. The words burned as they left his tongue. At one point, he strode to the corner of the garden and vomited, the despair scorching his throat.

"His name was David, and he was barely a man," Masabala whispered, knotting his hands into fists. "I should have helped him. He was engorged in bloodlust, blinded and immune to death. It was not his fault. It was mine!"

Akiva smoothed the tunic over his knees encouraging silence. He closed his eyes for a moment, rubbing his forehead and readjusting his head covering. "Moses smote an Egyptian. Yet the Holy One,

Blessed be He, chose him to lead our people from bondage. On Mt. Sinai, it was Moses who received the Ten Commandments. Moses found God's favor. Seek forgiveness, and it shall be given," Rabbi Akiva intoned. "Just as the clouds can block out the sun, clouds can hover over the mind. To set aside that which obscures your vision, you must turn to *teshuvah,* to repentance. In time and with age, you will find peace," Akiva offered.

Masabala was bewildered, wanting desperately to shove aside the self-condemnation that haunted his every move. But the idea of being worthy to find the Ark was beyond his capacity to reason.

Through his father's eyes and his words, he and Livel had spent their childhood days surrounded by stories of the Ark. He could hear his father's voice describing how the Jews carried the shrouded Ark containing the Ten Commandments for forty years as they wandered the desert. He could imagine the feel of the acacia wood beneath his fingers and could see the four golden rings and two golden poles used to carry the Ark. Moses honored his brother, Aaron, the man who always spoke for the stuttering Moses by placing Aaron's staff beside the Tablets inside the Ark. He also included pieces of manna, unleavened bread that God had sent from the heavens to feed the Israelites in the wilderness.

Akiva spoke of forgiveness, of *teshuvah,* repentance and how one day he would find peace. Yet Moses was never allowed to enter the Holy Land. Masabala shuddered. *What is going to be denied to me?*

"You are a descendent of Aaron and Moses," Bar Kokhba said, his expression intense. "Your lineage is holy. I have seen your resolve, your leadership abilities and your devotion to our cause, the land and our people. It will be you who brings the Ark of the Covenant into the light."

Chapter 20

Masabala strode beside Bar Kokhba as they scrutinized the thirty-five acres of rock-strewn ruins, the remains of the Second Temple. The air was crisp, signaling the approach of Rosh Hashanah, the Jewish New Year. Ten days later Yom Kippur would follow, the time when every Jew would repent and pray to God for his sins to be forgiven.

"I have brought you here today because there is much I need to tell you," Bar Kokhba said softly. "While you are searching for the Ark, I will be supervising the building of the Temple. Together our accomplishments will rewrite the history of our people." He watched Masabala for several heartbeats before he continued. "Right now, we are standing on Mount Moriah, the Temple Mount that is the Foundation Stone of Judaism's holiest site. At this very location, Abraham was asked by the Holy One, Blessed be He, to sacrifice his only son, Isaac. And it was here that Jacob dreamt of angels moving up and down between heaven and earth. He proclaimed that we would build the House of God right where we are standing."

Bar Kokhba aimed his eyes at Masabala. "Now that you've been chosen to partake in this extraordinary undertaking, I need to know that you are with me."

"I've made you doubt me," Masabala said. "For that, I'm sorry. I am your humble servant forever."

Bar Kokhba nodded. "As a rabbi's son, I know that what I am going to tell you may not be new to you. But I want you to see it through my eyes and to listen as if you have never heard it before."

Masabala nodded.

"The Temple was built on the highest point of this hill. To level the excavation, the stones were removed and used to build the large retaining walls that still remain." He pointed to his left. "Beneath us are huge vaults, massive structures." He took a few steps. "After the Jews had built the Second Temple, Herod the Great instituted a massive expansion. He constructed courtyards in the Greco-Roman style, and he erected the largest manmade platform in antiquity.

"The Romans instituted a plan to face every building in the Temple compound with marble. Herod arranged to have priests trained to work with the marble because gentiles were not permitted to pass through the central courtyard. Signs warned of their impending death if they reached the area where marble was being cut.

"The Temple compound was the largest structure ever built. After entering the compound, the levels of holiness increased. First, there was the court of the Israelites: then, the court of the priests followed." Bar Kokhba lifted his eyes heavenward. "Try to imagine what it was like when a Jewish farmer, living in Syria, made a pilgrimage to Jerusalem to pray at the Second Temple. He would enter from the underground south grand staircases. One staircase was used for going up, and the other staircase was used for going down to the exit. Walking up the stairway, the farmer would be engulfed in darkness as he moved through Solomon's stables. He would continue climbing up and up through the shadows finally emerging into the courtyard, into the Jerusalem light; a light so bright, it belied description."

Masabala felt as though he had been transported into the distant past. He was so enamored by the magical spell cast by the nasi's story, he was afraid to make a sound.

"Before our farmer stands the Temple, the dome covered in gold. It must have been like looking at a snow-covered mountain whose summit was a golden fire. At the time, it was believed that one who had never seen the Second Temple had never seen a truly beautiful building."

Bar Kokhba sighed and then walked over to a trough filled with water, cupped his hands and took a drink. He then looked at Masabala as if he had forgotten he was there.

"In the Five Books of Moses," Bar Kokhba continued, "there are explicit instructions on how the Holy Temple is to be built: from the size of the buildings, the design, the type of wood to the nails used. Our new Temple will not follow that design! This is causing great discord among my inner circle. Even the great Rabbi Akiva is distraught. But I am the chosen one, and the path I walk is being directed by the Holy One, Blessed be He. This is *my* right and *my* duty!"

Masabala was dumbstruck, unable to believe that Bar Kokhba would override the very word of God. *This will be a disaster! There are men that think Bar Kokhba is an impostor and disavow him as the Messiah. They have kept their displeasure quiet, a low murmur, like the buzzing of flies over discarded food. They won't remain docile when word gets out that Bar Kokhba is planning to build a Third Temple of his own design!* Masabala looked away trying to hide his dismay.

"I can see that even you are distressed," Bar Kokhba said. Disappointment colored his face a deep red as he pulled out a piece of parchment and placed it on a boulder. He smoothed it with an enormous hand. "This is what *I* instructed my architects to draw."

Masabala's legs trembled as he leaned over the design to better see the drawing of a miniature Temple facade. There was a curved arch above double doors and four columns stood in front of the doorway supporting the scallop-edged roofline. "These numbers, can you explain them to me?" Masabala asked, pointing to an archway on the drawing.

"The Temple will be twenty-two feet long on each side. That footprint is large enough to accommodate the Holy of Holies, the *Kodesh Ha Kodashim;* the sacred room where the Ark will be placed. The new temporary Temple will be a variation, but a necessary departure if we are to have a High Priest in attendance for Yom Kippur next year."

He pulled out another parchment from the belt-attached pouch and carefully unfolded it. This one was five times the size of the first. With great resolve and a steady hand, Bar Kokhba placed the new drawing over the temporary Temple drawing. On it was a sketch of all the buildings that would make up the Temple compound. The veritable size of the project caused Masabala to gasp.

"Perhaps by looking at this, you can now comprehend the enormity of this undertaking. As you can see," Bar Kokhba said, stabbing at the parchment with his pointer finger, "I still intend to rebuild the Azarah Courtyard that held the Altar and the Main Temple. Even now, great blocks of white malaki stone are being quarried outside Jerusalem, and cedar logs are being rafted from Lebanon by sea to Jaffa. But completing structures this massive will take decades."

Masabala grew up listening to his father describe what took place inside the sacred Temple, laws and rules followed without exception and without divergence. He envisioned the mystery of the Mercy Seat, the revered place where once a year on Yom Kippur, the Day of Atonement, the High Priest sprinkled the seat with blood from a sacrificial animal. This ritual symbolized the visible throne of the invisible presence of God. *This is without precedence. Father too will think this a travesty. A temporary Temple!*

Yet, listening to Bar Kokhba, it was impossible not to see his point. Doing it his way, the Jewish people would have their Temple restored within a year.

"I want your honest thoughts," Bar Kokhba said, leaning forward. "Don't vacillate or temper your words."

"I fear you will find great opposition," Masabala said, his heart pounding in his ears.

"Go on."

"You have detractors, people who question your authority." A droplet of perspiration fell into his eye. "I worry that your enemies will say you have overstepped your authority, and they will rise up against you."

Bar Kokhba laughed. "Every great man, in every age, has had his enemies. Do you know what sets me apart from them all?" he asked, making it obvious by his expression this did not require an answer nor was he particularly concerned. "*I* am the Messiah, and

I have the protection of the Holy One, Blessed be He." Bar Kokhba took Masabala's arm. "Let me show you something."

They walked the circumference of the entire Temple Mount nodding to the workers as they passed. It took them fifteen minutes. When they were standing in the eastern quarter, Bar Kokhba began counting off his steps as he headed toward the center of the rubble. It was then he began to gather rocks, placing them one on top of the other until he had formed a small mound of stones.

"Here is where we will lay the foundation for the Temple that will house the Ark." His voice took on the richness of shimmering light, his eyes glazing like ice on a frozen river. "Somewhere beneath us lie the Ten Commandments, written by God and given to Moses on Mt. Sinai." He pulled from his pouch yet another parchment. "This is the document I showed you when we were with Rabbi Akiva." He handed it to Masabala.

Masabala looked down at the folded parchment he held, and suddenly his hands felt as if they were on fire.

"To locate the Ark, you need to understand the following: Only a Kohen is permitted to touch the Ark of the Covenant. For anyone else, touch is certain death.

"When you study the drawings, you will see that there are five tunnels that snake beneath the Temple Mount. They were constructed at the time of the First Temple, and for one thousand years they have served to mystify and mortify anyone who tried to enter them. Yet we know that one of these tunnels leads to the Ark of the Covenant. It will be your job to find the one that does. You begin tomorrow!"

Tunnels! I can't do that! Masabala grew frigid; icicles of fear making him feel faint. He had expected to locate the chamber and then dig from above ground, having vowed to never enter another tunnel after barely escaping death at Herodion.

"One more thing that you should know," Bar Kokhba said. "My selection for *Kohen Gadol,* the High Priest, the only man allowed to enter the holy of holies where the Ten Commandments will be placed will be your father, Rabbi Eleazar."

Chapter 21

Five months later

Masabala spit dust from his mouth and took huge gulps of fetid air into his lungs. The temperature inside the tunnels had turned frigid, and the ground was frozen.

According to the drawing, there were five tunnels to breach. To accomplish this, he had formed five teams, each consisting of thirty men. They started their dangerous and tedious day at sunrise and continued until dark. Even with the long hours, they only managed to progress a few feet each day. The ancient stones resisted each cast of the hammer, guarding the pathways that no man had walked on for over a thousand years.

Discouraged by their lack of progress, Masabala rearranged the men's schedules. He had more men digging and less men hauling. Still, the results were always the same. A man could only dig into solid rock for a short while before exhaustion turned his arms to jelly.

Masabala periodically stopped the men from working so he could assess the stability of the dig. He wanted to avoid making a critical mistake that could lead to a cave-in. Unfortunately, after many months of backbreaking work, they still had at least a hundred feet to go before they would even be near the location where they believed they would discover the Ark.

At the end of each day, Masabala walked the circumference of the Temple Mount where thousands of workers labored. Their progress was miraculous, the structure rising before his very eyes.

At the rate they were building, the Temple would be finished before he found the Ark. Feeling as if he were failing, Masabala found
it impossible to keep his disappointment and frustration at bay.

Nightmares dogged Masabala constantly. In one recurring
dream, he saw himself crushed beneath a mountain of rocks
screaming for Sarah, believing he was going to die never seeing his
unborn child or wife again. In another persistent dream, Masabala
walked the length of each of the five tunnels searching for the Ark.
From end to end he traipsed, his eyes caked in grime, his hands
and feet bloodied and the foul dusty darkness enveloping him. He
searched every crevice, crawling on his hands and knees, never
finding the Ark! Each time, the nightmare would end with Masabala standing naked at the door of the Holy of Holies. Thousands
of people would be pointing, staring and hissing, screaming their
disappointment at his failure.

He would awaken trembling; dripping wet and wishing Sarah
was beside him. He wanted to go home, just for a night, to hold
her, to kiss her belly and tell her how much he loved her. Masabala knew it was a notion that would never come to fruition. He
was doing God's work, and that took precedence over everything!
Masabala sent messages home whenever he could, reiterating the
one promise he vowed to keep. He would come home for the birth
of his child.

Rubbing his hands together to alleviate the chill, Masabala
watched as his exhausted men made their way out of the tunnels.
They nodded to him as they headed toward the encampment
where they would warm themselves by campfires, eat whatever
food was available and fall asleep only to return again at sunrise. It
amazed him how they continued without complaint. Then again,
Masabala never voiced his frustration aloud to anyone even if God
seemed to be taunting him with failure.

* * *

Masabala watched as the familiar face of Joshua, a scout from
his regiment at the encampment outside of En-Gedi, walked toward

him. He waved while picking his way around mounds of rocks. For a moment, Joshua's presence seemed like a routine errand. Then something stirred inside of Masabala and a spasm gripped his gut. In that instant, he knew that something was wrong.

"What's happened? Why are you here?" Masabala shouted.

"It's your wife, Commander," Joshua said. "She's in labor."

Masabala thought it was too soon, but then he realized he might have lost track of time. "Time," the word screamed at him. Suddenly nothing mattered, not the Ark, not the Temple, not his mission. All that mattered was Sarah and how long it would take him to get home. "Wait here," he shouted, as he ran to tell Bar Kokhba that he was leaving.

* * *

The men rode hard following the worn jagged paths of the Negev. Overhead, the moon was a sliver in a night sky filled with flickering stars. Masabala said very little to Joshua, his mind reeling with a thousand thoughts. He was ecstatic at the prospect of fatherhood and allowed himself to envision holding a baby in his arms. But as the night wore on, he began counting the months. If his calculations were correct, the baby was not due yet.

I was chosen to unearth the Holy Ark; therefore, God will protect me. If I am protected, then so are the people I love.

Masabala looked at Joshua wishing that Livel were by his side. His brother's face appeared: the coal colored eyes, pointy chin and angular face punctuated by a protuberant nose. His smile melted the features together in perfect harmony, like the notes of a favorite song.

Masabala missed Livel so much it hurt like a wound in his heart that always ached. He needed to talk to Livel, to tell him what was happening. Masabala knew it was a futile thought–a foolish man acting the fool–but in the vastness of the desert anything seemed possible.

Livel, I married Sarah–beautiful Sarah–the little girl that we both loved so much. Do you remember how I would send her away when-

ever she came pestering me for attention? Do you remember those mischievous eyes and how her freckles would turn bright whenever she didn't get her way? Masabala fought back his tears. *Tonight, my blessed brother, I am to become a father! Do you believe that? Oh, how I wish you were here to share this moment with us. How I wish you were here to watch my son grow; yes, a son. You could teach him the games we played as children.* His thoughts returned to his wheezing horse. He signaled to Joshua that they stop for a rest. He slipped off the saddle and held a skein of water for the animal to drink. Joshua did the same.

Masabala's desire to push on was intense, but he knew the animal needed time to rest. Masabala tore off a piece of stale bread and took a drink of water as he looked into the horizon.

Come back to us, Livel! Find your way home!

The enclave of En Gedi

When they reached the house, Masabala jumped off his horse and threw the reins to Joshua. He charged into the birthing room, his legs weak, his heart hammering. Sarah lay on a mat, her eyes wild, her mother and mother-in-law crouched beside her, the midwife standing at her head.

"Masabala!" she cried, trying to sit up.

Miriam and Alma backed away as he put his arms around Sarah. "I love you," he whispered, burying his face in her sweat-soaked tangled hair.

"You've been gone so long," she whimpered through cracked swollen lips. "I was so afraid you weren't ever coming home."

"I will always come home," he said, kissing her forehead.

Sarah stiffened and twisted from his arms as a contraction seared through her body. She screamed.

Masabala had never watched someone he loved suffer, and the helplessness of it all overwhelmed him. He had done this to her, and all he could think about was how to make the pain stop as she screamed again. Horrified, he caught the eye of the midwife, a woman he had known all his life. It was then that he knew something was terribly wrong.

"How long has this been going on?" he asked.

"Almost two days," the midwife Naomi said, shaking her head from shoulder to shoulder, sadness hooding her eyes.

"Is that too long?" Masabala grew cold.

Sarah shrieked, "I can't do this anymore!"

Naomi stroked Sarah's brow. "I will hear none of that kind of talk from you. You can do this! You will do this!" Naomi pointed a bony finger at Masabala. "You're a distraction. Sarah needs to concentrate. Go. We'll call you when the baby is born."

* * *

Just as the pewter sky tinged to early morning pink, Masabala moved into the yard where he was greeted by owls hooting and wind slicing the trees. He found his father sitting on the bench that Livel and Masabala had carved from a felled olive tree when they were boys. The rabbi arose and opened his arms to Masabala.

"It's good that you have come in time," the rabbi said, his face washed in trepidation as they hugged.

"I'm so frightened and feel so useless," Masabala said.

"Your wife and child are in the care of the Holy One, Blessed be He. Your only job now is to pray," his father said.

Masabala rested beside his father on the bench and bowed his head, conjuring up every prayer he could remember, praying so hard his body trembled, every invocation peppered by the aching cries coming from the room not thirty steps from where they sat.

Just as the sun neared its zenith, Sarah's mother, Alma, and Masabala's mother, Miriam, approached. They held on to each other for support, their pinched-pale faces revealing the words not spoken. Masabala jumped to his feet and raced past them.

Inside the room, Naomi held something tiny and ghost-white in her arms. Masabala's eyes darted from that image to his wife. Her eyes were squeezed shut, her face so pale that the skin seemed translucent, her breath coming in short little pants that were interspersed by pitiful sobs. Masabala did not know what to do, what to say, where to look.

Naomi moved to his side. "I am so very sorry that we couldn't save him."

Masabala let out a cry as he held the tiny, naked infant in his hands.

"Please, you must go and do what you must do. Sarah needs to rest now," Naomi said, her eyes bloodshot and sad.

Masabala stumbled from the room and out into the yard with the dead baby in his arms. Rabbi Eleazar stood back, hands at his side, bowing to the rules of God–a Kohen did not touch a dead body. He spoke to his son, but Masabala could not comprehend a word. The same held true when his mother and mother-in-law spoke. He could see their lips move, but the thundering in his head drowned out their voices. By virtue of hand motions, Masabala realized they wanted to see their grandchild. He held his son for them to view, but only for a few seconds before he clutched his dead son to his chest. There was no time to share, no time at all.

Masabala walked toward the groves where he and Livel had played as children. He stopped at an open patch of ground under the canopy of ancient olive trees, took off his tunic and wrapped the baby in it. Then on hands and knees, he dug with bare hands until his fingers were bloodied stumps. He raised his dead son over his head and screamed to God, "Is this what it means to be chosen?"

Masabala would never be able to remember if he cried, and he would never be able to recall if he said prayers over his son before placing him into the grave. All he would remember was the agony of loss and the fury he felt.

Masabala heard his name called, not once, but twice–a reverberating voice that surrounded him in an echo.

He swirled around. "Who's there?"

There was no reply, only a sudden rustling of the trees and the blackened call of the ever-present desert wind.

"Go back to Sarah. You are the only one standing between her and the Angel of Death," the voice commanded.

"Who are you? Where are you?" Masabala screamed, looking into the shadows thrown by the olive trees.

"Waste not another moment!" the resounding voice decreed.

His sanity in great peril, Masabala fled the orchard.

* * *

Masabala stood over Sarah, his heart breaking as he watched her chest rise and fall, her breathing labored and shallow, her eyes shuttering open and closed like a butterfly's wings. The acrid smell of blood and death suffused the room, reeking from every surface. Alma knelt beside her daughter, clutching Sarah's hand to her breast. Masabala's parents stood in the shadows near the doorway.

"She's lost too much blood," Sarah's mother, Alma, whispered. "I'm afraid we're losing her."

"Come, my son," his father bade. "It's time to pray for Sarah.

Masabala stood near his father and together they chanted, their bodies moving forward and back in unison like puppets swaying as if pulled by mystical strings. They recited psalms and when they finished praying, Masabala moved toward Sarah. He could see her essence–the blood flowing through her body, her heart beating, lungs fighting for breath. The voice in the orchard came back to him: *You are the only one standing between her and the Angel of Death.* Masabala knew what he had to do.

He placed his palms together and turned to his family. "Please, I beg you. Leave me alone with my wife."

"This is not a man's job! She must be bathed and kept clean," his mother-in-law said, panic cutting her words.

"Mother Alma, I beg you to trust me. I know what must be done if Sarah is to live!" Masabala reached out his hand to help her stand.

"We will leave my son with his wife," the rabbi said, his tone allowing no room for further discussion.

Once alone, Masabala lifted strands of sweat-tangled hair from Sarah's ashen face. "I will not let you go!" He leaned over and kissed her, his tears bathing her face. "Fight with me, Sarah."

There was a fresh tunic lying next to a pile of clean rags and a bowl filled with water. His own hands were raw and bleeding as he lifted Sarah's arm. He washed and dried it and then washed the other arm. Then, he lifted the blanket that covered Sarah, his heart aching as he washed her breasts and distended belly. Between her legs lay a cloth seeped in blood. With gentle hands, he turned Sarah on her side and washed her buttocks and vagina, his blood and the blood of their son mixing together. Turning Sarah to her back again, he placed a clean rag to catch the flow of clotting blood. When he had completed all of this, he wrapped his damaged hands, damaged from digging the grave for their son.

He then lay down beside her. In a soothing voice, Masabala sang the songs that Sarah loved. He told Sarah stories, reminding her of their youth, the life they would have together–how much he loved her. He talked until his voice was raw. His head resting against hers, he fell into a troubled sleep. Hours later, he was awakened by moans.

"My baby," she whimpered. "Where's my baby?"

"Our son is gone," Masabala whispered, holding Sarah as she wept. Her cries were inconsolable. Eventually, Sarah drifted off only to awaken a short time later to weep again.

Over the next three days and nights, they remained sequestered, accepting food but allowing no one to enter. They talked of their dead son and of the Jewish law not obligating them to mourn for an infant who had not survived for thirty days. Masabala and Sarah chose to follow their own hearts, and together they mourned their son.

On the fourth day, Masabala told Sarah about his sacred mission to find the Ark of the Covenant.

"I will lose you again, just as I have lost my son," she said, strangling on her tears. "But you must go back! Perhaps it will be a way to win the blessing of the Holy One, Blessed be He so that our next child will live and thrive and know us in our old age."

"When my obligation is complete, I will never leave you again," Masabala vowed, holding Sarah as she wept.

They would begin again.

Chapter 22

Rome

Livel ran down the steps of Doctor Galen's house, his heart joyous and his mind dancing. He was a free man, declared so by Hadrian, the emperor of Rome himself! He mounted one of the Galen horses and moved into the crowded street. For the first time in years, Livel was able to go where he pleased, when he pleased.

It had never occurred to Livel, not even for an instant that he would leave Rome one day by simply deciding to do so, but that was exactly what he intended to do. Despite Doctor Galen's expectation that Livel would stay and run his school, he knew he must leave. Arria anticipated Livel would remain in Rome, taking half her inheritance as the adopted son of her famous and moneyed father. However, she was wrong. He had served his last master, and only one ambition remained: to gather enough money for passage to Judea. Livel was going home!

The sight of the Gracchus villa shocked him; he could not remember riding there. He dismounted, tied the horse to a post at the back of the estate and walked toward the servants' entrance. He vowed it would be the last time in his life he ever entered through a slave's doorway.

Climbing the stairway off the kitchen, Livel entered the hallway that led to his room. Everything seemed so different. He felt more in control. As if he had grown taller and the ceilings had lowered, the floors had leveled, and the light had turned brighter. His mind meandered over the past years and how the experiences had expanded his mind and body. Stoicism and philosophy served to enrich his love and appreciation for Judaism, and mastering the sword had given Livel confidence. When injury ended his soldier-ing, he turned from teacher to Doctor Galen's student. As a result, he was now a physician. As a young boy, Livel had dreamed of serving his Creator as a sage, studying the Torah and seeking the ultimate truths. In Rome, he learned there was more than one pathway to the Creator. Through his hands and intellect, guided by the One above, he could bring solace and healing to those who suffered.

Livel thought about Arria's accusation that he intended to steal Doctor Galen away from her. The allegation was false, but Livel could certainly understand how it must have looked to Arria. Doc-tor Galen had mentored him, affording Livel the opportunity to learn from the greatest physician alive. To repay that trust, Livel had worked tirelessly with only one intention: to be worthy of the great doctor's confidence and praise. It never occurred to Livel that his dedication and admiration would result in his adoption.

Hesitating on the threshold of his classroom, Livel stepped inside. He was instantly encapsulated in a cocoon of memories, the hundreds of hours he spent here, first living with Zosima and then tutoring Domitius and Scipio. With determined attention, he dusted the top of his desk with the open palm of his hand, caress-ing it one last time. He moved slowly around the room collecting drawings, quills and ink but decided to leave everything else in place. When Livel closed the door to this room, he would be leaving all it represented including oppression and servitude. The yoke of bondage was shattered. He would bow to no man ever again!

"I was hoping to see you before you left," Scipio said, hanging in the doorway, his eyes alight and a devilish smirk on his face. "May I come in?"

"It's your house," Livel replied, not sure if Scipio was teasing or challenging him.

"And free men go where they choose," Scipio said grinning. "I heard that you will be taking over Doctor Galen's school. Congratu-lations. You may not believe this, but I am really happy for you. I have much to thank you for. Now that we are going to be related, I hope we can remain friends."

Livel scrunched his eyes. "Related?"

"You haven't heard? Domitius intends to wed Arria. That means, we will both have a new sister." The bitterness in his tone sliced the air. "Too bad for me, she chose the wrong brother."

"She can't be that foolish!" Livel blurted. "You must pursue her and win her away from Domitius!"

"You have not seen Arria with Domitius, have you? She is smitten and totally under the guise of his charms. I don't believe anyone could dissuade her." Scipio perched against the desk, assessing Livel. "Would I be wrong to assume that you too are smitten by the enchanting and beautiful Arria Galen? Or are the renderings you incessantly draw of her done for some other reason?"

Livel blanched. *Scipio has been through my sketches and seen everything, including the drawing of Arria participating in our surgeries.*

The two men studied each other in the prevailing silence.

"Take that downtrodden look from your face. Your secret is safe with me. Besides, are you anything more than an illustrator working within a fantasy?" he winked at Livel. "Although, I hope Arria realizes all of her learning will be useless to her. Even if Domitius allows her to continue to learn the practice of medicine, my stepmother Athena would never allow it. I certainly hope Arria has thought about the consequences of her decisions."

"I have no idea what Arria is thinking or intends to do," Livel said, settling on the sofa, clutching the portfolio of his drawings to his chest. "I am certain of only one thing. She hates me."

"And you detest my brother as much as I do," Scipio said. "May I ask you a question and count on your honesty in the answer?"

Livel felt their relationship shift, like the sliding of a chair from one place to another. This man was his friend, and he could trust him. "I shall do my best to answer you truthfully."

"Something happened between you and Domitius before you arrived in Rome. What was it?"

The question transported Livel into the past. The rancid smell of death and decay in the hold of the swaying ship, the chirping monkeys and the low growl of lions assailed him. He felt a tightening in his chest, and the fury he had fought to quiet rose like a blown volcano. "On my way to Rome in the bowels of a slave ship, I befriended a tiny little girl who had been stolen from the jungles of Africa. One night soldiers came, and they took my little Tillie away along with many other young children, both male and female. When they finally returned them to us, they were all on the brink of death, torn and bleeding, defiled and broken." Livel's face had gone ashen, and his voice broke. He buried his face in his hands. When he finally looked up, his grief was so deeply apparent Scipio had to look away. "Tillie died in my arms. Domitius and I had an altercation, and I struck out at him. In punishment, he made me watch as Tillie was fed to a lion." Livel broke down then, sobbing in a grief that he had tucked away for so long. When his composure returned, he stared into the distance and said, "I have been taught, you shall not hate your brother in your heart." Livel swallowed hard. "This is an edict by which I cannot abide. For in my heart, I do truly detest Domitius for his inhumanity to Tillie!"

"In this we are united," Scipio said, putting an arm around Livel. Together, they walked from the room.

* * *

Livel headed toward the Galen home, his drawings and supplies tucked neatly inside a leather pouch tied tightly to the saddle. He neared the Forum, the political and religious center of Rome. It was located in the valley between the Capitoline Hill on the west and the Palatine Hill on the south. Suddenly, Livel had an overwhelming urge to stop and taste the fruits of his equality. Intoxicated by self-determination, Livel dismounted and tied his horse to a tree.

Livel wandered through the massive grass-covered square. He was surrounded by hundreds of shops where the Roman elite fed their unquenchable appetites for every type of luxury item one could imagine. There were pearls from China, silks and rubies from India, gold and turquoise bracelets and beaded necklaces of sliver and lapis. For the intellectual of means, there were many rows of stores selling books. In the offices, businessmen made deals, financiers discussed loans and land was traded and sold.

Feeling secure with the parchment declaring him the adopted son of the famous Doctor Claudius Galen tucked neatly inside his pocket, Livel made his way through the late afternoon crowd. He had heard so much about this place and was delighted to be standing amid the wooden platforms. Here the intellectual men of Rome stood and espoused their thoughts on philosophy, law and the injustice that surrounded them. They spoke of anything and everything that might entice one to tarry a bit and listen. It was a spectacle of passion and discourse, and Livel found it mesmerizing.

He stopped at one platform where a silver-haired man, dressed in the purple stripes of a senator, was reciting Epictetus. "*Some things are in our control and others not. Things in our control are opinion, pursuit, desire, aversion and our own actions. Things not in our control are body, property, reputation, command and whatever are not our own actions,*" the senator said.

Epictetus was Livel's favorite stoic philosopher. He was a freed slave who had been beaten and severely injured as a child. He suffered his entire life from those wounds. At Livel's darkest moments, his thoughts often turned to Epictetus for solace and inspiration.

Livel listened intently until he heard the words Jew and Judea sifting from a conversation behind him. He turned to locate who had uttered the words. Two men stood off to one side, each wearing the robes of equestrians. Livel made his way closer.

"The Jews have control of Judea," the taller of the two men said.

"Our troops have been slaughtered," replied the other.

The two men nodded to Livel as he approached.

Pulling back his shoulders and lifting his chin to give off the airs of an aristocrat, Livel asked, "What grave news do you speak of?"

"The Jews have defeated our troops. The war in Judea is a scar upon all of Rome!"

"I had not heard," Livel replied, keeping his voice steady. "This news is surely grave," he said, as he forced a frown upon his face.

Walking away, Livel looked toward the east, toward Jerusalem. *My people have defeated Rome!* Pride filled his heart. Longing for home, he envisioned the walls of distance and separation disappearing, replaced by a golden thread that connected him forever with his heritage.

The home of Doctor Galen

As Livel moved over the stone driveway, he eyed a coach flying the flags of the Royal House of Hadrian. It was parked under the canopy of a weeping willow tree. Continuing on to the back of the Galen home, Livel was surprised to find a half-dozen wagons being loaded by men dressed in the livery of the emperor's palace.

Spotting the doctor standing amid the chaos, he waved. "You're not leaving so soon?" Livel asked, suddenly terrified that teaching for the great doctor was now falling upon him.

"It wasn't my intention, but a message was delivered shortly after you left. The emperor expects me in residence by this evening. He is not feeling well, and since I have been commissioned . . ." The doctor left the sentence unfinished as he stared over Livel's head, his shoulders scrunched up to his ears. "It seems that you have been freed, and I have been enslaved, no longer the master of my own life."

"You are the greatest physician alive. I'm certain you'll ascertain ways to maintain your independence once you endear yourself to the emperor."

"Thank you, young Livel. How could I have ever doubted my importance to the emperor of Rome?" The doctor's laugh was sarcastic, and his eyes mirrored uncertainty. "Come with me." Doctor Galen turned toward the house. "I have much to say and to show you before I leave."

For the next hour, Livel followed the doctor from room to room. He was shown secret passages, stores of hidden food, money tucked into crevices and a box that was placed under the floorboards in the wine cellar that held the deeds to all the doctor's properties throughout the kingdom. With every revealed secret, Livel felt his excitement grow. If all of this was now partly his, he could just take the money he needed for passage and leave.

As if the doctor was reading his thoughts, he turned to Livel as they entered his private chambers. "I know that you want to go back to your family."

"It is my most fervent desire," Livel replied.

"I do not intend to stand in your way. I have come to care for you as if you were my own son, and I only want what is best for you. But there is something I must ask of you before you go. It was my intention to spend the waning days of my life teaching new generations of doctors. That all changed when Hadrian called me into his service, and I lost control of my destiny. If my school shuts down, the stream of information ceases, and thousands will die who need not die." Galen paused, desperation creasing his brow. "I am begging you to stay until we can identify a suitable replacement for me."

Livel wished he had put his hands over his ears to block out the doctor's pleadings, but he had not. Now it was too late. This kindly man had saved his life and changed it forever. Because of Doctor Galen, Livel would return to Judea carrying healing gifts to his people. No matter how badly he wanted to leave right now, he was raised with the deep and abiding traditions of Judaism. The Ten Commandments decree that one must honor thy mother and thy father. The rabbis teach that this decree includes stepparents and even teachers. Livel knew he had a debt to repay to his esteemed teacher, and the reality of that obligation was impossible to deny.

"You have been my mentor, protector and friend. I will be honored to remain until a replacement is found."

"Thank you," Doctor Galen said, hugging Livel in a rare show of emotion. Embarrassed, he stepped away and dropped his hands to his sides. "You should be aware Arria's wedding to Domitius Gracchus is imminent. In the mean time, you will be sharing this villa with her. I hope you two can become friends."

"If I were in control of that decision, there would be no problem. But in case you have forgotten, your daughter detests me. And this adoption has not helped my cause."

Doctor Galen scowled for a moment and then shrugged. "She is used to getting her way. Just be patient and try to ignore what she might say to you. In time you will win her over."

A week later

Livel perched on the sofa in the enormous room that served as both his classroom and library. Scattered about him were a dozen books, articles and notes that Doctor Galen had left for him, information that Livel was expected to memorize before the first group of student doctors arrived in less than a month.

Overcome by the realization that time was running short; Livel attacked his studies with a zealous intensity. He ate only enough to sustain himself and slept for just a few hours at a time. Yet even in his fatigued state, every moment of discovery thrilled him.

Livel was beginning to develop some theories of his own about surgery. To test those theories, he needed an actual cadaver. He made inquiries, even though it was illegal in Rome to experiment on the dead. He refused to think about the rules that forbade him, as a Kohen, to have physical contact with the deceased. He had let that law slide by long ago because, as a surgeon, he would have no choice.

Deep in contemplation, Livel looked up with a start. "How long have you been standing there?" he asked, stunned by Arria's presence. They had been living under the same roof for days, and this was the first time he had set eyes on her. According to the servants, Arria had breakfast served in her room hours past the normal breakfast time. Then she would dress and leave, not returning until the wee hours of the morning.

Arria stared at Livel, hands on her hips, a look of utter disdain on her face. "This was just delivered by a man who looked to be an undertaker to the devil himself," she said, throwing the note on the table. "It's forbidden to use human bodies for experimentation. You should know better!"

"It is also considered highly rude to read another person's private correspondence!" Livel replied, furious at her intrusion in his private affairs.

"What sneaky, underhanded thing are you planning?"

"If I can get a body, you mean?"

"Are you going to tell me or not?" Arria demanded.

Livel did not cower in her presence as he had in the past. In fact, he found her haughty behavior a distraction and had no intention of being drawn into an argument. "Are you about to throw one of your notorious tantrums?"

Arria stamped her foot. "Either I'm part of this, or I'll call the authorities and then . . ." She stopped in mid-sentence. "Until I'm married, I intend to be part of everything you do."

"In that case, perhaps you would care to join me later. At your father's behest, I am going to visit Doctor Matthia's patients in the Jewish quarter." Livel drew out the word Jewish, baiting her to reject his suggestion.

Arria looked at him, defiance in her stare. "What time shall I be ready?"

Chapter 23

Arria was moody and withdrawn during the entire ride to Doctor Joshua Mattia's house, her mood a reflection of the dreary winter eve, the raging wind and the tumultuous clatter of wheels over the muddy rutted streets. She had cancelled plans with Domitius to prove a point to Livel, but the decision weighed heavy upon her. When she was with Domitius, he distracted her with lovely gifts, wonderful parties and plenty of drink making the departure of her father almost tolerable. Being here with Livel changed all that. He represented learning and medicine, reminding her of all that she might have been and all she was giving up. As often as Arria told herself being a physician was in the past, the pull of medicine was still strong, like a drug she could not resist.

She wondered what Domitius would say if he knew what she was doing this night. He was indulgent, and yet he could also be rigid in his beliefs. Once she had tried to broach the subject of medicine, hinting at her participation at the school with her father and Livel. Domitius had grown incredulous and angry, so she had quickly changed the subject.

Arria knew that just as she was attracted to the dangerous underpinnings of Domitius' personality, he was attracted to her headstrong ways. It might take a bit of time, but she felt certain he would indulge her after they were married. In the meantime, Arria fully intended to do exactly as she pleased.

The carriage rolled to a stop in front of the doctor's house. Livel climbed down, took his medical bag and then offered a hand to

Arria. She refused him with a look of disdain, moving to the ground effortlessly.

Livel had to restrain himself from rebuking her rudeness. He was already angry that Arria had kept her head turned away from him for the entire ride and had sat as far away from him on the seat as possible. He had no misconceptions as to why Arria was here. She wanted the opportunity to practice medicine on real patients. But she could at least show some gratitude. After all, he was risking a great deal bringing her to the Jewish Quarter. The very idea of a woman doctor was repellent in a society where men ruled. If they were discovered, it would mean the end of his career.

Together Livel and Arria climbed the three steps of the stoop. Livel knocked. In the distance, they heard the scraping of a chair and footsteps.

Doctor Mattia pushed open the door. He was dressed in a stained tunic, and there was a splotch of dried food at the corner of his mouth. "Could it be?" he laughed. "Are these old eyes playing tricks on me?" His face crinkled into a smile as he folded Arria into his arms. She tucked her head against his chest.

"I've missed you so much, Uncle Joshua. I'm sorry it has been so long since I last visited."

Doctor Mattia lifted Arria's chin. "Don't be silly. Guilt has no place in our relationship."

"Oh, I do so adore you," Arria said, hugging him again.

Livel felt like a fool. He should have realized Arria would know Doctor Mattia. The man introduced Doctor Galen to medicine when Arria was a young girl.

"Come in before you both freeze to death," he said, shaking Livel's hand. "We have little time to waste. I have five very sick patients that need attention. Let me get my coat and medical supplies so we can go."

"How are you feeling?" Arria asked, as the doctor gathered his things, trying to push aside the obvious: the grayish cast to his complexion, the yellowed eyes and labored breathing.

"Tired, my little one. This will be the last time I venture out now that Livel has offered to take over for me. Perhaps you will assist him? It is too much for one man. Take a look at me. I am proof of that."

Arria felt a shiver go down her spine. She had thought it would be just this one time. It never occurred to her that she might actually be allowed to practice medicine. Her father had always said it was a foolish dream. *But was it? Who would care for the sick down here in the Jewish quarter? Who would see her practicing medicine? Who might try to stop her?"*

* * *

They trudged through the narrow garbage infested alleyways. It was freezing. The icy wind from the river assaulted them as they tried to navigate the puddles and filth of human waste that littered the gutters. Arria pulled the sheepskin wrap tightly around her, striding between the doctor and Livel.

"I have a theory as to why this area is so ridden with disease," the doctor said, speaking loudly above the howling wind. "When the routes opened from the Indian Ocean and the South China Sea to Rome, the cargos were infested with insects and rats, and the seaman often arrived desperately ill with diseases we had never seen before." His breathing ragged, he continued, "Now our people have come down with these infirmities, and we must find ways to treat them."

The doctor moved to his left and stood in front of a stoop. There was lamplight seeping past the corners of a boarded up window.

He knocked, and the door was opened by a little girl with big brown eyes, sunken cheeks and hair the color of midnight that hung in stringy tangles down her back. Her nose was running, and she sneezed, wiping her nose with the back of her tiny hand.

"Good evening Miriam," the doctor said, bowing slightly. The little girl laughed and bowed back. "How is your mother feeling today?" he asked in a gentle voice.

Miriam averted her eyes and shook her head.

Doctor Mattia took the lamp from the table. "Never lose faith child. I have brought two very smart doctors with me tonight, and I am certain that between us we can find a way to make your mother feel better."

Livel and Arria followed the doctor and the little girl as they moved through the short hallway that led to the only other room. Lying on a straw mat near a sputtering fireplace was a waif of a woman. "Her name is Leah," Doctor Mattia said. He knelt on the mat and put a hand to her forehead. Leah moaned, opened her eyes for a moment and closed them again.

"She's burning with fever," the doctor said, moving aside so Arria and Livel could get closer.

Out of the shadows, a man appeared. "Thank you for coming," he said, his voice heavy with emotion. "I don't know what to do. She can't eat. It hurts her too much!"

"Amos, this is Doctor Livel and Doctor Arria Galen. They have come to help me." Doctor Mattia turned to Livel. "Feel her neck."

Livel probed gently, feeling swollen nodes so large they would surely block the passage of food and even her ability to breathe.

Arria put a finger on Leah's wrist and felt for the pulse. "It is weak."

"Any ideas?" Doctor Mattia asked.

"Herbs to lessen the pain so that she can take liquid," Livel offered. "They will reduce the fever."

"A charcoal poultice for her neck and chest," Arria added. "And steam. We must have steam. It will open the passages in the nose!"

"All good ideas, but they will need to be ministered," Doctor Mattia said.

"I will stay with her. You can come back for me when you have finished," Arria said, pulling out a small pouch that hung around her neck. "I have the herbs I will need."

Livel opened his medical bag and took out clean rags and two pieces of charcoal for the poultice. He handed them to Arria, and their eyes met. It was a moment of truce. For whatever else they might think or feel about each other, in the ministering of healing, they were united. "Your wife is in good hands," Livel said, rising and putting a gentle hand on Amos' shoulder.

"May the Holy One, Blessed be He, bring healing through those hands," Doctor Mattia added. "We will be back in a few hours."

* * *

Livel and Doctor Mattia knocked on a door only three houses away.

"It saddens me to tell you that this next patient is beyond our help. I come here as comfort for the family. I stop by every few days just to let them feel that something is being done."

"What are the symptoms?"

"High fever, weakness, hallucinations, black urine. I see it often yet Galen tells me he rarely has cases like this. That fact has led me to believe this disease is regional, occurring mostly near the waterfront."

Livel and the doctor spent ten minutes with the family, leaving herbs to ease the patient through his impending passing.

At the next house, the doctor put a hand on Livel's shoulder. "I must warn you before you enter this house. I have been here often and have not been stricken. But this illness has felled the entire household. There is a rash, swollen throat, fever, cough and runny nose. The mother was near death, but she recovered. The father died a week ago. The three children are still ailing."

"What are you doing for them?' Livel asked, his pulse quickening. Doctor Galen had spoken of plagues, illnesses that killed thousands. He had never questioned if he would have the courage to expose himself in this way. At least, he now had the answer. "Have you tried poultices and steam?"

"Again my boy, those treatments are labor intensive and for an old man, impossible. I am lucky enough to have the neighbors leaving food on the doorstep; otherwise, they would all have starved to death by now."

"I will stay with them and see what I can do."

"You could be felled by this illness."

"And if I am, I will recover."

Livel thought he knew what to expect. According to Doctor Galen, illness had a pattern like a roadmap. Yet, upon entering the one room house, he was overcome by the scene before him. The children were all under five, and they lay scattered about the room crying. These were not the howls of babes looking for attention. These were the pitiful cries of suffering as they dug at the rashes that pocked their skin. The mother had a haunted, yet determined look in her eyes, a woman fiercely defending her family from the Angel of Death.

Doctor Mattia made the introductions. The woman's name was Sapphra.

Livel wasted little time. He took out a mortar and pestle, placed a piece of charcoal in the dish with some water and ground it into a paste. He made three portions, placing each mixture on a square cloth. Folding the cloth, he made three poultices. Then he mixed a pinch of herbs into three portions of water.

"Please, give this to the children to drink. It will ease them to sleep."

The mother cooed and sang, urging her babies to drink. Within minutes, the room was still. Sapphra came to Livel and sat cross-legged beside him. Her eyes were wide in wonder and gratitude. "This is the first time in days that no one is crying."

"I am sorry for the loss of your husband," Livel offered.

Sapphra pushed the hair from her eyes. Her expression was bold and determined. Livel could see that once she had been lovely, before grief had stolen the gleam from her eye and the smile from her lips. "My children must survive! They are all I have left."

Livel moved from child to child, placing the poultices on the babies where the skin was most ravaged by the rashes.

Removing a pestle and mortar from his bag, Livel ground enough herbs to last for the next day. He scooped them into a small clay bowl and handed the medicine to Sapphra. "Just put a pinch in a cup of water every few hours. It will lessen their pain and keep them sleepy so they don't scratch their wounds," Livel said. "When they wake up, feed them a broth of this." He placed the pouch filled with dried ground vegetables on the table. "This will give them strength. I will come back every day until they are well."

Sapphra brought a fist to her mouth to hold back her tears. "How do I thank you? What do I say?"

Livel smiled. "We are going to get your babies well. That is all the thanks I need."

Doctor Mattia turned his back and wiped away his tears. God had brought him a healer.

Chapter 24

The stress of living two separate lives was beginning to take a toll on Arria. Circles shaded her eyes from lack of sleep, and she had grown thin and waif-like. Yet regardless of her exhaustion, she ventured out each night to meet Domitius, with her hair coiffed, tunic perfectly draped and body perfumed.

They spent their evenings at boisterous parties where Domitius often drank too much, becoming moody, rude and dismissive towards servants and even friends. He remained respectful to Arria, so she forced herself to disregard his behavior, even though she found his arrogant streak unsettling.

After the parties, they found creative places in the Gracchus villa to be alone: in an empty room in the guest quarters, the library, any unoccupied space they could find. He was a passionate lover and in that regard, Arria remained content.

* * *

In the attic above the library of the Gracchus villa, a feathered couch was washed in lamplight. An inebriated Domitius poised above Arria, his hands grasping her arms. Nearing climax, he disregarded the force in which he was moving or the strength by which he held her. Arria cried out and tried to squirm away, but she was pinned. Domitius was lost in lust, riding her violently. When he was spent, Arria shoved Domitius off her and grabbed for her tunic. Once dressed, she stood nursing the bruises on her arms, so furious her entire body shook.

"How dare you treat me as if I were some common whore? I'm leaving!" she raged.

Domitius jumped from the couch. "Please, you must forgive me," he begged, reaching for her. Arria stepped back, swatting his hands away.

"It will never happen again. I swear to all the gods!"

"You mean it will never happen again until the next time you have too much to drink?" she hissed, so upset the words burned like fire as she spoke them.

"Arria, I love you. You must know, I would rather die than harm you."

"Well you did!" She offered forth her bruised arms for him to see.

Domitius hung his head, hiding the rage that burned in his belly. He felt no remorse for hurting Arria; only regret that she was in a position to threaten him with leaving. Once they were married, he would never have to deal with this behavior again. In the meantime, he had to do whatever was necessary to soothe her. "I am infinitely sorry. Tell me what I can do to make it up to you."

An inner voice warned Arria that evil lurked here. She was in danger. Domitius could harm her one day. She was frantic, half of her wanting to flee from this place, never setting eyes on him again and the other half being in love with him and daydreaming of a beautiful life together. In the end, there was no decision to make–Arria would never quit, not ever. When she wanted something, she got it. When things were broken, she fixed them. Without her father, Domitius was her future.

I will change him once we are married.

She pointed her raging eyes at Domitius. Arria had little choice but to trust he had learned his lesson. Besides, she questioned her right to judge Domitius harshly. He might not be perfect, but neither was she.

Arria continued to care for the sick in the Jewish section, lying to Domitius about how she spent her days. While Domitius found her headstrong attitudes challenging, Arria was certain he would never approve of her caring for the sick. If Domitius ever discovered her deceit, she was certain it would be the end of their relationship.

"Forgive me?" He smiled, gently taking Arria's face in his hands. He kissed her forehead, eyes and lips. Arria resisted, but not for very long.

* * *

Livel's life was full. When he wasn't attending to the sick, he was studying and preparing for the arrival of his students. The opening of the school meant he would teach all day and then see patients at night. That change of routine would mean the end of Arria going with him. Her evenings were set aside for Domitius. It would also mean the end of Arria's visits to the Jewish section; it was too dangerous for her to go there on her own. The realization saddened him. To add to his anguish was the fact that her absence would double his responsibilities. In his heart, Livel knew it was for the best, as things could not continue this way. Arria had a life to live, and he needed to get over his infatuation.

Still, in the middle of the night, when nothing stirred and darkness cloaked his room, reality abated. It was then that Livel imagined Arria throwing Domitius aside, proclaiming her love for him.

In the morning light, when he caught a glimpse of his reflection in the mirror, Livel was reminded of his foolish folly. Domitius was a handsome, virile man who obviously satisfied Arria on levels Livel could only begin to imagine. He knew nothing of pleasing a woman; his only encounter was with a stranger, one who had snuck into his bed as a gift from Scipio. It remained a poignant memory and a reminder; he needed to get home to find a wife and end his obsession with Arria Galen.

* * *

An hour before sunset, a coach pulled into the driveway. Doctor Galen climbed down from the carriage. He wore a tunic weaved from the finest wool, and around his neck hung a thick gold chain with the likeness of the emperor engraved on a golden disk. His gait was slow, hoping to forestall what lay ahead of him.

Livel and Arria had just returned from doctoring. They were heading down the hallway towards the stairs when they heard the front door open and a slave greet the doctor.

Arria ran down the corridor and threw herself into her father's arms.

"Why didn't you send word you were coming? I would have prepared a feast! Oh Father, I have so much to tell you. Wait until you hear about my patients. I have cured so many, I lost count. Do hurry. Come in!" she said tugging on his arm.

Doctor Galen looked over his shoulder at Livel and smiled. He could not remember when he had seen Arria so happy. He hoped that these memories would last her a lifetime.

Doctor Galen put his arm around Arria as they moved into the foyer.

"Everything you taught me was right! But I do have questions, things that Livel and I have yet to figure out," Arria said.

Livel stayed a few steps behind. He had been writing to the doctor, keeping him abreast of their activities. He told Galen that he and Arria traveled to the Jewish section of the city every day except the Sabbath. He disclosed that while they each had their own patients, they consulted with one another when necessary, discussing the various treatment options. He assured the doctor, he and Arria had established a mutual respect for each other's intelligence and competence.

In a return letter, the doctor warned Livel to be careful not to be seen by anyone who might recognize Arria. With that comment, Livel knew it had been a very long time since the doctor had spent any time in the Jewish section. The people there were hard working, poor and never passed into the city proper. There was little chance anyone would recognize either of them.

"I'll make myself a drink and rest in the library while you both go and change," the doctor said.

Arria kissed him on the cheek. "I won't be long."

* * *

Livel was the first to return fifteen minutes later. He shook Doctor Galen's hand. "It is really good to see you."

"As it is to see you," Galen said, offering Livel a glass of wine. "Come and sit with me."

There was something in the doctor's tone that concerned Livel. "Is everything all right?" he asked as they settled on a couch near the fire. The logs crackled and sparks flew as a servant tended the wood. Another servant brought platters of fruit and cold chicken and placed them on the sideboard under a portrait of the doctor and Arria.

"There are rumors swirling around the palace. Hadrian is furious with the situation in Judea. He is convinced there are spies in Rome and intends to send soldiers into the Jewish area dressed as peasants to seek them out," Galen said.

"Spies? That's absurd! The people there are just trying to survive; they care nothing of politics or Jerusalem," Livel replied.

Doctor Galen's expression grew pensive. "It matters little what you or I or anyone else may think. If the emperor's obsession intensifies, I can assure you beheadings will follow. You must stay away from there! And as of this day, Arria is never to set foot in the place again. Is that understood?"

"I empathize with your concern, and I agree that Arria should not return. As for me, it is not a request I can comply with," Livel remarked, his expression set.

Galen wanted to insist. He knew the kind of carnage that could take place at the emperor's whim. He had seen beheadings occur simply because Hadrian was in a foul mood. "If you are caught—"

"That won't happen."

"What won't happen?' Arria asked, entering the room. She wore a blue tunic dyed with the root of a ginger plant, and her hair was tied back with a velvet ribbon.

Doctor Galen rose and kissed his daughter. "Please, have a seat," he said. "May I pour you a cup of wine?"

"Thank you," Arria said, moving to a chair opposite the couch. She smiled at her father as she accepted the drink. "You should know Livel and I have been getting along quite famously."

"As I expected you would," Galen replied, sitting next to Livel. "If nothing else, I knew you would find commonality in your love of medicine. And that is one of the reasons, I have come here tonight." He told her about the rumors and about his concerns.

Arria chewed at her lip, worried about her sick patients and disappointed she would be forced to quit before she was ready. She conjured up a scenario to get around the dilemma: how she might go to her patients before sun-up disguised as a man. In the end, she realized the idea was foolish and dangerous. If she were caught, it would disgrace her father and be the end of his career. Always resilient, Arria settled on the thought the gods had intervened just in time. Now, she had no decision to make about when she would stop going into the Jewish area–the resolution had been made for her. "What about the people who are ill? What will become of them? Who will take our place? You know Uncle Joshua is too frail and—"

"I will continue to go," Livel said, noting the look of relief wash across Arria's face.

"There is another matter we need to discuss," Galen said, sipping the wine while mustering his resolve. "Hadrian is growing restless. His closest advisors tell me that restlessness precedes his desire to travel. It could be two weeks, a month or six months from now. I don't know when, but my departure is imminent." He looked at his only child; the greatest treasure in his life. The possibility he might never see her again was inconceivable.

Arria leaned over and reached for her father's hands. Until this moment, she had always held onto the belief he would never be too far away to come to her rescue. Even in deciding to marry Domitius, she felt there would be safety in her father's nearness. "I don't want you to go. You can't go! I need you." She fell into his arms crying. "Take me with you. Please take me with you."

Livel felt like an intruder, not wanting to be witness to their anguish, yet unable to look away.

"My precious Arria, you know I cannot take you with me. And even if I could, it would not serve your best interests. You are to become the wife of Domitius Gracchus," Galen said, wishing instead he could tell his little girl he would never leave her. But the time had come for Arria to move on with her life. It had been her decision to do that with Domitius Gracchus. As the father, he had a duty and an obligation to put his emotions aside and remain resolute. "You will always be cherished, my child, and never far from my thoughts." Doctor Galen wiped the tears from his daughter's face with his fingertips. "But soon you will have a husband to love and protect you, as it should be.

"I have been to see Marcus Gracchus and have told him of the situation. We have agreed your wedding will be held ten days from now."

Arria stepped away from her father. Her eyes dull, she appeared to collapse within herself. It was all happening too fast. She had yet to decide if Domitius was kind or cruel, considerate or thoughtless. That uncertainty terrified her. Arria knew that to voice her concerns would only distress her father and would do nothing to change the outcome. She had made a commitment, and her fate was sealed.

Livel forced a smile, but inside his heart was breaking. It was over. Arria was lost to him forever.

Chapter 25

From En Gedi to Jerusalem

Five days after the death of his son, Masabala rode alone into the Negev Desert. The sun illuminated a cloudless, sapphire sky, bands of light reflecting off the sand creating an illusion of flickering diamonds. All around him lay the barren, desolate, rock-strewn mountains, a monotone landscape depicted in shades of white, neutrals and charcoal. For a moment, Masabala thought about the followers of Moses, how they had trudged over these very same paths. It was a vista that had remained unchanged for thousands of years.

Masabala had never felt so lonely, insignificant and sad. Leaving Sarah behind had broken his heart. He could still see her eyes, the lashes covered in tears, feel her arms around him, clinging for one last embrace. His chest tightened making it hard to breathe. Sliding from the horse, Masabala fell to the ground. All the anguish and anger he had pushed away suddenly surfaced, his screams shattering the silence.

"Why didn't you just punish me?" he howled, shaking his fist at the heavens. "I transgressed! I am deserving of your anger! But my Sarah, how could you do this to my Sarah?" His eyes glowed furiously as he pounded his chest. "You knew nothing would hurt me more than seeing Sarah suffer."

Masabala fell prostrate on the ground, crying until his tears were as dry as the grains of sand where he lay. Sitting up, he stared at his calloused hands, the very same hands that had placed his infant son into the earth. He squeezed his eyes shut.

"Question if you must, but do not lose faith."

Masabala jumped up, his mind afire. He knew that voice; he had heard it in the grove when he buried his son.

"Who are you? Why can't I see you?" he cried, turning in circles, searching the barren landscape.

"Is it not enough that I have come to you? There is so much you do not understand. But you will," the angel called, its voice drifting away with the breeze.

* * *

Masabala arrived in mid-afternoon. Even in his great despair, he was cognizant of his surroundings–how the sun's rays cast a golden glow over the ancient city of Jerusalem and how the air smelled sweeter here than anywhere else. He entered the tent city and handed the reins of his horse to a soldier standing watch. Masabala then headed toward Bar Kokhba's headquarters.

Silhouetted in the shadowed doorway of the command center, he stood rooted in place, unable to move. Masabala knew he had to go back to work, but it seemed so overwhelming, as if his mind had disconnected from his body and his will.

Torches hung from the walls bathing the room in light. The *nasi* stood in the center of the room with the renowned architect, David Ben Shira, at his side. They were discussing reinforcement points in the Temple walls. A few feet away, men sat at tables with feather quills and wax working in silence.

Rabbi Akiva and three other rabbis were gathered around a table off to the right. They were arguing, their eyes intent and their voices urgent as they discussed implementing a government based on religious rule.

Bar Kokhba glanced toward the doorway. His eyes widened and then slid away as if he needed a moment to find the right expression. A messenger had arrived days before, alerting him that Masabala had lost his son. Bar Kokhba had been preparing himself for this moment. When he looked again at Masabala, his face was mournful. He did not wave or speak, but just made a slight dip of his head as he strode closer. He touched Masabala's chest with an open palm as if to heal his broken heart. He then turned and walked out the door. Masabala followed.

Masabala and Bar Kokhba remained mute trudging through the narrow streets of Jerusalem, past barking dogs and a maze of street vendors. They continued up ragged steps that led to the courtyard surrounding the construction site of the Third Temple. Thousands of men toiled piling stones and breaking rocks. The noise was like the roll of thunder.

"Come this way," Bar Kokhba said, leading Masabala away from the bedlam. Standing in the vast expanse of quarried stone, Bar Kokhba leaned against a rock and looked at Masabala. "I am so sorry." His eyes clouded as he looked into the distance. Crossing his arms over his chest, Bar Kokhba pointed his chin at Masabala. "I know it is difficult, but we must accept the will of the Holy One, Blessed be He without question."

Masabala's stomach soured. He rubbed his beard; anguish coloring his face.

Bar Kokhba continued, "We cannot know the Lord's reasoning when a life ends before it has begun, anymore than we can understand when a young soldier dies." He looked intently at Masabala.

Masabala did not need reminding. He continued to grieve for every man that had died at the cave-in at Herodian and for all the men he had lost in battle. Their cries still pierced his heart.

Bar Kokhba shook his head, his expression drawn. "Without faith, Masabala, you will never find solace. Accept that your son is safe in the arms of the Holy One, Blessed be He, and you shall find peace."

Masabala wanted to believe, needed to believe. He thought about the conversation he'd had with his father just before leaving En Gedi. The rabbi had cried when he learned that his son was chosen to unearth the Ark of the Covenant. He begged Masabala to pray with him before he left, but Masabala had refused, his heart hard as stone. Now he was sorry. Perhaps prayer may have helped him find comfort.

"Give yourself time," the *nasi* said, putting his arm around Masabala.

Masabala did not know if time would heal his pain. He was certain of only one thing: the Ark beckoned. He had a job to do, and do it he would!

* * *

Masabala returned to the tunnels with renewed vigor. His goal was to find the Ark before the Temple was completed. His men agreed to work in shifts throughout the day and night. Once their bodies adjusted, it made little difference if it was light or dark outside; inside the tomblike bowels of the tunnels, there was perpetual darkness.

He moved from excavation to excavation. His life was becoming one long day interrupted by intervals of sleep lasting no more than a few hours at a time. The hard work served as a salve for Masabala's misery. Although he was too busy to think, he was not too busy to ache for Sarah. That drove him on, knowing that once his task was completed, they could be together again.

Three months later

An hour before sunset, on the eve of the Sabbath, an elated Masabala, along with Simon Bar Kokhba and Rabbi Akiva, entered the town of En Gedi. Flocks of birds floated on the gentle breezes and the scent of blooming flowers and balsam sweetened the air. It was not long before they were recognized, and a throng gathered vying for the opportunity to be in the presence of Bar Kokhba, the Messiah.

Masabala, riding alongside the nasi, had only one thought in mind. Sarah. Moving amidst the crowd, they turned a corner and stopped in front of the only two-level structure in all of En Gedi, home to the family of Rabbi Eleazar.

Masabala dismounted and rushed inside. So much had changed in his life, but here everything remained the same: the furniture, the walls reflecting the light, the familiar sounds. Masabala knew his father would be coming from the synagogue at any moment. Birds and lamb would be roasting over the fire, and the table would be set for the Sabbath with a tablecloth, the Sabbath lamp and wine.

He stepped inside and quietly moved into the kitchen. Sarah had her back to him, arranging something on a platter. His mother kneeled at the hearth, basting the pigeons and meat. He moved behind his wife and touched her shoulder.

Sarah looked up. She began to cry the moment she saw her husband. Her prayers were answered. Sarah fell into Masabala's arms, breathing in his smell, the feel of his arms around her, his heart beating against her chest. She hugged him as hard as she could. She needed to be held, to know love once again and to find her lost spirit. Masabala gently kissed Sarah's lips and wiped away the tears with his fingertips.

Miriam rose from her knees, her gratitude and joy boundless. The past months had been such a desperate time in their home. Once Sarah recovered her strength, she continued on as if everything was normal. But the girl with the indomitable spirit had disappeared, replaced by a serious, unsmiling and wounded young woman. Perhaps now that her son had returned, Sarah would emerge from her despair.

While holding Sarah's hand, Masabala reached for his mother's hand and brought it to his lips. "It's so good to be home."

"And such a wonderful surprise!" Miriam said. Her eyes crinkled with a smile.

"I'm not alone, Mother. Bar Kokhba and Rabbi Akiva are here as well."

"Here? You mean in my house?" Miriam asked, tugging at the scarf around her head.

Masabala nodded.

"Oh my! We must not keep them waiting." Miriam rushed into the hallway, thankful that extra food was always prepared for the Sabbath.

Sarah whispered, "Why didn't you send word you were coming?"

"Because I didn't know until last night. I'll explain later." He faced Sarah and touched her face with trembling fingers. "I love you, and I am so sorry that I have not been here with you."

"That is not true," Sarah said, her expression resolute. "You have been with me every moment of every single day." She took his hand and placed it over her heart. "In here."

* * *

Rabbi Eleazar gathered his esteemed guests in the dining room. An oblong table and chairs filled the center of the room. The sideboard was located against the west wall. Masabala approached his father and bowed. He kissed the back of his hand, a custom Rabbi Akiva encouraged.

"I am joyous at your return, my beloved son," the rabbi said, hugging him.

Miriam and Sarah lit the Sabbath lamp. They covered their eyes as they sang the ancient melody. The flickering lamp, his mother and wife in sacred unity, the continuance of the traditions, all represented faith to Masabala. He would memorize this night and recall it when in doubt of God's presence.

Prayers were said over the wine, and the cup was passed from person to person. The pious men washed their hands and said in unison, "*Barukh atah A.donai E.loheinu melekh ha'olam, asher kid'shanu b'mitzvotav v'tzivanu al n'tilat yadayim.* Blessed are You, Lord, our God, King of the universe, who has sanctified us with His commandments and commanded us concerning the washing of hands."

The bread was sanctified, and then everyone sat. Rabbi Eleazar was at the head of the table. Rabbi Akiva and Bar Kokhba were to his right, and Miriam, Masabala and Sarah were to his left.

Servants offered platters of pigeon and lamb seasoned with mustard, capers, dill and rosemary. Plates of plump olives and figs were served along with bowls filled with lentils, cucumbers and onions.

"I am honored to have you at our table," Rabbi Eleazar said, raising his wine goblet in a toast.

"As we are honored to be here," Rabbi Akiva replied.

"The Temple nears completion, and I feel certain that under the guidance of your son we will soon find the Ark of the Covenant." Bar Kokhba smiled at Masabala. "It is a momentous time in the history of our people, and that is why we are here."

Sarah wanted to feel joy at their progress, and certainly, she was proud of her husband. But she had given too many years away. Sarah believed she was entitled to have Masabala in her life every day, and she was lonely and tired of feeling guilty about her needs. Brooding, she was distracted until she heard Bar Kokhba say, "My decision will not only affect you Eleazar but your entire family."

Masabala smiled at Sarah.

"Rabbi Eleazar, I am here to appoint you the Kohen Gadol, the High Priest of the Jewish people. You and you alone will approach the Ark of the Covenant on the High Holy Days." There was not a sound in the room. Even the lamps ceased their flickering. "Animal sacrifices will again become a part of the sacred daily rituals. During Yom Kippur, you will present the sin offerings and peace offerings and all the sacrificial prayers of repentance that attain atonement for our people. Your prayers will become the golden connection between man and the Holy One, Blessed be He." Bar Kokhba's eyes were radiant.

Rabbi Eleazar bowed his head, trying to grasp the magnitude of the great honor being bestowed upon him. He tried to imagine what it would be like to approach the Ten Commandments, to stand as Moses stood–to be in the presence of God's words.

At the time of the First and Second Temples, only the priests communicated with God. Individual prayer was nonexistent. But over the past two generations, Judaism had changed; the rabbis founded synagogues, and the Jews began to pray directly to God.

Judaism had thrived for thousands of years because the religion was rarely dogmatic or stagnant. It was always moving forward. Even the ways in which the Jews prayed to the Lord had been altered. In the beginning, they prayed to God the King. Now He was worshipped as God the father.

Will the people and the rabbis be willing to relegate communication with God back to the priests? Perspiration creased the rabbi's brow. *And what about the rabbis who do not believe that Bar Kokhba is the true messiah? Will they break away? Judaism cannot afford a rift from within—not now, not when freedom is finally ours. I will not let that happen!*

Miriam watched her husband. She could see the emotions play across his face. Joy. Concern. Determination.

Eleazar looked from Bar Kokhba to Rabbi Akiva. In that moment of reflection, Eleazar vowed to himself and to God that as the Kohen Gadol, he would unite his people. With great solemnity, he lifted his eyes toward heaven and said, "May the sacrificial offerings of Judah and Jerusalem be pleasing to the Holy One, Blessed be He." His face resolute, he placed his hand into Miriam's hand.

The family of Eleazar would be moving to Jerusalem.

Chapter 26

Jerusalem

While the trees birthed their spring leaves the days grew longer, the weather warmer and the ground softer. Wild orchids, irises, roses and poppies turned the mountainsides and hillsides into a celebration of colors.

They were nearing the location of the Ark, and Masabala was anxious to the point of distraction. He was unable to concentrate or sleep for more than a few hours at a time. No longer content to oversee the excavations, he commandeered an ax and a pick and selected a different tunnel to work in each day. For weeks, he toiled beside his men, his hands bandaged, his eyes and hair perpetually caked in dust and dirt.

It was nearly nightfall, and Masabala was working in tunnel number three. The shift was about to change, and his men were gathering their tools. Suddenly, an exhausted but resolute soldier decided to swing just one more violent blow into the facade of the rock wall. A chunk of stone shattered. A piercing blast of wind hissed through the hole, extinguishing every torch. The men were plunged into darkness, shouts of terror filling the black void.

Masabala, always nervous in the tunnels, now faced his own worst fear of becoming trapped. He took slow deep breaths, willing himself to remain composed. Putting his back to the wind, he shouted, "Hold close to the walls, stay together and follow my voice."

Heading toward the exit, Masabala used the wall as a guide. Running his hand over the rocks, he was shocked by the heat that seemed to emanate from the surface of the walls. Too frightened and confused to comprehend what it might mean, he hollered, "Call out your names." When all six men were accounted for, Masabala said reassuringly, "You dug this cave so you know every inch. There is only one way in and one way out. Follow me. There is nothing to fear."

"Tell that to my shaking knees," a voice shouted back.

"Or to my pounding heart," said another voice.

"Just keep talking," Masabala replied, knowing his most important task at this moment was to keep himself and his men distracted from their terror.

The banter continued until they cleared the tunnel. For all the men, it felt like the longest walk any of them had ever taken. Excited and relieved to be breathing fresh air and to have their sight returned, the soldier-diggers all began to talk at once. "Did you feel that? The walls were burning! It has to be the Ark! We must go back!"

Masabala's mouth went dry, and his heart hammered. *We have found the Ten Commandments!* There was just no other answer for walls that sizzled to the touch or a wind strong enough to extinguish every torch. The magnitude of the moment swirled about him like a tornado.

"What are we waiting for?" a soldier demanded.

The men exiting from the other four passageways heard the urgent voices and gathered around. When they were informed of the possible discovery, they too insisted upon returning to the tunnel. In mass, the soldiers headed back toward the opening.

"Stop where you are!" Masabala yelled, placing himself between the advancing crowd and the tunnel entrance. He held up his hands for silence. "Only a Kohen may approach the Ark!"

"You're a Kohen!" a voice called.

"Go back in. We want to know!" another soldier hollered.

Masabala remembered Bar Kokhba's words: *A good leader planned ahead.* He had been so preoccupied with finding the Ark, he forgot to formulate a plan for what was to be done once the Ten

Commandments were found. He knew he had to retake control. He could not have an unruly mob anywhere near the site.

"I pray that we have found the Ark," he said loudly. "But it is not my decision or yours as to when we may proceed. Only the Kohen Gadol and Bar Kokhba can make that determination. Only they have the right!" He let the words hang for a few moments. "Everyone back to camp now!" he ordered, his inflection leaving no doubt there would be no further conversation.

Soldiers grumbled, and some began shuffling away. Others stubbornly refused to move.

"Now!" Masabala screamed. "Or I will have you arrested!"

Masabala watched the crowd hesitate and then begin to disperse. Once alone, he could not take his eyes off the entrance to the tunnel. The urge to return was so strong; it pulled at him like an aphrodisiac encourages lust in a man. *I have to go back inside.*

He went into the makeshift storage hut twenty yards from where he stood and pulled out a torch. He lit it from the embers left over from the day's cooking fire.

Holding the torch high, Masabala moved hesitantly toward the entranceway. His thoughts turned to Sarah and how much his life had changed now that she was here in Jerusalem. Each night, they sat together by the hearth in their cozy kitchen. Sarah would serve him and then listen as Masabala talked about his day. Because of her unwavering love, his nightmares were beginning to subside, and there were even nights he no longer awakened drenched in sweat.

As Masabala stepped into the tunnel, he felt the presence of his father, Bar Kokhba and Rabbi Akiva, as if they were standing beside him. His first tentative steps were met by air so thick, he found it hard to draw a full breath. Staring into the darkness beyond what he could see, Masabala moved slowly forward, the only sound the drumming of his heart.

There was a scream so loud it pierced his ears, and he turned to see if someone had followed–but there was only the wind. His torch extinguished, he was thrust into total darkness yet he could see the walls of the cave melting. The ground vibrated beneath his feet and then stopped. He moved forward, walking in a river of liquid silver. Light reflected off every surface as luminescent as the sun. He shut his eyes and blinked several times. The surrealistic scene remained unchanged. He was too stunned to be afraid–his only emotion, wonder.

Lost in determination, Masabala continued on until the path ended. He approached the breach in the surface of the stone. Lifting a discarded pick from the silvery ground, he gently began tapping at the opening. Small pieces of rock crumbled beneath his fingers. Dazed, he worked without regard for place or time, just tapping and watching the slivers of stone pile at his feet. When the hole was the width of four hands, he placed his eyes at the opening.

A mist of billowed pewter clouds drifted in the haze, and for a moment, he could see nothing. Then the mist shifted becoming a kaleidoscope of hues and images: the sea, the sky, mountains and valleys, infinite stars–the entire universe passing before Masabala's eyes. Suspended in wonderment, having moved beyond rational thought, he could see the present, past and future. His arms expanded into wings, and his legs transformed into talons.

Masabala was an eagle spiraling into the night, shooting past stars, sailing around the moon, bouncing off the sun as he flew towards forevermore. Accompanied by angelic beings, his mind was afire. He watched in horror as countless images assaulted him–surreal and terrifying. The cities were burning, the dead lay unburied, children begged for food and water, their mouths poised in a perpetual scream. The streets of Judea had become rivers of blood.

He awoke from the dream-state sometime in the middle of the night and lay curled in a fetal position crying like a baby. He had seen the future, and he believed it to be true.

Masabala sat up and tried to stand. His legs gave way. He began to crawl along the stony floor. In shock, he had only one thought in mind: bring his father, the Kohen Gadol, to the throne of the Ten Commandments. Masabala prayed aloud as he inched along the ground, "Please, please," he begged, "show me how we can alter this unthinkable future. I will do anything. You must not let this happen!"

Masabala could not remember leaving the excavation grounds. When he realized he was walking down familiar roads, he felt bewildered. He knew where he was, but he could not remember how he got there.

He heard a loud groan and a dragging sound. His eyes flitted from side to side as he turned in a slow circle. In the gutter, he saw a rat with a lacerated tail. He heard the rodent cry as it limped past. Masabala placed his hands over his ears and quickened his pace. Even with his ears blocked, he was inundated by sounds and sensations–trees sighing in their sleep, awakening to spring and flowers grunting as they delivered their buds. He passed doorways and discerned the energy from those inside, knowing if they were happy, hungry, grieving or tormented.

He found the doorway to his home and stumbled inside. The house was asleep yet deafening sounds assaulted him. He could see and feel Sarah, a witness to her dreams and the depth of her love for him.

Trancelike, he moved to his parents' door and pushed it open. The room was a reflection of their lives. The days clothing lay folded neatly and stacked on a table. Parchments were lined up like soldiers against the eastern wall. His father's worktable, where he studied the words of the great prophets and wrote his commentaries on those words, was arranged in perfect order.

His father lay on his back, his mouth open, snoring softly. His mother was on her left side, an arm thrown across her husband, her mane of silver hair spilling over the pillow.

Masabala stepped softly toward the bed and with a trembling hand touched his father's shoulder.

Rabbi Eleazar's eyes flew open. Masabala felt his father struggle to coax his body from sleep. He felt the ache in his father's bones, how his right knee had stiffened and how the joints of every finger were swollen and sore. Masabala wanted to embrace him and ease the pain of his suffering, but Masabala instinctively understood that his gift of seeing did not come with the gift of healing–if it did, none of them would be facing the future he had seen.

The rabbi looked at his son, put his finger to his lips and pointed to his wife. He reached for his head covering that sat on a table beside his bed. Sitting up, the rabbi placed it on his head, closed his eyes and mouthed the prayers he said upon awakening. "*Modeh Ani Lefanecha Melech Chai Vekayom Shehechezarta Bi Nishmati Bechemla Raba Emunatecha.* I offer thanks to You, living and eternal King, for You have mercifully restored my soul within me; Your faithfulness is great."

Only then did the rabbi slip from bed. Shivering, he grabbed a sheepskin and wrapped it around his frail shoulders, following his son to the kitchen. The rabbi looked into his son's eyes glowing with the transcendent light of God. He did not need words to know what had happened. He put his arms around Masabala and embraced him. The sensation was startling, like trying to embrace a cloud. Tenderly, he released him.

"May God bless you, my son."

They settled in chairs across from one another, their knees touching, "Tell me everything!" the rabbi implored.

Masabala did not know how to put into words what was indescribable. What could he say? How could he say it? Could he tell his father he had soared into the heavens, and he had not wanted to return? Dare he say he had the ability to see beyond himself into another realm?

"Just tell me what you can," the rabbi urged.

"The trees and flowers call to me. I hear the thoughts of strangers." Masabala hesitated, bile rising in his throat. "I have seen the future. It is unspeakable!" he whispered, his eyes distraught.

"You must not be afraid. Just as the Holy One, Blessed be He parted the sea freeing us from bondage, the future is always alterable through penance and prayer." The rabbi reached for Masabala's hands. "We have a sacred mission before us. When the Temple is ready, the Ark of the Covenant must be moved into the *Kodesh Ha Kodashim*, the Holy of Holies within the Temple structure." He touched Masabala's arm, his eyes glowing reverent. "If the ancient whisperings are true, anyone other than a Kohen will perish if he touches the Ark. So I will assemble the Kohanim, the rabbis descended from Aaron, the brother of Moses. As it is written, the Ark will be wrapped in a veil of sheep's skin and then a cloth of blue. Our first concern is to conceal it from view, even from those chosen to carry it."

The rabbi rose. Before dressing, he would take a ritual bath of purification in the Mikvah located one floor below. "I will prepare myself, and then you and I will do what must be done. We will seal off the opening until the Holy of Holies is ready to receive the Ark of the Covenant."

Chapter 27

Rabbi Eleazar stepped into the tiny room at the end of the hall where the ceremonial clothing was stored for the Kohen Gadol, the High Priest. Finding the magnificence of the moment overwhelming, his hand hovered motionless over the eight garments. With prayers on his lips, he stepped out of his nightclothes.

Fully aware that each movement was now sacred, Eleazar lifted his right foot and then his left, as he stepped into white linen pants. Extending his arms, he slipped the tunic over his head. Around his waist, he tied the linen belt that was woven with blue, purple, scarlet and white threads. Next came a sleeveless blue robe decorated with thirty-six tiny golden bells and scarlet, purple and blue tassels shaped like pomegranates sewn to the bottom of the hem. Over the robe, the Kohen Gadol placed an ephod, fashioned like an apron. Then he added a breastplate attached to shoulder straps. It was adorned with twelve precious stones, each one representing one of the twelve tribes of Israel. With a tremulous hand, he placed a golden plate on his forehead inscribed with the words, *holy to God.* It was held in place by a ribbon of blue linen. Lastly, he took the long strip of white linen fabric and wound it around his head.

Eleazar was profoundly affected by the sacrosanct duty that lay before him. With head bowed, he recited prayers only known by the Kohanim.

Walking from the chamber, Eleazar continued to pray as he moved into the kitchen.

Masabala felt tears stinging his eyes as his father entered the room. He imagined an adjacent world where a parade of angels floated on the breeze beside the Kohen Gadol. Beyond the boundaries of self, Masabala heard a thousand voices singing, their heavenly music radiating from harps played by hundreds of unseen fingers.

Masabala reached for his father's hand and brought it to his lips.

"We will go to the Ark now," the Kohen Gadol said, taking Masabala's arm.

They walked through the night in silence down the winding passages and along the deserted colonnaded streets towards the Temple Mount. Every step the *Kohen Gadol* took was accentuated by the numinous sounds of swishing fabric and tinkling bells.

Masabala surrendered to the mystical trance-like state. He embraced the yellow crescent moon with his mind feeling its gravitational pull. The night sky sang a melody to him, each star having its own vibration and color.

"The sun is still hours from appearing," the rabbi said. "I wish to approach the *Aron ha-Kodesh,* the Ark, in the solitude of night."

Masabala was overcome by the awe-inspiring weight of responsibility that lay upon his father. He was searching for words to express his feelings when the hushed night exploded in the prodigious sounds of a dozen footfalls.

As soldiers came into view, Masabala recognized them as Bar Kokhba's personal entourage. These men guarded the *nasi* when he worked and when he was at home with his wife and son. That they were standing here in the middle of the night was definitely not a good sign.

A guard Masabala recognized as Abel stepped forward. Upon seeing the *Kohen Gadol*, he gasped, averted his eyes and bowed his head at the glorious sight of the High Priest of Israel.

"What is all of this?" the rabbi asked, his palms tapping the air.

"We are here to escort you to the excavation site," Abel said softly. "Rabbi Akiva and Bar Kokhba await you there."

* * *

When Masabala and his father arrived at the courtyard of the excavation site, they were awestruck. There were hundreds of torches and thousands of soldiers milling about. The noise level was deafening. Then as if an unseen hand was raised, the din of conversations began to ebb. An eerie silence prevailed as one man after another bowed his head at the sight of the High Priest moving amongst them.

Bar Kokhba stood near the entranceway of the tunnel. He had been awakened an hour earlier by a senior officer informing him that the Ark had been found, and Masabala's men had entered the tunnel without authorization. Rabbi Akiva stood nearby amidst a group of rabbis.

Bar Kokhba was the first to approach the *Kohen Gadol.* With great reverence, he kissed Eleazar's hand as Akiva and the other rabbis crowded around.

"The Holy One, Blessed be He has deemed us worthy to receive His most sacred of gifts," Eleazar said, embracing his role as the representative of God's connection to the Ten Commandments. He placed his hand on Bar Kokhba's shoulder. "As you must know, it is imperative we reseal the opening until the Ark can be placed inside the Holy of Holies."

Masabala stood beside his father watching the exchange. He had moved to a place beyond reason, and he was being bombarded by disjointed phrases and thoughts of the men surrounding them. He sensed that something bad had happened, but he could not filter out the information. Determined to shut out the frenzied staccato of words, he squeezed his eyes shut and focused all his energy on Bar Kokhba. *Just him,* he thought. *Just let me read what the nasi is thinking.*

Masabala began to tremble as he absorbed Bar Kokhba's feelings of trepidation and fear. Masabala forced himself to go deeper, to see more so he could understand the true meaning of the nasi's anxiety. The answer came to him in a rush.

Bar Kokhba is afraid to be in the presence of the Ark. Masabala was stunned. *God's emissary on earth should be ecstatic for the opportunity to encounter the Lord.* Reality struck like an arrow piercing his heart. *Bar Kokhba is a fraud!* Masabala bit down hard on his lip drawing blood.

He snapped his eyes open. His father was watching him, a look of concern in the worried creases around his eyes. Masabala blinked several times shoving the reprehensible information aside, to be dealt with at another time.

Bar Kokhba stepped away from Eleazar. "Because I was not alerted the moment the Ark was discovered, we now have a very unfortunate situation." His words were accusatory as he focused his eyes on Masabala. "We have men inside the tunnel."

"That is impossible!" Masabala blurted. "I ordered them to go back to camp." The tunnel passage appeared before him obscured by swirling pewter clouds. He cringed. "If the men inside approach the Ark, they will die!"

Bar Kokhba shifted his feet into a determined stance. "Let us pray that you are wrong. In the meantime, it is obvious that my presence is needed here to maintain control. The soldiers will not dare disobey *my* command as they did *yours*." He scowled at Masabala.

You are afraid, Masabala thought. *You know that and now so do I.*

* * *

Masabala and Eleazar walked into the tunnel side by side. Ten paces in, the bells on the *Kohen Gadol's* skirt ceased their tinkling, and the passageway filled with light. Eleazar began to pray as they moved forward. Five minutes later, they came upon the soldiers. All eight men lay dead at their feet, their eyes burned out, their skin blackened as if set afire.

Forbidden to touch a dead body, the rabbi took two steps back as he intoned the blessings for the dead. Masabala had lost count of how many men had died in his arms. He no longer considered that the Kohen rule applied to him. He knelt and laid his hand on Jonah, the youngest of the soldiers. "This makes no sense," Masabala whispered. "The Ark is fifty paces from here. These men have been felled without having ever touched it."

Masabala moved to stand. As he did, the ground undulated hurling him upwards. He threw his arms over his head to keep from crashing into the ceiling. There was no need. His body had evaporated into a wisp of smoke, his shape morphing into the diamond-sliced light that reflected off every surface. He was a beam of light, with no past, present or future. He just was.

The *Kohen Gadol* felt a sudden whoosh as the weight of his body evaporated. Like a puff of smoke, he drifted on a breeze floating higher and higher. He soared amidst the souls from a hundred generations. Their wisdom became his knowledge. He heard their songs and rejoiced in experiencing the exaltations of triumph. Like a rainbow sweeping across the heavens, Eleazar was immersed in the color of love. For only an instant, a beat of the heart, the *Kohen Gadol* transcended into communion with God, the creator of all things. It was a moment in time that would change him forever.

Lightning flashed and thunder roared, pulling Masabala and Eleazar back to the present. Dazed to be standing next to each other on holy ground before the gap in the wall, the two men began to pray.

It was time to seal off the Ark from view. Eleazar touched his son's hand passing the message without uttering a sound.

Masabala picked up a stone and held it against his chest before gently placing the rock into the hole in the wall. The light, radiating from behind the barrier, diminished slightly. He picked up another rock and another until the breach was sealed shut. When the Temple was completed, they would return and escort the Ark of the Covenant to its rightful place within the Holy of Holies.

*   *   *

Masabala and Eleazar shielded their eyes from the blinding mid-morning light as they stepped from the tunnel. Masabala's head ached, and he was so thirsty he could hardly swallow.

The Kohen Gadol lifted his head high, his soul in a state of inexplicable celebration. He had transcended to a sacred place and touched the illusions. There was no separation, no past and no future. All were part of the One.

Sarah and Miriam stood amidst the crowd in the shadows not far from the entrance. They had been at the site since dawn when they were awakened by a neighbor who told them that the Ark had been found.

"They are coming out!" Sarah cried upon seeing her husband. She took a step forward and stopped when her mother-in-law put a firm hand on her arm.

Miriam shook her head from side to side. "No child. We must wait here."

"But—"

"You are the daughter-in-law of the Kohen Gadol. I know you did not ask for that responsibility. Neither did I. But it is our lot in life, and we must act appropriately. We *will* wait here."

Sarah did not like restrictions and rules but as she shifted to her left for a better look at her husband and her father-in-law, she gasped. Eleazar, a man she had known her entire life, had been transformed. Everything about him, from the look in his eyes to the way he held his head seemed holy.

Miriam moved beside Sarah. "Look at him. My Eleazar is the High Priest of Israel," Miriam whispered, reaching for Sarah's hand.

Eleazar moved with determined purpose towards Bar Kokhba. He placed his palms together and bowed his respect to the nasi. "The wall has been sealed. Unfortunately, the laws of the Holy One, Blessed be He were disobeyed, and good men have died as a result," the Kohen Gadol said, his face drawn in grief.

Bar Kokhba hunched his shoulders forward and inhaled deeply. He saw the deaths as an ominous warning that he too would be smitten if he approached the Ark. Bar Kokhba shrugged the thought aside and rose to his full height. "I need volunteers to go inside and remove our dead," he shouted.

His request was met with trepidation and defiance. No man lifted a hand.

"There is no further danger!" Masabala shouted, his voice carrying to the outer ridge of the crowd.

"You have nothing to fear," the Kohen Gadol called. "My son and I will accompany you inside.

Slowly men began to come forward, most of them friends of the deceased. It was a long and very sad few hours as the bodies were removed.

* * *

When the last man was shrouded and removed, the crowd began to disperse.

Sarah and Miriam approached their husbands. Shyly, Sarah slipped her hand into Masabala's and squeezed hard. She did not speak, sensing that while he needed her presence, he was grieving for his men and needed solitude.

Miriam faced her husband and took his trembling hands in hers. This was the man who had shared her life, and yet looking at him now, he seemed a stranger. She could see him and touch him, but he was somehow beyond her reach.

Rabbi Eleazar stumbled, so exhausted he could barely walk. Miriam whispered something in his ear as she took his arm. Sarah held the old man's other arm. Masabala followed behind as they slowly headed for home.

"I cannot take another step," Eleazar said, after they had climbed the steep uneven stairway leading from the excavation. He moved from the path. "Assist me with these," the rabbi said, tugging at the breastplate that hung heavily around his neck.

Miriam helped him remove the layers of clothing and ornaments. Once he was down to just his tunic, he sat on the ground and leaned against the trunk of an ancient olive tree. Miriam sat beside him, and together they folded each piece of clothing and stacked the precious symbols.

Masabala and Sarah sat opposite his parents. They remained silent waiting for the Kohen Gadol to speak.

After what seemed an interminable length of time, the rabbi cleared his voice. Enunciating each word very slowly like a tailor sewing each stitch he said, "I have been searching for a way to express what happened to me in the presence of the Ark. I find that it is impossible to describe that which is indescribable. There are no words." He sighed, tenderly taking Miriam's hand.

Masabala leaned forward, desperate to know what his father had seen. He squeezed his eyes shut, blocking out everything as he focused on his father's thoughts. At first there was a flash of light, then a triangulated vortex of sounds and images. Then, there was nothing. Certain that his father was shielded from attempts to part the curtain of his mind, Masabala turned his thoughts towards Sarah and his mother. Nothing came. His gift of insight was gone.

Downcast that he no longer had his extraordinary gift, Masabala felt empty, a vessel spilled of its contents. Then he began to think of all that had happened over the last hours. God had touched him. He had traveled beyond himself. Masabala let a tiny smile play upon his lips. In truth, he did not want to know what others thought or to see beyond the present.

The *Kohen Gadol* placed his hand over his heart. The glint in his father's eye told Masabala his thoughts had just been read.

Sarah gazed at her husband. "You were in the presence of the Ark twice. What can you tell us?'

Masabala started to speak, and then he decided against it. What would he say? Could he tell them about the unspeakable future that awaited them? Could he disavow Bar Kokhba as the messiah?

Not now. Not yet. Perhaps, not ever.

Chapter 28

It was springtime in Rome. Every home had a flower box and every yard its garden, no matter how poor the inhabitants. Peach irises, yellow poppies, red rhododendron and blue campanulas scented the air like the perfume of gods, their colors painting the landscape with joy. Bougainvilleas encircled their prickly arms around fences and walls, their vibrant flowers turning the dullest home into a treasured villa. It was the time marriages were celebrated; the dates chosen with care to avoid the demonic omens of displeased gods.

Arria sat at the dressing table in her room as two servants twisted her ebony tresses into curls and weaved rose petals into her hair. It was her wedding day.

She looked around the bedroom. Her eyes lingered on the crack in the wall where she had heaved a brass pitcher in a fit of anger. *I can't be doing that anymore.* She ran her hand over the arm of the chair remembering how many times she had moved the chair in front of the window to daydream about her future.

Arria had spent her life surrounded by the unconditional love of her father, a man who understood her curiosity and need for independence. She always knew that the day would come when she would find a husband and leave the protection of her home; she just never imagined it would be so difficult.

Livel's homely face flashed in Arria's mind. They had spent every afternoon ministering to the sick in the Jewish section of Rome. Being a physician was the fulfillment of a life-long dream for Arria, however fleeting it might be. During that time, she and Livel had become friends. Arria massaged the back of her neck in contemplation, grudgingly admitting to herself that Livel knew her better than Domitius ever would. Yet ever since the date for the wedding had been announced, Livel had barely spoken to her. She found his silence confusing and hurtful.

"Leave me now," she ordered her servants, when the last wisp of hair was pinned into place. Once alone, she disrobed. Standing before her mirror, Arria admired her milky-white body and firm full breasts. She turned to the side and ran her hands along the gentle slopes of her hips.

Arria could not help but wonder if the doubt she felt about her marriage to Domitius was reflected in her emerald eyes. She moved closer to the mirror satisfied that even she could not discern the apprehension she felt.

Her father's pending departure as Emperor Hadrian's personal physician had forced the wedding date to be moved ahead. With little time to prepare, Arria found herself overwhelmed with decisions. She spent countless hours going through all her things, trying to decide what to take with her to the Gracchus villa and what to leave behind. In the end, she decided to take it all: clothing, parchments, jewels and even toys she had played with as a small child.

Arria pulled the white linen tunic over her head and slipped on the white silk stola with its embroidered hem. Staring at the veil she would wear as a bride, Arria allowed her thoughts to meander over the past ten days. She had been forced to spend time with her future mother-in-law, Athena, and scowled at the mere thought of the woman as bits of conversations came flashing back.

Athena had insisted that Arria accompany her daily to the public baths. The baths Athena frequented were bastions of luxury. There were vaulted ceilings, marble columns, walls and floors covered in vibrant colored mosaic tiles, marble benches and baths with silver faucets.

"This is how young women from refined homes spend their mornings," Athena had said one day as they moved into the changing room.

Arria detested the public baths. She was totally uninterested in the gossip and silly chatter of women who had nothing better to do. She much preferred to bathe at home in solitude and privacy.

Every day was the same. Wrapped in sheets, Arria and Athena would move into the unctuarium, where they were rubbed down with fragrant oils. The entire time, Athena never stopped talking, smiling and sharing banalities with every over-ripe, under-loved, highbred woman within hearing distance.

Another day while moving into the steam room, Athena leaned into Arria and said, "As I am sure you know, Domitius is to be your first priority! When he is home, you must always be available for him. Your duty as a wife is to please my son in all things."

Arria felt the color rise in her cheeks. Her thoughts venomous, she wanted to shout, *I don't need you to tell me how to please your son!* Instead, she nodded and smiled.

"And when you are not serving your husband, I will expect you to make yourself available to me." Athena had put a flabby arm around Arria and kissed her cheek. "Isn't this going to be wonderful? I will finally have a daughter, and you will have the perfect mother."

My mother is dead, and you can never take her place! Arria remembered the haughty eyes and imperious grin on Athena's reed-thin lips. *Does she really expect me to be available whenever she wants me?* Arria had visions of pulling the woman's stringy black, over-coiffed hair right out of her head. She trembled at the recollection.

After the steam bath, they would spend time in the cool waters of the enormous swimming pool that could easily hold a few hundred people. Arria tried her best to remain pleasant. She glued a smile on her face and managed to hide her anger by blocking out every other word her future mother-in-law said.

Then one day, Athena brought up the responsibilities of running a home properly. Arria knew Athena would be mistress of the house, and she had no choice but to accept that. But the woman had prattled on and on about keeping the servants in line and not getting too friendly, or they would take advantage of you.

She spoke about keeping every room in the villa immaculate and filled with fresh flowers. She continued to insist beds were to be changed regularly and described how meals should be prepared and served.

"I managed my father's home for years," Arria retorted. Anger and sarcasm dripped from her tone. "And I—"

"Really, my dear! Have you ever entertained Thracian royalty? I am speaking about sophistication and elegance. So please, there is really no point in discussing your role as a hostess. It may have been adequate, but it will do little to serve you at this level of refinement."

Leaving the baths, they always passed jugglers and acrobats and stood for a while listening to the poets recite their writings. Arria took little notice. After a morning with Athena, she had only one over-riding thought in mind, imaging how wonderful it would feel to slap Athena's painted face.

Thinking back, Arria was not sure how she had maintained her composure. The only answer she could think of was most of the time, she was really too furious to speak.

Arria forced herself back to the present. She pointed a finger at the mirror. *Enough! You are not marrying Athena. You are marrying Domitius.*

Arria checked herself in the mirror one last time. She placed a wreath of flowers on her head and gathered the flame colored veil draping it over her arm. Moving from her room, she softly closed the door.

She walked down the staircase and made her way through the house. Servants were everywhere, arranging flowers, washing floors, dusting windows, lighting lamps and placing trays for the feast that would follow the ceremony.

Out in the garden, the morning sun tinted the sky pink, and the trees rustled in the breaking breeze. Arria stood beside a statue to the god Jupiter listening for the first signs of her father's arrival. She heard the clattering of wheels on the driveway and knew that he had come. Her first thought was to run to the front door to greet him. But on this day, even Arria Galen had to follow the rules of decorum.

Arria heard doors slam shut and the familiar voices of their servants as they greeted Doctor Galen. A few moments later, he appeared. Dressed in his finest white wool tunic, Claudius Galen strode to his daughter's side and kissed her offered cheek.

"This is a portentous day for my little girl," Galen said, studying her with tender eyes. "If only your mother had lived to see this." He swallowed hard.

"I have had you, Father. It was enough," Aria said, tears pooling in her eyes.

Galen opened his hand to present Arria with a white linen belt interspersed with golden threads. With trembling hands, he encircled Arria's waist with the belt and tied the knot firmly. "I perform this rite of passage to symbolize the *knot of Hercules*," his voice broke as he said, "our guardian of wedded life. The only one who can untie this knot will be your husband."

Arria caressed the sacred knot with tremulous hands. "I'm so scared," she wept, snuggling into her father's arms.

Galen hugged Arria, fighting back his own tears.

Composing herself with great effort, Arria pulled away and stared at her father. "How do you know if you really love some-one?" *I mean really love them!*

Galen tugged at his beard. "Love is an enigma. It wears many masks. With the blessings of the gods, you will have a husband who will walk through life with you." Galen paused and stared into the distance. He shrugged. "I am a scientist. What do I know? I loved your mother. I love you. That is all I have to say on the matter."

* * *

Pink, white and yellow roses were tied to a dozen trellises that hung in the Atrium of Galen Manor. Scattered throughout the newly planted gardens were tables laden with bowls of the ripest berries, grapes and melons. There were roasted hens, plates of chickpeas, cucumbers, stuffed olives and bread seasoned with coriander.

Arria looked tiny standing beside Domitius. He was dressed in a wool toga that was draped over one arm leaving the other arm free. He wore a flowered wreath on his head, and gold chains hung from Domitius' neck. Regal in appearance and stature, he smiled at Arria, his handsome face punctuated by jade colored eyes that seemed more threatening than loving. Arria winced, and for an instant, she contemplated fleeing.

Then Arria glanced at her father positioned to her left. Seeing the joy and contentment on his face put an immediate end to the notion of running away. She could never shame or disappoint him in such a manner.

She shifted her gaze toward Livel standing on the other side of her father. He stared back at Arria, his expression sad and withdrawn.

Try as he might, Livel could not understand how Arria would willingly agree to such a doomed union. He dug his nails into his palms. Watching Arria marry Domitius was Livel's worst nightmare, tantamount to Arria plunging off a cliff to her death. He could not help thinking he should not have come.

Sensing Livel's dark mood, Arria gave him her most radiant smile. Livel was immediately beguiled by Arria's attention, and despite himself, he smiled back.

Domitius watched the exchange between Arria and Livel, and his jaw clenched. Livel had single-handedly done his best to undermine Domitius' opportunity to become consul. In secret, he had taught Scipio Aramaic and Hebrew, and then Livel had gone to his father, Marcus Gracchus, with the information. That Arria would dare even look at his most hated enemy made Domitius furious. He decided in that moment that after today, he would make sure that Arria never set eyes on Livel again.

Scipio was positioned to Marcus Gracchus' left. He too saw the look that passed between Livel and Arria, noting the black glare of jealousy that shot from Domitius' eyes. Scipio detested his half-brother, so he felt gratification in watching his obvious discomfort. But the pleasure was fleeting, resentment burning through Scipio's veins as surely as if he had been injected with boiling oil. Arria should have been his prize; he was the more worthy brother.

Marcus Gracchus stood beside his wife, Athena. They smiled, confident that their son had chosen well.

As was the rule of law in Rome, there were ten witnesses present. The family consisted of five and five were invited guests, friends of Doctor Galen. Presiding over the ceremony were two dignitaries and a priest.

A hand servant placed red scarves over Domitius and Aria's heads veiling them both.

Arria chanted the words, "*Quando tu Gaius, ego Gaia,* when-and where-you are Gaius, I then-and there-am Gaia." The ritual words were rooted in the Roman belief that Gaius was a name favored by the gods.

Domitius repeated the libretto with a powerful voice, proclaiming to all present that he was taking Arria as his wife. Domitius and Arria walked hand in hand to a carved marble altar. On top of the pedestal was a silver tray that held two lamps and a salted spelt cake known as *far.*

Holding hands, the bride and groom sat on sheepskin-upholstered stools before the sacred altar. The priest lit the lamps. With practiced solemnity, he made an offering of the *far* to Jupiter, the deity of good faith in all alliances.

The veils were removed, and the cleric offered the cake to Arria and Domitius. It was believed that the potency of the god Jupiter dwelt in the *far,* and by tasting the sanctified cake; the couple would assimilate the power of the god. After tasting the sacred loaf, the couple stood.

"Do you take this man, Domitius Gracchus as your husband?" the cleric asked. It was the final ritual; the bride was required to consent to the nuptials.

"Yes," Arria replied, her voice a trembled whisper.

The priest crumbled the loaf and sprinkled the crumbs over the bride and groom's heads, invoking the prayers for fertility and abundance.

Facing one another, Domitius kissed Arria. It was the symbolic end to the ceremony; representing the beginning of their lives as husband and wife. Arria leaned heavily on Domitius as they moved toward their family, her hands icy and her legs unsteady. Putting his arm around Arria, Domitius read the behavior as a bride's nervous reaction to the excitement of the day.

They were met with shouts of congratulations and applause. Arria caught site of Livel as she moved past. He alone among the guests was not smiling; a bad omen that would displease the gods. Livel's impropriety infuriated and empowered Arria. She took a slow deep breath, gathering her resolve. Domitius was a good man. The marriage was not a mistake. She would not let it be a mistake.

Chapter 29

Four months later

Arria was in the stables preparing to mount her favorite horse, a white palfrey. She always rode early in the day because her mother-in-law was horrified someone might see her partaking in such an unladylike activity. Arria wondered what the witch would say if she ever found out what else her daughter-in-law had been up to.

Over the past months, Arria had spent days following Athena around the villa, ashamed of the mean-spirited woman berating the slaves over the most minor infractions. Worse still, Athena showed no compassion; forcing sick slaves to work and leaving injured slaves untreated.

Arria had tried to speak with Domitius about the mistreatment, offering to help the wounded and sick.

"What could you possibly know about treating the sick?" Domitius had said laughing. "It is the profession of men."

Arria had never told Domitius about her training, and while she knew it was a secret worth keeping, she could not stop thinking about the suffering that was going on around her.

"I grew up in my father's classroom," Arria had said, relieved to be claiming her past. "I am an accomplished physician and surgeon."

Arria could still see the incredulous look on Domitius' face. At first he said nothing, and Arria thought he was simply disseminating her words. It was not until Domitius balled his hands into a fist and slammed them on the table in their sitting room, that Arria realized how angry he was.

"This is unheard of! I forbid you to interfere!"

"Why not?" Is it better to leave these poor defenseless people to suffer?" Arria said. But Domitius' face was set, his attitude unmoved by her pleadings.

They had continued to argue, but in the end, Arria pretended to acquiesce assuring her husband that she would obey his wishes.

The very next day, Arria began ministering aid in secret to the sick and injured slaves.

A servant suddenly charged into the stables, running to her side. "There's been a terrible accident in the kitchen. Please, we need your help."

"Get my bag," she said to her groom. "And make sure no one sees you."

"What happened?" Arria asked as she ran with the slave toward the kitchen.

"The boiling water, it spilled on Nonus! She is in a bad way!" the slave replied.

* * *

Arria knelt beside the injured child. Only twelve years old, the young girl had lost her grip on the boiling caldron. The liquid spilled scalding the skin on her legs, arms and hands. She lay whimpering in agony. The minutes it took for her medical supplies to arrive seemed like an eternity to Arria.

Compared to broken arms, cuts that needed stitching and fevers, this was the most disastrous situation Arria had yet to face. Horrified and wishing her father or Livel were here to help, Arria mixed the herbs that would ease Nonus into unconsciousness. She administered the medicine and sighed in relief when the girl's eyes finally closed.

Arria applied salve to the blood-raw skin. With the help of the head cook, she wrapped the legs and arms in bandages. In her heart, Arria knew the ministering was futile. The girl would either die of infection or spend the rest of her life disfigured and crippled.

The door banged open. Arria was too intent in her work to care who may have entered. It was not until she heard a familiar booming shout "What goes on here?" that she bothered to glance up.

"What do you think you're doing?" Domitius shouted. His face was purple with rage as he grabbed Arria by the arm and yanked her to her feet.

"Trying to save this girl!" Arria defiantly shouted back as she twisted to break his grip on her arm.

"Are you mad?" Domitius' eyes were dark pools of fury. "I warned you about this!" He shoved Arria roughly away. She stumbled landing on her behind with a cry.

The cook ran to help Arria. Domitius kicked the old woman and sent her sprawling.

"This slave is damaged and beyond repair," Domitius pronounced, sliding his dagger from its sheath.

"No!" Arria howled, her brain refusing to comprehend what her eyes were seeing. She jumped to her feet, but it was too late.

Cavalier as a butcher slaughtering a cow, Domitius leaned over and ran the blade across the unconscious child's throat.

* * *

Arria groaned as she opened her eyes. She was lying in her room on a feather-stuffed mattress that sat on top of a crisscrossed frame of leather straps. She squinted toward the glass- paned windows that overlooked the courtyard. The light hurt her eyes. Shifting away, she momentarily lost herself in the mural of a maiden walking in a garden, leading a small child by the hand. She glanced at the frescoed ceiling where nymphs and flying horses pranced.

The first word that formed in Arria's mind was innocence. She could almost taste the word dissolving. Her husband had murdered an innocent child. The realization struck Arria as if a part of her had died as well.

How could I be so stupid? How could I not know he was such a monster? She heard Domitius moving about in his bedroom next door. Arria leapt from the bed, retrieving the scalpel she kept hidden in a chest.

Seconds later, Domitius swaggered into the room. "Your behavior yesterday was abominable."

"My behavior was abominable? You murdered a defenseless little girl!" Arria shrieked.

"Whose life was no longer of value," Domitius replied, as nonchalant as if he were discussing the weather.

Arria grasped the handle of the scalpel hidden in her tunic. She could not help but imagine how easy it would be to gut Domitius and end his life.

"Had you not interfered, that child might still be alive. I hope you learned your lesson."

"You dare blame me?" Arria glared. There was no point in continuing the argument. She could not win, and it no longer mattered. Domitius was dead to her now.

He moved closer. His stance warrior-like, he pointed a finger in Arria's face. "Do not disobey me again, or you will live to regret it!"

"The only thing I regret is that I married you in the first place. Now get out and leave me alone!" Arria hissed.

"So sad you have still not learned your lesson." Domitius sneered at Arria. "But you will, my love. You will."

* * *

Livel paced back and forth in the hallway near the front door. Doctor Galen had arrived earlier in the day, and Arria was due any moment. Livel could barely think. He knew that memory and infatuation can make things bigger and better than they are. But he also knew that would not be the case with Arria.

"There you are," Doctor Galen said, blocking Livel's path. "Let's go into the classroom. This old man needs a few moments to reminisce."

When they entered the room, both Livel and the doctor were bombarded by memories. Livel pulled out his old stool from the corner and dragged it to the front of the room. He perched there just as he had done when Doctor Galen was instructing the class. Silence prevailed, melancholy settling over them like a mantle.

Galen unrolled a parchment on the table and ran his fingers over the words. "It has been too long since I've been home. I can assure you, it has not been from the lack of trying. Every time I made a plan to visit, Hadrian came up with some new and mysterious ailment that prevented me from coming. The only reason I am here today is the emperor is obligated to appear before the senate prior to our departure. And our departure in imminent," Galen said, fidgeting with the parchment.

"I'm sorry to hear that," Livel said, greatly saddened his mentor would be leaving Rome.

"When I was appointed Hadrian's personal physician," Galen continued, "I feared becoming indentured. And that is exactly what has happened. I cannot scratch my nose without permission!"

"What of your work?" Livel asked. "The emperor must know how important it is."

"That's the only good news I have. Permission has been granted for me to start writing again. Of course, I don't have my illustrator or my able assistant to help me."

That comment said, the door flew open and Arria entered. Accompanied by her slave, she had left the Gracchus villa without permission. Disheveled, her clothing wrinkled, her eyes red and swollen, Arria ran into her father's arms. The moment they embraced, she started to sob.

"What is it child? What's wrong?" the doctor asked. "Has something happened?'

During the carriage ride over, Arria had practiced exactly what she would say. She had intended to tell her father how Domitius had murdered the child and how he had threatened her. She would reclaim her wedding dowry, divorce Domitius and move back home. She had to do it before she found herself pregnant. Roman law recognized the father's rights to all children in a divorce, and Arria would never leave her child. But now that she was faced with admitting her marriage was a failure, Arria found she could not do it. At least not yet.

Fighting to compose herself, Arria finally managed to say. "I'm just happy to see you." She caught Livel's eye over her father's shoulder. His look was so intent and the concern so real, she was certain he understood her plight.

The doctor took Arria's arm, studying her not as a father, but as a physician. She was pale, tense and much too thin. Galen wanted to believe her fragile state was the result of adjusting to a new life, but he knew his daughter too well. Something more was going on. He tenderly touched her face and kissed her cheek.

The doctor decided this was not the time to pry. Tonight, they would enjoy their reunion. In a few days, he would speak with her. If he was right and Arria was unhappy, then together they would find a suitable resolution before he had to leave.

* * *

Arria sat beside Livel on a bench in the atrium. The last time she had been here was on the day of her wedding. She shuddered. The sun was beginning to set, and Arria knew she would have to leave soon.

"How is Uncle Joshua?" she asked, deciding that was the best way to open the conversation.

"Doctor Matthia is strong in spirit, but I'm afraid he is failing," Livel said, breathing in Arria's scent, her nearness making him feel light-headed.

"I've been thinking about joining you in the Jewish quarter again," Arria said without preamble, intent on getting her point across quickly.

Livel's eyes grew incredulous. "That's impossible. It's much too dangerous. Everyday there are more and more soldiers roaming the streets. I have no idea what your husband would say, but I can assure you that your father would never approve."

"No one needs to know. It can be our secret," she said, her smile alluring.

"I can't do that!" Livel said, refusing to be enticed by her charm.

"You can't or you won't?" Arria challenged. "I intend to start seeing patients again. Now, the only question that remains is whether I do this with you or without you?"

"Why would you risk everything? What's going on? Is it Domitius?" Livel asked, conjuring up a hundred sordid scenarios all of them making him wince.

Arria shook her head. "I just can't continue to live the way I've been living. My life has to have meaning. I am a doctor, a healer. It is what I do. It is what I have to do." Tears filled her eyes. "Please, don't question me anymore. I just need you to be my friend."

Arria's anguish overwhelmed Livel. He had seen her crying in fits of temper, and those tears had angered him. This was different. He could feel and see her desperation. "I am your friend," he said, patting her hand. "I only hope we won't both be sorry for that friendship." He blinked several times before saying; "I go to the quarter each day at daybreak."

"I will meet you at Uncle Joshua's," Arria said.

* * *

It was still dark the following morning when Arria's slave saddled the white palfrey. Dressed as a man wearing pants and a dark cloak to hide her face and hair, she rode through the deserted streets of Rome. At sunrise, she arrived at Doctor Mattia's home in the Jewish quarter. Livel was waiting outside. He helped Arria dismount and then tied the horse up next to his in the side yard, away from prying eyes.

"I have only two hours to visit six patients. Four of them are fairly routine, sore throats, bellyaches. The last two are more complicated. One is a hand amputation and the other—"

"An amputation? Who did the surgery?" Arria asked in wonder.

Livel pointed to himself.

"By yourself?" Arria was stunned unable to imagine taking on such an onerous surgery. "Weren't you terrified?"

Livel shrugged. "I had no time to be afraid. You were not there to assist, so I had little choice but to proceed. Had I not, the man would have died. As you will see, he is still critical."

"I would have given anything to be there!" Arria said.

Livel smiled. "Despite everything I said yesterday, I want you to know, I'm happy to have you back. But, I'm also very concerned. The soldiers have been merciless attacking without regard. The amputee I told you about, his hand was the result of trying to keep his wife from being raped."

Arria pulled open her cloak. Around her waist was a sheath that held her scalpel. "I can take care of myself," she said, defiance daring Livel to question her resolve.

Livel reached over and pulled the cape closed, anxious that someone might see. It was obvious Arria thought she had a need to protect herself. What concerned Livel was her trepidation seemed to run deeper than the obvious danger of being in the Jewish quarter. Livel hoped with time she might reveal what had happened to provoke such fear.

* * *

Domitius and Scipio were dressed in woolen tunics and trousers and wore leather boots with iron hobnails in the soles. Each wore a scarf around his neck to protect him from the chain mail armor. Each carried a sword and javelin.

At dawn, the half-brothers arrived at the Coliseum to participate in war games. They were highly respected by their peers for their expertise with dagger and sword. Domitius was renowned for the length and accuracy of his throws with a javelin. Scipio was an excellent archer. Standing in formation waiting for inspection, a legion staff officer approached Domitius and Scipio.

"Come with me," he ordered.

The two men fell into line with twenty-five other soldiers. Marching in formation, the men were led to the stables where the commander of their regiment waited.

"Jewish spies have infiltrated our city," the commander spat, his voice enraged. "Previous raids have been unsuccessful, so I am now turning to my best soldiers for help. I want you to go from house to house interrogating those Jews who have been giving refuge to the spies. Use whatever means necessary. Do not disappoint me! I want heads dangling outside the senate by week's end!"

Scipio fought to keep his breathing steady. Livel had told him he was treating patients in the quarter every day. He had to get a message to him. He had to warn him!

Chapter 30

Scipio spent the morning glued to Domitius' side. The joy his half-brother displayed during the interrogations disgusted him. Torturing innocent people, who obviously knew nothing, was an abomination to Scipio.

With each house they entered, Scipio dashed from room to room hoping to find his friend Livel before Domitius found him. At the home of Mattia, the Jewish doctor, Domitius seemed even more enraged.

"You are obviously too sick and feeble to care for the sick. Who assists you, old man?" Domitius demanded, pushing the doctor against the wall, his hand around his neck.

"I work alone," the doctor said.

"I warn you. Do not lie to me!" Domitius slapped his face and then applied more pressure to his neck. "Others have told me there is another doctor that visits. Give me the bastard's name now!"

The old man's eyes began to bulge. He tore at the hands strangling him, his face purple, his mouth foaming.

"Who is he?" Domitius shouted. The doctor gasped for breath as his eyes rolled back.

"You're going to kill him," Scipio hissed, moving in to stop Domitius.

It was too late. The doctor was dead. Domitius threw him to the floor in disgust and barged from the house.

Scipio was shaken. He lifted the doctor and carried him to the couch. He closed the frozen stare in the doctor's eyes and covered the old man with a blanket. On hands and knees, he began reciting the prayers he had heard Livel say so often.

* * *

Arria and Livel had just finished with their last patient, a father of three who was unable to urinate. He was in horrendous pain and would not last the night.

"I wish there was something more to be done," Arria said, as they moved into the morning light. The quarter had come alive; the streets were crowded with peddlers, and the merchants had opened their stores.

Livel looked around, his skin prickling. His instincts told him something was not right, but he could not figure out what it was. He made eye contact with a cobbler whom he had treated. The kindly man shook his head and then looked away.

"Wait here," he said to Arria. Livel approached the cobbler. "What's going on, Jacob?"

"The solders are here searching every house. One was asking for you by name. You should go before you are caught!"

Livel ducked his head rushing back to Arria. He grabbed her arm. "It's not safe. We have to go! Keep your face covered and stay close to me."

The plan was to reach Arria's horse and get her out of the quarter. Doctor Mattia's house came into view. There were soldiers everywhere, pounding on doors, swarming like wasps. Arria and Livel stepped into an alley and crouched in a corner.

"What now?" Arria whispered, her blood racing.

"We wait." Livel opened his medical kit and removed the scalpel. Arria unsheathed hers and held it in trembling hands.

All around them were the sounds of torture: women and children screaming, the curdling shouts of denial and the heartbreaking pleas of men and women begging for mercy.

They heard a shout and the sound of heavy footsteps. Livel and Arria moved further into the shadows. Arria held the knife so tight her fingers grew numb.

"I need to take a piss," a soldier shouted, ambling into the alley. Two other soldiers followed. The men laughed and joked seemingly oblivious to Arria and Livel's presence.

Livel looked left and right hoping for any means of escape. There was nowhere to run and no place to hide.

As they turned to go, one of the soldiers leaned into his comrade and whispered. A heartbeat later, they advanced toward Arria and Livel.

"Don't say a word," Livel whispered, stepping out in front to protect Arria, doing his best to hide the limp. "I am a physician and a citizen of Rome," he called to the soldiers. "We have come to the quarter to treat the sick."

"Are you a Jew?" the tallest and meanest of the soldiers shouted spraying spittle in Livel's face.

Before he could stop her, Arria hid the knife behind her back and sidestepped Livel. "I am Arria Galen, daughter of Doctor Claudius Galen, personal physician to the emperor," she said feigning confidence. "This is my brother, Livel." Arria realized it might have been more prudent to use Domitius' name for protection, but that would not have saved Livel.

"I don't give a shit who you are! I asked this man a question, and I want an answer!" the soldier demanded holding Livel's arm in a vice-like grip.

"I am a Jew," Livel said, struggling to keep the terror from his voice. "I am also the adopted son of Doctor Galen."

"Isn't that the perfect ruse, you sniveling Jew. You hide out here under the guise of a doctor. That way, you can pass what you learn from the emperor's physician back to your traitorous brothers in Judea!"

"That is a stupid lie!" Arria hissed.

A soldier with a thick beard and rat-like eyes licked his lips. "I like a fiery woman. And this one's a beauty. Let's get rid of the Jew and give ourselves a reward!"

Everything that Livel was–doctor, soldier, son of his parents and brother–slid away as he plunged the scalpel into the neck of the solder restraining him. Before the man had even fallen to the ground, Livel lunged forward, his instincts feral, his military training excelling under the passion of his intentions. No one was going to hurt Arria. Not while there was a breath in his body.

Both soldiers reached for their swords. Attacking with no regard for his own life, Livel swept his arm in an arc. Before the soldier to his left could retrieve his weapon, Livel sliced across his throat.

The second soldier swung wildly barely missing Livel's head. Livel knew his scalpel was no match for his attacker's weapon. There was only one opportunity to save Arria and himself. He cocked his arm and with all his might, Livel threw the blade at the soldier's face. It found its mark between the fighter's eyes, and the man collapsed dead within seconds.

With the realization of what he had just done, Livel began to shake uncontrollably as he removed the scalpel from the dead soldier's forehead. He was a healer, a doctor who had taken the Hippocratic Oath to do no harm. Yet, he had just killed three men. The stain of death dripped over him. Arria fell to her knees sobbing, the carnage overwhelming her.

Livel lifted her gently. With one arm around her waist he said, "Listen to me. We can't stay here." He reached for his medical bag. "If we're found, they will kill us both."

Arria nodded, the instinct to survive coursing through her like a lightning bolt. Staying near the walls, they managed to move around a corner without being spotted and entered an open area behind an adjoining row of houses.

With hand gestures and silent steps, they wound their way into Doctor Mattia's back yard. "We need to check on Uncle Joshua," Arria whispered. "He might be hurt."

"It's too late for that," Livel replied. "We have to get out of here, and we have to do it now!"

Arria and Livel snuck into the side yard. They froze in mid-step. Standing before them, one hand on the palfrey's mane, the other hand holding a sword, was Domitius.

"Imagine my surprise when I came across my wife's horse," Domitius said sarcastically, shooting Livel a murderous look. "All along, I thought she was at home." Domitius seized Arria before she could react. He grabbed her by the hair bringing her face to within inches of his own. "Dressed like a man?" He clucked his tongue in disgust. "I warned you Arria, but you would not listen. Now, I'm going to kill this insignificant little Jew, and you are going to watch. Just so you will be prepared for what is about to happen, I have no intention of killing him quickly. In fact, I will relish watching you both suffer!"

Arria leaned into Domitius freeing her right arm. With all her might, she aimed the scalpel at his chest. The metal of the blade struck the metal chain mail of his armor. Sparks flew. Uninjured, Domitius laughed as he disarmed Arria. Holding her by the neck, he pressed the blade of Arria's scalpel into her cheek drawing blood.

Livel howled, leaping toward Domitius, his own scalpel still in hand.

"Stop!" Domitius ordered. "Or I will take out her eye!"

Livel pulled back.

"Drop it!" Domitius shouted.

Livel let the blade fall from his hands.

Arria tried to squirm free. Domitius put his lips to her ear. "Hold still my beloved, a blade is a dangerous thing in the hands of an angry man." Grasping her chin, he kissed her on the lips. "That will be the last kiss any man will ever want to give you." With careful calculation, he ran the tip of the blade down Arria's face, beginning at her ear and ending at the corner of her mouth. "Now you will never forget me or this day," he said softly, as the blood gushed from the wound. Arria screamed, dropping to her knees.

Livel was overcome by rage. Ducking his head, he plowed into Domitius. The ensuing struggle culminated with Domitius kneeing Livel in the stomach, knocking the wind out of him. An uppercut to Livel's jaw landed him on his back. Domitius pinned Livel to the ground with his foot. "Perhaps I should cut off your hands before I kill you?" he said, lifting his sword.

Blinded by fear, Livel recited the *Shema*, proclaiming his belief in one God as he waited to die.

Scipio had been searching for Domitius when he recognized his voice amidst the screams. He ran to the side of the house. He could not believe his eyes. Arria's face was a bloodied pulp, and Livel was on the ground about to be impaled by his half-brother's sword.

Domitius' back was to Scipio, and with no time to contemplate his actions, Scipio snuck up behind him and smashed Domitius over the head with the handle of his sword. The thud was sickening as he crumpled to the ground, unconscious.

Livel scrambled to his feet rushing to Arria. Her eyes were glazed, and she was barely conscious. Livel held his hands to the wound applying pressure to stem the blood flow. "She's in shock. We have to get her somewhere where I can treat her!"

Scipio retrieved Livel's medical bag. Together, they lifted Arria on to the horse. Livel then mounted behind her, Arria's head lolling against his chest. Scipio tied the medical supplies to the saddle.

"Go to the waterfront. There's an inn on the northeast corner near the bakery. The owner's name is Faustus. He's a friend of mine. Wait for me there, and make sure no one sees you. I'll bring Doctor Galen with me." Scipio swatted the horse's rear.

* * *

Doctor Galen and Scipio entered the inn through the back door. It was late afternoon, and there were few people about.

"I have given them my room," Faustus said, greeting Scipio with a smack on the back. "And I have hidden the horse. But I'm afraid the lady is in a bad way."

They climbed a half-rotted staircase. The stink of fish was overwhelming.

"Sorry," Scipio said. "It was the best I could think of on short notice. At least they are safe for now, but I don't know how long. "

The innkeeper unlocked the door and then stepped aside. The room reeked of stale food and dampness. Arria was asleep, lying on a tattered, stained mattress. Livel greeted Scipio and the doctor with a sullen nod.

"I have to go back before I'm missed," Scipio said. He was gone before Livel had the opportunity to thank him for saving his life.

Galen stood in the doorway, his heart pounding and his legs threatening to give way. Tears blinded his eyes. Galen never prayed, but he prayed to the gods now as he fell to his knees beside Arria. With gentle hands, he forced himself to examine the wound. It was not life threatening; she would recover.

Arria's eyes shot open. "What happened?" she mumbled, her wounds making it too painful to speak.

"You've been injured," her father said. "It's nothing that Livel and I can't fix."

"This will help with the pain," Livel said. He had mixed water, poppy juice, a pinch of henbane and hemlock into a cup. He dripped the medicine into Arria's mouth.

Once she had fallen asleep, Doctor Galen and Livel worked in unison stitching Arria's torn face back together. Neither man spoke for fear of breaking down, for even with their combined talent as surgeons, the right side of Arria's face would be forever disfigured.

* * *

Scipio returned to the inn around midnight. He called Livel and the doctor into the hallway. "Domitius has reported Livel to our superiors," Scipio said, frantically. "He is claiming that you not only murdered three soldiers, but you kidnapped Arria. The city is crawling with soldiers looking for you. You can't stay here. It's too dangerous."

"Scipio, you will come with me." Galen glanced back into the room where his daughter slept soundly. Lifting his chin with resolve, the doctor said to Livel, "We will be back soon. In the mean time, if Arria awakens, try and get her to drink something."

Arria awakened an hour later. Livel offered her water, but she brushed his hand aside. "How bad is it?" She asked, moving to touch her face.

Livel cupped her hands in his. "You are still beautiful," he said, absolute in his belief that Arria was still the loveliest woman alive.

* * *

Hours before sunrise, Livel and Galen rode together inside a carriage borrowed from the innkeeper. Arria lay on the doctor's lap, her face and eyes so swollen she appeared a grotesque caricature of herself. To deal with the emotional trauma and pain, she was medicated every few hours.

Scipio sat at the reins managing to circumvent all the main streets. He arrived at the front of a boarded-up house five blocks from the waterfront. The doctor knocked. A huge black man opened the door. Bolo was Galen's most trusted servant, and he had practically raised Arria. When Doctor Galen told him what had happened, Bolo did what needed to be done. With determined steps, the slave moved to the carriage and lifted Arria, carrying her as he had when she was a baby.

Arria opened one eye, wrapped her arms around Bolo and fell back to sleep.

His face contorted in sorrow, Bolo placed Arria on a bed of blankets in a corner of the main room that he had swept clean for her arrival. Galen covered her with a sheepskin. It was dank and cold, and every little while, rats the size of kittens scurried up a wall.

Livel sat on a rickety chair that threatened to tip over if he did not balance perfectly. He stared at the pots and pans, mattresses and bedding, salted meats, breads and grains piled in the center of the room.

Scipio whispered something to the doctor and then left.

Doctor Galen lay down beside his daughter. He inhaled, taking in her fragrance, a memory to be held as one holds a precious gem. There was no choice. He had to let her go. Yet Galen could not help but think it was his fault. If he had never exposed Arria to the practice of medicine, she would not be in this horrible situation; attacked by her own husband and now forced to run for her life. Galen caressed her swollen face with his fingertips. Arria sighed and shifted toward him, opening her tear-filled eyes. She murmured the word *daddy* and then drifted back into a drug-induced slumber. Galen held Arria in the crook of his arm. He fell asleep with his face nestled in her hair.

Bolo prepared a bed for Livel, but sleep would not come to him. He kept envisioning the dead men. Livel knew there had been no other choice; it was the only way to save Arria and himself. Still, he could not reconcile how he, the son of a rabbi, had become a murderer. Certain that escape from Domitius was impossible, he saw himself dangling from the gallows.

* * *

Scipio returned a few hours before dawn, his expression triumphant. "The gods were with us. Just as you said Galen, a ship was in port that is captained by a friend of yours. He was more than willing to take on three more passengers, for the right price. It's all been arranged. The ship sails for Alexandria tomorrow morning!"

Boat, Alexandria, after dark, they–the words danced in Livel's head. He had never imagined even for a moment that such a miracle was possible. He was going home, and Arria Galen was going with him.

Chapter 31

Scipio arrived home an hour after sunrise. In his possession was a dispatch from Doctor Galen to Marcus Gracchus. The doctor had suggested that a servant deliver the letter, but Scipio had refused, adamant that he become the messenger. Domitius had almost killed Livel, and he had maimed his own wife. It was time to expose the heinous actions of his half-brother.

Scipio managed to enter the house unseen. He found his father in his office still in his nightclothes, his hair not yet combed.

Marcus Gracchus looked up from his writings and scowled. "Where have you been all night? Do you have any idea what has happened to your brother and Arria?" he yelled, sucking in his cheeks and narrowing his eyes.

Scipio paced in front of his father's desk. Despite himself, he was trembling. He handed him the letter.

Marcus Gracchus held it up to the light before opening it. As his father read the letter, Scipio watched his expression move from incredulous to furious. He threw the letter down on the desk and smashed it with his fist. "This is outrageous! All lies! Domitius never injured Arria or threatened Livel!"

"Not lies, but the truth," Scipio said, his head pounding.

Marcus hunched forward half out of the chair, his eyes wild. "Why was this letter in your possession? I want answers, and I want them now."

Scipio grasped his hands to keep them from shaking. Marcus Gracchus' eyes shifted toward the doorway. Scipio turned.

"I too am anxious to hear what you have to say," Domitius hissed. His head was bandaged and his eyes glassy as he crossed the room, a panther in pursuit of its prey. He loomed over Scipio, bloodlust oozing.

"Sit down!" Marcus ordered, sneering at both his sons.

Domitius moved to within inches of Scipio's face, so close Scipio could smell his wine-soaked breath. He grabbed the front of Scipio's tunic. "Admit it! You attacked me!"

"I did, and I would do it again!" Scipio was enraged. He shoved Domitius away. "I had to stop you. You would have killed Livel! And what about your wife? Should I describe how you sliced her face open with a scalpel?"

Domitius threw himself against Scipio wrestling him to the ground. Howling, the veins in his face popping, he grabbed Scipio by the neck strangling him. His eyes that of a madman, he screamed, "She is my wife! My wife! What I do is none of your business!"

Marcus flew from behind his desk grabbing Domitius by the shoulders. "Desist now!" he shouted. "Now!"

Domitius let go kicking Scipio as he stood.

"You bastard," Scipio sneered, rubbing his neck as he rose.

Marcus pounded the desk. "Silence both of you!" He held the letter up to Domitius like a hangman holds a noose. "Claudius Galen is demanding dissolution of marriage and the return of his daughter's dowry."

"Never," Domitius shouted. "There will be no divorce!"

"Do you have any idea what you have done?" Marcus asked, his look one of anger and disgust. "Claudius Galen is the private physician to the emperor of Rome. The emperor!" he repeated again for emphasis. "You attacked Galen's daughter and his adopted son. One word from him to the emperor, and you are a dead man!"

"There is no proof. It would be the word of the Jew against the son of Marcus Gracchus."

"You fool," Marcus spat. "If Galen brings charges against you, you will hang."

"And if they want testimony, they would have mine," Scipio said, hate oozing.

Domitius seethed with rage and took a step toward Scipio.

Marcus held up his hand. "Enough!"

Scipio could see the fire burning in Domitius. There was no question; there would be long-term consequences for taking a stand against Domitius. They had spent their lives in daily competition to win their father's approval. But today, Scipio changed the rules exposing Domitius for the reckless fool that he was. There would be no turning back. When in combat, they would not be allies. He would have to watch his back. Domitius would take the first opportunity to kill him.

Domitius turned brushing Scipio's arm as he passed. His face was beet red, and his fists were clenched. "This is not over," he said in a low and menacing whisper. "It will never be over."

* * *

Livel and Scipio stood a few feet from the gangplank, both men reserved, aware that their time together was drawing to an end. Livel thought back to their first meeting, how he had been so broken, lost, angry and desperate. His life had felt as though it was over. He was a slave, and his every dream had died.

He pictured Scipio with his classic Roman face, steel gray laughing eyes and black curly hair. He had seemed so self-confident. Scipio had said, "I didn't expect you to be so young. With me as a student, you will age quickly." He had poked Livel and laughed. "You have about as much chance of making me a scholar as I have making you a soldier." Livel remembered being charmed by this man who began as his master and was now his friend.

"Thank you," Livel said softly, breaking the silence. "You saved my life."

Scipio moaned. "True. But I almost got you killed as well."

They both paused. Livel could not forget that fateful day: wargames, Domitius stepping on his leg, the indescribable agony. He would limp for the rest of his life.

"Had that not happened, you would never have become a doctor," Scipio retorted, suddenly overwhelmed. Scipio had few friends, and losing his best friend was so much more difficult than he had anticipated.

Scipio offered Livel his hand. Livel looked at the outstretched hand for a few heartbeats but did not take it. Instead, he clasped his arms around Scipio and embraced him. It was a powerful hug, intense and over in seconds. When their hands dropped back to their sides, they were both speechless. They stared at the grimy water.

"I should go," Livel said, breaking the spell.

"It has been a great honor to know you," Scipio said, finding it difficult to maintain his composure.

"Perhaps we will meet again one day," Livel said, knowing that while he would not miss Rome, he would miss his friend.

"We must both pray that never happens," Scipio replied. "If it does, it will be my people against your people."

* * *

Livel held tightly to the ship's railing as the horizon softened into an indistinguishable line, and Rome disappeared. Only then did he sigh in relief. Arria stood a short distance away, burrowed into her coat like a turtle burrows into its shell. She had not uttered a word since leaving her father on the dock. Tears streamed down her anguished face, the freezing wind turning her skin raw and blotchy. Livel wanted to put an arm around her, to say something that would bring her some solace. He might have done it, if not for the warning Bolo, the servant, had given him.

"Please allow me to give you some advice," Bolo had said, pulling Livel aside as they oversaw the crewmembers carrying their mattresses, pots, pans and food aboard, more than enough to sustain them on their voyage. "I have been with Arria since just after her birth. I lived with the family in Greece, then Crete, Cyprus and Cilicia. When we finally settled in Alexandria, where her father taught at the medical school, I was the one to see to her daily needs.

"I know Arria better than anyone, other than her father. The scars on her face will be a challenge Arria will overcome. Of that,

I am certain. It is her intellect that Arria always treasured, not her beauty. But leaving her father is going to be a much more difficult task. She appears headstrong and confident, but beneath that bristled exterior is a very sensitive young woman who has always depended on her father for guidance."

Livel was struck by Bolo's intelligence and eloquence. It was certainly obvious why Galen had trusted him with Arria's care. "Your advice?" Livel asked, certain he had just heard the longest discourse of Bolo's life.

The wise old black man had smiled. "Give her a wide berth. She will come around when she is ready."

Livel tightened his grip on the railing. The seas were growing angrier by the moment, with waves cresting, curling and crashing, causing the strong wooden hull to dip and sway. He was determined not to get seasick. Not this time. There was so much to look forward to and so much to forget. The smell of seawater and the flapping of sails pushed Livel into the past. Like a waking nightmare, he could feel the darkness closing in and all reason evaporating. He could smell the lions and hear their terrifying growls. For an instant, he could feel Tillie's tiny hands dripping water into his mouth, her body curved into him as they slept. Forcing himself back to the present, he realized his entire body was trembling. He shook his head to dispel the visions. *It's behind me. I am going home a free man, a better man, a doctor.*

Livel imagined the looks on the faces of his parents and Masabala when he appeared in their home in En Gedi. With concentration, Livel could almost feel their arms embracing him. He knew so much would have changed. *Did Masabala become a soldier? What of Sarah? Did she ever get over her childhood infatuation with Masabala?*

He allowed himself a moment to reflect on what it must have been like for his family after he disappeared. He had so often thought of how devastated his parents and brother would be. But now, it was almost over, and all their lives would be made whole once again.

Rome

Domitius was inconsolable. He loved Arria, and in his deranged mind, he believed that his willingness to forgive *her* would be the first step in reconciliation. It did not even occur to him that he was at fault, or that slicing his wife's face was a loathsome deed she would never forgive. He thought himself justified, a lesson given to a wayward, misguided wife and hopefully a lesson learned. He just wanted to make things right for them, and in order to do that, he had to find Arria.

Obsessed and unable to sleep, he hid in his carriage across the street from the Galen manor. Domitius knew all he had to do was simply walk up to the door and knock, demanding to see his wife. But he also knew Doctor Galen would never allow him near his daughter. Still, if Arria were there, eventually she would have to come out. When she did, Domitius intended to be waiting.

Domitius maintained his vigil all night and the following day. As evening fell, a carriage approached with the insignia of the emperor. The front door opened, and servants began loading boxes into the coach. Domitius moved closer fearful that Arria might slip past without him seeing her. What he saw instead was Galen shaking hands with his servants, bidding them farewell before climbing into the carriage. Domitius slammed his fist into his open palm, baring his teeth like a rabid dog. Galen was returning to the emperor's service. That could only mean one thing: Arria was no longer in Rome.

Wandering the streets like an errant beggar, Domitius found his way to the waterfront. He was confident that Livel would head toward Judea. What remained uncertain was whether Arria would accompany him. He stopped seamen at every wharf, questioning them until he knew the name of every ship that had departed Rome in the previous two days.

His hands numb from the cold and his belly rumbling its hunger, Domitius headed toward the Black Lion Tavern. It was a place he frequented often for a good meal, a fair glass of wine and a woman willing to do his bidding. More importantly, it was clearly the best place to glean information about the comings and goings of men and goods on the docks.

It was mid-day when he entered, and the place was beginning to get crowded. Domitius approached the barkeep, a man with long grey hair and a beard of silver. "What can I get for you?" the barkeep asked, his enormous belly jiggling as he moved.

Domitius placed a handful of coins on the table. "Information."

The barkeep eyed the money. "I'm here to serve."

"I'm looking for a ship that took on two passengers at the last minute."

The barkeep smiled showing stained crooked teeth. "That would be the *Isis*. I heard the gubernator wrangled for a hefty price to take on a woman, a man with a limp and their slave. They say the lady is nobility." He moved to pocket the coins. Domitius slapped his hand on top of the barkeep's hand.

"Not so fast. Where is the ship headed?" Domitius demanded, his nostrils flaring.

"The *Isis* travels between here and Alexandria." Domitius lifted his hand, and the man pocketed the coins. "Anything else?"

"Food and drink," Domitius said. He moved to a couch nearest the back door, fighting his instincts. He wanted to charge from the tavern, find the next ship sailing for Alexandria and book passage. But as he was commissioned to serve in Britannia, leaving would be desertion, and desertion was punishable by death.

Domitius recalled the conversations he had with Arria about her years in Alexandria. She was overly impressed he thought, with what she referred to as the intellectual elite. As far as Domitius was concerned, the Greeks were a bunch of philosophical imbeciles, more impressed with literature than with worldly pursuits. Yet, given Arria's penchant for the Grecian way of life, he was convinced she would stay in Alexandria.

Domitius' insides vibrated. He was not a man of patience. He liked immediate satisfaction, and yet, there was nothing he could do. He imagined Arria living in a lovely villa surrounded by servants and the scrolls she loved to read. She would make a new life. Happy and secure, she would forget about him. He took a deep breath and felt himself grow hard. How sweet his revenge would be when he found her and took it all away from her.

His thoughts turned to war. *As for Livel and my brother, they are both dead men!*

Chapter 32

Scipio had only been able to secure one cabin for their journey. The room was tiny, six strides in each direction, with one bed and a wooden plank seat, all bolted to the floor.

Punctuating the air with his finger, Bolo pointed to Livel. "You can sleep here." He threw a mattress on the floor. "And you, my precious, will sleep on this nice soft bunk that I have prepared for you. As for me," Bolo said, "I will make my bed just outside the doorway, in case you need me for anything." He shot a challenging look at Livel. "Now, with your permission, I will go and prepare your midday meal."

Arria sat on the bed, her eyes lost in a vacant stare. Livel's stomach twisted in waves of nausea.

"I need fresh air. I get seasick," Livel admitted softly. "But first let me take a look at your face."

Arria glanced at him as if she had forgotten he was there. She pulled the scarf off. Her ebony hair had come loose, falling over sleepy eyes, dusting her alabaster skin. Livel tenderly tucked the strands behind her ear before palpating the swollen ridges surrounding the stitches. With a gentled touch, he applied the salve Doctor Galen had mixed.

"The swelling will be gone in a couple of days."

"Will it matter?" Arria asked, her voice dead.

Livel decided that a response would sound trite. Instead he stood, exaggerating his limp as he moved toward the door.

A small smile appeared on Arria's face, his point obviously made. He had overcome his disability and so would she.

"Come with me. " He offered his hand. "The fresh air will do us both good. Besides, if I'm in this cabin another second, I can assure you I'll be sick."

Arria donned the scarf and stood. She squared her shoulders, throwing a defiant look Livel's way. She had grown up motherless, moving from place to place, always having to bid farewell to people and places she had grown to love. She had always managed to make a new life, and she would again. Arria wiped away a tear that trickled down her face. With silent resolve, she vowed it would be the very last tear anyone would ever see her shed.

* * *

Arria held Livel's arm as they walked around the deck of the lurching ship. On the starboard side, they stepped gingerly around the hundred or so boisterous passengers: men, women and children, who would sleep in makeshift tents on the deck of the ship, until their arrival in Alexandria. Livel cringed, wondering how many might die, unable to withstand freezing nights on the open seas. A group of boys playing with flimsy wooden swords careened past, lost in the naiveté of their youthful games.

A man with a flowing white beard and a huge belly approached. His face had peaks and valleys, lines so deep his eyes all but disappeared in a crevice of weathered skin. A gold medallion, identifying him as a man of authority, dangled from his neck.

He bowed to Arria and then Livel. "Please allow me to introduce myself. My name is Lucian Caelio, *gubernator* of the Isis."

"It's a pleasure to meet you, Captain. I am Livel son of Eleazar and this is Arria Galen."

"I know, I know," the gubernator said, his frown changing to a smile as it curved into the creases of his beard. "I want to apologize in advance for the inclement weather. Under other circumstances, I am certain you would have chosen to wait until the weather changed." He gave Livel a knowing nod. "When sailing with the summer Etesian winds blowing across my bow, I have been known to make the crossing from Rome to Alexandria in ten days. Ah, but this is not the circumstances in which we find ourselves now. So our voyage will surely be longer."

"How much longer?" Level blurted.

The gubernator laughed. "Am I to assume you prefer traveling by land?"

"You would be correct in that assumption," Livel said, noting the unsympathetic glint in Arria's eyes.

"Please, do me the honor of accompanying me to my cabin, so we can speak in private."

* * *

The gubernator's cabin was three times the size of theirs, yet it seemed even more cramped. Every inch was covered in parchments, charts, old food and dirty clothes. The foul smell of sweat permeated the air.

The captain swept a pile of dirty clothing from the bench that ran across the leeward side of room. "Please," he said, motioning for them to sit. "I do not have much time. With weather like this, we are often forced to reset our course in order to keep the sails full. A moment of distraction, and the Gods can send us to the rocks." He shifted his massive body into a chair and rubbed his stubby hands together, pointing his eyes at Arria. "You don't remember me, do you?"

Arria blinked several times. "I doubt that we've ever met. If so, I certainly would remember."

He smiled, showing a mouth filled with gaps, more gum showing than teeth. "You were about four years old when I first met you, a tiny thing with the loudest wail I ever heard." The gubernator chuckled.

Arria squinted her eyes, trying to remember. *Had she ever heard his name mentioned, seen him? Maybe.* "You knew my father?"

"I was captured while sailing off the coast of Egypt and sent to Rome to become a gladiator. And a gladiator I became! A great one! The crowds loved me!" His belly jiggled with his laughter. "I was to fight just one more battle, and if I survived, I would be given my freedom." His eyes grew dark. "I took a gruesome slash to the chest, and while I made it out of the arena alive, I was all but dead.

"That was when your father appeared. He stitched me up like one would darn an old sock. We became friends. I can tell you, if not for the doctor, the Isis would be under another's command. And I would be rotting in a nameless grave. So needless to say, when your father's emissary approached me, I could do nothing less than offer my assistance. When we get to Alexandria, I will arrange for your safe passage to Judea."

"Your help is greatly appreciated," Livel said, still finding it impossible to believe he was going home.

"I have something for you," the gubernator said. Kneeling, he removed three wooden slats from the floorboard. He reached in and hefted out a wooden box. He handed it to Livel. "When you've gone through the contents, please return it to me for safe keeping. Amongst my crew are scoundrels and thieves and while they make the best sailors, you don't want to tempt them with riches or a beautiful woman."

The gubernator looked hard at Livel, swiping a hand across his beard. "Just one more thing, before you go. You introduced yourself to me as Livel, son of Eleazar. That was a critical mistake that could cost you your life!"

Livel scowled. "I am sorry to contradict you, but that is exactly who I am."

"I know who you are! I also know that the documents you carry list you as Livel Galen, the brother of Arria Galen. If you intend to arrive in Judea alive, it is imperative you use that name. If the Romans find out you are a Jew, they *will* kill you!"

It took Livel a few moments before he nodded.

"When we reach land, I intend to arrange passage for you with a trader I know and trust. The man's loyalty lies with his friends, not with the Romans or the Jews. But I must warn you, these are dangerous times–the Roman army is resupplying, and war with the Jews is imminent."

He opened the door. "Remember, return the box to me when you've gone through it."

* * *

The contents of the box lay between them on the bed. Doctor Galen had sent two of every instrument used for surgery. Livel's hands trembled as he examined each one. There were hooks of various sizes for dissecting, for raising blood vessels and for tissue excision. There were vaginal speculums for diagnosis and treatment of vaginal and uterine disorders and tile cautery. And perhaps the most important of all instruments was a scalpel used for destroying tumors.

Arria watched without speaking, trying to imagine what her father must have been feeling and thinking as he assembled these instruments, knowing that he would never see her again. To some, it would look like nothing more than a bunch of strangely shaped tools. For Arria, they represented her life. She remembered learning how to hold the tile cautery, how to make an incision with the scalpel. Each new skill had represented a milestone in her life, a memory to be treasured.

Livel gently lifted a sewn-together manuscript from the box. They were the writings of Claudius Galen. The meticulously copied pages included hundreds of essays written in Greek, each subject so discerning and detailed, anyone with a medical background could learn from them.

"Once these are translated, thousands of lives will be saved," Livel said, his tone incredulous.

Arria lifted a velvet-covered box from the chest. A letter addressed to her was attached to the top. With trembling fingers, she gently unfolded it.

To my beloved daughter:

Bidding farewell to you is like losing half of myself. And yet, I know if you are to survive, we have no other choice. I believe with all my heart this is your destiny, the path you were meant to travel. You have great strength of character and resolve. I have no doubt you can begin again, because you must! What brings me solace is knowing that I am sending you in the company of a good man.

Livel will keep you safe and protect you. Of that, I am certain. As I contemplated losing you, I realized that even in my grief, there were matters that had to be attended to. I sent Scipio to the home of his father with two demands: the dissolution of your marriage, and upon my insistence, the return of your dowry. He has complied. You are now free to marry again, and you have enough money to be always independent. If you ever find yourself back in Rome, all of my worldly goods will be here waiting for you. Be happy my child. You will forever be in my thoughts.

Your loving father.

Arria blinked several times, banishing her tears. There would be time to cry later. She slid back the tiny hook on the box. Inside were dozens of emeralds, diamonds and sapphires. She held them with both hands.

"Where we are going, you will not need riches," Livel said. "There are no villas to buy, and our women don't wear brooches."

"Fine," Arria said, dropping the gems, one at a time, into the jeweled box. She slid the hook back into place. "All I ever wanted to be was a physician." She removed the scarf. "And that is what I intend to be!"

Off the coast of Alexandria, Egypt

Seventeen days into the crossing from Rome to Egypt and ten miles out to sea, the top of the Great Lighthouse of Alexandria came into view. Considered one of the Seven Wonders of the World, it sat on the island of Pharos. It was the tallest building on earth at four hundred and fifty feet, and it took twelve years to build. A giant mirror sat at the apex of the lighthouse. During the day, the sun reflected off of it, and at night huge fires were lit in the furnace. The reflection from the fire served as navigational markings for the ships.

Livel and Arria stood amidst the excited passengers as the *Isis* made port in Alexandria, Egypt. A dory filled with weathered

sailors met the ship, their powerful backs arching as they manipu-
lated the heavy oars. With much swearing and shouting, a line was
thrown from the *Isis* and secured to the tug. The ship was towed
into the southwest basin set aside for commercial use. Taken to the
dock forecastle first, she was moored to an enormous stone ring
on the quay.

Instructed by the gubernator not to leave the ship until he
personally came for them, Livel and Arria lingered at the rail. The
gangplank was lowered, and dozens of stevedores teemed aboard
to begin unloading the cargo. Alexandria was a waterfront like no
other. On the dock, musicians played flutes, rattles, clappers and
drums. The frenetic melodies added to the chaotic reunions taking place as the exhausted passengers ran into the arms of waiting
friends and family. The faces were exotic. Indians, Arabs, Persians
and Ethiopians shouted greetings in their strange-sounding
languages.

For Arria, the sight almost took her to her knees. Her only
thought was that there would never be anyone to greet her, ever
again.

The gubernator waved as he neared, his eyes darting from side
to side as he watched his passengers disembark. "This is a wonderful city," he said, sweeping his arm toward the bustling waterfront.

His words carried Arria into an undulating current of memories. She had spent ten years in Alexandria as a young girl. Her
father had taken her to every site. She could still remember her
feelings of revelation as she explored the tomb of Alexander, the
temple of Serapis and the sanctuary of Pan.

But Arria's most cherished memories were the times she spent
at the Museum. Founded by Ptolemy, it was the most advanced
school in the world. Arria would hold her father's arm as they stood
in the cloister listening to an ambulatory lecture. On other days,
they would sit in the theater, her hand in his as they listened to
the greatest minds of their time discussing literature, mathemat-
ics, astronomy and medicine. Arria understood little of what was
being said, but it had not mattered. She was with her father, bathed
in a sea of intellectual excellence.

"There is talk of war breaking out in Judea. Perhaps you should consider remaining in Alexandria?" the captain offered, interrupting her reverie. "My wife would be happy for the company. And it would give me an opportunity to settle my debt with your father. He saved my life. I will save yours." The gubernator crossed his arms over his chest, staring at Livel. "Judea will be at war soon. She should remain here."

Livel hated the truth of the captain's words. But he was right. In good conscience, he must try and shelter Arria from the impending danger. "You would be safer here," Livel said, the words stinging his tongue.

Arria gazed into the distance, letting her scarf play into the wind as she massaged her healing wound. The offer was tempting. This was a city she knew, a people she understood. She would be immediately accepted into the aristocracy and live among the brightest minds in the world. But thanks to Domitius, there would be no suitors for a woman with a scar crawling over her face like the imprint of a serpent.

She tried to imagine what it would be like in Judea. From what she had learned, it was a completely foreign land with strange customs and stranger people. She spoke Hebrew and had practiced with Livel for hours. That would make the transition a bit easier.

Her father's letter came to mind. He wrote: *What brings me solace is knowing that I am sending you in the company of a good man. Livel will keep you safe and protect you. Of that, I am certain*

Arria studied Livel. She hated to admit it, but her father was right. Livel was a good man and a gifted surgeon. More importantly, he had protected her at the risk of his own life, not once, but twice. The first time, when he killed the soldiers in the alley, and then again when he stood against Domitius. If she remained with Livel, there was a chance she could use her skills. A country at war would not care that she was a woman.

Her decision made, Arria said, "I will follow my father's wishes. Livel is my brother, and my place is beside him."

Livel's mouth went dry. Arria Galen had just declared that she would rather be with him than stay in Egypt. He knew he should protest her decision, but instead, he remained silent.

The gubernator scowled, practically growling at Livel. He said, "If anything happens to her, I will hold you personally responsible."

Chapter 33

Bolo, Arria and Livel stood dockside with the gubernator while he negotiated with the trader, Draco. He was an ox of a man. He was missing an ear and had a scar that traversed his pockmarked face from his mutilated ear to his broken nose.

It was an entertaining few moments as the two men argued with great flourish. From the very first words, it was evident Draco had the upper hand.

"That is my price," Draco insisted. "If you have other options, take them my friend. I will not be insulted. For while it might seem a steep price to pay, we both know I will deliver them healthy and with all their limbs attached."

"I will exact my revenge," the gubernator vowed, a grin tilting his mouth. "When you bring me gold and ebony from Egypt or silver, ivory and spices from far off lands, I will cheat you, as you cheat me now! Be assured, I will regain my leverage. When you pay me in Roman coins for a wagon-full of whatever my magnificent *Isis* happens to be transporting, grain, spices or slaves, you will pay dearly."

"We will see. But does it matter?" Draco said with a smirk. "In the end, we shall both make fortunes. Now, as for all of you," he said, pointing his nose at Livel, Arria and Bolo, "I have no loyalty to any country or man. I'll trade with Roman, Egyptian or Jew. The gods bless me, but even they do not have my loyalty." Draco laughed. It was not an unpleasant sound.

Arria glanced at Livel, unable to hold back a smile as she readjusted the scarf over her face.

"I travel fast and will stop only long enough to trade and buy. You are expected to keep up, not complain and stay out of my way! As for you," he said, pointing to Arria, "my men leave Alexandria with their sexual needs satiated but a week from now, they'll begin to grumble. Two weeks from now, they'll become dangerous. So here are my rules: you do not speak to or even look at any of my men." He turned his attention toward Livel. "I will place your tent beside mine as protection, but when darkness falls, she is not to leave the tent."

"You control your men. I will take care of Arria," Livel said, his tone leaving no room for further discussion.

"I have preparations to make. I will meet you here an hour from now," Draco said, turning to leave.

"Take good care of them, or you will answer to me!" the gubernator warned.

Draco laughed. "Have I ever let you down?" he called, melting into the crowd.

"Now, I must take my leave. It has been my honor to serve the daughter of Doctor Claudius Galen." Smiling at Arria, the gubernator crossed a fisted hand over his heart. "I pray the gods keep you safe," he said, shaking Livel's hand.

Arria, Livel and Bolo stood in silence, each lost in their own thoughts. The stillness was ended when Bolo asked, "If you do not mind, I would like to have a look around?"

"Of course," Arria said, thinking that Bolo must be as excited as she was to be in Alexandria again.

"Stay close," Livel said. "We don't want to keep the trader waiting."

* * *

When Bolo returned, three men accompanied him, all the color of ebony. They were chattering in a tongue neither Arria nor Livel had ever heard.

"These are my people," Bolo said proudly, his eyes dancing.

"Where are their masters?" Arria asked, nodding to the men.

"They have no masters. They are sailors, having just arrived on a trading ship from Africa. The large ship," he pointed to his left, "over there."

Arria glanced at the ship. As she watched Bolo converse with his countrymen, a thought planted itself in her mind, tugging at her like a child tugs on its mother's skirt. She had never seen him so animated, gesturing with his hands as if they were branches of his heart. For an instant, Arria remembered the Bolo of her childhood. He had sparkling eyes that still held hope. That same look was on his face now.

"Bolo, a minute please," she said, beckoning him to follow her. As they walked, Arria linked her arm with his. "I wanted a private moment to thank you for a lifetime of loyalty," she said, her voice catching.

"It was not loyalty. It was love," Bolo replied, leaning down to kiss the top of her head. "Stop looking so sad. My life is with you. It is too late for it to be any other way."

Arria shook her head. "No Bolo. It is *not* too late."

The old slave's eyes flew wide. "I don't understand. What are you saying?"

"You are free to go home, Bolo."

The slave dropped to his knees, a wail emanating from deep within. His body shook as he wept. Arria knelt beside him. Placing her arm around his waist, she helped him to his feet. Livel moved to assist, but she waved him away.

Facing each other, Arria said, "Never kneel before anyone again." She stood on tiptoe to kiss Bolo's cheek. Arria slipped her hand into the pouch beneath her cloak where she kept the jewels her father had sent to her. "I want you to have these." Arria pressed an emerald and a diamond into Bolo's palm. "Sell them when you get to Africa, and you will never want for anything for the rest of your life."

Lost in emotion, she embraced him with her head against his chest. Always having Bolo in her life had been taken for granted. Now he would be gone; the last thread attaching Arria to the only life she had ever known. That part of her life was over.

* * *

Fifteen ruffians rode in the caravan of thirty mules and ten wagons. True to Draco's word, they moved with great purpose, beginning each day at sunrise and continuing until it was too dark to go on. They crossed northern Egypt and then followed the coastline east toward the triangular-wedged Sinai. It was a vista of craggy plateaus, broad sand-filled wadis, pointed granite peaks, scattered palm trees, white and beige sand and sapphire-shaded skies. Thus far, it had taken them twenty days.

Once in the Sinai, they came upon an encampment of Roman soldiers. Draco turned greedy-faced, his weasel eyes crinkling with his smile. "Oh, how I love a lone regiment traipsing through the desert! It is like discovering gold. Dismount and circle the mules," he yelled to his men as he rode off toward the camp.

It was almost dark when Draco returned, a triumphant look on his face. "You have brought me luck. In the morning, my donkeys will have lighter loads to carry!" he said, patting Livel on the back. "I have learned some things that will be of great interest to you. Have you heard of Julius Severus?"

"I know who he is." Livel tugged at his beard, his thoughts reeling. Had he not been freed, he would have accompanied Scipio to Britannia to serve with the commander.

"According to my new good friend, Cato the centurion, Severus will arrive in Judea within six months. He will be joined by twelve army legions from Egypt and Syria. I am sad to say this to you, but with them they bring an edict directly from Emperor Hadrian: Annihilate the Jews."

Livel began to tremble. "Just get me to En Gedi, Draco. Just get me home."

Jerusalem

Masabala awakened with a start. The dream was so real it had to be a vision. He nudged Sarah awake.

"What's wrong?" she mumbled, burrowing deeper under the covers.

"I saw him, Sarah. I saw Livel!"

Sarah opened one eye. "You had a dream, my beloved, just a dream. Go back to sleep."

"No Sarah. It was too real to be a dream," Masabala said, his voice edging near frantic.

Sarah sat up crossed-leg on the bed. Masabala stood and began to pace.

"I could see Livel's face. He is a man, different and yet the same. His shoulders are broad, and his stance seemed full of confidence. He stood at the railing of a mighty ship." Masabala closed his eyes. "He was beside a woman and while they were not touching, I know they are together. Livel is coming home!" He wrung his hands. "I must talk to my father."

"Now?"

"Now," Masabala said, reaching for his sandals.

* * *

They sat in the kitchen near the hearth. The rabbi was wrapped in a shawl, his hands folded neatly in his lap as he watched his son. Sarah hung back near the doorway. The lamps gave off a tender glow like the sun when it is setting in a powder sky.

"I had a vision. Sarah thinks it was a dream, but I don't. I saw Livel on a ship. I believe he's on his way home!"

The rabbi shifted in his chair as he beckoned Sarah with a trembling wave of his hand. She moved from the shadows and knelt beside her father-in-law.

"Do you think it could have been more than just a dream?" she asked, wanting to believe Masabala but finding it so difficult.

A tear fell from the rabbi's eye. "The LORD said to Moses, I will do the very thing you have asked because I am pleased with you, and I know you by name. If my son believes that the angels of the Holy One, Blessed be He have given him a vision, then it is so." He touched Masabala's arm.

Miriam entered the kitchen, readjusting her scarf. "What's going on?" she asked, her voice thick from sleep. "Why are you all here in the middle of the night?"

The rabbi rose and moved toward his wife. He took her in his arms. "Our son *is* coming home."

"My Livel?" she cried. "When? Where? How do you know?"

"Masabala had a dream," the rabbi said, understanding how foolish it must sound to Miriam.

"A dream! That is what you had, a dream?!" she wailed, her hand over her mouth.

"A vision given to our son by the angels of the Holy One, Blessed be He," the rabbi proclaimed.

* * *

Masabala camped near the western shore of the Dead Sea, an area he knew well. He had climbed these mountains in the smoldering heat of summers and shivered through the darkness of the nights. The desert of Judah was his friend.

All around were rock formations, shapes worn by wind and sand. He fashioned a tent by hanging a blanket over two large boulders and then tugged his stubborn mule over to a palm tree to tether it for the night. The animal carried his supplies: enough dried food and water to last a week.

The sun had set hours earlier, and the temperature dropped precipitously. Shivering, Masabala lay on a blanket wrapped in sheepskin. He could not sleep. His happiness was overshadowed by the knowledge that Livel was returning to a place and a people on the precipice of destruction. Masabala would be welcoming his brother into the arms of the Angel of Death. He had often heard his father say that God hears the laments of the tormented. If that were true, then Masabala intended to wail and pray and beg God to protect the people of Israel. Masabala believed, had to believe, that as long as there was life there was a possibility for change. He screamed, and he wept, his cries echoing in the stillness until his voice was so raw his shouts became but a whisper. Teetering on the edge of exhaustion, Masabala said a final prayer before closing his eyes.

Fighting off the need to sleep, Masabala began to ponder what it would be like meeting his brother again. Time and life experiences would have changed both of them. Yet, Masabala knew they would reconnect; they would transcend the song and silence through honesty and authenticity.

Masabala let the book of his life unfold. So much had happened; so much he could not wait to share with his brother. He had unearthed the Ark and stood amidst the wings of the Ten Commandments. He was a warrior, a digger of tunnels and a soldier who had seen too much death. He lived behind a wall of self-protection; the only way he could keep the dead eyes of a thousand men from haunting him. He had married Sarah and buried a son. Livel would understand. He would reach across time and help him extinguish the black fire that had scorched his soul.

Masabala's legs began to cramp from the cold. He stood, picked up a handful of kindling and was about to add it to the fire when he noticed sparks in the distance, like fireflies dancing on the horizon.

Livel was near.

Masabala began to pace back and forth making a path in the sand. It was impossible to estimate how far it was to Livel's camp. It could be a full day's trek. Riding alone in the desert at night was a foolish man's endeavor. Every soldier knew that. But the thought of waiting until morning seemed unbearable. He forced himself to lie down. Eventually, Masabala slid unwittingly to sleep, the kind of sleep that belies a feeling of rest and renewal.

The dawning light of morning released him from his anguished sleep. Like a somnolent child, he doused his face with water, packed his mule and headed into the desert. Masabala rode until the animal was so tired it refused to move. He dismounted, cursed the stubborn creature, gave a hard tug and began to walk, pulling the beast behind him. By day's end, Masabala could clearly see the sand kicked up from the caravan.

He tied the mule to a knurly tree and began to run. His legs ached, and his lungs felt as if they would explode, but he kept going. Masabala was chasing his past; aching to see his brother, to let go of the shame and guilt that had been eating him from the inside ever since the day he abandoned Livel in the desert. He had dreamt of this moment, prayed for it.

Like a mirage rising from the barren sand, he spied the outline of tents and could smell burning wood. Seeing no guards on watch, his heart pounding in his ears and overcome with emotion, Masabala moved slowly to the edge of the encampment. Over a dozen men were scattered about, all seasoned warriors, their faces contaminated by harsh weather and too much sun. He searched every face. Livel was not among them.

It cannot be! My brother is here. I know it. I can feel his presence.

Masabala moved into the shadows making his way toward the two tents that were separated from the rest of the camp. The first tent was dark and silent. He moved toward the second one. He heard voices, a man and a woman. His knees shaking, Masabala lifted the flap. The interior was bathed in lamplight. His brother was sitting on a mat and across from him sat the girl Masabala had seen in his dream.

Masabala was not sure when he entered the tent, and he would never be able to recall those first few moments. What he would always remember was the astonished look of recognition on his brother's face.

Livel dropped the plate he was holding, and his entire body began to shake. He rose as if in a trance. Stunned and in shock he cried, "*Ach sheli, ach sheli*, my brother, my brother." He ran into Masabala's outstretched arms.

They held on to each other, both so overwhelmed in their joy, they could do nothing but cry. They slapped each other's backs to affirm that neither was an apparition.

Masabala knew what his first words would be. He had rehearsed them a thousand times over their years of separation. He kissed Livel's cheek and whispered, "Please forgive me for leaving you. I am so sorry."

Livel drew back and touched his brother's face with an open palm. "You did not abandon me. You saved yourself because I insisted. I never blamed you. Never."

Masabala felt the anguish of guilt lift. Unable to control himself, he buried his face in his hands and wept. When he regained control, he looked up at Livel. His brother was smiling through his own tears.

"Mother and Father, are they well?" Livel asked, his hands pressed together in supplication.

"They are both fine and waiting anxiously for your return," Masabala said.

"Baruch Hashem, thank God. Now tell me, by what miracle did you find me?"

Masabala sighed. "It's a long story; one of many I have to tell you."

Arria watched the scene unfold through tear-filled eyes. She stood pulling the scarf over her scar. Masabala turned to her and smiled as she approached him.

"My name is Arria Galen. It is an honor to finally meet you," she said in perfect Hebrew.

Masabala did not know how to react to her forthright behavior; women of Judea would never introduce themselves. His face turned crimson. He looked at Livel hoping for direction, but his brother had a foolish grin on his face. Captivated by her beauty and confidence, Masabala finally managed to say, "*Shalom.*"

"Arria is one of my long stories," Livel said, his tone teasing and mischievous.

"I hope we can be friends," Arria said, instantly liking this bear-of-a-man with his tender eyes, huge calloused hands and ingratiating manner.

"We will be family," Masabala replied, touching his heart with an open palm.

Chapter 34

At daybreak, Arria, Livel and Masabala bid farewell to Draco and made their way into the desert. Walking side by side, leading a donkey carrying their belongings, they maintained a slow but steady pace to accommodate Livel's limp. The raw beauty of the majestic mountains, the cerulean sky and the glittering sun made the perfect backdrop for sharing what had transpired during their separation.

Livel began at the moment of his capture and did not take a breath until he had described the nightmarish details of his tiny friend Tillie's rape and how her dead body was fed to a lion. To spare Arria, he left out the fact that Domitius had been on the boat.

Arria stared at Livel. "I am so sorry!" she said, burying her face in her hands.

Masabala put his arm around Livel but remained silent. He was miserable. Livel had left En-Gedi an innocent boy and returned injured in body and mind. It broke Masabala's heart.

Livel shared the stories of his life as a teacher and soldier and how he was injured during war games; again not naming Domitius as his assailant.

He elucidated in great detail how he became a doctor and how he and Arria had worked together in the Jewish Quarter. He talked of his adoption by Doctor Galen and the circumstances surrounding his freedom from slavery.

Arria felt ashamed. She had never bothered to wonder about Livel's life, his feelings or his travails. For the first time in her life, Arria saw herself as she really was: self-indulgent and self-centered. She had no close friends, and no one really knew her deepest longings, dreams or fears.

Arria thought about the slaves that had served her. She knew nothing about their lives. Even Bolo, whom she loved, until the docks at Alexandria, she had given no thought to his past.

Yet, here was Livel stripping away all pretenses, trusting them enough to expose his deepest feelings. Just as her father said, Livel *was* a good man. She had just been too blind to see.

Livel stopped walking, his face steeped in misery. With tears in his eyes, Livel spoke of the overwhelming guilt he felt for no longer praying three times a day or celebrating the holidays. He had turned his face from God: letting medicine become his religion.

Feeling as if there were pieces of broken glass in his mouth, Livel told Masabala how he had been forced to take the lives of the three men who had accosted him and Arria in the Jewish Quarter.

When he had uttered his final words, Arria put her hand on Livel's shoulder. She yanked the scarf from her head revealing the angry red scar slithering down the side of her face. "This is why we fled! My husband would have killed both of us. Livel saved my life!"

For many moments there was silence, each of them deep in their own thoughts. When Masabala finally began to speak, it was with slow deliberation. He shared how he too had been overcome by guilt, blaming himself for Livel's capture. He talked of the death of his infant son, cave-ins, preparing for war, the fear and horror of combat and the helplessness of watching so many young men die. He did not mention his actions in taking the life of a fellow soldier. He never would.

Masabala's narrative turned to the victorious defeat of Rome and how a Jewish nation emerged from the tyrannical rule.

Arria felt conflicted: torn between her feelings as a citizen of the Roman Empire and now as a woman who would be living in Judea.

Masabala used his words as a canvas to paint a picture of the Temple. There was a subtle shift, and the energy around them softened. He spoke of finding the Ark, seeing the future and being able to hear the thoughts of others. He concluded his saga with the story of how their father was now the *Kohen Gadol.*

For Arria, the nonbeliever, it was but a colorful tale exaggerated beyond all possibility of truth. People did not hear other people's thoughts or see into the future.

For Livel, it was a revelation, every sentence and every inflection in his brother's voice bringing Livel deeper into the arms of the Judaism he had all but forsaken.

* * *

They arrived at the spot where Masabala had left his mule and supplies. "Before we continue," Masabala said, "father asked me to give this to you." He retrieved a pouch hanging from the saddle and handed it to Livel. Inside was a lamb's wool tunic. At the four corners were tassels of white wool interspersed with a cord of blue threads. The vestment was worn by Jewish men to fulfill the biblical commandment, *speak unto the children of Israel and bid them to make fringes in the borders of their garments throughout their generations.*

Livel removed the Roman tunic and slipped the garment over his head. The moment he did, he was drawn into the past. He was thirteen again standing in the synagogue beside his father. They were bowing and swaying in unison, immersed in the holy prayers. Livel chanted the words and melodies from memory imprinted on his heart forever.

Trancelike, Livel reached into the pouch again and removed a set of *tefillin,* two square leather boxes smaller than the width of two fingers. Inside the boxes were tiny pieces of parchment inscribed with chapters from the Torah, the Five Books of Moses. Attached to the boxes were leather straps. It was commanded in the Torah that this ritual be carried out every day except on the Sabbath and holidays. It served as a sign of remembrance that God delivered the children of Israel from bondage in Egypt.

And you shall bind them as a sign upon your arm, and they shall be as a symbol between your eyes.

Livel had not touched *tefillin* in years. His hands trembled as he placed the *Shel Yad* on his upper arm facing his heart and tightly wrapped the leather strap to keep it in place. He held the second box, the *Shel Rosh*, on his forehead between his eyes wrapping the leather straps around his head.

The veils separating him from God were lifted. The prayers came to him, the words dancing before his eyes. He was no longer standing in the sand of the Sinai. He was soaring over the holy mountain of Sinai. He was no longer wrapped in the *tefillin*. He was wrapped in the arms of God.

Masabala watched his brother closely. He could see Livel was moving again toward the purpose of Jewish life: you shall be holy. Livel had not lost his Judaism, and his Judaism had never lost him.

Arria could not believe what she was seeing. She had thought of Livel as an intellectual, a man beyond the reach of such foolish rituals. She believed in medicine and science and thought that Livel was of the same mind–until now.

* * *

Fortress walls of sand-colored stone surrounded the city of Jerusalem. Mount Moriah lay to the north and to the east sat the Kidron Valley and the Mount of Olives.

Long before they walked through the Dung Gate that led to the Temple Mount, they could hear the shouts and sounds of a thousand men.

As they neared the Temple Mount, what had once been ruin was now the site of a nearly completed Third Temple. Livel shook his head from shoulder to shoulder finding it inconceivable. He longed to walk the perimeter and touch the sacred ground.

"Tomorrow, you must bring me back here and show me everything," Livel said, his excitement bursting like floodwater overrunning its bank. "The Ark. The Temple. Tell me this is not a dream."

"Oh, but it is a dream," Masabala said, "And now, you will be a part of that dream."

Arria had no understanding of their religiosity or their fascination with a mere building. Still, it was hard not to be impressed by the industrious Jews.

Smiling, Masabala continued to lead Arria and Livel. They walked up steps and down arched alleyways for another five minutes, their sandals slapping against the stone walkways. They moved past shops and houses that had stood for centuries and then stopped at an entranceway set into a thick rock wall. Entering, they walked through a well-tended garden with rustling palm trees. The massive house folded back from the street. It was built of Jerusalem stone and Lebanese cedar.

He led them into the foyer and down two hallways before turning right and pushing open the door. The study was bathed in the temperate light of a waning day. There were five tables lined up like soldiers. On the tables were parchments, oils lamps, menorahs and vials that had once been filled with fragrant oils, all from the Second Temple period.

When they entered, Rabbi Eleazar was standing with his back to the door, studying an incense shovel. He turned and his face went crimson. "My son!" he cried, reaching out for Livel. The rabbi's entire body shook as he held Livel in his arms. "I can't believe it! I can't believe you are here!" The rabbi pulled away to study Livel's face and then hugged him again, laughing as he turned to Masabala. "The Holy One, Blessed be He chose you as his messenger. Thank you, my son, for never doubting, for following your heart and bringing your brother home."

Livel was shocked by how time had marked his father. The eyes were cloudy, the brow deeply creased, his beard and hair gone silver. But when his father smiled, as he was doing now, all the years melted away.

The rabbi noticed Arria for the first time. He squinted at Livel.

"This is my friend, Arria Galen."

Arria nodded, clutching the scarf closer to her face.

The rabbi sensed the strength and determination in Arria. He also saw the fear in her eyes. "It is an honor to welcome you into our home." He took Livel's hand. "Your mother," was all the rabbi said, tilting his face toward the doorway.

* * *

The four of them entered the kitchen. Sarah was the first to notice them. "Livel!" she wailed, her mind trying to comprehend what her eyes were seeing.

Miriam dropped the dish she was holding and screamed. Until this very moment, she had not allowed herself to believe that Livel was coming home. She could not bear the possibility of disappointment.

Losing her son had been the blackest time in Miriam's life, a sword impaling her heart. Every day of her life, she fought against the darkness. She had managed to make a life, but the struggle was staggering, the pain unbearable.

Miriam gasped, finding it difficult to breathe as she blinked her eyes and swiped aside the tears. "Tell me this is not a hallucination. Tell me this is my son!" She opened her arms, and Livel moved into his mother's embrace. Time had been gentle with her. The hair was grey, and her skin was mapped by a lifetime of experiences. But Miriam was still lovely.

The feeling of love was inexplicable: a mother's heart beating against the heart of her son. He had come from her womb and for that brief moment, Livel felt the sacred bond of coming from and being part of another human being.

Miriam held Livel's face as she kissed his cheeks and embraced him. Then she reached for Masabala's hand. "Look Eleazar, we are whole again!"

The rabbi laughed as he hugged his wife and sons.

Sarah took a tentative step forward. "Welcome home," she said, nuzzling Livel's cheek.

"Little Sarah," Livel said softly, looking into her eyes. It was like looking at the sun on an overcast day. The impish sparkle was still present, but there was also sadness in her big brown eyes. It was obvious Sarah was still mourning the death of her infant son. They hugged.

Livel suddenly realized he had yet to introduce his mother or Sarah to Arria. He went to Arria's side, introducing her to his mother and then his sister-in-law, Sarah.

Arria fidgeted with the scarf covering half her face and nodded as each woman welcomed her.

Chapter 35

Masabala led Livel into the courtyard of the *nasi's* home. He had not wanted to interrupt the family reunion and felt guilty about taking Livel away, even for only a short while. But what Livel had to say to Bar Kokhba was of paramount importance, and it could not wait. They knocked on the door. A servant answered and bade them to remain in the garden. Bar Kokhba appeared a few moments later, looking askance at Livel.

"This is my brother Livel," Masabala said.

"The one taken by the Romans?" Bar Kokhba asked, remembering that sad day so many years ago when he had gone to En-Gedi and learned that Rabbi Eleazar's oldest son had been captured.

Masabala nodded.

"Baruch Hashem!" He shook Livel's hand. "Welcome home."

"I'm sorry to disturb you," Masabala interjected. "But my brother has vital information, information I wanted you to hear directly from him."

Bar Kokhba studied Livel. "What is it?"

"Hadrian is amassing troops from Britannia, Syria, Arabia and Italy. He is vowing a full-scale attack to annihilate Judea. Tens of thousands of men will be dispatched to insure his success."

Bar Kokhba began to pace, hands behind his back. He stopped after a few turns. "Let them come! Let them bring their mightiest warriors! I fear no man! Israel was born in the desert, growing from the dust. God reigns. He is clothed with majesty, His power infinite. We will be victorious!"

Masabala shuddered. The prophecy was shown to him. He had seen the destruction of Israel, seen the people of God weeping. Shimon Bar Kokhba was the false Messiah.

Israel would be defeated.

* * *

By the time Livel and Masabala returned, the sun was nearing the horizon on the grey winter day. Livel found his father in a private room used only by the rabbi. It had whitewashed walls, a mosaic floor and was sparsely furnished. A small window overlooked the shadowed garden gone dormant for the winter.

They sat across from each other at a table that served as a desk. A servant brought wine and cakes, placed them on the sideboard and left quietly.

"It is imminent. Rome will attack!" Livel said to his father, anger slicing his words as he recounted his conversation with Bar Kokhba.

Eleazar turned his head so Livel would not see the knowing reflected in his eyes. Just as Masabala had seen the desecration of Judea in his vision so had the rabbi. Disaster was imminent. Like a fissure in the earth, it would split apart and swallow the Jews.

Reciting prayers, the rabbi's body bowed and swayed. He called upon the angels, begging them to be his emissary, to intervene with God so that He might reverse His decree.

Livel watched his father closely. When he was a young boy, he too might have turned to God at a moment like this. But that innocent boy and those days lay in the past. If the Jews were to survive, they could not sharpen their swords against the wind. Decisions had to be made, and plans implemented. He had seen firsthand, the power, determination and might of the Roman military. Regardless of the eventual outcome, the results were inevitable: thousands would die and be maimed. He had only one thought, one mission, to use what he and Arria knew to save lives. Doctors needed to be trained in the newest techniques, and the medical instruments they would need had to be made.

The rabbi crossed his legs, his eyes never leaving Livel's face. "This is not the homecoming I envisioned when Masabala foresaw your return. I wanted you to be bathed in gentle days of prayer and reflection, to stand beside me in the Temple as we offered sacrifices to the Holy One, Blessed be He."

"Father, there is so much you do not know about me. Things I must tell you so that you can understand who I am, what I have become."

He is blood of my blood. He may have been away, but a father always knows his son. The rabbi combed his beard with trembling fingers. "Whoever you think you have become, you are still a Kohen from the lineage of Aaron, and those bonds can never be broken." The Romans were a pagan society with radical philosophies. He had seen the way Livel looked at Arria. He was in love, and that was the strongest influence in a young man's life. If his son had turned away from his faith, then it had to be because of the girl.

"Not broken, Father, just rearranged," Livel said softly. Livel began his story from the time of his capture to the present. Unlike the version he told to Masabala, he left nothing out: not Domitius' role in the injury to his knee, Arria's disfigurement or the murders Livel committed to protect Arria.

The kaleidoscope of images painted by Livel's words was difficult for the rabbi to hear. There were instances when Eleazar grew so pale Livel feared he might faint. But each time Livel paused, the rabbi became agitated, insisting he continue.

"That is who I am now," Livel said, when he had uttered his last sentence.

The rabbi could not find his voice. That Livel was alive seemed the greatest miracle of all. It was a rabbi's duty to give honest council, speaking as a messenger of God's words. To council wisely, Eleazar needed to remove his emotions from the situation and not see himself as Livel's father. Their world would soon be one of strife and destitution, starvation and death. Doctors would be needed if lives were to be saved. God's decree might not be irreversible, but Judaism would not perish. It was God's promise to the children of Abraham.

The rabbi readjusted his skullcap. He placed his hands on the table as if to gain some balance before speaking. "I am so sorry for all that you have been through. It breaks my heart. I know now that my dream for you to stand beside me in the Holy Temple must be laid aside. There is no other choice. A violent storm is approaching, and many will be swept away. There is little time to waste. If the girl can help you, then she must. There will be resistance by some of our priests and rabbis, but our history is filled with women of great courage: Sarah, Rebecca, Rachel, Leah, Deborah and Esther. This young woman has been sent to us as a gift. That she is not one of us must not be viewed as a deterrent, but rather as a blessing from the Holy One, blessed be He."

* * *

The drafty hallways of the enormous villa were painted with scenes of luxurious gardens, fountains and preening peacocks.

"This villa was built by the Romans. My father-in-law would never have chosen to live in such luxury," Sarah said matter-of-factly, as she led Arria toward the room set aside for her. "It was cast upon him because of his role as the High Priest of Israel."

Arria did not reply. She was too disorientated by the layout of the house, so familiar yet seemingly so incongruous, like a rose blooming in the desert.

The atrium separated the north and south wings. It had four marble-faced columns, a high ceiling with an open square roof and a shallow pool in the center to collect rainwater that drained into an underground cistern. There was a semicircular bay with seats and an array of stools where the rabbi often greeted guests, when the weather was warmer.

"Watch your step," Sarah said, as they entered the north wing. "This section of the house has eight bedrooms. One of them will now be yours." She smiled. "The others are kept mostly for visiting rabbis. There are also two sitting rooms, and here is the library." Sarah pushed open the door.

The room had hundreds of parchments stacked on shelves. There was a row of windows near the ceiling, and stools were positioned around the room along with several reading desks.

The smell of parchments, the pervasive knowledge that seemed to be seeping from the pages and surrounding Arria, brought visions of her father. The grief struck so suddenly and with such intensity, she gasped. Arria missed him, missed the comfort of knowing that he could always make things right. Yet here she was alone and frightened. She blinked away her tears as she turned away from Sarah's gentle eyes.

"This must be so hard for you," Sarah said. "Leaving your family behind."

Arria nodded, seeing no need to speak when her remarks could change nothing.

"I know you must be tired. Let me take you to your room now," Sarah offered, wishing she could find a way to reach Arria.

Arria's new quarters were two doors down from the library. The room was large with a small window and a mosaic-tiled floor. There was a cabinet for clothing and a couch. Two single beds were nailed to opposite walls–both with feather mattresses covered in blankets, the feathers sticking out between the wooden slats. There was no bathroom, only a chamber pot sitting in a corner. Some unseen servant had lit the fireplace and unpacked Arria's things laying them in neat piles on the bed.

Sarah leaned against the doorframe, reticent to enter. Arria had been anything but friendly.

Arria glanced toward Sarah, really looking at her for the first time. She was taken in by her beauty–the round almost cherubic face filled with tiny freckles, her straight nose and slightly crooked smile accentuated by perfect teeth. Her eyes were exquisite, thick-lashed, inquisitive, sensitive and intelligent. Suddenly, Arria did not want to be alone.

"Would you like to come in?" Arria asked.

Sarah grinned. "I would love to."

The girls sat primly on the couch. For a few heartbeats there was only the sound of the crackling fire. Then Arria said, "It was very hard to leave my father. He is all I have."

"I'm so sorry. This has to be so horrible for you."

Arria imagined her last confrontation with Domitius. After that, not much seemed horrible.

Sarah pulled the shawl from her shoulders and the scarf from her head. Arria went to do the same and then hesitated.

"It's alright. Masabala told me what happened," Sarah said softly, patting Arria's knee.

Arria slipped the scarf off revealing her face, waiting for Sarah's reaction.

Sarah paled, and then her faced flushed. "He must be a very evil man," she said, tentatively touching the tiny ridge that traversed Arria's face. "But you are still a beautiful woman."

Arria shrugged. "It does not matter. The scars I carry are deeper and uglier than anything that can be seen from the outside." The bitterness was abiding. Arria felt the fool, still trying to understand how she could have ever loved such a malicious, hideous man. Knowing she was incapable of seeing wickedness where it lurked, she had lost confidence in herself, doubting she would ever trust her instincts again. Yet, her instincts were calling out, urging her to see that Sarah was suffering.

"Please forgive me," Arria said. "I certainly did not mean to upset you."

A tear slipped down Sarah's face. "Did Masabala tell you about our baby?" she whispered.

"Yes. And I am so sorry."

Sarah closed her eyes, talking softly as if to herself. "For months, he wiggled and kicked inside my belly. We were one, inseparable: my body nourishing him, his soul nourishing me. And then he was finally born." Sarah hesitated. "It must have been my fault!" she cried, her words jagged. "I must have done something wrong!"

Arria took Sarah's hand and held it. "It was not your fault, Sarah."

"He never took a breath. I never held him or felt his heart beat against mine. I am supposed to be over this by now. Jewish women are resilient: we are proud and strong and are taught to accept the Lord's will. But my heart was not ready for his heart to stop."

Arria squeezed Sarah's hand. "I know. I really do. I also know each of us mourns in our own way and in our own time. My mother died the day I was born. I never knew her, and yet I hold her in here," Arria said, placing a hand over her heart. "That's where we have to keep them Sarah–in our hearts."

Their eyes met and held for a second.

"Will I live long enough to have another baby? Is war coming? Is that why Masabala and Livel went to see Bar Kokhba?" Sarah asked, her voice a strangled cry.

Arria nodded. "I am afraid so."

They were two women standing at separate ends of a very long bridge, both in desperate need of honesty, hope and a friend. Whatever lay before them, they would have each other.

Chapter 36

Scipio Gracchus sat on a wooden crate in the kitchen of a ramshackle house built of crude mud walls with a dirt floor. Located within the borders of Moesia, the place belonged to the tribal leader of the village. The warrior's name was Gar. He had intense black eyes, a thick black beard and arms the size of tree trunks.

"You have cut us off from our water supply and now you come to me!" Gar slammed his fist into the palm of his hand. "You want to talk! Talk about *what*? How my crops are dying and my people are starving?"

The accusations were true, but Scipio held the man's gaze refusing to acquiesce for fear of appearing vulnerable. Hadrian had ordered a fence to be constructed in the northern frontier. It served as an artificial barrier between the Rhine and Danube Rivers, protecting Rome from the neighboring barbarian tribes of Germania, Moesia, Dacia and Scythia. The fence blocked access to the precious waterways, resulting in conflicts and frequent attacks.

"I did not come here to fight you," Scipio said. "I came to find a peaceful solution. Your village needs water. I will allow you access to that water as long as your tribesmen do not try to draw my soldiers into conflict."

The leader laughed: his gruff voice ominous. "Why should I trust you? Do you know how many of my people have been slaughtered in the past few months by soldiers of Rome?" His jaw jutted forward and his massive chest expanded. Fury steamed from his eyes. "Not just my men but innocent women and children! If I had good sense, I would kill you right now!"

A little boy about five wandered into the room. He had bare feet and a runny nose. The child stared up at Scipio with eyes too old for his years. Gar lifted the child onto his lap, studying the guiltless, trusting face of his little boy. "My men will put down their arms as long as we have a right to the water."

"You have my word. I will instruct my men to allow you safe access to the waterway." Scipio stood. The men faced off in an uncomfortable moment.

Scipio was pleased he had negotiated successfully with his enemy. It was a challenge carrying the mantle of a virtuous commander. Domitius mocked him, as did most of the other commanders. But Scipio had remained altruistic, vowing he would return home with as many of his soldiers as possible.

"Are you my friend now?" the little boy asked, pointing a finger at Scipio.

Both men smiled.

* * *

Scipio stood near the riverbank while the tribesmen dug a trench that would allow water to flow toward their fields. Children splashed in the muddied water as the women of the tribe roasted rabbits over crackling flames. The day was mild, but the sky threatened rain as charcoal singed clouds gathered overhead. Scipio could not help but congratulate himself at the peaceful scene. He allowed himself a few precious moments of reflection.

He and Domitius had been sent by their father to Britannia to serve under the legendary commander, Julius Severus. They trained with twenty-five other soldiers: all young and all from the finest Roman families.

The commanders studied engineering: learning how to build roads, bridges, canals and defensive walls. They were taught how to assemble siege engines, some capable of breaking through city walls and others capable of spewing stones and fire.

The young commanders perused maps and studied the topography they would encounter as they moved their troops toward

Judea. The movement of tens of thousands of soldiers was held under the direct logistical prevue of Severus. He personally devised the intricate plans that would be used to house and feed the legions.

Scipio stretched, looked around and decided it was time to take his troops back to camp. "Mount up!" he shouted. Taking the reins of his horse from an aide, Scipio went in search of Gar. He found him knee deep in a trench. "I will be back in the morning."

Gar lifted his arm in salute.

* * *

Scipio led his twenty men on a slow retreat, inspecting areas of the fence that had been breached and would require repair. He was issuing instructions when he glanced over his shoulder and squinted his steel gray eyes into the distance. Scipio felt the hair rise on his arms as a shiver shot down his spine. There was a haze on the horizon, red and ominous, coming from the direction of Gar's village. Scipio screamed for his men to follow him, kicking his horse into a canter.

As if the gods themselves were weeping, torrents of rain began to fall. Scipio's thick ebony hair lashed across his face, momentarily blinding him as he charged through the torrential downpour.

At the encampment, Scipio slid from his horse. There were mutilated bodies everywhere, innocent victims of a massacre. Guilt, such as Scipio had never experienced, assailed him as if he were being devoured. He had told Gar his warriors had no need for weapons. Scipio had given his word. Infuriated, his scream was primal, coming from the depths of his soul.

In shock, he carefully moved among the dead. He found the great warrior Gar splayed in the mud, eyes wide and mouth frozen in an unspoken cry. Gar's little boy sat beside his father, holding the cold dead fingers of his father in his tiny hand. The child stared at Scipio, pain oozing from his incredulous eyes like blood runs from a fatal wound. His look of betrayal would remain with Scipio Gracchus for the rest of his life.

Scipio turned away, fury crashing like symbols in his head. He had no need to ask himself who was responsible for the slaughter. The violence had a familiar footprint: men beheaded, arms lopped off, pregnant women with bellies sliced open. Only one commander would encourage this type of carnage. And only one officer would have had the audacity to impinge on another commander's region.

He did not care if it cost him his own life, he would take revenge!

"Move out!" he shouted to his men.

* * *

It was growing dark by the time Scipio reached Domitius' encampment on a hilltop overlooking the Danube. There were three thousand soldiers under Domitius' command: cavalry, auxiliaries, engineers, artillerymen, craftsmen, service personnel along with camp followers, paid servants and slaves. Tents stretched in every direction.

Domitius had set up his headquarters at the apex of the hill. As Scipio approached, he saw his half-brother standing in the entranceway of a tent, lazily scratching his thick curly beard, a signature guise worn by every officer in Hadrian's army.

Scipio placed his hand around the hilt of his sword as he faced Domitius. "Those villagers were under my protection! You had no right—"

"I had every right!" Domitius hissed. "I was heading back to my camp when I came upon barbarians stealing water." He turned his face and spat on the ground. "I eliminated the problem."

"There was no problem!" Scipio's rage prevented him from organizing his thoughts. "They were in my region. They had *my* permission!"

"And that is exactly the problem," Domitius said. "We are warriors, and our mission is to prevent incursions through the fence. If you can't keep our enemies at bay, then I will simply do it for you."

"Does it make you feel powerful, Domitius, killing innocent women and children?" He brought his face to within an inch of his half brother's, lowered his voice and spat out through gritted teeth,

"Is that why you carved your wife's face? Was that your reason for trying to kill Livel? Did it make you feel powerful, Domitius?" Scipio taunted. "Or was it because they saw you for who you really are?"

Domitius' face turned blood red. Balling his fists, his green eyes spewed hatred. "I should kill you right here and now. But it would spoil my fun. So let me warn you, Scipio. When we reach Judea, remain vigilant. Your biggest threat may well attack when you least expect it."

"As might yours," Scipio said, a smile turning his lips. "As might yours."

* * *

Arria and Livel walked through the ancient streets of Jerusalem on their way to the blacksmiths. They were picking up the last batch of surgical instruments being made for them to distribute to other doctors.

"I don't think a school is the right way to proceed," Arria insisted, turning as she moved in front of Livel.

Livel shook his head. "Jews value education. If I am going to convince doctors to change their method for treating patients, I must do it methodically and with great erudition. Otherwise they will not listen. Believe me, I know my people and how they think."

"If you want them to follow you, then you must lead. Open a clinic near the Temple Mount. With all the injuries happening there every day, you will have the opportunity to perform surgeries, save lives and teach more than just theory," Arria said.

"I never considered a clinic," Livel said, rubbing his beard. "It just might work."

"It will work. The methods being used here are archaic. Imagine what we could do."

Livel recalled his father's words, *if the girl can help you, then she must.* In theory it sounded so simple, but Livel knew that change took time. That was the one commodity they did not have.

"Arria, I would be honored to have you beside me, but in Israel, the rules are even stricter than in Rome. A man would never allow a woman, who was not a family member or his wife, to touch him."

"And yet a man can treat a woman!" Arria said, the rebuke turning her expression grim. "When someone is dying, do you really think they will care if I have breasts?" she said, as much as to shock Livel as to alleviate her anger, frustration and bitter disappointment.

Livel blushed and hated himself for it.

Arria had come to this place with high expectations that things could be different. But Livel was right: no matter her qualifications, she was a woman and would never be accepted as a physician. Yet despite everything, she had come to admire the Jews and their unwavering faith in only one god, a god they could not even see.

In their piety, they prayed three times a day and chanted before and after each meal. But it was on the Sabbath that Arria found herself wishing she believed what the Jews believed. By sundown on Friday night, the tables were set for a lavish feast. The women lit the Sabbath lamps, and the men said special blessings over the wine and bread. It was a time when the Jews of Israel paused as if taking in a very long breath and holding it.

For the ensuing twenty-four hours, all work ceased: it was a time of rest, prayer and contemplation. Arria sensed the gentleness that cloaked the family during this time. They would sit together and talk or read or just be in the silence.

Their daily rituals only served to magnify Arria's lack of belief in any god. She questioned her existence and her reason for coming to Israel. She had begun to wonder if she came so she could be with Livel. Did she care for him simply because he was the only one who honored her skills and accepted her, or was it something more? And did it really matter how she felt about him? Arria Galen was an outsider, and even if she would consider embracing the religion, it was too complicated and too confusing. She would not know where to begin.

After paying the various blacksmiths and arranging for the instruments to be delivered, Livel and Arria hesitated. There was so much to do, and yet the day was glorious. Neither one wanted it to end. In the gentle silence of companionship, Arria and Livel wandered through the crowded street, stopping at a spice stand, enchanted by the colors and aromas of the cumin, saffron and coriander.

At one of the many perfume stalls, Arria began testing the fragrances. "Israel has a lot to learn about what smells good." She scrunched her nose. "In Rome, my favorite was a mixture of sandalwood and musk combined with cinnamon, ginger and vanilla."

"Smell this one," Livel said, passing a vial of blue glass to Arria.

She passed the vial under her nose. "I actually like this one," she said grinning.

"It's made in En Gedi, where I come from. The main ingredient is persimmon that grows near the Dead Sea." Livel dug into his pouch and handed two coins to the merchant. "We'll take this one."

"I can't accept . . . "

"I want you to have it. Maybe when you wear it you will think of me?" Livel felt like an inept fool the moment the words left his mouth.

Arria took the bottle and dabbed a few drops on her wrists. The scent would forever bring this moment back to her: the dogwoods and olive trees, the crisp honeyed air and the red-faced woman scolding her dusty children.

Chapter 37

One month later

Masabala's heart was heavy as he waited for his father at the base of the Temple Mount. The burden of the coming war was so debilitating, there were times when just the simple act of getting out of bed in the morning seemed crushing. Sarah was despondent as well: terrified because Masabala was leaving and certain she would never conceive or know the joy of motherhood.

He did not want to go, did not want to fight again. But Masabala was a soldier in the army of God, and he had no other choice. Yet even in the depths of Masabala's despair, in the gruesome visions that replayed over and over again in his mind's eye, he knew the Torah and the Jewish people would survive.

His great challenge was to make sure Sarah and his family were among those survivors. Masabala intended for his family to go to the Negev and hide in one of the caves. It was the perfect solution. There was just one problem: convincing his father to leave Jerusalem.

Off in the distance, he watched the rabbi approach. His steps were slow and heavy, a man moving with the weight of a great burden upon him. As he neared, the rabbi lifted a hand and waved for Masabala to come to him.

They kissed, their smiles forced. "Over here," the rabbi said, leading Masabala to a secluded patch of dirt about to become the foundation for a house.

He glanced at the Temple Mount with disdain. "We should have stopped this long ago." The rabbi studied his knurled aching hands. "According to prophecy, only after the Messiah comes can a Third Temple, the Eternal Temple, be built," the grief-stricken rabbi said. He kicked his foot into the dirt like a petulant child. "We were led astray. Bar Kokhba is not the Messiah! We cannot, we must not break with God's covenant. It is our solemn responsibility to make sure the Ark is not placed within the Holy of Holies!" His face contorted in fierce determination.

"How, Father? Yom Kippur is upon us. Bar Kokhba is expecting the Ark to be moved within the next few days. If you refuse and try to expose him, I am afraid what might happen," Masabala said, drowning in his father's desperation. This was not the first time they had talked about this, but it was the first time Masabala had seen his father so indomitable.

The *Kohen Gadol* intertwined his fingers. "I have no intention of exposing Bar Kokhba. We can do nothing to stop a wave roaring toward shore. Our country will soon be at war and disavowing him would only destabilize and demoralize our army. But we can prevent the Ark from being moved into the inner sanctuary without anyone ever knowing."

* * *

Masabala left his father and was heading back toward the Temple Mount when he felt the earth tremble beneath his feet. His first thought was an earthquake. Then he heard the sound of crashing stones. What followed were the heartbreaking cries of anguish that reside within the nightmarish bowels of a disaster. A wall of ashen dust shot into the sky and spread out like a whirling sandstorm. Masabala felt his heart pounding to the rhythm of his steps as he ran towards the howling cries. A half-built retaining wall had collapsed, and men were pinned under the massive stones.

Masabala felt his emotions go numb as he assessed the situation. He had been here before, seen the carnage of destroyed and bleeding bodies. Later he would grieve, now he would organize.

He shouted for shovels, assigned men to dig and others to bring stretchers. He ordered tents to be brought so the wounded could be treated.

A hundred yards away, Arria and Livel were inside their make-shift clinic, a series of tents set up along the perimeter of the Temple Mount. The clinic had been in existence for two months. During that time, doctors came by the dozens to watch him perform surgeries they deemed impossible, using instruments they had never seen before. When the patients lived, and many did, the doctors began to ask if they could assist in the procedures. Livel agreed, teaching the techniques in a setting of practicality, just as Arria had suggested. Afterward, Livel dispensed the surgical devices and copies of Doctor Galen's book translated into Hebrew by scribes.

Arria was always present and always ignored. She mixed the medicines, made sure there were clean bandages and was available when Livel needed a consultation–out of earshot of the other doctors, of course. Being ignored and disregarded day after day upset her. But she held her tongue. The practice of medicine was Arria's breath.

Arria and Livel were storing their supplies for the night when they heard the roar of the collapsed wall. Arria felt her knees give way. She was certain they were under attack. They ran into the dusty day, suffocated by the barrage of flying sand and pebbles and the horrendous cries of the injured.

"Do I come or stay?" Arria shouted above the pandemonium.

"Have the servants gather everything we need and then meet me there!" Livel hollered as he ran toward the fallen wall.

Livel spotted Masabala and ran to his side. "How many are hurt?" Livel shouted.

"My guess, forty to fifty men. I'm having tents set up over there." Masabala pointed behind him. "What can I do to help?"

"Just make sure the most critical are brought in first."

Within the hour, every available doctor in Jerusalem was at the site. Twelve men were dead, and another forty were seriously hurt. Seven men had escaped with gashes and other minor injuries. One was still missing.

By the time his last patient was sutured and the broken bones splinted; Livel was covered in blood. Arria had assisted from the shadows, encouraging him when his determination wavered or he doubted his abilities. No man died under Livel's care.

It was nearing midnight, and the doctors were assembled to arrange a schedule for sharing responsibilities throughout the remainder of the night, when an unconscious fourteen-year-old boy was carried in on a stretcher. His mangled leg was dangling and crushed. The hysterical mother was holding her son's hand and weeping. She was a slight and waiflike woman with a heart-shaped face contorted and grief-stricken. "You must do something!" she wailed.

"Please, let me examine him," Livel said, kneeling beside the injured boy. "What's his name?"

"Tobiah," the woman mumbled, her midnight eyes shining pools of tears as she stared at Livel. "He's my only child. . . a good boy . . . such a good boy."

Doctor Ezekiel moved to the mother's side. He was an elderly man with a jowly chin, leathered face and a full head of silver hair. Recognition and hope dawned on the mother's face. "You have known Tobiah his whole life. It's not his time to die! Please, find a way to save him," she begged tugging on the doctor's bloodied sleeve.

"If only there were something we could do," Doctor Ezekiel replied, defeat showing in the way his shoulders sagged and his eyes darted from side to side.

Arria could no longer remain silent. She moved to the stretcher and knelt, feeling for the unconscious boy's pulse. It was weak and irregular, and his lips had a bluish tinge. "You are wasting precious time!" She burrowed her eyes at Livel. "The leg has to come off now. It is his only chance!"

Doctor Ezekiel shot Arria a murderous look. He had put up with her annoying presence long enough. "You are a stranger among us. You do not know our ways. It is the will of the Holy One, Blessed be He. We must let Tobiah go in peace." The other doctors muttered their agreement.

"No!" the mother howled. "If there is a chance he can survive, I want you to try!"

Arria held her breath waiting for Livel's response. She knew it would not be easy to stand up to the pressure of the doubt surrounding him. She watched Livel closely as his jaw jutted forward and his lips seemed to disappear. It was a look of determination she knew well.

"We have to move quickly," Livel said, sliding a rapid glance toward Arria.

Arria felt triumphant as she gathered three small glass jars brought from the clinic. She put two drops of poppy juice, a pinch of henbane and a pinch of hemlock into a cup, adding water and mixing them together until the mixture dissolved. She dripped the solution into the unconscious boy's mouth, massaging his throat to get a swallow response.

"That will help dull the pain, but it won't be enough," Livel said. "We are going to have to restrain him." He flashed his eyes at two of the doctors. "I need you at his head and you at his feet."

Livel had only performed one other amputation and he was terrified, his mind refusing to focus, his heart thumping in his ears.

Arria moved beside Livel, ignoring the murmurs of disapproval from the doctors waiting to watch the operation. She leaned in close to Livel and whispered, "Make the incision here." She pointed to the thigh. "Where the healthy tissue is. You'll have to work quickly because you'll only have three to four minutes before he bleeds to death." She took the saw from the tray and handed it to Livel. "Make a circular cut first through the skin, then the muscle, tendons and nerves."

"What else?" he asked, "what am I forgetting?" Perspiration dripped into his eyes.

"Hot oil," she whispered.

Livel looked at Doctor Ezekiel. "Please, prepare some heated oil to control the hemorrhaging once the leg is removed."

Arria murmured her approval. "You know what to do. Just don't cut through a joint and when you're done, be sure you leave enough skin to cover the end of the extremity." She patted him on the shoulder, shot a look of defiance toward the doctors and backed away.

"Hold him down," Livel ordered. He placed the saw on Tobiah's thigh.

The boy's eyes shot open. "What's happening? What are you doing to me?"

Livel yanked the saw away.

Arria rushed to the mother and grabbed her hand. "He needs to hear your voice."

Kneeling beside her son, the mother said, "Tobiah, you've been hurt, and the doctor is going to fix you." Her voice stuttered as she swallowed her tears. "I love you son. I will be right here when you wake up."

"I have to begin now! Please, wait outside," Livel ordered.

Arria led the weeping mother from the tent. One doctor held Tobiah's arms and the other held the good leg. One of the doctors positioned a wooden stick in Tobiah's mouth to keep him from biting off his tongue. The assault of the saw brought an agonizing scream. It lasted only seconds before the boy lost consciousness.

Livel's body tensed as the saw made contact with the femur. Gripping the saw with all his might, his actions turned automatic. His intellect was now in control of his racing emotions.

When the leg was off and only the stump remained, Livel applied the hot oil cauterizing the oozing blood vessels. The bleeding ceased within minutes. Arria handed Livel a needle and thread. He sutured the gaping hole where once there had been a leg.

Arria assisted with wrapping the stump in a pressure bandage. "Excellent work," she said under her breath.

"If I hadn't seen this with my own eyes, I would never have believed it possible," Doctor Ezekiel said, shaking Livel's hand. "Look, the boy's color is already improving, and his breathing is steady."

The doctor looked at Arria. His expression was filled with contempt as he turned away.

Chapter 38

On the edge of the city sat a two-room house designated as a place of learning and study. Rabbi Akiva often came there to discuss the commentaries on the Torah he was writing with the greatest rabbinic scholars of the time. The learned men would scrutinize every word and every possible meaning, the discussions often turning heated.

In the evening, the *Beit Midrash*, the house of learning was deserted. It was the perfect place for Rabbi Eleazar and his sons to meet. They sat together at a long table. A single lamp burned at one end casting strange shadows.

The three of them chanted blessings as Rabbi Eleazar took a Torah scroll from the cabinet against the wall. The rabbi then placed the scrolls on the table and closed his eyes, his lips moving in silent prayer as he swayed forward and back. When he had finished, he opened his eyes and looked at Livel.

The rabbi blinked several times. He pointed to the Torah. "The Five Books of Moses are not in heaven but in the hands of man as our compass, giving us the path to conduct our lives.

"Prophet Ezekiel said the consecration of a Third Temple could only occur with the appearance of the *Mashiach*, the Jewish Messiah. While Bar Kokhba has been a great leader, a man who empowered our people to defeat Rome," the rabbi squinted as if in pain, "it saddens me to tell you, he is not the messiah."

Livel was astounded, finding it impossible to take in all the repercussions resulting from this revelation. His eyes shifted from his father to Masabala and then back to his father. "Have we incurred the wrath of the Holy One, Blessed be He? Will He turn from us and allow the destruction of Israel?"

"That we have incurred His wrath seems evident," the rabbi said softly. "But I believe the Holy One, Blessed be He is a merciful God, always ready for us to repent. But we must not break further with His commandments. To ensure that does not happen, I need your help."

"I will do whatever is required," Livel replied, his thoughts reeling.

The rabbi's eyes burned with determination. "As the *Kohen Gadol*, it is my obligation and duty to prevent the Ten Commandments from being placed within the Holy of Holies."

"Father, I do not want to seem insolent," Livel said, staggering under the implications, "but the Ark is being moved into the Holy of Holies tomorrow. All of Jerusalem will be there!"

"And they will see the Ark being taken into the sanctuary. What they will not know, what no one will know other than you and your brother is that the Tablets of Ten Commandments will not be inside the Ark."

"The holidays? What about the holidays?" Masabala fought to keep the incredulous look from his face. As far as Masabala knew, his father had never lied in his life. Yet here he was planning to perpetrate a deception of such magnitude, there were no words to describe it.

"As the *Kohen Gadol*, I will perform the holy rites on Yom Kippur. I will present a sin offering, the sacrificial blood that serves as a conduit to purify the Israelites and sanctify them to God. On that day, I will repent and pray in the name of the people of Israel. I will make this sacrifice to the Holy One, Blessed be He with the full knowledge that I am an impostor. I do this for one reason only; to assure the Tablets do not fall into the hands of our enemy. Now, let me tell you what must be done."

* * *

In the open expanse surrounding the Temple Mount, thousands had gathered playing flutes, tambourines and lutes, dancing and cheering. Shimon Bar Kokhba, Rabbi Akiva and the *Kohen Gadol* ascended the steps leading to the entranceway of the Third Temple. Eleazar was dressed in the turban, breastplate, robe, apron, sash and breeches of the *Kohen Gadol.*

Following close behind were other distinguished members of the rabbinate, all descendants of Aaron: men who would serve as priests within the Temple walls.

Bar Kokhba raised his arms for silence. "This is the destiny of the Jewish people!" He swept an arm toward the Temple. "In recognition of this momentous occasion, I am commissioning coins to be inscribed with the façade of the Third Temple. At the top of each coin will be a star representing the prophecy of my coming, *the son of a star.* And on that coin will be the name, Shimon."

The crowd roared their approval. Bar Kokhba basked in the moment.

The *Kohen Gadol* moved beside Bar Kokhba. He rested his hand on the nasi's shoulder, an act meant to show allegiance. Even though Bar Kokhba was the great pretender, he was the military leader of Judea.

* * *

Twenty-eight Kohanim entered the sacred underground passageway that led to the Ark. They lined the tunnel, each standing ten paces from the other. The rabbis offered prayers as the *Kohen Gadol* and his sons passed by.

When the *Kohen Gadol* reached the wall separating him from the Ark, he spoke to his followers: "Turn your backs and avert your eyes." He then spoke to his sons: "Masabala, Livel, remove the first stone. The moment it's removed, turn from the light and wait over there," he said, pointing to a crevice in the wall. "When I've prepared the Ark for transport, I'll call for you; then and only then will you approach. If something happens to me," he said, lowering his voice, "You are to escort everyone to safety, allow no one to pass. Then seal off the cave entrance."

The two brothers each took a chisel, and with coordinated movements, they dislodged a large stone from the wall. Beams of light shot from the hole and illuminated the tunnel.

Masabala longed to look into the light, and for a moment he contemplated disregarding his father's instructions to turn away. Then he thought about the visions, the terror that accompanied him day and night. He closed his eyes and turned toward the wall.

Livel could not turn away, held in suspension as surely as if God was forcing him to peer into the luminescence. He had the sensation of oneness, floating into eternity: important, unimportant, everything and then a part of everything. Then Livel found himself standing in the middle of a huge field. All around him was incomprehensible devastation: the fields afire, bodies everywhere, the sounds of silence louder than a thousand drums. Livel bit his lip to keep from crying out. *This can't be God's mandate for the Jewish people!* As quickly as the images appeared, they disappeared. Livel shut his eyes to the light and waited.

The *Kohen Gadol* used hammer and chisel to remove more stones. Empowered now with the strength of Samson, he was able to lift the heavy stones as if they were weightless. When the opening was large enough to walk through, he entered the chamber.

The Ark rested in the center of the room surrounded by a golden light. The words from Exodus came to his mind:

And they shall make an ark of acacia wood; two and a half cubits shall be its length, a cubit and a half its width, and a cubit and a half its height. And you shall overlay it with pure gold inside and out you shall overlay it, and shall make on it a molding of gold all around. You shall cast four rings of gold for it, and put them in its four corners; two rings shall be on one side, and two rings on the other side. And you shall make poles of acacia wood and overlay them with gold. You shall put the poles into the rings on the sides of the ark, so the ark may be carried. The poles shall be in the rings of the ark; they shall not be taken from it. And you shall put into the ark the Testimony, which I will give you. You shall make a mercy seat of pure gold;

two and a half cubits shall be its length and a cubit and a half its width. And you shall make two cherubim of gold; of hammered work you shall make them at the two ends of the mercy seat. Make one cherub at one end, and the other cherub at the other end; you shall make the cherubim at the two ends of it of one piece with the mercy seat. And the cherubim shall stretch out their wings above, covering the mercy seat with their wings, and they shall face one another; the faces of the cherubim shall be toward the mercy seat. You shall put the mercy seat on top of the ark, and in the ark you shall put the Testimony that I will give you. And there I will meet with you, and I will speak with you from above the mercy seat, from between the two cherubim which are on the ark of the Testimony, about everything which I will give you in commandment to the children of Israel."

The realization that he stood only steps from the Tablets that represented God's Testimony, words that established morality in the world, made the *Kohen Gadol's* legs weak. Acutely aware of his thundering heart, the rabbi had to concentrate and remember to inhale and exhale as if his body had forgotten how. He fell to his knees, crawling toward the Ark, uttering prayers.

The *Kohen Gadol* touched a corner of the Mercy Seat, a golden surface that looked solid but quivered under his touch. He lifted the covering no more than fist high.

Lying on a bed of shimmering gold were the Tablets: beside the Tablets lay Aaron's staff and manna.

The rabbi had only a glimpse before the chamber exploded into flames. Kneeling in the midst of a blazing inferno, the *Kohen Gadol* felt no heat, no burning, he was in union with the Source, his body one with all there was, all there ever would be.

The flames dwindled. A profound silence followed. The rabbi stood, shuddering in his enlightenment. He imagined placing his hands on the Tablets, touching what Moses had touched; what God Himself had written. Then Eleazar looked down at his hands. He was not imagining holding the Tablets. He was holding them. The rabbi knew that God, may His name be blessed forever and ever, had placed them into his hands. Knowing what was expected of him, although no words were spoken, the rabbi knelt and laid the Tablets on the leopard skin that was lying on the floor near his feet.

He draped the skin over the Ten Commandments, and the room fell into total darkness. He went to the Mercy Seat and removed Aaron's staff and the manna and placed them on the ground beside the covered Tablets.

"Masabala, Livel, approach," the rabbi called, his voice echoing in the stillness.

His sons crept into the chamber. It was like stepping into the abyss, the absence of light absolute.

The rabbi could see beyond the darkness. He took each son by the hand and then placed their hands on the poles attached to the Ark.

"I'll carry from this end. Just walk straight, it's only a few steps," the rabbi said.

Masabala and Livel moved into the corridor, the absence of light diminishing with every step. After ten steps, Livel transferred the Ark to the next priest waiting along the corridor to receive it. Another ten steps and Masabala did the same. And so it went until each of the Kohanim had taken part in escorting the Ark of the Covenant from its home beneath the Temple Mount.

When the Ark was brought into the daylight, a hush fell over the throngs. People prostrated themselves and wept as the Ark passed by and was carried up the steps by the *Kohen Gadol* and his sons. Hanging across the entranceway to the Holy of Holies was a thick linen curtain of blue, purple and scarlet embroidered with cherubim. The Kohen Gadol pulled the veil aside. He smiled at his sons as he placed the empty Ark of the Covenant inside–thereby rewriting the history of the Jewish people.

Chapter 39

Livel and Arria sat at a desk in the far corner inside the main tent of the clinic. Shabbat was less than an hour away, and for the first time in a week, there was no background noise coming from the Temple Mount. The silence was almost eerie.

"The patient we saw today with the severe pain in the lower right quadrant of his belly," Arria said, rifling through a stack of parchments where she recorded every patient they treated and every surgery they performed. "This is the third time we have seen these same symptoms. In every instance, the patient has died." She picked up the book her father had given them and began turning pages. "Ah, here it is," she said, handing the book to Livel.

Livel studied the page for a few moments, although he had memorized the entire book. "You think it's this worm-like append-age causing the illness and pain?" Livel asked. "If so, there is noth-ing we can do."

"You could take it out."

"Arria, cutting into the belly is almost always fatal. Perhaps one day it will be possible, but now we just don't know enough."

"And how will we ever know if we don't try?"

Livel stood signaling an end to their nightly ritual of discussing the day.

"You need to be more open-minded," Arria insisted, stacking the parchment.

"And you need to be more realistic," Livel retorted as they left the clinic and headed toward home.

The waning afternoon was suffused with a lace-like stream of golden sunlight. From every open window and doorway came the mouth-watering aroma of freshly baked bread, roasting fowls and simmering stews.

"I love the Sabbath," Arria said as much to herself as to Livel.

Livel stopped mid-step to look at Arria. She always seemed so aloof, as if the daily rituals practiced by the Jews had no effect on her. And yet, here she was professing her love of the Sabbath. Livel could not help but speculate that Arria might be stepping into the embrace of Judaism.

Unbeknownst to anyone, Arria had been spending long nights studying Judaism in the rabbi's library. It had begun out of curiosity; out of the need to understand the people she lived with and had come to love and respect. She poured over the texts, memorizing the daily prayers and dozens of Psalms. Arria never intended to embrace the religion, but over the weeks and months, something shifted within her. Medicine could explain only so much. She could cut open a body, but something greater caused that body to heal.

Arria slipped her arm through Livel's arm. It would have been an innocent gesture in Rome, but in Israel, unmarried men and woman did not touch in public. Livel thought he might drown in the nearness of her body, in the touch of her hand.

A tiny voice within his head whispered, *if you love her, then you must protect her.*

Livel knew what he had to do. If Arria remained in Judea, she would be caught up in the war. As a citizen of Rome and with the jewels given to her by her father, she could go to Alexandria and live a life of safety and security.

"Arria, there are decisions that need to be made," Livel said, using every ounce of his willpower to pull away from her. "Judea is going to be attacked. The war will be devastating, and an incalculable number of people are going to die." Livel swallowed hard, determined to say what must be said. "I think the time has come for you to leave. You can go to Alexandria. You'll be safe there."

Arria tensed, her expression turning bleak. She could not believe Livel wanted to send her away. The hurt turned to anger. "If

I mean so little to you . . . if I am such a burden . . . then I will leave tonight."

"Arria, please. You are not a burden! You could never be a burden. If anything—," Livel refused to finish the sentence. Professing his love would be selfish and foolish.

Arria's eyes filled with tears. Until that very moment, feeling Livel's apparent rejection, she had not realized she was in love with him. Arria castigated herself for being so outspoken and stubborn, making it impossible for Livel to love her in return.

"If you want me to leave your parents' home, I will. But I will not leave Judea. I belong here! It is my home now, and you cannot force me to go!"

"Please, Arria. Go to Alexandria. Start your life over again," Livel begged.

Arria removed the scarf and turned to face him. Her stance was defiant. "I am not leaving!"

Livel had loved Arria through all her temper tantrums, jealous rages and even through her marriage to Domitius. He didn't know what to do or say to make her listen. "This is a mistake. I can't protect you!" Livel barked, more frustrated and confused than he had ever been in his life.

"You don't have to protect me. You just have to want me!" Arria shouted, biting her lip to fend off more tears.

"*Want you*?" Livel felt as if his heart might burst. "You are all I have ever wanted."

Livel looked around, needing a place of refuge. He took Arria's hand and led her down an overgrown path that led to the side yard of a half-built house. They stood face to face, their breathing ragged. Livel desperately wanted to take Arria into his arms and never let go. But he was terrified of ruining the moment: afraid if he touched Arria, she would come to her senses and turn from him.

Arria sensed Livel's fear and understood at the deepest levels of her being that this was a life-altering moment. She leaned her head against Livel's chest and put her arms around him. They stood that way for several seconds before Arria looked up at Livel. Their lips touched, the connection was so intense that they both struggled for breath. Their love needed no words. Their destiny was sealed.

* * *

The *Kohen Gadol* stood in the courtyard at the bottom of the Temple steps. "No one saw you?" he whispered as Livel and Masabala approached.

"No one, Father," Livel said.

It was four hours until sunrise as they climbed the steps. With his sons guarding the entrance, the *Kohen Gadol* trembled, as he entered the darkened Holy of Holies. The rabbi was distraught, having no other choice, he had removed the Tablets from the Ark; the first time since Moses had placed them there.

Prostrating himself on the floor, the rabbi wept as he chanted prayers of sacrifice for the empty Ark. For when Jerusalem fell, foreseen in his visions, the Romans would not search for words written on a block of stone: they would search for the golden shrine: a shrine now being sacrificed in order to save the Ten Commandments.

When Eleazar left the Holy of Holies he walked backwards, paying homage not to a structure made from wood and gold but for all that the Ark represented.

His eyes were filled with tears as he led Masabala and Livel toward the tunnel where the Tablets were hidden. They spoke not a word as they walked the passageway. In silence, they placed each stone back into the wall. When the wall was sealed, the men stepped away.

"Master of the Universe, accept our prayers," the rabbi said. "Your Tablets, words that gave light unto the nations, may Your Commandments be safe in this place, beside Aaron's staff and the manna you bestowed upon Your followers as they wandered the desert.

"It could be thousands of years from now, but the *Mashiach*, the anointed One, will appear. On that day, we will celebrate the ingathering of exiles and the restoration of the religious courts of justice. It will be the end of wickedness, sin and heresy. The righteous shall be rewarded. Temple services will be restored and the Ten Commandments will be found," the *Kohen Gadol* proclaimed, bowing his head in supplication.

* * *

The rabbi stood between his sons, allowing each one to hold an arm as they walked toward home. The night had taken its toll on Eleazar, and he felt as ancient as the olive trees they passed.

"Livel, there is much I need to tell you, things Masabala already knows," the rabbi said, proceeding in gentle tones to tell the story of how and why the Ark had been hidden away before the destruction of the First Temple. "In each generation, three men have been designated as keepers of the secret, the only ones entrusted with the location of the Tablets. Each of those three men was allowed one holy man as his confidant.

"It was stipulated that one of the keepers of the secret must always live within the borders of Judea, and the other two must live outside of Judea. In my generation, I was the keeper of the secret within Judea, and Rabbi Akiva was my confidant. But that was then." The rabbi turned to Livel, his look intent. "My son, your participation in what took place this night has only just begun."

Livel was anxious to hear his father's next words, anxious and frightened.

"*L'dor vador*, from generation to generation, we have survived. It is now going to be your responsibility to carry this secret out of Judea."

"You want me to leave my home?" Livel was aghast, refusing to believe what he was hearing, not when he had been through so much just to get back to Judea.

"When the time comes, yes. Your mother, Sarah and her mother, Masabala and Arria, if she so chooses, will go with you. In the mean time, you will leave Jerusalem within the next few days. A cave in the desert near En Gedi has been stocked and prepared for your arrival. You will live there until I send word for you to leave Judea," the rabbi said, fighting to keep his emotions under control.

"And you, Father? What of you?" Livel asked.

"If I can come to you, I will."

"Father, I have never disobeyed or even questioned you, but I am a commander in the army of Israel. I cannot leave!" Masabala said.

"And you will remain a commander for now. But when I tell you to go, you *will* go to your family," the rabbi said. "It has been decreed. Our lineage must survive." He seemed to hold his breath before continuing, "If something happens to Livel, as a Kohen it becomes your right and responsibility to carry the secret into a new land."

Masabala would say no more. His father was doing what he had been told to do. One did not question the word of God.

* * *

Julius Severus and his commanders gathered on a plateau overlooking the vast expanse known as the Negev Desert, a region of dusty mountains and dry riverbeds. A sea of tents spread out below them, the voices of ten thousand soldiers vibrating on the wind like the gathering of a storm preparing to rain down upon Judea.

Amassing to the south and west of Severus' location were fifty thousand more soldiers deployed under VI Ferrata from Arabia, X Fretensis, XXII DeiotArriana and II Traiana Fortis. In the north, three legions were stationed in Syria: III Gallica, IV Scythica and XVI Flavia Firma.

Scipio and Domitius had ten men separating them, but still they glared at each other. Since their confrontation, neither one had uttered a word to the other.

"I selected you!" Severus looked from man to man, the eyes of twenty-five commanders staring back at him. "In the morning, you will gather your men and ride out. You are to impose full military discipline at all times," Severus said, placing his massive arms across his chest, "including full marching maneuvers, weapon inspections and practice maneuvers. Winning means preparation!" He took a few steps and faced his men. "It's imperative that you never underestimate your enemy. The Jews fight like fierce warriors and are willing to die for their faith. Without a doubt, our troops are a superior force, but passion is an able enemy."

Severus began to strut, stopping in front of each officer for a moment as he spoke. "Like rats, these Jews hide in underground tunnels and lurk in caves, running out when least expected. Do not allow your troops to be ambushed!"

He cleared his throat and continued, "To cut off the head of these snakes, we must attack where they least expect us to attack.

"There are almost a thousand villages in Judea, all small and vulnerable. Your job is to strike each of these villages in the areas you are patrolling and wipe them out. Eventually, this will drive the Jews into their cities. That is when victory will be in our grasp."

Severus put an arm across his chest. "I ride now to give these commands to my other legions. I trust you will follow my orders without deviation. May the gods protect you, and may it not be long before the head of Bar Kokhba is placed at Emperor Hadrian's feet."

Chapter 40

An hour past dawn, Masabala entered Bar Kokhba's headquarters. It was chaos. Maps were nailed to walls and spread out on every available table. Commanders gesticulated, poking fingers at the maps and shouting orders. Searching for a familiar face, Masabala spotted Asher. His heart pounding, he moved to his side. "What happened?"

"The Roman army crossed into Judea just north of Tiberias yesterday. Reports have been coming in all night. There are tens of thousands of troops amassed along our southern, northern and western borders." Asher took a deep sad breath. "We fight again, my friend. It is—" Asher shifted his eyes and froze mid-word as he watched Bar Kokhba approach.

"Gather your men," Bar Kokhba said without preamble. "I want you to be ready to depart by morning! I am depending on you," the nasi said, the intensity of his stare so powerful, Masabala felt as though Bar Kokhba was reading his every thought. A loud argument drew the nasi's attention. He turned and walked away.

Masabala watched him, his mind reeling. He was responsible for the southern region of Judea. Of the ten thousand soldiers under his command, most were already in hiding in fully stocked tunnels and caves throughout the Negev. Their orders: lie in wait and strike with all the might of Israel, then retreat.

Masabala disagreed with the strategy. Rome was a virulent enemy being led by able commanders. An ambush could only be effective if it was a surprise, and the Romans were not stupid. They would not fall prey to the same tactics Israel had used in the last war against them.

Masabala's strategy was to populate the towns, enclaves and cities with heavily armed soldiers. His suggestion had fallen on deaf ears. Under other circumstances, he would have argued vehemently. But in the end, he knew the fate of Israel was sealed. A false messiah ruled, and Judea would be conquered.

* * *

Livel stood at the doorway to his father's study, rubbing the sleep from his eyes. He knocked gently and pushed open the door. The rabbi was facing east saying his morning prayers. Livel joined him. When they were finished praying, the rabbi took a small leather pouch from his pocket. He threaded the end of the pouch through a leather cord and tied off the ends.

"You must wear this around your neck and never take it off," the rabbi said, handing it to Livel. "Inscribed on the parchment is a coded map made up of random Hebrew letters and numbers. They correspond to words and numbers in the Torah and to the six hundred and thirteen commandments. Only a learned Torah scholar will ever be able to decipher the meaning."

Livel grasped the tiny pouch in his trembling fist, overcome by the enormity of the responsibility before him. He was now one of only three people being entrusted with the location of the Ten Commandments. The Tablets stood as proof of God's existence, the most important testimony on earth, the ineffaceable connection between God and man. Chanting prayers, Livel slipped the necklace over his head.

"Take no unnecessary risks, my son. With the Lord's blessing, one day you will pass this down to your son, and he will pass it down to his son. And so it will continue from one generation to the next," the rabbi said softly, "until the time when the *Mashiach*, the Anointed One, appears."

The rabbi hugged Livel, patting his back endearingly. Stepping back, he smiled. In his son's eyes, the rabbi saw elation and expectation. "What a monumental day this is for you!" Go now and prepare!"

Late Afternoon

Arria half ran and half walked down the hallway on her way to the atrium. With Rome bearing down on Judea and time running out, she and Livel had decided to marry immediately. In preparation, she had just returned from the mikvah, a ritual bath of purification and supplication required for conversion and marriage. Dressed in a yellow wool tunic, her damp hair was tied into a bun under a veil of white silk.

Livel waited for Arria at the doorway of the atrium. When she arrived he kissed her cheek, his lips lingering. Arria slipped her hand into his, and together they entered the atrium. Overhead the sun shone through the open skyline, reflecting ribbons of light across the shallow pool of the garden. As if walking on air, they moved to stand beneath the *Chuppah*, a wedding canopy fashioned of braided wool and silk. Masabala moved next to his brother. Miriam and Sarah stood near Arria.

Rabbi Eleazar held a Torah in his arms. Chanting softly, he placed the Torah on a table and moved to stand before Arria and Livel.

"In the book of Leviticus it is written," the rabbi began, "*When a stranger resides with you in your land, you shall not wrong him. The stranger who resides with you shall be to you as one of your citizens; you shall love him as yourself, for you were strangers in the land of Egypt: I the Lord am your God.*

"I shall begin by telling you the story of Ruth," he said, smiling at Arria. "She was the great-grandmother of King David, the second King of Israel." He smoothed his beard, his face serene. "Ruth was not a Jew but a Moabite woman whose people lived east of the Dead Sea. She converted and was brought into the tribe of Israel when she proclaimed her intentions to her mother-in-law, Naomi. Today Arria, you have chosen to follow in Ruth's footsteps. By doing so, you vow to follow the laws of Torah. And so, if you are ready, I ask that you declare yourself."

Arria drew a prolonged breath, reeling in the momentous implications of becoming a Jew by choice, at a time when the full power of Rome was about to come down upon Judea. How easily she could proclaim herself Roman and leave this land before the sand turned to blood. And she might have done just that, if not for Livel. She squeezed his hand.

For the first time, Arria understood the kind of love the poets and psalmists wrote about. Livel's smile brought her joy, and his gentle presence made her feel protected. She trusted, adored and respected him.

Arria lifted her head and in a loud clear voice she said, "Your people shall be my people, your God my God."

The rabbi placed his hands inches above Arria's bowed head. "By repeating the words said by Ruth fifteen hundred years ago, you now enter into the covenant with the Jewish people." With his palms facing outward and the thumbs of his outstretched hands touching, the remaining four fingers on each hand were separated into two sets of two fingers each; denoting the letter *Shin* in the Hebrew alphabet. It was the emblem for *Shaddai,* God Almighty. The rabbi gave the priestly blessing, "May *Adonai* bless you and guard you. May *Adonai* make His face shine upon you and be gracious unto you. May *Adonai* lift up His face onto you and give you peace."

"Mazel Tov!" Masabala, Sarah and the rabbi said in unison, each hugging Arria in turn.

Livel took Arria's hand and brought it to his lips. "I love you," he whispered.

Struggling to maintain composure, the rabbi said, "In the presence of the Divine let us now begin the sacred ceremony binding you forever as husband and wife."

* * *

The gentled song of the wind drifted through the open window, and the moon cast the room in silken shades of gold. Livel pulled

Arria closer into his embrace, overcome by her touch. They kissed, their passion exploding into desire that took on a rhythm of its own. Arria was lusty and sure of herself, guiding Livel when his confidence and knowledge waned.

For hours they made love, exploring, touching, kissing.

Legs intertwined, Arria's head on his chest, she touched the pouch around Livel's neck. "What is this?"

Livel kissed the top of her head. "The only secret I will ever keep from you," Livel whispered, before falling to sleep.

During the night Arria got up and stood naked before her sleeping husband. Livel sensed her absence from their bed and awoke. He slipped from beneath the blankets and went to his wife. The gloriousness of her body, the way her hair cascaded over her breasts, the curve of her buttocks made Livel hard again with need and desire. He lifted Arria into his arms and carried her back to bed. The scent of her, the way she sighed and cried out captivated him. It was as if Livel had been asleep his entire life, awakened by this magnificent creature that was now his wife. On the morrow, danger, sorrow and fear would become their companion. But tonight, they were in communion with God. Tonight the angels rejoiced in their love.

* * *

At dawn, they gathered in the dining room for their last meal together as a family. It should have been a celebratory breakfast to honor Livel and Arria's marriage, but it was more like a feast of sorrow. Even the air inside the room was stale, as if the angels had ceased to breathe. Masabala had been issued his orders. Today was the day he would lead his men into war and escort Sarah, his mother, Livel and Arria to the foothills of the cave.

Sarah sat beside Masabala, her eyes red from crying. Every few seconds her glance shifted toward him as if to make sure he was still there. As a young girl, and again as a married woman, Sarah had waited for Masabala's return from war. She knew then as she knew now, he was the only man she would ever love. Over the years, her devotion intensified, growing stronger through the grief they shared with the loss of their infant son and through the long months of separation. Despite the hardships, Sarah always believed in their future, in the family they would one day raise in Judea. Then her father-in-law decreed his sons must leave the land of Israel, and on that day, Sarah's dreams died. When she begged Masabala to explain why they had to go, he was vague, saying only that it was *as it must be*. As a dutiful wife and a daughter of Israel, Sarah did not want to leave the country of her birth. But she would remain silent and question him no more.

Masabala watched the fear of uncertainty slide across Sarah's face. He put his arm around her, patting her back as if she were a child. He felt Sarah take a sharp intake of breath and then relax against him. How he longed for the carefree times they had shared, for the freckle-faced girl who feared nothing. Masabala blamed himself for the life they had lived, for the lonely times, the battles he fought not only in war but afterwards, when he couldn't find his way back into Sarah's life. He wished he could do it all over, recapture the lost months when he had been distant and self-absorbed. Masabala studied Sarah's profile, the way her lip protruded and her nose crunched when she was deep in contemplation. He vowed to himself that if he lived through the next few months, he would find a way to make it up to Sarah.

Arria and Livel moved their chairs as close together as possible, hands intertwined, knees touching. Livel knew too well the calamity of separation; he had lived it firsthand. But this was different. There would be no coming back–there would be no home to come back to.

He felt like a man cut in half. When he thought about Arria, his heart soared. When he envisioned saying goodbye to his father, his heart broke. Livel wished it were different, but he understood why his father would not come with them. Eleazar was the High Priest of Jerusalem, protector of the Third Temple.

The rabbi sat at the head of the table watching his family, seeing them as he had never seen them before. He imagined it was how a dying man viewed life in those final moments, with clarity so intense it was almost blinding.

The rabbi drifted from the present to the future. Like being caught in the jaws of a lion, grief almost took the rabbi to his knees. As a holy man, it was not death he feared, viewing one's passing as he viewed birth, moving from the known to the unknown, from the darkness into the light. But he was terrified of losing his family, the anguish that lay ahead of him made all the worse because he was the one insisting they go.

The rabbi's training taught him to be reserved. He listened, taught the word of God and rarely voiced his own thoughts or opinions to his family. Today would be different.

He pushed himself up, placing both hands on the table for support as he fought for composure. "The darkest day of my life was the day you were taken from me," the rabbi said, riveting all his attention on Livel. "Now you must go away again." A tear slipped from his eye as he turned to Masabala. "I pray you never know the anguish of having a son at war. Every time we heard about a soldier dying, our hearts broke, knowing it could have been you. And now, it is all happening again. Please my son, stay safe." The rabbi walked around the table and stood next to his wife. Miriam looked up at him, her eyes filled with tears.

Sarah laid her head on Masabala's shoulder, stifling a sob.

"In my old age, I have come to realize something," the rabbi said softly. "Separation is only an illusion. Love has no boundaries. Even in death, love survives. Wherever we go, we will always be connected." The rabbi placed a hand over his heart. "In here." He readjusted his head covering and sighed.

Miriam held on to Eleazar's every word, using them as a catalyst to strengthen her resolve. She had married him when she was fifteen, and he was twenty-seven. They had spent thirty-five years together. It was a good marriage. He was her friend, mentor, confidant and lover. Miriam could not imagine a life without Eleazar in it.

Tucking stray hairs into her scarf, Miriam watched her sons, how the sunlight streaming through the window highlighted the shading of their hair, the way they moved their hands, their heads. She wanted always to remember how Livel slouched, and Masabala sat ramrod straight.

There were so many things Miriam still needed to say to her boys, motherly things, things you would say to little children: remember to eat, get enough sleep and be careful you don't get hurt. Perhaps she would tell them when she kissed their bearded cheeks and bid them goodbye.

Miriam stood and faced Eleazar. She was a timid woman, content to stand in the background. Yet here she was pale and shaking, determined to speak her mind. "*Your people shall be my people, your God my God*, those were the words Arria spoke when she declared herself," Miriam said.

Alarmed by how sickly his wife looked, the rabbi moved to put his arm around Miriam. She shrugged him away whispering, "I'm fine." Miriam swallowed, gathering her courage. "Ruth also said, *Entreat me not to leave thee and to return from following after thee; for whither thou goest, I will go; and where thou lodgest, I will lodge.*"

"Miriam, this is foolishness. Please," the rabbi pleaded. "I have no choice, but you do!"

Miriam shook her head slowly. "I have no choice, my beloved. I will not leave you. Not now. Not ever." Miriam slipped her hand into Eleazar's hand. "Wither thou goest, I will go."

* * *

Miriam and Eleazar stood on a ridge overlooking the valley surrounding Jerusalem. Neither said a word. They just held hands and wept as their family melted into the crowd of soldiers. Eleazar prayed, his lips moving, his body swaying like a fragile old tree that seemed about to fall. Miriam held up her hand and waved. She knew they would not see her, but it did not matter. A mother must always wave goodbye to her children.

Chapter 41

Like the spreading of a wildfire, Roman soldiers crossed into Judea. Each commander had his orders; crush, exhaust and exterminate the Jews. Once every village was annihilated, they were to attack the larger towns: Sidon, Nazareth, Samaria, Caesarea Phillippi, Jericho and Hebron, Gaza, Lydda, Joppa and finally, Jerusalem.

Scipio led his men into the southern region of Judea, a desolate place devoid of color, bleak yet awe inspiring. Surrounded by barren peaks and deep gorges, its soaring cliffs loomed overhead like ominous gargoyles. As the sun dipped below the horizon and the temperature dropped, Scipio walked among his troops. He could sense their eagerness, soldiers so hungry for a fight they were like starving bears emerging from hibernation. Scipio appreciated this kind of impassioned urgency; it turned soldiers into warriors.

It was dark by the time they made camp five miles northwest of En Gedi. Within hours, fortifications were being constructed around the encampment, ditches were dug as protection from attack and raised walkways were in place and guarded by soldiers. The campsite was laid out as all Roman encampments were, in the shape of a square. Each tent held eight soldiers and including the slaves' dwellings, there were over four hundred tents in all. As the commander, Scipio's tent was placed in the center.

Scipio lay on a feather-filled mattress covered with sheepskin. An oil lamp illuminated the tent with rugs thrown over the sandy floor. There was a couch in front of a wooden plank that sat atop two boulders. The plank served as a table where he could eat, read maps and plan maneuvers.

Exhausted, Scipio tried to quiet his mind but could not. He kept thinking about the moment when Severus announced each commander's assignment. To Scipio's absolute disdain and disbelief, Severus had ordered both Scipio and Domitius into the southern quadrant of Judea. Scipio recalled the menacing self-satisfied grin on Domitius' face.

"The gods certainly do have a sense of humor. Let me think," Domitius had taunted, stroking his beard. "En Gedi is in southern Judea. Isn't that where Livel is from?" His voice dripped sarcasm. "Perhaps your friend will be *very* lucky, and you will find him before I do!"

Scipio came back to the present with a start. His scouts had reported that Domitius attacked seven villages during the day. Word of the attacks had spread amongst the Jews like the sweeping waters of a flash flood. Hundreds were fleeing into the mountains and others north towards Jerusalem. Scipio shivered and drew the sheepskin closer. He could not dispel the feeling Domitius was watching him, although the notion was without merit. Domitius was three hours away, his encampment in a valley halfway between En Gedi and Beersheba.

Alone with his thoughts, Scipio could not help but ask himself why he had not also engaged in warfare on his way south. Had he avoided confrontation out of some kind of misplaced loyalty to Livel? Did he hope if the Jews were given enough advance warning of an invasion into their territory, they might be better prepared, put up a better fight?

With a heavy heart, Scipio threw off his cover and moved to the couch. Sitting at the table, he drew lines on the map circling the closest villages. He made an "X" through En Gedi.

He had twenty-five centurions prepared to lead twenty-five hundred men into battle. He would issue directives, but once the fighting began, he knew his orders would become obsolete and havoc would rule. Survival was instinctive. Men killed to keep from being killed. When arrows flew and swords were drawn, the old, the feeble and the young all became victims.

Scipio intended to take a force of fifteen hundred men to En Gedi, enough soldiers to subdue the enclave. In honor of his friendship with Livel, he would not obliterate the entire population. The able-bodied would be taken as slaves and mothers with young children would be spared.

Mothers, children–the words brought the image of another time when Scipio had good intentions. The memory still made his blood boil. Domitius striking like a fox attacks a rabbit, slaughtering the tribe after Scipio had promised them protection. He had no doubt Domitius planned to do the same thing again, if given the chance. But Scipio would not give him the chance.

Not this time! Scipio pounded his fist on the desk. *Not this time!*

* * *

Domitius moved among his legions like a graceful panther watching as thousands of men toiled, erecting a city in the sand. He found it difficult to keep a self-satisfied smile from his face. The day had been a great success. Hundreds of Jews were dead, and fear had been shot into the very heart of Judea.

Domitius intended to embrace his destiny, returning to Rome a hero. He would be the lone survivor of his family, in line to inherit all that was rightfully his as the son of Marcus Gracchus. But first, he had a score to settle.

He squeezed his eyes shut conjuring up an image of Livel. Domitius imagined cutting out Livel's tongue, punishment for his treachery to undermine him in his father's eyes while praising Scipio. His emerald eyes glazing over, Domitius envisioned cutting off Livel's hands, filthy hands he used to help his wife Arria touch the sick and diseased.

Domitius would save those hands to throw at Arria's feet, when he found her. And find her he would! Arria had lived in Alexandria as a child and had spoken of the place often. When the war was over, he would travel there. It was a huge city, but Arria was not the type of woman to fall into the shadows.

Domitius opened his eyes and shook his head. First, he would have to find Livel. Domitius was not one to delude himself. The chances Livel had returned to En Gedi were slim. But having been raised there as the son of a rabbi, someone would know where to find him. Domitius had no doubt the information would be easily attained: torture was a great revealer.

Domitius headed back toward his tent. He needed rest. When Scipio struck En Gedi in the morning, he would be there with fifty of his most loyal men. And if his half-brother happened to take a Roman arrow in the back, well those things happened, the sad consequences of war.

* * *

Livel, Arria and Sarah moved among the soldiers, a boisterous mass of men and boys swaggering in their insolence. Soon their small group was engulfed into the army of zealots, just three insignificant people pushed along like waves moving with a rising tide.

Sarah searched for Masabala. She looked for his midnight stallion, hoping for just a glimpse of him. She tried to imagine how he must feel with so much to do and so many people depending on him. She wondered how he was dealing with saying goodbye to his parents. And even though Sarah knew it was selfish, she hoped he was thinking about her. Looking around, Sarah felt desperately alone and insignificant, realizing that being the wife of the commander and the daughter-in-law of the revered *Kohen Gadol* of Israel meant nothing now. She was just another remnant displaced by war. With her world coming apart, Sarah knew she was at a crossroads. She could be weak and fearful or strong and resilient. In truth, there was no decision to make. Sarah would be what she had always been: a woman of valor.

Arria too searched for Masabala but saw only the bouncing heads of soldiers. *Please God, protect him*, she prayed silently. She moved beside Sarah and took her hand. She was sad and frightened.

Even in her great joy at becoming Livel's wife, Arria could not help but worry about her father-in-law and mother-in-law. If Jerusalem fell, as surely it must, how would they survive? Arria castigated herself for being so morose. She could not know the future, and it was wrong to mourn for those still alive.

"We will make it through this," Arria said, squeezing Sarah's hand.

Fierce determination creased Sarah's brow as she softly intoned the words from Deuteronomy: *Be strong, be bold, do not be afraid or frightened of them, for Adonai your God is with you. He will neither fail you nor abandon you.*

* * *

Five hours into the Jewish army's trek across the Negev, the troops came upon a terrified horde of fleeing refugees. Masabala and the zealots ceased to march, and an eerie silence descended. Women carried children on their backs, dragging their meager belongings, food and water in rickety carts. Old people limped over the stony desert, their expressions frozen in shock and fear. The Roman incursion had not only begun, it had begun with virulent intensity and carnage. Masabala listened to testimony of villages overrun and bodies thrown into burning pyres.

He kicked his horse into a trot. "Move along!" he shouted, moving through his men, skirting mules, wagons and an army of two thousand Jewish soldiers. When he found Asher, he was in the midst of organizing the first phase of their military operation, culling out half of their men, ordering wagons and mules to a staging area a quarter mile south. From there, Asher would lead his men toward the southern center of Judea to protect Beersheba and the surrounding villages.

Masabala moved beside his second-in-command and closest confidant. "It has begun! Ride swiftly, my friend. Leave no village unprotected, but do not tarry. Beersheba will no doubt be attacked with the full might of Rome."

"To victory!" Asher shouted, raising a defiant fist in the air as he began shouting orders.

Masabala turned his steed back toward the remaining troops. "Stay in tight formation and be alert!" he shouted, zigzagging a path in search of Sarah, Arria and Livel.

He found his family gathered beside a large boulder. He dismounted and was beside Sarah in two long strides. Looking at her, the world stood still. There were no raucous shouts, no wagon wheels crunching across desert stone, no neighing horses, no fights to come, men to bury or tears to shed. There was only Masabala and Sarah. Their future finite: infinite. Gently he cupped her chin in his enormous hand, kissing her forehead, cheek and then her lips. "I will love you forever."

Sarah tried to block out the feelings threatening to overwhelm her. She had vowed to herself to be strong. But looking at Masabala, the way his sable eyes reflected love, the essence of his presence, strong, indomitable. Falling into his embrace, she crumbled and wept. Slowly, Sarah regained her composure. Slipping the scarf from her head, she tied it around Masabala's neck.

"So you won't forget me," Sarah said.

"I will never forget you. And I will come to you in the cave as soon as I can," Masabala promised.

"I know you will." Sarah hugged him one last time. "And please, when you see my mother, convince her to leave En Gedi and come to me."

Masabala nodded but knew it would be a futile conversation. Alma, Sarah's mother, had been adamant about not leaving the only home she had ever known.

"You should be at the cave before nightfall," Masabala said, taking a sword from his saddle. He handed it to Livel. "Try not to hurt yourself," he teased.

"This weapon has never been in more capable hands," Livel said, grasping Masabala's hands in his. "He who blessed our forefathers; Abraham, Isaac and Jacob, may he bless you and all that serve with you."

Chapter 42

Sarah, Arria and Livel were but tiny figures moving over the rocky ground, dwarfed by the majesty and magnitude of the flat-topped mountains of stone that were the Negev Desert. They each carried a skein of water, medical supplies and food for one day.

Sarah and Livel had grown up with the mountains as a backdrop to their lives. But Arria was a city dweller; buildings, trees, plazas, baths and people were what she knew and understood. She found the desolation, enormity and silence of the desert unsettling.

Livel took out the map given to him by his father, studying the jagged lines on the parchment. He tilted his head back as far as he could, peering with disdain at the treacherous ascent that lay before them. His father had obviously selected the cave because it was so inaccessible. Now one question remained: could Livel make it? On most days, his knee did little to hinder him, but this climb was going to be a great challenge.

Arria slipped her hand into Livel's hand, reading his thoughts. "We'll go slowly," she whispered.

From the foothills, they began their climb toward the cave. "Be careful," Livel urged, following behind Arria and Sarah, the path shifting beneath their feet.

They hugged the mountain wall as they trekked breathless and tense, knowing a misstep could send them careening over the side. Two hours into their ascent, it became obvious they would not make the cave by nightfall. Livel was in pain, and Sarah and Arria were too tired to go on.

They made camp on a ledge as dusk turned to night. With the stars as their blanket, they lay down beside each other.

Tomorrow they would begin again.

* * *

Masabala had watched his family walk away, watched until they were but dark silhouettes on the horizon. He knew it was time he could ill afford to waste, but he could not tear himself away. He finally turned aside when a scout approached, returning to report that not two hours ahead was a huge contingent of Roman soldiers directly in their pathway.

With no choice, Masabala set a new course: a convoluted path that added hours to their journey. Driving his men hard, they arrived in En Gedi near midnight. With great purpose and a firm voice Masabala moved among his men, dispatching the Jewish zealots to set up a deep defensive boundary around the still darkened sleeping enclave of En Gedi. He then rode the perimeter, adding more men where needed.

With a thousand soldiers in place, Masabala ordered the rams' horns blown, just as Joshua had done in the battle of Jericho. The *shofars* aching mystical sound awakened the inhabitants of the enclave as if the world were weeping.

Carrying torches, the frightened and bewildered residents poured into the streets.

"Women, girls, boys under twelve and the infirm," Masabala shouted as he searched without success for his mother-in-law. "Go to the synagogue! You must hurry! Bring food and water with you and nothing more!" He turned to the men and boys who had not joined the rebellion in order to protect En Gedi. "Gather every weapon you can find and bring them to the synagogue! It will be up to you to protect your families!"

Masabala was acting now without emotion, a soldier with only one thing on his mind: the survival of his people. When the last group entered the synagogue grounds, he began stationing the villagers, who carried everything from axes to anvils around the myriad of one-room buildings that made up the complex. Crying babies and weeping mothers sat on the hard stone floors and sprawled on benches. Others found space within the walled courtyard.

Masabala found his mother-in-law in the courtyard sitting amongst a group of children, holding one on her lap, rocking back and forth and cooing to the child. The desolate look she gave him needed no words as she gently took the child off her lap and stood. She offered Masabala her cheek. "A very sad day," Alma said, biting her lower lip, a habit Sarah had when she was nervous. "How is my daughter?"

"Disappointed you refused to go with her to the cave."

"Defeat the Romans and then I will," Alma said, bending over to pick up a wailing child whose mother was busy with another of her offspring. "Don't let anything happen to these children, Masabala. They are the future of Israel."

"I will do my best," Masabala said, bowing his head to her. "I must go."

"Be safe," Alma said, and turned back to the children.

Masabala moved into the night. The chaos that had been everywhere had now died down. All speaking was in hushed tones, as if the wind were listening and might carry the words to their enemy.

Masabala shook hands with the men and boys who would defend their families. He knew no one would fight more valiantly or have more to lose.

* * *

Scipio stood in the doorway of his tent. The sun rose, nestling into the sky in slivered streaks of red. Throughout the night he had tossed and turned, fighting the opposing emotions assaulting him. It was easy when your enemy was faceless, but Livel had put a face to the Jews.

Scipio wished he had refused to go to Britannia to compete with Domitius for their father's favor. If he had turned his back on that challenge, he might not be in this situation. But it was too late for that now. It was time to prepare for war.

Scipio raised his hands above his head as a slave put the chain mail metal shirt over his head. Torso armor was then put in place. He slipped the leaf-shaped dagger into its sheath. Then he ran a finger lightly over the blade of his sword, checking for nicks.

Placing the helmet on his head, Scipio moved from the tent into the vast expanse of men and never-ending sand and rock. A scout ran to his side, his breathing labored; sweat dripping down his dusty face.

"Permission to report?"

"Permission granted," Scipio barked.

"The Jews have set up a protective ring around En Gedi. I saw no defensive walls or moats."

"How many men?" Scipio inquired.

"Close to a thousand."

Babudius, Scipio's most trusted centurion, drew near. Scipio used the tip of his sword to draw a circle in the sand.

"I want the enclave surrounded with a soldier placed every three feet. It makes no difference if the Jews see us, as long as we remain out of range of their arrows. Scipio moved closer to Babudius. "When we break through the line, no one enters the city until my command. Women and children are to be spared. I will have no massacre of the innocents! Be sure our troops understand my orders. If I see otherwise, the consequences will be dire."

Babudius was confused. Why would Scipio go against orders from Severus to kill everyone? Regardless of his misgivings, he raised his arm straight in front of him, palm down. "As you command." He took three steps back and turned.

* * *

Domitius observed the sunrise from a ridge overlooking Scipio's encampment, perched like a majestic eagle, seeing all. He maintained his focus on the center of the camp where he knew Scipio's tent would be located. He watched him come out, speak with someone and then move among the soldiers.

Domitius knew his decision to intrude into a territory not under his command was frivolous but felt the rewards were worth the risk. But Scipio must not see him coming. Timing and the element of surprise would be everything now. He could not move too soon or wait too long if his twofold plan was to work: burn En Gedi to the ground, and in the ensuing havoc, kill Scipio. If the gods were smiling, he might even find Livel. If not, Domitius would not leave En Gedi until he found someone who could tell him where to find Livel.

* * *

Livel and Arria slept with their backs towards the mountain, snuggled in each other's arms. Sarah could not get comfortable, the rocks a loathsome bed. She managed to fall asleep intermittently, but it was never for more than a few minutes at a time.

When the first rays of sun swept away the dawn, Sarah stretched her arms above her head, fought the kink in her neck and stood. She rubbed her sore bottom, staring into the distance. She could not believe what she was seeing.

A massive Roman encampment was clearly visible, an oozing boil festering in the heart of the Negev. *How? When? It was not there last night!* She had no idea the number of men a camp like that could hold, but her gut screamed too many.

"Livel! Arria!" she shrieked. They were both on their feet in seconds.

Sarah pointed in wide-eyed horror. Livel caught glimpses of the sun reflecting off the armor as thousands of men began to congregate outside the encampment. His heart all but stopped.

"We have to warn Masabala," Sarah cried, slipping towards the edge of hysteria.

Livel felt as though his entire body was vibrating. He was a man of logic, a consequence of his genius. But at this moment, he did not care about the pouch around his neck and the sacred assignment it represented. He was incapable of reasoning, only reacting. "Let's go!" he cried, heading down the mountainside.

Chapter 43

Masabala stared helplessly as thousands of Roman soldiers surrounded the enclave, dressed in full armor while the Jews wore nothing more than flimsy tunics. He frantically tried to formulate some type of defensive strategy. It was an exercise in futility. They were outnumbered by a thousand men and without the tri-pointed arrowheads that could pierce through body armor; there could be no effective offensive strategy.

The enemy was better equipped and outnumbered them by a thousand men. Still he shouted, "Hold the line!" as he passed among his troops, bows held at the ready, lips quivering, arms trembling.

No matter how brave they might be, no matter how deep their faith, how resolute their dedication, no one wanted to die. And if they managed to live through this day, they would awaken tomorrow thankful to be alive but disillusioned and changed forever.

"Make every shot count!" Masabala shouted, as a black wave of arrows arched toward the Jews. The screams that followed were harrowing. Too enraged to comprehend the catastrophe surrounding him, Masabala shot arrow after arrow into the air, watching in disbelief as they bounced off shields, doing no harm.

The Romans began to advance.

"Hold your positions!" he howled to no avail. The surviving troops had broken position and were taking refuge behind boulders or running toward the olive groves. "Jews are not cowards!" he howled, shoving those he caught back into the line of fire.

The arrows kept coming, bouncing along the ground or finding entrance in an arm, leg, head or chest. There was blood everywhere, men bellowing for help, ripping arrows from their wounds, the blood spurting and turning the ground crimson. His army was being obliterated.

This night, every mother in Israel would mourn. Thousands of families would rend their clothing and weep.

He had only one thing left to do: *get back to the synagogue and save the children.*

* * *

Domitius and his men were gathered on an incline near the waterfall that flowed into the oasis of En Gedi. He observed the massacre, likening it to watching games at the Coliseum. And just like those games, the Jews had no chance. When it was over, there were bodies scattered everywhere, the carnage engorging his men with bloodlust. Domitius' fifty soldiers were the best of the best, expert marksmen, killing machines, eager to participate. Domitius smiled as his warriors doused their cloth-wrapped arrows in sulfur and oil.

He was moments away from giving the signal to set fire to En Gedi when he spotted Scipio moving methodically between the dead and wounded.

"Stand down!" Domitius shouted.

* * *

Scipio was not aware of his hot tears or of the black-winged vultures circling overhead. He searched for Livel in every face, every step taking him closer to the precipice of insanity.

"*Azor lee be'vakasha,* help me please," came the echoing Hebrew words, each plea sending Scipio deeper into the nightmare. "*Ima, Ima,* Mother, Mother," the childish voices cried in desperation.

Scipio's men watched their commander in confusion. No one approached him or asked what he was doing. They just stood in clusters, keeping their distance from the corpses, awaiting their orders.

In the end, whatever relief Scipio felt knowing Livel was not among the deceased was now lost, his heart broken. Overcome by grief and guilt, he stood before the enclave loath to enter, wanting to never take another life.

"Are you not well, sir?" Babudius asked, venturing near.

Scipio stared at the centurion, stunned by the innocence of the question. He wanted to scream *no!* He yearned to walk away from his post as commander and never look back. One day he would. But not today. He had a vow to keep; there would be no more killing in En Gedi. "We are done here. Whoever is within the compound will be left to bury their dead. Lead the men back to camp," he commanded. Then he turned away from the slaughter. "Tomorrow is another day."

* * *

Domitius watched in disbelief as Scipio's men retreated from the perimeter of the enclave and headed into the wilderness. Every fiber of his body triggered disgust as Scipio lagged behind his army, distancing himself as if he were a mere foot soldier rather than a commander of Rome.

With jaw clenched, Domitius balled his fists and faced his small troop of stone-faced armored warriors. "Split up. There will be no resistance. I want fire to rain down upon the Jews. Burn the enclave to the ground and then return to camp!" He raised his arm and brought it down as if he were cutting off the head of a snake.

The soldiers rode away, excited shouts and the echo of horses' hooves breaking the haunting silence. He kept his attention riveted on Scipio. This was his chance. There would be no witnesses and no one to report how their commander had died. He kicked his steed. The horse was skittish and circled in resistance. Fighting the reins, he glanced toward the horizon. Three people were on foot, zigzagging across the desert. At first, he was not sure what he was seeing. He stilled the horse.

Domitius swallowed a triumphant howl as he studied the distant limping figure, knowing it was Livel. Then his breath caught when he spotted the second figure. He would recognize Arria anywhere, the curve of her body, the way she held her head, defiant and proud. He had no idea who the other woman was nor did he care.

Torn, he shot a quick look at Scipio. He knew there should be a moment of contemplation, to evaluate going after Scipio or taking down Livel and Arria. Yet, there was really no decision to make. He hated his half-brother for usurping his favored position with their father and for stealing his wife. It was time to exact his revenge and reclaim what belonged to him. He kicked his horse violently.

Sarah was the first to spot the soldier bearing down on them. "What do we do?" she screamed.

Livel had no options. They were in the middle of the desert, and there was nowhere to hide. "We have to divert the rider. It's our only chance!" Livel shouted. He was momentarily transported back in time. He and Masabala were playing in the desert when they spotted the Romans coming after them. They had split up then, as Livel was ordering his wife and sister-in-law to do now. He prayed that this time it would end differently. "Sarah run towards En Gedi! Arria, run back toward the cave. *Go*!!!!!"

Arria's eyes flooded with tears. She shook her head violently. "I am not leaving you!"

"Please, my beloved." He unsheathed the sword Masabala had given to him. "I will not give up without a fight, but I cannot protect you and save myself. Arria, I am begging you!"

Arria threw her arms around Livel.

He hugged her hard and then forced her away.

Sarah caught Arria by the arm. "Trust the Almighty. He will protect us," Sarah said. The look that passed between the two women transcended words.

Sarah gave Livel a furtive look. "Thank you," she mouthed, her intentions and courage focused on escaping the rider and finding her husband.

"Run like the wind!" Livel shouted, holding the sword ready.

Domitius was amused as the threesome separated. Despite himself, he felt a transitory flash of respect for Livel. He had taken an impossible situation and tried to make the best of it. In doing so, at least the stranger among them would survive. A smile turned his mouth as he charged towards Arria.

Livel was aghast as he watched the rider change direction. He began running toward Arria, his leg buckling beneath him as he pumped his arms. He tripped, jumped up and sprinted toward the stallion.

Arria heard the horse approaching, the ground vibrating beneath her feet. She kept running, refusing to think, needing to believe she could outrun her pursuer.

Domitius slowed his horse, wanting to enjoy the final moments of his pursuit. He circled Arria, cutting off her route of escape. She froze, hugging herself and dropping into a squat.

He slid from his horse and pulled Arria to her feet by the hair. She recognized the smell of him and her head snapped up, defiance cloaking her fear.

"How I have dreamed of this day," Domitius said, kissing her hard on the mouth, biting her lip and drawing blood. "Look at you! Dark just like one of the Jews," he hissed in disgust, drawing her face near. "Ah. The scar. My mark," he said, tracing his fingernail along the soft flesh surrounding the scar. "But still, you are beautiful."

Arria sneered at him, overcome by a hate so complete she was blinded. She spat in Domitius' face. He slapped her hard.

Livel thought he was seeing an aberration, his worst nightmare realized as he recognized Domitius. "Leave her alone you bastard!" he howled, racing forward, his sword drawn.

"Ah. The hero comes to rescue you." Domitius pressed the dagger to Arria's throat. "Drop the sword or I will finish what I started back in Rome."

Livel fought debilitating desperation as he let the weapon fall from his hands. "Let her go!"

"I don't think so," Domitius taunted, pulling Arria closer until his manhood was pressed against her back. "You are mine now," he whispered.

"Why? Because you're too much of a coward to fight Livel like a man!" Arria challenged.

Domitius laughed, yanking the helmet from his head. "Is this what you want?" Keeping the dagger pressed against Arria's neck, he unsheathed his sword and pointed it at Livel. "The lady wants a fair fight: let's give her what she wants." He shoved Arria away, and she fell to her knees.

Domitius placed the dagger in the sheath on his hip as Livel retrieved his sword. The two men faced off. Domitius was a head taller and a massive presence as he sliced the air with his sword, delighting as it whooshed past Livel's head. Arria screamed.

Livel ducked and then lunged, his sword reverberating off the chainmail armor protecting Domitius' chest. Domitius' eyes shot open, and the smile evaporated from his face. He swung left and then right. Livel jumped sideways, spun around and charged. Their swords clashed and crossed, and clashed again, metal crashing against metal, tendrils of sparks flying.

Livel weaved and dipped, moving forward and back, an agile moving target. His armor cumbersome in hand-to-hand combat, Domitius was quickly tiring of the sparing. It was time to finish this. His arm extended, he lunged toward Livel's heart and missed. The swords crossed and the two men pushed away.

Arria blocked out all sound and thought as she focused on the dagger stuck in the belt at Domitius' side. She leapt out of her crouch like a panther chasing its prey and yanked the dagger free. In one fluid motion, she sliced the blade across the side of Domitius' neck. The cut was precise, severing the artery. Blood gushed, spurting to the rhythm of his stuttering heart. Domitius grabbed his neck and turned, his fingers oozing a river of blood. His mouth was frozen in a silent scream as he crumbled to the ground.

* * *

Scipio fell farther and farther behind his men, lulled by the constant swaying of his horse and lost in nightmarish mind-numbing visions. Riding up a rocky incline, he turned in his saddle. There were fifty Roman soldiers heading toward En Gedi. Scipio knew without question, Domitius was the culprit. He scanned the surrounding rises expecting his half-brother to be watching the attack from a safe perch.

It was only when he looked into the barren void just beyond En Gedi that he recognized the white steed. Domitius was fighting a tunic-clad Jew. A shiver shot through Scipio. He did not need to see his features to know it was Livel. He roared at the sight, digging his heels into his horse.

Livel held a quaking Arria in his arms, Domitius dead at their feet. Suddenly Arria pulled away screaming and pointing. A Roman soldier was charging over the sand, spear in hand.

Livel grabbed Domitius' horse and yanked the bow and arrow from its latch. He forced himself to breathe, to concentrate, and to see nothing but the approaching rider.

"Livel! Livel! "Don't shoot!" Scipio wailed. But his shouts went unheeded, lost in the crying wind. He tore the helmet from his head. "Look, it is I! Scipio!"

Livel was focused on protecting Arria, his thoughts numb as he drew back the string releasing the arrow.

Scipio lifted his hand, palm flat, patting the air as if he could halt the flight of the projectile. It struck him high in the thigh.

Livel shot another arrow, missing Scipio completely, hitting the horse in the neck.

It all happened so quickly. The animal's legs buckled, sand kicking up like splashing rain. As the rider fell from the horse, Livel recognized the face of his victim.

"No! No! This can't be happening!" Livel screamed, racing toward Scipio. They were but moments apart and yet for Livel, they were the longest few seconds of his life.

The horse was on its side, neighing his cry of death. Scipio was pinned beneath him. Livel leaned against the animal with his shoulder, digging his feet into the ground. He shoved with all his might, but the steed would not budge. Arria slid in the sand beside him. She knelt next to Scipio, putting a gentle hand to his neck. His face was grey, his pulse erratic and his breathing shallow. She looked at Livel and shook her head. His body was crushed, the damage too acute for him to survive.

Livel fell to his knees beside Scipio. "I didn't know it was you," he cried. "I didn't know. . . I would never hurt you." Desperate, he lay down beside his friend, sliding an arm beneath him so that he could hold Scipio.

"No . . . more . . . killing . . . It's . . . over . . . now." Scipio gasped, his body shook and then stilled as he fell into the abyss, dying.

Fury coursed through Livel's body as the realization struck him that Scipio had butchered his people. Then their eyes locked, and Livel remembered the brother he once knew. Livel wept as his friend slipped away.

Chapter 44

Livel closed Scipio's unseeing eyes. It was a torturous moment, hate and heartbreak colliding with the force of a tornado. With his bare hands, he scooped sand over his friend, crying, unable to stop thinking that he was smothering Scipio. When the body was covered, Livel added stones, wanting to believe the rocks would keep the sand in place. He knew the entire ritual was a fool's errand; the wind would blow, the sand would disseminate and the scavengers would feast upon the fodder of Scipio's remains.

Livel stood silent watch: with a hardened heart, he refused to pray.

Tears flowed from Arria's eyes as she watched Livel standing beside Scipio's sand covered body. She was now a Jew, and Scipio was a soldier of Rome; her enemy and a man to be loathed and cursed. But he had once been her family, a brother-in-law and a beloved ally. Whatever Scipio had become, he died trying to save them from Domitius. For that, she would always be grateful.

Arria let the memories cascade over her, remembering that day in the Jewish quarter when Domitius took a knife to her face, the disfigurement a daily companion. She could still see him standing with his foot on Livel's chest, sword in hand. If not for Scipio, Livel would have died that day.

She glared at Domitius lying fifty yards away. Hot arid breezes kicked sand into swirling orbs as she strode towards the body. He was sprawled on his back, head turned askew like a broken toy, congealing blood pooling beneath him.

Arria stared, hating him. He was a monster, an animal that deserved to die. She touched the tiny ridge of scar that traversed her face. She had dreamt of revenge, and in those dreams she had watched as he grew cold and stiff. Arria was not sorry he was dead. Not sorry at all.

She turned back toward Livel, saw the heartbreak etched into his every move and knew that neither one of them would ever stop thinking about this day. But they would have each other; have their love.

"We have to find Sarah!" Livel said, shaking free from the claws of regret. It was time to leave Judea.

Riding tandem on Domitius' steed, they galloped toward En Gedi. As they moved into the open expanse, Livel looked back, finding the strength to ask God to have mercy on his friend.

* * *

Sarah ran across the great divide that separated her from the oasis of En Gedi. She sprinted with her mouth open, gulping air. Never had she known such terror, demons everywhere.

Where was the rider? Was he coming for her? Did he capture Livel? Arria?

She was too afraid to look back, darting past woody shrubs, dense tangles, pointed rocks and etched gullies. At a rocky sand dune she rested, forcing herself to think.

What if the Roman army has already attacked En Gedi? What then?

For a better look at what lie ahead, she crab-crawled to the top of the dune. Twisted bloodied bodies were everywhere. Sarah slipped into shock, unable to fathom the catastrophe that had transpired. She put her hand to her mouth to silence the scream. *A thousand dead! It cannot be!* She cowered, hugging herself against the reality. *I have to save my mother. I have to find Masabala.*

With determination born of desperation, she navigated her way from the dune into the desert. Time splintered into fragments as Sarah headed north of the enclave toward the hillsides. She moved among the gnarled trunks of soaring trees crowned with foliage. She skirted shrubs laden with tiny pink, yellow and white flowers, the beauty unnoticed by a heart torn asunder.

Her steps cautious, her senses pulsating, Sarah found her way to the edge of the olive grove. This was a place of innocence, where as a child she explored, climbed trees and fell in love with Masabala. For Sarah every tree was familiar, every path well remembered. With aplomb, she crisscrossed the grove leading her into the enclave.

There was a whoosh overhead, and Sarah stopped in her tracks. A flaming arrow skimmed the treetops, igniting the tinder-dry leaves. Sarah screamed as more arrows fell, the grove turning into an inferno. She yanked her tunic above her knees and ran.

* * *

With a heavy heart, Masabala left the fields of carnage behind, fighting his way through the smoke-smudged alleys of En Gedi, his arms pumping wildly as arrows struck the wooden-beamed straw roofs and the houses caught fire.

He charged into the synagogue compound, howling like a madman, ducking and weaving to avoid the spitting fire. People were panicked, pushing and shoving, fighting to escape.

"One at a time!" he shrieked, smashing his fist through a planked window before dashing into the adjoining building. "Get out! Run!!! Don't turn back, just go!" He kicked out doors, sprinting through the spreading blaze. Masabala was David fighting Goliath, beyond pain, beyond awareness.

By the time he finally escaped the fire and collapsed near the base of an olive tree, the arrows had stopped. Only then did he realize the brutal extent of his injuries. Masabala held up his smoldered hands. *How will I ever hold and touch my Sarah again?* He riveted his attention on his charred feet. *What good is a man who cannot walk?* The agony was indescribable; the desire to close his eyes forever all consuming, as the angel of death hovered near. Those were Masabala's last thoughts as he glided into a place where pain held no purchase.

Sarah felt as though she had taken only one breath since running from the grove. Her eyes burning from the ash, she found herself among the fleeing residents of En Gedi. Swept up in their wake, shoved along unwittingly, she edged past families weighed down with what meager belongings they could carry, pulling wagons, leading donkeys, carrying those too old or too ill to walk.

"Alma, Alma!" Sarah yelled, calling for her mother. There were so many people, each face familiar, strangers now clouded in masks of grief and fear. A gentle hand touched Sarah's shoulder. She turned.

"My baby, my only child!" Alma wept, taking Sarah into her arms, kissing her checks, hugging her. "I never thought I would see you again."

"When I saw the fire," Sarah stammered, "I was so worried, so afraid you'd been hurt. Masabala? Have you seen him?"

Alma's head bobbed up and down. "The synagogue."

* * *

Masabala lay on the ground just steps from the smoldering synagogue, his massive body so vulnerable and still. Sarah fell to her knees, crawling to his side. He was so pale, his breathing so shallow. Sarah could not bear to look at the burns as she took his head into her lap, his brows, lashes and hair singed off. "Masabala," she whispered. "I'm here. Talk to me, my beloved." When there was no response, Sarah began to weep, fingering the burned tattered scarf she had given him for protection. "Mother, I don't know how to help him. I don't know what to do!" Convinced her husband was dying in her arms; Sarah's vision refracted, her world now a prism where nothing existed but Masabala.

Alma sat beside her daughter murmuring assurances, telling her she was loved, wishing it were otherwise but believing there was nothing to be done.

* * *

As Livel and Arria neared En Gedi, they dismounted and ran the rest of the way. The sand was stained with blood, bodies everywhere, the sight before them incomprehensible. Livel went cold and began to tremble. Masabala's voice called to him from a distant place, begging for help. As if being pulled by an unseen hand, Livel turned towards the synagogue, knowing where his brother lay. He grabbed Arria by the hand and began to run.

Tears blinded Livel as he laid his head on Masabala's chest listening to the muffled heartbeat. "Sarah, you must move, I need access to my brother!" he said, looking to Alma for assistance.

Livel examined Masabala's hands. Three fingers had bone exposed, one of them the finger Masabala intentionally severed to prove he was worthy of joining Bar Kokhba's army. The palms and backs of his hands were leathery swollen globs of white, yellow and black.

Livel moved to his brother's feet, turning pages in the imaginary book that resided in his memory, looking for information on how to treat burns. "We are going to need bandages for compresses, cold water, wine and vinegar," he said, as Arria knelt beside him. Livel shot a look in Sarah and Alma's direction. The two women ran into the smoke filled streets and vanished.

Livel stared at Masabala's damaged feet and legs where the straps of the sandals had burned into his skin. "We have to get these off," Livel said, his hands shaking as he moved to undo the leather straps.

"Let me," Arria said.

Livel grimaced as Arria worked, looking over his shoulder every few minutes, willing Sarah and Alma back. Arria removed the second shoe just as the two women returned.

Their instincts and skill overriding their emotions, Arria dipped the cloths into a mixture of wine and vinegar while Livel dripped water over Masabala's burns. Livel laid a compress over his brother's feet.

Masabala's eyes shot open and he tried to sit, wailing a foreign sound detached and disembodied. He gazed up at Livel, wanting to beg for help, trying to move his lips, but he was unable to get past the unbearable pain.

Livel placed his hand on Masabala's chest. "I know it hurts, but you must not move," he said, choking back tears. "I am going to take care of you." Livel knew if they could manage to keep Masabala alive, to keep infection at bay, he would lose some of his fingers. As for his feet, he might never walk again.

Masabala fought against Livel, begging God for his voice, begging to see Sarah just one more time.

"Touch him, Sarah. Let him know you are here," Livel said, forcing himself to look away from the ebbing light in his brother's eyes.

Sarah stroked Masabala's head, placed her open palm on his cheek, his forehead. She brushed her lips across his mouth. "Please, don't leave me. I need you. I love you."

Masabala closed his eyes merging into the warmth of Sarah's love. He was at peace.

Two weeks later

In the waning dusk, hundreds of forlorn and silent Jews headed west, destination unknown. In the distance, they could see an ocean of green trees beckoning them forward. Their leader was a man known as Livel. Around his neck, he carried the most treasured map ever written: a map that a thousand generations would search for and dream about.

Moving beside Livel were three women: the widow Alma, Arria and Sarah. Inside of Sarah, a tiny fetus was growing; the miracle of a new life. A horse-drawn wagon followed them carrying a gravely wounded soldier, a man fighting the greatest battle of his life, his fate in the arms of the Creator, blessed be His name.

The End

Epilogue

The Bar Kokhba rebellion ended in the summer of 135 C.E. The definitive battle took place in Betar, the location of Bar Kokhba's final headquarters. The city was under Roman siege for a year. Deprived of food and water, those Jews who did not starve to death were slaughtered when the Romans finally entered Betar. The city fell on the *ninth of Av,* the same day the First and Second Temples were destroyed. Bar Kokhba was executed and some sources say his head was laid at Hadrian's feet. Rabbi Akiva met with a horrendous death, his skin flayed with iron combs. The High Priest, Eleazar was also executed.

As with all historical fiction, the writer sometimes takes liberties with actual people, time and events. To cut down on confusion, I used the United States system of measurements rather than Roman and biblical measurements. I use the abbreviation C.E. (common era) rather than A.D. (anno Domini) in the year of our Lord, to avoid using a religious reference to the time period.

To elucidate on what was real and what was not in *And So It Was Written,* Doctor Claudius Galen was a Greek physician born in 131 C.E. I borrowed him for my story by having him born a bit earlier. I gave him a daughter but the facts about his medical prowess are based on historical fact.

As for a Third Temple, you decide. Some of the Bar Kokhba coins discovered by archeologists had an illustration of the Holy Temple. While it was common practice among the nations to portray temples on coins, nonexistent structures were never depicted. Maimonides states that during Hadrian's rule the Roman governor,

Tinnius Rufus plowed up the Temple Sanctuary and its environs. The Second Temple was destroyed 70 years earlier, so what Temple was Maimonides referring to?

As for the Ark of the Covenant and the Ten Commandments, it was lost with the destruction of the First Temple. Is there a map? Could the Holy Tablets be lying under what is today the Al-Aqsa Mosque in Jerusalem? Perhaps one day we will know.

Acknowledgments

And So It Was Written was a huge undertaking that could not have happened without the guidance and help of so many people who gave unselfishly of their time and expertise. To my editor, Maxine Cahn, thank you for the hundreds of hours and the dedication you gave to the details. Sherry Gold, thank you for all your hard work. I am forever grateful. To my writing group: Deborah Weed, Lily Prellezo, and Orlando Rodriguez. We met weekly, pouring over every word and nuance. They are brilliant and talented, and I could never have done this without them. A special thanks to Deborah, for pushing me so hard and for not letting me ever take the easy way out!

Thank you to: Professor Erik Larson, Department of Religious Studies, Florida International University for your insight and ability to bring the Holy Temple alive for me and to answer my questions with gentle patience. Rabbi/Cantor Marc Philippe, who came into my life as a spiritual leader, opened the door to Judaism for me and then became my friend. Your advice and opinions helped me from making critical errors. Doctor Susan Baker-Weiner, who validated all the medical information, reminding me when I forgot to put the stitches in! Marjorie and Alan Goldberg for always asking and always listening.

Writing is a solitary affair and without the love and support of family it would be so much more difficult. My husband, Mel is the love of my life. His guidance and support is the touchstone of my existence. We have been blessed with an incredible blended family. My children and grandchildren are the joy of my life. Each one is special and gifted and I honor them. Todd Brazer and his girls; Jordyn and Emma, Carrie Brazer and Steve Woodby and their children Nikki, Maxwell and Jacob. Judd and Ayda Brazer and their girls; Tiffany and Julia. On Mel's side there are Barry and Ellen Brazer, Dr. Jordan and Heidi Tacktill and Dylan, Samantha Brazer. Mitchell and Becky Brazer and Mathew and Megan. Bonnie and Joe Grote, Rachel, Alexandria and Ryan. Friends and family are often neglected and so I want to thank the following people for a lifetime of always being there for me: Barbara Glicken, Judi Wolowitz, Miriam Matloff and Michele Kabat.

I lost my beloved father as I neared the end of this book. Irving Glicken, of blessed memory, lived every moment of his life as an example. His loss changed everything, teaching me about endings and beginnings. We miss you daddy, but we feel yours and mother's love shinning down on all of us.

My thanks to the authors of the following books I used for research:

Yadin, Yigael. Bar Kokhba New York: Random House 1971 Print

Marks, Richard. The Image of Bar Kokhba: False Messiah and National Hero. Pennsylvania State University Press, 1994 Print

Potok, Chaim. Wanderings: History of the Jews. New York: Fawcett Crest 1978 Print

Reznick, Leibel. The Mystery of Bar Kokhba. New Jersey: Jason Aronson 1996 Print

Freund, Richard. Secrets of the Cave of Letters. New York: Humanity Books 2004 Print

Yourcenar, Marguerite. Memoirs of Hadrian. New York: Farrar, Straus and Giroux 1974 Print

Adkins, Lesley and Roy A, Adkins. Handbook to Life in Ancient Rome New York: Oxford University Press 1994 Print

Casson, Lionel. Travel in the Ancient World. Baltimore: John Hopkins University Press 1974 Print

Veyne, Paul. The Roman Empire. Cambridge: The Belknap Press of Harvard University Press 1997 Print

Cowell, F.R. Life In Ancient Rome New York: G.P. Putnam's Sons 1961 Print

Carcopino, Jerome. Daily Life in Ancient Rome.
New Haven: Yale University Press 1940 Print

I want to acknowledge and thank **Wikipedia** and all the scholars who contribute to that incredible Internet website.